Praise for S.P. SOMTOW

"S.P. Somtow doesn't write like anyone else—which is unusual in this time of unimaginative and imitative fiction. His is a fresh voice, as engaging as it is unique."
—Dean Koontz

"[*Vampire Junction* is] the closest thing to a nightmare ever put on paper."
—Robert Bloch

"Terrible things happen in [*Vampire Junction*]—murders, tortures, rapes, abandonments . . . it's about rock music, about mass hysteria, about vampires, about horror . . . one comes out knowing, and caring about, a panoply of new friends and acquaintances, living and dead, and un-alive."
—Theodore Sturgeon
The Washington Post

"*Moon Dance* offers a complex horror experience, rich in atmosphere and history, not to mention animal sexuality and a great deal of gore."
—*Publishers Weekly*

"Somtow's sheer inventiveness, his marvelous use of language, so often turning the vernacular into chilling beauty, his ability to leap across time without losing a beat, and those beautiful twists of plot—I can only marvel at it all."
—Robert Cormier

Also by S.P. Somtow

Valentine

❧❧❧❧❧❧❧❧❧

S.P. SOMTOW

A TOM DOHERTY ASSOCIATES BOOK
NEW YORK

VALENTINE

Copyright © 1992 by Somtow Sucharitkul

Cover art by Joe DeVito

A Tor Book
Published by Tom Doherty Associates, Inc.
175 Fifth Avenue
New York, N.Y. 10010

Tor® is a registered trademark of Tom Doherty Associates, Inc.

ISBN: 0-812-51240-5
Library of Congress Catalog Number: 92-25100

First edition: October 1992
First mass market edition: February 1995

Printed in the United States of America

0 9 8 7 6 5 4 3 2 1

The action of VALENTINE takes place in a reality almost identical to, but subtly different from, our own. A number of well-known historical personages and situations appear in this book, but they are used fictitiously. All other characters and events are solely the product of this author's imagination. None of this really happened; the people herein depicted do not exist, and never have existed, except within these pages; and any resemblance to actual persons, places, and events, is purely coincidental.

To the cast and crew of *The Laughing Dead*

Nothing that happens on the set of *Valentine* could be as bizarre as the things *we* went through!

CONTENTS

PART ONE

❧ ❧ ❧ ❧ ❧ ❧

ANGEL

En una gota de agua
buscaba su voz el niño.

In a droplet of water
The little boy searched for his
voice.

LORCA

1

FIRST IMPRESSIONS

MOSAIC STONES

Sissy Robinson, age 12:
The first time I saw Angel Todd I was like standing in the lobby of the Sheraton Universal and the elevator door opens and he's standing there looking way past me with dreamy eyes and he doesn't even see me and I'm all "Are you Angel Todd?" and he's all "Yeah," like that, only the way he says it means a thousand different things like, "Wanna make something of it?" and "Get the fuck out of my way," and like, "I'm more beautiful than you are."

But I didn't care because I love him and I want to take him home with me but I know I can't so at least I got this poster plastered on my wall next to Freddy Krueger.

Gabriela Muñoz, agent:
The first time? I took one look at him. Stars in his eyes. Dollar signs in mine. First thing I said to him was: Timmy Valentine.

Valentine? he said. Jesus, he'd barely even heard of him, that's how naïve he was. Could there still be a town in the universe where Timmy Valentine was unknown? Shit, even the fucking Ayatollah had called him a tool of the Great Satan.

Listen, I said, listen. I sat him and that redneck slob of a mother of his down on my twelve-foot leather sofa and flicked on the stereo, and I fast-scanned from station to station until that voice came bursting into my office, oh Jesus what a voice . . . sweet, pure, soaring, serene yet concealing so much pain . . . twisting the scalpel in your heart, that's what that voice does to you . . . the voice is as beautiful as childhood and it hurts you like the memory of childhood, knowing you can never have childhood back again.

> Don't matter if you hitch a ride,
> Don't matter if you pay;
> I'll be waiting at Vampire Junction
> To suck your soul away.

So I watched Angel Todd as he sat and listened. Angel was no Timmy Valentine. There could never be another Timmy Valentine. But he sat up straight, drinking in the music, and there was something in the way he sat, the way he *concentrated.* The way he closed his eyes and his dirty blond eyelashes quivered as he breathed in time to the music. Kid had something. Self-assurance. I could make something of him.

The mother paid no attention. She stared out of the window onto Melrose, probably pricing the Porsches and Ferraris as they zoomed by. The kid was all concentrated though, bundled up inside himself. I liked that.

You'd have to fix the hair, of course, and dye it black, and change the clothes. But Angel definitely had possibilities. His demo tape proved that abundantly even if he'd picked all the wrong music to record. Country and western yet! And some fucking Rogers and Hammerstein ditties. Well, maybe his mother or his seventh-grade music teacher had done the picking.

And even if he couldn't sing, there were his headshots. The camera loved this boy. I couldn't believe my luck. I was glad I hadn't pulled the agency from the yellow pages after all.

The song died away. Seven years since Timmy Valentine's disappearance, and the music was fresh as ever, and the voice still haunting, still unforgettable.

You really think I can sound like that? Angel said. I could tell he was awed.

I'll be frank, I said. I don't know.

What I do know is I can make you a star.

Jonathan Burr, director:

I had a feeling he would be difficult. I mean, beneath his polite yessir, nossir attitude there was a kind of arrogance. I didn't like him. I didn't like him at all.

Elena Horsting, schoolteacher:

I was glad I wasn't going to have to be his studio teacher.

Petra Shiloh, journalist:

I remember the first time I saw Angel Todd. It was way over on the other side of the hotel coffee shop. There were a dozen other Timmy Valentine look-alikes swarming through the lobby, each one of them with his entourage in tow, agents in shades, managers in business suits, mothers and sisters and big brothers staring at each other with ill-concealed animosity.

I was hunched over my notes. It was only when I moved the plastic flower vase that I saw him. He wasn't like the others. There was nothing childlike about him. The way he sat, his body language, as he listened to his

mother and his agent, was grave and confident. He was
a grownup in a child's body. He didn't look that much
like Timmy Valentine, but he had the same poise, the
same sense of balance. And he had something that
Timmy Valentine didn't have—a barely submerged adolescent sexuality, smoldering, raring to erupt. An embry-
onic James Dean kind of a thing I guess. He didn't have
the Valentine mystery—he was somehow more blatant,
more on the surface. It was precisely because he wasn't
slavishly imitating Timmy Valentine that my gaze was
drawn to him.

And also he reminded me of my son.

I remember thinking: This kid's going to win the look-
alike contest hands down. There's no comparison with
the others. He's going to get the part. Even if he can't
sing and dance . . . they'll lip-synch his voice, they'll use
stunt dancers . . . they'll do anything just to get in a few
close-ups of those eyes.

I had to stop thinking of my son. Perhaps I would go
down to Forest Lawn later and lay some more flowers by
his grave. I could do it that afternoon, between the get-
acquainted lunch and the producers' press conference.

Jonathan Burr:

But even though I didn't like him I could tell that there
was something of myself in him. Maybe that's why we
always fought.

Brian Zottoli:

The first time I saw Angel Todd was on MTV. I'd had
a shitload of downers. It was the day they were going to
take away my cable box and turn off my phone.

I remember thinking: What bullshit! If they wanted to
know what Timmy Valentine was really like, why didn't
they come to me? Shit, I could have used the money, sold
an option, been able to move out of this one-room shit-
hole above a toy-store front.

No one's ever going to believe that Angel Todd was Timmy Valentine, not in a million years. Ask me why don't you? Ask me.

I knew him. I was close to him, real close.

I was this close to driving a stake through his heart.

Gabriela Muñoz:

Some kids, when you say that to them, they'll turn white and red and start to gibber and pant. Angel Todd didn't.

His mom was doing all those things. Pacing up and down and looking out of the window and smoking like a fucking chimney.

Angel looked me straight in the eye and said, Why, ma'am, I'd like that very much.

Timmy Valentine:

The first time I saw him I envied him.

He was already bursting with incipient sexuality. He was warm, full-blooded, full of enthusiasm. He was alive.

These were all things for which I would gladly have exchanged my immortality.

2

SÉANCES IN THE SAND

❦ ❦

VISION SEEKER

Despite her talk-show notoriety and her frequent appearances in the pages of the *Enquirer,* Simone Arleta, it was rumored, liked to think of herself as a private woman. She had no palace in the Hollywood hills, no glitzy office on Rodeo Drive. To reach her, a person had to drive fifty, sixty miles, and not on the freeway either. But Petra Shiloh didn't mind the drive, didn't mind the canyon road and the blistering Mojave Desert sun. There wasn't much that Petra cared about anymore. Jason's death had changed everything.

The silver Nissan didn't have much pickup and she found herself flooring constantly as the road snaked uphill. The air conditioner was stressed out, the engine was stressed out, *she* was stressed out. She was tempted to pull in somewhere, call the estate, put off the interview.

Not that there was anywhere to pull into, and not that one would ever dictate to the flamboyantly dictatorial Simone Arleta, self-proclaimed queen of psychics, doyenne of daytime talk television. Petra tried to stay calm as the sweat began running into her eyes.

If only she could put it off for another week . . . another day. Her forehead burned. She rummaged in the glove compartment for an Advil. It was too early for PMS, but then again nothing had been regular lately. She fumbled with the radio. New Age synth music played softly beneath the hum of the air conditioner. It didn't make her more restful. She put the radio on auto-search. Newsmen mumbled. Preachers ranted. Metallica pounded. Then, as though crystallizing out of the dense air, there came the voice of Timmy Valentine. Why did it have to be that song? She tried to detach herself. Valentine was part of her story too, after all. Valentine was the reason she'd demanded the story. The answer to her grief was somewhere in the music of the boy who, supernova-like, had blazed briefly in the early eighties, only to vanish mysteriously in what was widely regarded as the publicity stunt of the decade. Was he dead? Was he in hiding, along with Elvis, in the caverns of Mars or the mists of Venus? Only the music remained.

She drove on. The boy's otherworldly voice overpowered the song's sugary harmonies and trite lyrics. There was something there besides the music itself . . . an overwhelming sense of thwarted innocence, of tragedy. At last the song ended. Its final cadence lingered like the memory of an intense erotic experience.

The car wheezed its way to the top of the hill. Then it began gathering speed as the road swept down an incline, hugging the side of a sheer sandstone drop that overlooked a desolate vista of sand and scrub. The sun was in her eyes. She was going blind. Oh God, she thought, the road's shaking, the road's swaying back and forth like a snake charmer's snake, oh God I can't see and I can't see and—

A boy stood in the road. A boy with headphones in his ears.

She honked madly at him to get out of the way.

He looked up at her with hungry eyes. A flaxen-haired boy in a T-shirt and dirty jeans. She honked again. He didn't move.

Jesus, he *wants* me to kill him, she thought, and then the sunlight was in her eyes again and she panicked—

Petra slammed on her brakes. Stones pelted the windshield. A thud, and then he rolled up the hood with his arms outstretched. The boy's face squished against the glass . . . a hanged boy . . . his tongue protruding . . . his skin blue-green . . . his eyes bulging out of puckering sockets . . . Jason.

The car skidded to a halt in the middle of the road. There was distant rumbling. A tremor racked her body. Was it an earthquake? She didn't know if the earth was shaking or whether it was just her.

"Jason," she said aloud.

Jason was gone. It had been another apparition. There was no earthquake. It was just like that when she had found him dead. No earthquake. No comets to trumpet his passing. A quarter-inch in the local paper. Another occult teen suicide, another statistic. My son, she thought.

Stop haunting me, she said to him. Stop haunting me. I loved you so much. You had no right to leave me. Oh Jesus, what did I do to you? Jason, Jason. She closed her eyes and saw him again, a boy and a lemon tree and her ex's leather belt, the only thing he had left behind when he'd driven off into the night, nine years ago.

A boy hanging from a lemon tree. The air heavy with the fragrance of semen-tainted citrus. The CD Walkman was still buzzing in his ears. The name of the song was "Vampire Junction."

In the middle of the highway, drenched in suffocating sunlight, Petra Shiloh began to weep bitterly. No cars passed in the road as she vented her grief and anger. She was alone.

Alone with the memory of her son.

SHAMANESS

A turtle crawled across the marble-faced writing desk in the room without walls at the center of the Arleta mansion. Idly, Simone Arleta petted the creature as she searched through a fat file folder marked "Muriel."

Candles burned everywhere. There were tall candles and fat candles and candles shaped like mythical beasts and candles that spelled out I LOVE YOU in wax. Candles with the fragrances of jasmine and lemon and pumpkin and blueberry and pine and musk. In one corner of the room burned a row of votive candles bearing the image of Saint Barbara, the decapitated saint, who in reality is Shangó, the god who gives power over others. Shadows danced across the walls as Simone brushed the blue-white curls from her eyes and leafed through Muriel Hykes-Bailey's old letters.

Muriel had been a silly old woman really, a dilettante; she had never known what she had gotten herself into. At least she'd managed to die in a spectacular manner, getting herself blown to smithereens on stage at a rock concert, with half the audience convinced they were just the latest stage effects from Timmy Valentine's ever-inventive production designers. Muriel and her withered friends from her Cambridge days . . . old things who wanted to inject a few final thrills into their decadent existences . . . how pathetic they had been. Muriel Hykes-Bailey was no witch. But she had shown Simone the way to Timmy Valentine, a source of almost limitless diabolical power.

He is, she read, *an elemental of some kind. Am convinced after he visited me in my dreams. Many characteristics of an incubus—or is it succubus? Can never keep the damn terminology straight.*

Or perhaps a vampire.

Muriel's friends, the Gods of Chaos, had been no match for the dark forces. But when it came to dark forces, Simone Arleta had their number. Hadn't she turned a woman into a toad right there on "Oprah"? Mass hypnosis, they called it.

Simone smiled. She adjusted her robes. That reporter or whoever she was would be arriving soon, and everything had to look just right. The black arts were ninety percent show biz.

But now it was time for the other ten percent.

She lifted the turtle up in her cupped hands. Its feet were curiously dry; she had never shaken the notion that these creatures should be slimy. It didn't try to escape; she had reared it since it hatched, after all.

She stroked the little head with her forefinger a couple of times. Blew the creature a kiss. And whispered the words *Eternity, eternity, eternity.*

Then she bent down and bit off its head.

She spat the head out along with a mouthful of blood and bile. Dark fluid was gushing from the stump. The torso convulsed as she gripped it in both hands and began asperging herself, the walls, the writing desk. Blood fizzed as it struck candle flames and ran into wax. She whirled, she chanted gibberish, she leaped.

At last the headless creature grew still. Its life force was gone. Wiping the blood from her lips and cheeks with a fold of her robe, Simone sat down again. She tossed the torso into a slop pail under her writing desk, and threw in the head as well. It plopped against the packed carcasses of other headless turtles. Thank God, Simone thought, I've managed to keep all my teeth. She picked a speck of raw turtleflesh from one of her molars and flicked it into the pail. Tomorrow would be rats; mammals were always more satisfying anyway.

There was no way of telling time in the room without walls. But Simone could sense that the reporter was near. Out here on her estate there were so few souls that each presence could be perceived quite distinctly, as, in a still pond, one could gauge the size and number of pebbles being dropped in by the pattern of ripples in the water. This was to be just a routine interview; one of those *Enquirer*-type journals that would end up making up its own story anyway. She closed her eyes and concentrated. The stench of blood almost overpowered the hundred mingled fragrances of candles.

She tried to reach out with her mind. She liked to know people before she faced them. It was a woman, she realized. Since her days on the stage circuit she had learned that women were much less easy to read than men; it was as though they spent their entire lives in concealment, and made a habit of hiding things that really did not need to be hidden.

This woman was in turmoil. Something was impelling her toward this meeting with Simone Arleta, something far more urgent than an assignment from a newspaper— some yet unspoken need within the woman herself.

That was good. Simone enjoyed enigmas. She loved to watch the workings of Fate as the threads of individual destinies stranded and unstranded.

The woman would be here within the hour. Right now she had stopped for some reason. It was easy to get a fix on her. She was sitting somewhere drowning herself in grief. Simone siphoned off some of that raw emotion and savored its taste. It gave her an instant rush, like a candy bar; grief was one of her favorite emotions.

The woman knew nothing of this at all. And yet . . . there was a bond between them now . . . puppeteer and puppet . . . hunter and hunted.

She shrieked with maniacal delight. She swept her arms across the table. Candles went flying. Oh, she felt warm, she felt protected by layers of another's feelings . . . at last she found the intercom, the thing that connected her to the rest of the universe she owned.

"Jacques," she said, "Jacques! Prepare for yet another guest. Moderate to semi-ostentatious scenario, I think.

And . . . it's getting toward suppertime . . . we had better have one of those candlelight dinners you do so well."

She glanced at the slop bucket at her feet. "Turtle soup, I think," she said. "It's about time you emptied the trash."

VISION SEEKER

There was the estate, the exterior of it so integrated with the sandstone that it seemed almost like the cliff dwellings of ancient Indians. She parked her car; inside the nearest cave, concealed from view by a wall of rock, was an elevator that whisked her into the heart of Simone Arleta's lair.

A man in a butler's uniform ushered her into a waiting room. The décor was nouveau Southwestern. A mural depicted some kind of kachina ceremony, with masked dancers waving bizarre utensils. Petra sat down. The sofa enveloped her so thoroughly she felt almost as though she were floating in amniotic fluid. The lighting was muted and seemed to have no source. On the coffee table were the kind of magazines one might find at a dentist's office. She leafed through a *Time* magazine; there was a brief piece on the upcoming Timmy Valentine look-alike contest in Los Angeles.

Iced tea appeared as if by magic. It had a hint of passion fruit. Then, just as she was beginning to wonder whether the fabulous Simone Arleta would ever condescend to appear, the mural slid aside and she saw the queen of the psychics in the flesh, sitting on a papasan chair in a flowing robe, her plump fingers sporting a half-dozen Liberace-style rings, her towering coiffure a triumph of the wigmaker's art. New Age music tinkled away on hidden speakers. She was lit by candlelight. Unobtrusively, the fluorescent lights dimmed.

"Impressive," said Petra. It would not do to appear

daunted. After all, this gaudy creature might be idolized by millions, but Petra did not believe in psychics.

Simone Arleta, rising from her throne, waddled forward and extended her hand. Petra didn't know whether to shake it or kiss it. Simone sat down beside her and took her hand firmly. She did not let go. She sat uncomfortably close. She was, Petra saw, a tiny woman, less than five feet tall.

Simone didn't speak and didn't let go of her hand. Petra had the uneasy feeling that there was something going on . . . that the old woman was somehow . . . sucking something out of her. She shuddered.

"Poor, poor girl," Simone said. "How you have suffered." Her voice dripped with theatrical empathy. Petra thought, I should see through this charade, but somehow I feel she knows something. . . .

An image of Jason rose unbidden to the surface of her mind.

"A child, I see," Simone said. "Death, unexpected."

"How can you know such a thing?" Petra said. God, she's zeroing in and plucking it out of me, feeding on my grief . . . she's a voyeur. An emotional vampire.

"It's in your eyes."

"Please," Petra said, managing to wrest away her hand, "I didn't come here for a consultation. I was hoping to talk about you, not about me. I've been sent by *Entertainment World* to pick up the trail of Timmy Valentine, if I can . . . I understand the studio's asked you to appear at the look-alike contest they're sponsoring so they can find someone to play him in the movie, and"— Oh God, I'm talking too fast and I can't get away from her eyes—"and you've announced that there's going to be something really *big* going on, and there's some speculation you may actually attempt to channel Timmy Valentine himself as one of the judges for the contest. . . ."

She paused to take another sip of the tea. Looking away didn't help. She could feel the woman's eyes on her.

"You've come to see me," Simone said, "because I'm colorful, I'm always good copy, I'm a joke, a charlatan . . . and I've been on a lot of talk shows . . . I'm right up there with the Reagans' astrologer. Am I right? And you don't believe."

Petra stared past the wall that had been the mural, past the throne surrounded by hundreds of votive candles.

"There won't be any TV channeling of Timmy Valentine, Petra," Simone said. "You can only channel the dead."

"So you think he's alive!" This was what she had hoped for. Her editor wanted a Timmy Valentine sighting even if she had to manufacture one, but it was always better to preserve a semblance of good journalism.

"Alive? No, I didn't say that. But assuredly, my friend, not dead."

Simone turned away abruptly. With a start, Petra realized that she had been violated somehow. Her mind had been raped. Petra knew all about rape.

That was how Jason had been conceived.

"Let's have a bite to eat before the séance, shall we?" said Simone.

"Séance?" Petra felt a sudden chill. Weren't they rushing things a bit? She had only come to get an interview, not get sucked into a voodoo bullshit session!

"My dear"—once more came that hand, gripping hers, burning!—"you didn't just come here for a story. You could have waited until the look-alike contest next week to interview me. You chose to come here, to my desert lair. I didn't reel you in. You chose to come. Because you want to talk to your son."

Petra fought to avoid tears. "You must be right." Simone's hand offered no comfort. "I want to talk to Jason." She had resigned herself.

She reached for the Advil bottle in her purse. It was empty. From the distance came the thrum of helicopter blades. Were there to be other guests at this dinner?

Would there be others at the séance, eavesdropping on her grief? She hoped not.

"Headache, my dear? Let me get it for you."

Simone Arleta cupped her hands over Petra's forehead. She began to croon and mumble nonsense syllables. Then she said, over and over, "Drawing it out . . . releasing . . . drawing it out . . . releasing." What kind of New Age psychobabble have I let myself in for? Petra thought. Then, with appalling suddenness, the pain was gone. In its place there was . . . nothing at all. Empty space. Oblivion.

"Why, thank you," she said. "It's been bothering me all day."

"That's my job," said Simone, "easing the pain. Think of me as a kind of doctor."

DISSOLVE

Dinner was agony. There were thirteen at the table and the meal was served by an army of elegantly dressed waiters in matching uniforms; all of them had the look of having been plucked off Malibu beach. The meal was all exotica: from the turtle soup appetizer to the salmon soufflé and venison Wellington to the three kinds of coffee and the flambé dessert, this was not casual dining.

Petra was sandwiched in between a youthful Asian woman in a Dior suit and a bearded, corpulent man who looked familiar, and whose voice had something of a Kentucky twang. After puzzling awhile she realized that she had seen him on television now and then while playing cable roulette with the controller . . . he was some kind of televangelist. She wondered what one of those people was doing here; did they believe it was all Satanism?

Not many people conversed at the dinner table. Each one looked awkwardly at the others; Petra had the feeling that each one of them had come here thinking he had been granted a private audience with the queen of psychics.

Toward the end of the meal, the Asian girl turned to her and said, "I'm so nervous; aren't you? I've never come to one of these things before."

Despite the severity of her suit—it looked much too old for her—and the fact that she wore little makeup, she had the kind of fine-boned beauty that made men stop in their tracks—and even women. Her voice was barely a whisper. "My name is Premchitra," she said. "Just call me Chit, everyone does. I'm a sophomore at Mills College."

"A Thai?" Petra said, hoping she wouldn't offend her by guessing wrong; she knew, from her Berkeley days, how touchy Asians could be about their nationality.

Chit laughed prettily, covering her mouth with her hand. "You must be a writer; writers always know these things."

"Well, if you can call stringing for *Entertainment World* writing," Petra said.

"Don't sell yourself short," said Chit, and laughed again.

"Will we be called in separately for our séances?" Petra said. "Or is it some kind of group spectacle?"

"Oh, I wouldn't know. I am only here because my mother sent me. She had a visit from the family shaman," she said solemnly, "and then I had a fax from Bangkok, and here I am; I had to skip a final." She shrugged; clearly the exams were of no consequence to her.

"Sometimes it's together, sometimes it's separate," said the putative televangelist. "It all depends on how the spirit moves her. And I can tell you, the spirit that moves her ain't holy." He downed a glass of the Châteauneuf du Pape that had come with the venison.

At the head of the table, Simone banged for attention on a little gong. "We will retire to the drawing room for brandy, cappuccino, and—for those who absolutely *must* indulge in filthy Hollywood habits—little red, white or blue pills. Now, dears, we've sat through this long and elegant meal together, and the ice hasn't even begun to crack. I know many of you are not anxious to have your identity known; you have come here in secret."

At that moment, each of the guests was served a white card on a silver plate. They turned the cards over. They were name badges such as one might see at a salesmen's convention. Petra's said: "Hello, I'm TINKERBELL."

"Yes. To preserve anonymity, my friends." Simone Arleta had risen from the table and was being helped into an elaborate robe, embroidered with suns and moons and zodiacal signs, the sort of thing Merlin might wear.

Premchitra's badge read "PRINCESS." The preacher's read "MAMMON." Petra looked around and saw other badges being hastily pinned to lapels and breast pockets. She had a sneaking suspicion that each badge held a secret meaning, if she could only break the code.

The gong sounded again. Warily, the guests made their way into the next room.

NIGHT-MUSIC

Lady Chit had been getting more and more nervous as the dinner proceeded. Of course, she had obeyed the *phuyai* of the family and come to see this rather unorthodox spirit doctor; she was too well brought up to argue with the wishes of her elders. Ten years of American schools hadn't succeeded in transforming her into a barbarian, much as her mother might fret about her forgetting her roots.

In the drawing room, as they waited to be summoned one by one into the presence of Simone Arleta, there was little to soothe her nervousness. The only woman she had even been able to talk to was Petra Shiloh, a journalist, who had not bothered to hide behind the silly charade of pseudonymous badges. Apparently she was hot on the trail of some story to do with Timmy Valentine. Chit remembered how—back in the mid-eighties—she'd been so obsessed with Timmy that she'd even concealed a pinup from *Tiger Beat* inside her pillow at the New England boarding school she'd been going to at the time. She'd written a long letter to her grandfather about Timmy Valentine. He'd gone crazy shortly after that.

This drawing room—ridiculous! A Victorian conceit— plump loveseats, coffee tables with covered limbs, hunting etchings on the walls. Chit knew who half the guests were, but Simone's bizarre protocol forbade any show of recognition. Look—there was Benito Piscopo, a soap opera hunk—and that man sitting in a corner, downing a snifter in one gulp, wasn't that Ali Eslami, the Iranian dissident? And the fat man—wasn't that Damien Peters, the televangelist brought down by some pornography scandal?

One by one they were being summoned into a side room by Jacques, the butler. One by one they were coming out. They seemed dazed. Had they really all seen ghosts, or come face-to-face with some mind-boggling epiphany?

She felt horribly alone. She was by far the youngest person in the room, wasn't she? At length she sought out Petra and tried to engage her in conversation.

"So who have you . . . who are you in mourning for?" she said.

"My son," the journalist said. A string quartet was mangling Mozart's *Eine kleine Nachtmusik*. Rich though Simone Arleta might be, her taste in music was decidedly unrefined.

Lady Chit did not know how to respond. Petra Shiloh's loss could be read easily on her face. Americans never hid their emotions from outsiders, and this one seemed more disturbed than most. Her curiosity got the better of her and before she could stop herself the word "Why?" had already escaped her lips.

"He hanged himself," Petra said.

There was a moment of grave discomfiture; then, to her relief, Jacques came with the summons.

The curtain was whisked aside. She was in a room without walls, lit by thousands upon thousands of candles, their scents melding together like the humid Monsoon night. There was no furniture. Only a few cushions; the quiltwork was either Appalachian or Laotian hilltribe—the styles looked very much alike. Simone Arleta sat in lotus position on a large pillow at the four corners of which burned incense braziers. She clutched a bundle of rags to her breast as though she were suckling a baby.

"Princess," she murmured, "I've been looking forward to this meeting for a long time."

"I'm not a princess," Lady Chit said automatically; it was always hard to explain to foreigners the Thai system of devolving hereditary titles which made a prince's progeny into commoners in five generations. "My grandfather was the last prince in our family."

"It's because of your grandfather that you're here?"

"Yes."

"Prince Prathna. An old man who belonged to a secret society named the Gods of Chaos, founded at Cambridge in the years of the First World War. A voluptuary who possessed a garden of delights in Bangkok in which his guests could enjoy every conceivable carnal pleasure. A man who disappeared mysteriously, five years ago, in the tiny town of Junction, Idaho . . . while searching for Timmy Valentine."

"You seem to know more than I do, Madame Arleta. I barely knew my grandfather; I've been in America, going to school, since I was thirteen; my mother asked me to come to you. Our family shaman has told us that my grandfather's ghost is not at rest. He can't *bai phut bai koet*—be reborn into the karmic cycle—until he is exorcised. But she could do nothing since his spirit is somewhere on American soil. That's why my mother asked me to come and see you; you were recommended as the best American spirit doctor money can buy."

"How flattering," Simone said, putting her at her ease despite the strange surroundings.

"Well—she saw you on 'Letterman' once."

They both laughed. Then, as the laughter died away, as Chit reclined against a cushion and waited, she began to feel afraid. There was something cold in the room. Tickling the nape of her neck. Her hands were shaking. She watched as Simone rocked slowly back and forth, her eyes closed, murmuring to herself, sometimes bursting into snatches of song. Now and then she made cooing noises to the bundle.

"My spirit guide," she said. "Show me, show me . . . beyond the river of forgetting . . . beyond the bourn of death."

Then came another voice: high, pure, like the voice of a little boy.

"Premchitra," the voice said. She had heard the voice before. Was it only in her dreams? The old woman rocked back and forth, back and forth, and the song she sang was like a lullaby. "Premchitra," it said again.

"Do I know you?"

The voice laughed a little, and then was solemn again. "Take my hand." She reached out and touched the withered hand of Simone Arleta, but the sensation was of a young boy's hand, smooth, stealing the warmth from her own hand. Although she was still reclining at the medium's feet, she could feel herself being pulled forward, out of herself.

A cold wind seared her face. Snowflakes tickled her cheeks. She saw burnt buildings . . . a gas station with its pumps half-buried in the snow . . . a railway platform with no roof, and the track twisted into angry, angular sculptures . . . she was drifting over snowdrifts, drifting with the bitter wind that howled through the hollow houses of a ghost town, shaking the ice from the naked branches . . . and she heard the wind sigh her name, *Chitchitchitchit* . . . a door without a wall slammed over and over as the hinges screeched her name *Chitchitchitchit* and the moon was full and red as blood. . . .

"Where am I?" she whispered.

"This place is called Junction," said the voice of the boy. "It burned down years ago."

"Where is my grandfather?"

And then she saw him. Slithering down the snow-covered high street . . . a severed head with a trail of innards, propelling itself forward with its tongue . . . "Grandfather!" she screamed . . . it came toward her . . . the jellied eyes bulging, rheumy tears oozing into the snow . . . maggots tunneled around its nostrils . . . pus matted its hair . . . it stared at her with naked rage. Prince Prathna had become the most dreaded of the undead . . . a *phii krasue* . . . the lowest order of supernatural beings, so degraded that they lived on human excrement. He must have died in infamy or he would not have been condemned to such a fate. But wasn't a *phii krasue* supposed to be female? Was this a grim karmic joke about the prince's sexual ambiguity? "Grandfather!" she cried. "Don't you know me? I'm Chit, your littlest granddaughter. . . ."

She ran toward him, her feet skimming the cold snow. He looked at her. He didn't even know her! He began to wriggle toward her, his esophagus pulsating, his intestines steaming, moved only by his primal hunger. Wet smacking sounds came from his lips. He was after her! She felt the tongue now, sliding up her calf, moist and sticky and . . .

"No!" Abruptly she let her hand slip from her guide's. She began to fade out of the vision. In a moment she was back in the room without walls. She was sobbing, shaking.

Simone Arleta put down her bundle and opened her eyes.

"Did you see what you came to see?" she said. "Don't cry, my dear." She fished a Kleenex from somewhere in her robes and bent down to wipe Lady Chit's tears.

"It was so real!" Lady Chit said. "But this is the twentieth century and I don't believe in *phii krasues* or shamans or exorcists. . . . It's my mother, you see, it's all her doing. . . ."

Simone opened her arms to her. Helpless, Chit fell into the old woman's embrace. She was still shivering from the cold of the ghost town. Her cheeks were frozen. She wondered if the snowflakes were still clinging to them. Simone's arms were full of warmth and comfort, but there was something else there too . . . something that seemed to feed on her innermost emotions. She did not like this thing, she wanted to tear herself away, but somehow she felt dependent, unable to release herself . . . this woman was like a drug, she realized. That was the hold she had over her many adherents.

DISSOLVE: NIGHT-MUSIC

Petra said, "Look, we don't have to do this if you don't want to. I know you normally get . . . a substantial fee for doing this kind of thing and . . . well, *Entertainment World* isn't planning to cover . . ."

"It's all right to be nervous. It's only natural. Relax, Petra. Relax. You are afraid of what your son may say to you. Afraid he may . . . blame you somehow."

Of course she was right. It was armchair psychology of the most elementary sort. I have to forget about myself. Become part of the furniture and just observe. How Simone thinks, talks, her body language.

Petra looked around and began settling into her journalistic mode. Simone was seated, cross-legged, on a silk pillow. Everything in the room was black. The walls, the candles, thousands of them, all black; a low table or altar behind Simone, polished onyx, with a black idol, many-armed. The ruby in the idol's forehead was the only color in the whole room. There were no windows. There was no sense of size or proportion. It was as though the room were completely outside the universe. Nothing was real and everything was real.

Petra could see how carefully the room had been designed. The client would be disoriented. Squatting on the floor in the posture of a supplicant, her eyes would be drawn upward, toward the old woman's face. You couldn't help but feel her power. Petra wondered whether the room was rearranged between sessions—whether there was a custom-designed environment for each member of her exclusive clientele.

"Relax," Simone said. "Relax, relax . . ."

Was this hypnosis? Didn't hypnosis always begin with *relax, relax*? Petra tensed. She wanted to fight it. She was afraid of what would happen once she was in the power of this woman . . . this woman who seemed to be growing in stature, who seemed to have wreathed herself in a blood-tinged mist, who seemed to have awakened the wind and released the cold of winter into the room . . . what was happening to her?

"Let go of me!" Petra whispered.

"I'm not holding on to you. You are free to leave. But you don't want to. Come with me. On a journey. Back to the past. To the time when your son was still alive."

Birds were singing . . . the sun was bright, drenching the citrus trees . . . the light sparkled on the swimming pool . . . a buzzing sound . . . like the chirping of crickets . . . *dzzzt . . . dzzzt . . .* the sound of headphones on a hanging boy.

She felt a hand in hers. It was cold and smooth, a child's hand. Simone had not moved, and her hands were folded on her lap.

"Who are you?" she said. "A-are you Jason?"

"No. I am the spirit guide. The one who speaks through Simone Arleta." The voice was a child's voice. It was high and sweet and pure. But it held a hint of lasciviousness. It sounded so familiar . . . but she could not dredge up the memory of it. "Come with me. Come, Petra Shiloh." Simone smiled. Her face seemed unlined now, much younger . . . a trick of the candlelight, Petra thought, or of the medium's art. She had interviewed a multiple personality once. She knew they had the same uncanny ability to reshape the very features of the face into an alien persona. "Come, come." She felt the hand stroking her own. She was aware of the very blood as it raced through the capillaries of her fingers. And still Simone's hands rested on her lap. The hand of the spirit guide was a spectral hand. Like a marble headstone, it stole the warmth out of her skin. It sent a chill shooting up her veins like a drug.

"Who are you?" she said.

"I cannot say. I am something born in the night; I am darkness; I am cold; I am love unborn and memory undead."

The hand gripped her. She felt herself being jerked upright. And suddenly she was standing there, in the back of her house, under the streaming sun, and there was her child, his face blue, his neck craning at an inhuman angle, reeking of shit and vomit so that even closing her eyes she could smell he was dead, dead, dead. And the birds were singing.

"Jason . . . baby . . ." And she was running toward him, the hot tears blurring in her eyes, weeping the way she had not been able to weep the day she had found him dead. "Jason, why did you leave me? Why?"

You should have aborted me. Bitch!

She looked up. For a moment she thought she saw the lips move. Then the lolling tongue began to drool on her. "No!" she shrieked. "Let me out of this dream—"

And suddenly she was in the séance room again. And Simone was sitting there, utterly tranquil. "You're a fraud!" Petra screamed. "Jason would never say that to me—never never never!"

Simone's face wrenched into a leer. *Did you ever see me for what I was? Jesus fucking Christ, you make me sick. The martyr, the rape victim. You hooked my stepdad with that spiel. Did you know he used to beat the shit out of me with that belt whenever you were out of the house?*

"Oh Jesus, what are you telling me—I'll kill him—I didn't know, I swear—I'll *kill* him for hurting you—" What did this mean? How could she know it was true? Words spewed from the febrile mind of a Hollywood psychic . . . Wildly she looked around, and she realized she had never left the vision at all, they were superimposed on each other, the dark room with the candles and the summer sunlight in the orchard with the dead kid and she had her arms around him and was trying to rock him back to life and he was heavy as a sack of stones, heavy as only a dead person can be.

It was you, Mom. I've always known you wanted me dead. Go ahead, kill him. You should have aborted me. You should have fucking aborted me.

And he put his arms around her. Arms heavy with sluggish dead blood. Heavy. The arms tightened around her. Not human arms. Tight and unbending like the arms of a robot.

You think I'm dead but now I'll never let you go—

His tongue swayed to and fro like a snake. His eyes rolled. He pulled her into an obscene embrace and she could feel the cold tongue against her cheek, chill and moist and stinking of compost, forcing her lips apart, shoving itself into her as her gorge began to rise—

Don't you love me, Mommy? Mommy—Mommy—fuck me, Mommy—fuck me fuck me—

"No!" she shrieked. The vision began to fade. She found herself in the arms of the old woman. Her eyes had retreated into their sockets and her empty pupils glittered like polished stones. "You're not my Jason—you're an illusion—a filthy trick!"

Petra found herself panting and sobbing. Sweat slicked her forehead. Her heart was beating fast. God, let this be over soon. But the old woman didn't seem to be coming out of her trance.

"Jason?" she said softly.

Scared you, didn't I? It was Jason's voice. Unmistakable. The voice of a teenager, just cracking, surly and vulnerable at the same time. *Never did get a chance to act on my Oedipal urges while I was still alive.*

"Simone plucked you from my mind, manufactured you out of all the guilt I'm feeling, the guilt I haven't been able to unload."

Don't you wish!

The taste of death was still in her mouth. She disentangled herself from Simone's arms. The medium did not try to hold on, but settled back into her lotus position. Petra sat back and waited.

Presently there came the voice of the other boy, seductive, lilting: "Do not be sad, Petra. He has only been with us for a little while. He is bitter. But the pain will pass for him as well as for you."

Again she felt the hand in hers. Fading now . . . fading . . . as Simone slowly opened her eyes as from a deep and ancient sleep.

"Before you go," Simone said—smiling now, seemingly unaware of the terrors she had unleashed from Petra's unconscious—"fetch me my purse, will you, dear? Right there, on the coffee table, behind you . . . don't mind the incense brazier, just push it out of the way. My spirit guide wanted you to have something. . . ."

Numbly, Petra did as she was told and handed her the leather Gucci handbag. Simone fished out a business card. "There!" she said. "He wanted you to have this. He said you'll find healing there. And also you'll find a lot of other answers you never expected."

The card read:

San Fernando Valley Grief Counseling Center

There was an address in Encino. Had to be one of those hundred-dollar-an-hour New Age bullshit therapy things. She wondered if Simone owned stock in it.

Simone laughed. "I don't own stock in it, if that's what you're thinking."

Petra managed a wan smile as she stuffed the card into a pocket. Then—she couldn't help herself anymore—she began to weep, passionately and inconsolably. And the medium, stroking her forehead with a tenderness that was as sensual as it was comforting, said, "There, there . . . I know, I know."

DISSOLVE: LOOKING-GLASS

The room had been transformed once more. Soft light suffused it. The ceiling was white, the walls off-white, and Simone faced Damien Peters, her oldest friend, her confederate in the art of deception.

"Everything going all right?" he said. He was still handsome, she thought, even though the sex scandal and the IRS probe had rendered permanent the furrows in his cheeks and forehead, and his hair had gone quite white. "I wouldn't want you to overwork yourself, now, and leave nothing for me, you hear."

"You want to talk to Jesus tonight? Or don't you dare disturb him after all those revelations on Larry King last week? What a floozy! You really can pick them, Damien . . . it's a wonder your ministry wasn't aborted at the outset."

"Don't you be pinning a word like abortion on me,

honey," said Damien. "Sometimes it doesn't hurt to compromise a little with Mammon, but outright murder just ain't my style."

"What about your late wife?" Simone said slyly. "Although I know the inquest cleared you of any . . . complicity."

"Ah, but she was removed for the good of the greater whole. And I'm certain she's a-strumming her harp right this minute up there in the clouds."

Although she had known him for almost twenty years, Simone had never gotten any closer to fathoming this man. She did not believe in evil; he did, but he regarded his relationship with evil in very much the same light as an ongoing negotiation between union and management. That he was a hypocrite was clear—his very presence here, in league with someone who, from the viewpoint of his theology, could be none other than a servant of Lucifer, attested to this. But she could never be entirely sure how much was true religious feeling and how much the extravagant blandishments of the snake-oil merchant. One thing was clear—he understood, and wanted, power, and though fallen from grace his charisma was still commanding.

"Let's get down to business, Simone. My ministry is in bad shape—you know that. I need something big— something powerful—like one of them demons you got under your control." His eyes glittered. He took a slug of bourbon from the silver flask he kept in his jacket pocket.

"I have no demons," Simone said. She had to choose her words carefully; it would never do to upset a client's worldview too much, and Damien—despite his protestations of long friendship—was very much a client. "This war of yours between the sheep and the goats, it's none of my business. I don't take sides; I wouldn't dream of trying to predict the winner; I'm just a businesswoman, doing my own thing, speaking to whoever, in the world beyond, will speak to me. I'm no Faust, my soul is still my own. Angels and demons . . . that's a *church* distinction . . . some of them are my friends, some are not, that's all."

"You'll excuse me, honey, if I don't share your amoral view of the world. You truck with demons and if I have to truck with you to further God's work, then ay-*men* and let's get on with it."

And he smiled the smile that had once delivered millions to his mailbox, day after day.

DISSOLVE: VISION SEEKERS

She declined Simone's invitation to stay over at the estate. Champagne brunch, they told her. Morning dip in the Olympic Jacuzzi outside in the bracing desert morning . . . an experience not to be missed. Petra wanted to miss it. She wanted to get out of that place before Simone played more mind games.

She had a splitting headache and no more Advil. Simone's visions lingered in her mind. She could still taste Jason's rotting tongue against her lips. How could that woman do that to her, how had she managed to zero in on every piece of filth that lay submerged in her unconscious, beneath all that grief and guilt? How could she know that any of it was true?

There are no monsters, she told herself. The only monsters are the ones inside ourselves. They are part of us. We can control them.

In the parking lot, night had fallen. There were a dozen cars, some of them limousines. There was no moon, but shafts of light fell from upper-story windows. Cacti bordered the parking lot, their silhouettes threatening. The night was chill. You could hear coyotes far off somewhere. Her head was throbbing and she stumbled around for a few moments trying to remember where she had parked.

She got into the Nissan, rolled down the window, and turned on the ignition. The radio came on. It was the same Timmy Valentine song they'd been playing on the drive to the Arleta estate. Jesus Christ, did they have to play that boy's music every moment of the day? She was about to turn the radio off when she saw someone come out of the front entrance. It was that Oriental girl, that princess or whatever she was. She was walking toward a white Porsche.

She stopped a moment, seemed to be listening to something. Petra realized that it was the song on the radio. Angrily she cut it off. But Lady Chit was already walking toward her Nissan. "Ms. Shiloh, Ms. Shiloh—that music—do you realize what it is?"

Petra did not want to stay and discuss music. She was seized with a burning need to escape. She gunned the accelerator. But the woman was holding on to the window, leaning down to talk. What could be so important?

"The music—Timmy Valentine—the spirit guide— don't you recognize that voice?" Lady Chit said. "Some- how—the voice Simone speaks with when she's in that trance—it's *him.*"

It was true. It had to be true. How did she do it? Was Simone Arleta a brilliant mimic, or was it some kind of bizarre channeling deal? "Are you sure?" she said.

She nodded. "When I was thirteen I just lived for that voice. I went to bed at night dreaming about that voice. All us girls did. You know—all-girl's boarding school— you dream about boys a lot. You can't mistake the voice of a childhood idol. Ms. Shiloh, that voice was *real.* And somehow it knew—oh, so many things—things I sus- pected but never dared face. About my grandfather. Did you know that my grandfather was at Timmy Valentine's last concert, that he made a pilgrimage to Junction, Idaho, where Timmy Valentine had his personal fortress of solitude, from which he never returned? He was ob- sessed. I heard that voice again today. That's why I couldn't spend the night here. I was afraid it would haunt my dreams, make me into a little girl again."

She didn't sound like one of those Elvis-on-Mars types who were always trying to sneak into the offices of *Entertainment World*. Petra knew—intuited—that Lady Chit had not imagined this. It was true.

Timmy Valentine's music had accompanied her discovery of Jason's corpse. A story about Timmy Valentine had led her to seek out Simone Arleta. Timmy Valentine's music had haunted her on the long drive through the Mojave Desert.

And now Timmy Valentine had spoken to her. This confirmed it.

"Are you all right? Petra . . ."

"Oh Jesus, do you have an Advil? . . . I don't know what's got to me . . ."

Lady Chit pulled out a bottle from her purse and gave her a handful of pills. "Take what you want . . . I get these in Thailand, you can buy them there without a prescription."

What were they? Valium? Ludes? Petra did not stop to think. She swallowed a couple of them, the little round blue-and-white capsules. In the distance a coyote howled. It was chillier now, and the wind sighed as it sifted the shifting sand. She was tired but when she closed her eyes she could see Jason, waiting in the darkness with his arms outstretched . . . like a mutant cactus in a cloud of dust . . . coming to her and reeking of the grave.

"No, no, no," she whispered. I have to get out here! Before they drive me out of my fucking mind.

The last thing she saw before sliding into drug-induced dreamlessness was the slender young Thai woman walking toward her Porsche. She heard the soft tread of her footsteps on the gravel of the parking lot. At the door Lady Chit turned. The light from the overhead window lent her face an ethereal radiance, but she betrayed no emotion at all.

SHAMANESS

Simone Arleta sat in a room without windows. Alone in a black room. With the candles extinguished, she could no longer tell if the room was real or if she had already entered the inner chamber of her mind, the room of a thousand entrances and one exit.

Come to me, she whispered to the spirit she had held captive for the seven years that had seen her advance from carnival sideshow to television celebrity. Come, come, come.

Come to me, child of the dark, princeling of terrors, come, come, come . . . come to Mommy.

3

THE LOOKING-GLASS COUNTRY

❦ ❦

LOST BOYS

Death is not so dead a place when you get to know it well. Given eternity, dead eyes can grow accustomed to the dark, enough to see the slow slow dance of shadows' shadows, shadows that dance in the cracks between the quanta of darkness. No, death is not so dead a place.

And the place to which he has exiled himself is not even death; it is undeath. He has turned himself inside out and has vanished deep into his inside outside. And the others that came with him are gone.

He is nailed to a tree at the forest's heart. Where he bleeds onto the soil, hyacinths have sprung up. And his tears have brought forth white carnations. Those are thorned vines that lash him to the trunk. A circlet of barbed wire crowns him and his palms are pierced with long-stemmed roses, but they have not staked his heart.

He remembers:

The train that left from the burned-out shell of the

railway station in the town of Junction, Idaho. The old man and the woman sitting with him. They are the only three passengers. As he looks out of the window he sees the town in flames. He is burning up his past. What he had once thought eternal is coming to an end. He is merging with his two lost other selves to become a new kind of creature.

The train pulls away and they sit talking quietly. It is night. As long as they sit in the railway car it will always be night. Night thick as the cold blood that seeps from the necks of dead women, night dark as death and deep as the infinite sea. The kind of night they are journeying into is a night of the soul.

It has not been a sad journey. It is rather the past that has been sad. Trauma piled upon trauma. The mad conductor, Stephen Miles, always fleeing from those who tormented his childhood; the psychoanalyst, Carla Rubens, terribly afraid of the encroachment of death; and he himself, Timmy Valentine, an enigma even to himself.

When they speak to one another, they can hardly be told apart. They are an ancient trinity: Osiris, Isis, Horus; Mage, Sibyl, Child; Father, Son, Paraclete; Creator, Preserver, Destroyer. But now they are slowly merging into one being. In the days when Carla Rubens was treating the neuroses of the rich, she would have called what they were a Jungian triad, one in which each of them was the Anima of one and the Shadow of the other. She would have drawn charts and reveled in the symmetry of their relationships. Now the symmetry is dissolving. But she does not seem to care any longer. She welcomes entropy.

—Where are we going?

—Up. Down. Away. Within.

—It doesn't matter where we go.

—I can't quite get used to it yet.

—Listen! The ceaseless motion of the train. Downhill, downhill, deeper into the woods, away from the town. Can you still see the town?

—In my mind's eye. The past burning up. Joyful. The living and the dead and the undead, all of them, flowering in fireworks of blood and flame. Oh, I will see them always. I will think of them always. That family—what was their name?—

—Gish.

—Did they all die? I think not. I think there are survivors.

—Look around us. On this train reality is in a constant state of flux. Look! That mirror on the wall of the compartment. That was never there before. I think it was something else once—

—A tawdry reproduction of some stray Picasso.

—Look in the mirror. It's not a mirror.

—It's the window where I see the burning city.

—It's the window where I see my whole past whizzing by like the landscape from a speeding train: Cumae, Pompeii, Egypt, Rome, Kyoto, Tiffauges—

—New Jersey. The Upper East Side. Los Angeles.

—Backstage at a hundred opera houses rolled into one.

—Who are we now?

—Does it matter? Look. The forest is enfolding us. Embracing us. Drawing us ever inward. In the end, after the visions of other times, the looking-glass will show us only ourselves.

—Ourselves?

—Our Self.

The three of them continue to speak in turn. At times they are solemn and at times they laugh. They are not afraid of the forest that envelops the train tracks, thickening as they descend. They speak even though they no longer have the need to speak. But speech is a playful thing that reminds them of when they were all still human.

—I wonder what the world will be like when we emerge from the forest.

—How much time will have passed, I wonder! A hundred years?

—Perhaps there will be no more humans. Perhaps the world will have been overrun by vampires.

—How dull!

—How entertaining!

The world darkens.

The three of them have not spoken in a long moment, or perhaps an age, for time is completely subjective in this realm. And still the world is darkening. They feel the movement of the train but they can see nothing save an occasional flash, distant lightning perhaps, that illumines gnarled branches and knotty oaks. Sometimes they catch a snatch of a nightingale's song or the hoot of an owl. More often the only sound is the clatter of wheels and the screech of steel on steel.

A profound stillness shrouds them for a time that cannot be measured in human terms. The forest is the cocoon that sustains them and keeps them warm until that far-off moment when they will be reborn as a single entity.

The boy vampire is not afraid of relinquishing his self. He has been alone so long. He does not want to be alone again; the nightmare will return, the living death men call reality.

He sinks. He gives himself to the darkness. Even the sounds of the train have begun to fade. Even the sense of movement ceases. Even the memories begin to blur, to meld into motionlessness. Even music, which has kept him alive through centuries of torment, has become no more than remembrance.

He is at peace.

And then, abruptly, the peace is shattered.

He wakes. The brakes screech. The train screams as it halts. He is thrown out of his seat.

"Carla! Stephen!" he cries out. He sees no one.

The shutters fly up. He looks out. No one. Only forest. Not a leaf trembles in this time-frozen world.

Silence.

Where have they gone? He calls their names again. He

cannot believe they have abandoned him. He does not even know what this place is. He calls their names and does not even hear the echo of his own voice.

He steps out of the compartment.

There is a voice in the distance. He does not recognize it and cannot tell yet where it is coming from. But it is the only sound. It is the voice of a woman. It is a dry, echoless voice, and it knows his name and calls to him across the darkness: "Timmy Valentine."

Timmy Valentine.

At first he does not even know it is his name. He has had many names, no name for longer than a few years. And this is the forest where there are no names. To name is to control.

"Who are you?" he says. "What have you done with the others?"

Come to me, the voice says, *come to Mommy.*

There is distant thunder.

The boy feels fear. He cannot believe it is his own. How can he know fear? Fear is something only mortals can comprehend, because to fear is always to know that one stands in the shadow of death, a breath from oblivion; it has been centuries since he knew fear firsthand. He has smelled the fear of humans; pheromonal terror, carried by the wind, extruded by the sweat glands, racing in blood. Fear has fed his desire as blood has slaked his thirst.

The fear he feels now is different. It is *he* who is in danger. The blood in his veins, made sluggish by centuries of death, stirs, pumps to the beat of another's heart. Entranced, he walks from darkness to deeper darkness.

I call you back to the world, Timmy Valentine, says the voice. *You may call me Mother.*

"By what power have you reached out to me? By what sorcery do you control me?" the boy says. And still he drifts toward the jungle's heart.

Dark power, says the voice, *dark sorcery.* And laughs. *I have interrupted your journey toward inner harmony be-*

cause I have need of your ancient strength, your dark charisma. Do not struggle. You cannot defeat me. You have learned not to fear the garlic and crosses and silver of men's superstitions. It is not with the forces of light that I bind you, but with darkness deeper than your own. With yourself I bind you, with a thousandfold yourself.

All at once he is flung against the tree at the heart of the forest. The nails are twisting as they lance his palms. His tears are blood. He is alone with the pain of the world, for he has become the world's pain, and in this inner world he is alone. He is crucified.

"What have you done to the others, the musician and the mind magician?"

"They are shadows," says the voice. "You are the only one who has ever been real."

"Then who are you?" he screams to the force that binds him, the only voice that seems to come from beyond the dark.

"Call me Mommy," the voice says. There is no irony in the voice, no laughter.

He thinks: But Night is my mother.

Children of the night. . . .

What music they make.

He sings to himself, very softly. It is an ancient music. It is a song taught him untold centuries ago, in the time of his humanness; a song overheard from a shepherd boy as they visited the Sybil of Cumae in her cave of fog and eternal night. It is the first music he remembers hearing—a song that sprang unbidden to a young boy's lips as he waited for the oracle to speak, a tune at once haunting and dissonant, as the boy's untutored voice wavered between the Dorian and the Phrygian modes— as though he has only heard it moments before, he plucks the contours of the melody from the empty air. *Nox est perpetua una dormienda.*

He knows that his captor will use that music to cause others pain and death. But he cannot help himself. There is an emptiness that must be filled. Music is the prime imperative. Even the stars sing, and the motion of the cosmos is sustained by their music. Before all that was, before even the creation of light, music is.

The boy's is the sole consciousness in the dark universe of his imprisonment. It will only take a few notes to shape the formless void. Though there is no light yet, he can already feel the trees begin to blossom.

THERAPY

So what is it you dream about? Does anyone want to talk about dreams? Petra, you haven't said anything yet.

Crucifixion.

Can you elaborate?

I—I mean there's a forest, and a tree, and a boy nailed to the tree, and I try to talk to him but he can't answer me even though I know he's still conscious and I know he's my son but he's not quite my son. Oh, his eyes look down into mine. He's crying, crying blood I guess. Yeah. And I can't look away and I can't look into his eyes either. I'm afraid of him and I love him. It's a very dark place. It reminds me of Minneapolis. Don't laugh, when I was a kid I stayed one summer with a sick aunt in Minneapolis and she had the thermostat on ninety degrees when it was ninety degrees outside and she never opened the curtains and the air smelled stale and dying. Okay. We all have a place like this we think about when we're depressed and stone sober.

What do you think he would say to you? If you were that boy, in the middle of the forest, nailed to the tree, and you saw yourself standing at the foot of the tree looking up at yourself?

I think I am saying, "Fuck you you're not my mother get out of my life, fuck you fuck you fuck you fuck you—" No. I think I am saying, "Help me, help me." No no, I'm saying, "Lick the blood that trickles from my fingertips," I'm saying, "Save me, unchain me, free me, touch me," I'm saying, "You know not what you do."

So you don't know what your son is saying.

He's saying all those things. And he's not my son. He's not my son!

Are you a religious woman, Petra?

No. Well, I was raised Catholic. I haven't been to confession in thirty years though. Jason was an altar boy.

How often do you have this dream?

Even when I'm awake. I see him in the rearview mirror of my car when I'm going down the freeway, or downhill when the road slides down Mulholland when I'm on my way home from therapy.

Is the mirror important?

Yeah. Because when I'm dreaming everything is always reversed, left to right, light to dark.

When was the first time you had this dream? Was it after your son committed suicide?

It's not my son.

LOST BOYS

He woke up. Perhaps it was one of the nightmares. There were many nightmares. People burning. People suffocating. People freezing under the piling snow. Sometimes they were himself and sometimes they were other people, dim remembrances.

It wasn't one of the nightmares. He'd taken too many Valium for nightmares. Through the fog of semiconsciousness he realized it was only the phone. And the answering machine was already interposing itself between him and the world. The efficiency stank of alcohol and unchanged sheets. The neon clock on the far wall said 3:00 A.M.

"Brian," said the answering machine from the kitchenette. The voice was half-familiar. No. It couldn't be that voice. Not unless the voice had come out of the nightmare, the one that the Valium was supposed to drive away. "Fuck Brian, I hope it's you. There's only one Zottoli in the Los Angeles fucking phone book. Man, I've lost track of you, I don't even know if you're in this town, but Brian, if it's you, pick up the fucking phone. Brian, pick up the phone before this fucking *kills* me."

The voice—it had been a kid's voice once. It was older now, it had gone through adolescence, but there was still something childlike about it, frail. A young boy trying to be heard against the roar of a winter wind. Against the flames of a burning town. Even his cussing had a kind of desperate bravado to it.

Brian Zottoli yanked the phone off the hook and reeled the handset toward the bed. "PJ," he said. "PJ Gallagher, the half-Shoshone kid who—"

They'd come through the fire and the snow together, he and PJ and that Gish kid, the only three survivors of Junction. Him delirious, strapped to a travois, the two boys schlepping him downhill, the wind screaming, the ice flakes scraping his skin raw. And behind them the town burning up. The vampires turning to charcoal. "Jesus," he said, "I never thought I'd hear your voice again. How the hell are you, kid? But you're not a kid anymore." He was groping for something to say, woozy as shit from all the Valium. Why three in the morning for a reunion?

"Brian, listen. Terry's here."

"That's great, but where the fuck is here? And can't this wait till—"

"Fuck, Brian, Terry's standing on the balcony of my apartment, get it? And he's screaming to be let in. He's wearing a tuxedo. He's pale as . . . Brian, I just flew back from his fucking *funeral*. He's *dead.*"

"Jesus . . . don't let him in!" He fumbled for the light.

Light came suddenly, yellow against the dusty venetian blinds. The fear came back now, all of it, all at once.

Moonlight on silver-sharp fangs and—

He closed his eyes. A curtain of blood descended. Jesus I'm scared. I'm fucking scared. His hands were shaking.

"Can you come over?" PJ said softly.

"I don't even know where you are."

"It's the craziest thing, Brian. I found you in the white pages and you're two blocks away, on the other side of the boulevard from me. Jesus, Brian, I'm depending on you, you're my only hope."

In the background Brian heard a rat-tat-tat, a dead hand rapping on glass, and a voice: "C'mon. Lemme in. I won't do nothing. I'm your friend. Your best goddamn friend."

The last time he'd seen PJ: at a Greyhound station in Idaho Falls. A dirty-faced boy next to a bank of dirty snow, a boy with a cigarette, not inhaling. Terry Gish was there too, a redheaded kid who seemed strangely calm even though he'd staked his own twin brother through the heart and doused him with gasoline and set him on fire, had insisted on doing it with his own hands, out of love.

PJ stood there with the snow flecking his long dark dirty hair. He stubbed out his cigarette in the slush. The air reeked of gasoline and garbage.

"Don't ever call me," he said. "Don't ever fucking call me or set eyes on me again." He stalked on up the street, uphill, into the wind. Brian knew he had turned his back on them so they wouldn't see him crying. He was really into this macho Indian warrior thing.

"Why'd he say that?" Terry said.

"He doesn't mean it," Brian said. "Did you get a bus ticket?"

"Yeah. I got me a one-way ticket to Cheyenne. I got an uncle there or something."

Brian wasn't sure whether to believe him. "You can come with me if you want," he said. "Except I don't know where I'm going."

Terry smiled wanly and said, "It's okay."

Brian had given his last twenty to the boy so he could get his ticket and a sandwich. PJ was going to walk to the reservation, maybe two days' walk if the weather cleared. Brian had his Visa card but there was no money left on it. He decided to start hitching, and by April he had ended up in Hollywood.

He understood why PJ had said he never wanted them to meet again. He felt it too. They had been through fire together, the three of them, and they never wanted to see each other again. Not because the bonds between them had been severed, but because to return to that junction in their lives would be to relive more pain than should be borne again.

Don't ever fucking call me or set eyes on me again—

"I'll be right over." He was already pulling on his jeans, which he'd draped over his computer so that the On light wouldn't glare at him in the dark. On the monitor was a half-finished sentence from a half-finished novel. It was eight months overdue.

"You can walk it. I'm on Argyll and you're on Cherokee."

"Don't let him in." He pulled open the bottom drawer of the desk. He knew the things were all still there. A thermos flask full of holy water. A couple of crucifixes he'd picked up on Olivera Street. A sharpened stake and a battered croquet mallet. A five-strip of Valium and a handful of ludes.

Rat-tat-tat-tat-tat—

I never thought I'd see them again. And now I'm going to have to kill one of them. The little redheaded boy with freckles standing lonely and vulnerable in the bitter wind of an Idaho winter.

He was shaking so hard he decided to take a few more downers before venturing out onto the boulevard.

LOST BOYS

"Come on back to bed, Angel honey."

"Don't want to."

"Well, turn that noise down."

"I can't, Momma. You know I gotta study." One
more notch on the remote . . . yeah. That voice. Shi-it,
how he hits that high one, dead on, pounces on that high
A-flat like it was nothing more than a little mouse. But I
can do it too. I can, I can. My voice won't crack at all,
not unless I grow six inches by Sunday.

Reach for that A-flat. Yowl! Play with it a bit—cat and
mouse—and then toss it away 'cause it's dead now, lifeless, chase after the next note. Shi-*it,* but that boy can
sing.

"Aw, Momma."

And suddenly the voice is gone. You can't hear nothing but the hum of the air conditioner. The magic's gone
too. The wallpaper is peeling and the blue and orange
neon's winking outside the window and you know it's
just another HoJo's in another goddamn city on the road
to stardom. She's turned off the stereo.

"Fuck, Momma. You know I have to be perfect. I
have to try it one more time."

"Momma's tired, Angel. Your voice'll be all tired out if
you keep straining after them high notes. Why don't you
take one of the blue pills the agent gave us? Go on. Lord,
look at you. They really done it to you, you couldn't look
more like those old photographs of Timmy Valentine if
they'd gone and dug him up out of his grave."

"What if he isn't dead?"

"He won't be dead, son, not after tomorrow. You're
going to bring him back to life. And we're going to get us
the biggest old house in Paris, Kentucky, the biggest you
ever did see. Lord, you are beautiful, son. Just look at
yourself in that there mirror. Your blond hair all dyed
black and your face all pale like on the cover of that

album. I sure wish you'd put on that cloak one more time before you come to bed."

"It ain't *me*, Momma."

"Come on."

"You're a sight. How many of them pills did *you* guzzle down?"

"Get into bed."

"Got my own bed, Momma, come on, I'm too old for this, we're in the big city now."

"I'm lonesome, Angel. Since your daddy run out, you been the only man in my life. C'mon, Angel. Give me a kiss."

"Too much liquor on you."

"Kiss me, Angel. Don't leave your momma now. Don't leave me."

"I love you." But my mind's floating in a far 'nother place. I can still hear Timmy's voice behind the traffic and the faraway siren and the chatter of folks in the street. I can hear his voice and I want to follow. His voice is cool, like the darkest part of the forest where the sun don't come even in the heat of summer.

LOST BOYS

Terry Gish was still standing at the balcony when PJ put down the phone. His face was garish in the flashing blue and pink of a neon sushi bar sign. He was still tapping on the pane.

"Go away. I know what'll happen if I let you in."

"Let me in, dude."

"You're not Terry Gish anymore. You're not the Terry Gish I buried yesterday—"

The funeral. Hadn't seen Terry since . . . since Idaho. Didn't even know if he'd made it down to Cheyenne, not until he got the phone call from Terry's Uncle Winslow and cadged a free flight to Denver by hanging around the pilots' lounge at Van Nuys Airport. He'd only just made it to the funeral. The leaves were raining down—PJ hadn't seen autumn in three years—the acrid smell of it caught him by surprise. He remembered the three of them—him and Terry and Terry's twin brother David— racing down Main Street over in Junction with the leafy wind whipping at them, the leaves all sticky and rotten. Remembered David burning up too, crying to them as he turned to charcoal.

Caught a glimpse of Terry's face before they shut the coffin lid. It was the same face now as then: not really that much older—what was he now, nineteen, twenty?— God, PJ thought, his face is all thin and all wore out, like a dishrag. And now it's all waxy. They do that to you in embalming.

"Jesus, at least talk to me, PJ."

"You're not Terry. You're just inside him. You're just—"

How had Terry Gish managed to become a vampire?

He heard footsteps. "Door's open." PJ left the bedroom and went into the living room, which was also the office, the dining room, and the studio. There was no balcony. He could still hear the tapping but he wouldn't see his friend.

And Brian Zottoli stood there in the studio. He'd slid downhill too. He seemed too fucking old to be only around forty, forty-one. He looked like the archetypal aging hippie with his graying ponytail, his torn denim jacket. PJ wondered if he'd managed to sell any of his writing in the last seven years.

Brian said, "You paint now, I see."

"Yeah." He started to make room, moving the dry canvases out of the way so as to clear a path to the sofa.

"Is that Shannah?"

"Yeah." But he didn't want to look at the portrait of his mother, done from memory in dry-brush acrylic, because it didn't do her justice, so he leaned another paint-

ing over it, an abstract. Brian was standing in the middle
of the room and PJ became conscious of the dust, the
way it drifted in the beam of light from the open refrigerator, the way it shook with each tap on the pane in the
bedroom.

"You look just the same," said Brian.

"I know," PJ said, "the Irish eyes and the Indian hair.
Standing here in my shorts and flexing like a muddy
Greek god. Shit yeah, I'm a stud. These tattoos are new,
though." There was a circle on his chest, and inside that
circle a red cross. "Protection magic." Brian nodded.
"You haven't changed much either." But he was lying
and he knew Brian knew it. Things were awkward between them. There was so much pain to remember to
forget. I shouldn't have called, PJ thought, I should have
dealt with it myself somehow. . . . Jesus why did it turn
out he was living in the same town, the same fucking
neighborhood? Almost like it was meant to happen. Almost like he wasn't in control anymore.

So there was Brian, looking at all the stuff in the living
room, the lava lamp, the moth-eaten sofa, the buffalo
shield, the dumbass paintings.

"Do a lot of Indian-style paintings?" Brian said. As if
it wasn't obvious—three or four identical Sitting Bulls
lined up against one wall.

"I sell them at the Saugus swap meet," PJ said. "Hey,
I gotta eat. Gotta pay for art school, too. They ain't what
you'd call, you know, my *real* stuff."

"I get it. Like the stories I used to write for *True
Confessions.*" They laughed a little.

Rat-tat-tat-tat-tat—

They stopped laughing. Brian said, "Look. I got all my
stuff." He pulled out a stake and a mallet from under his
jacket. "Maybe you'd better sprinkle some of this around
too." He handed PJ the thermos of holy water.

*"Oh Jesus no dude I can smell the holy water coming—
don't burn me up don't hurt me—"*

Brian looked up, startled. "It's Terry."

"In the bedroom."

"Yeah." Brian was shaking hard but after he swallowed a couple of pills he seemed to calm down a bit. "Downer?"

"No, thanks." A pause. "I've given up drugs."

"PJ noooo—"

"Jesus, we're not gonna just, like, kill him, are we?" PJ said. "I didn't set eyes on him since that one day, and he was lying in his coffin and now we're just gonna—"

"You were the one who called me, PJ. Even though you told me never to call you. Remember what we went through. Remember—"

Brian was weeping now. How were they going to go through with it? Gingerly PJ opened the bedroom door. Terry was still standing there with the pink and blue neon strobing against his pale features.

"Enough of this bullshit, PJ, just let me in, I mean, we've known each other since we were born and— Brian!—what a reunion! The fearless vampire killers. But like, you're not planning to use that stuff on me, are you?"

Brian said to PJ, "We can't leave him out there all night. And you know as well as I do that we're not going to shove this thing through his heart."

"All right. Give me the holy water." PJ took the thermos from Brian. He dipped his finger in the water and drew a circle around the futon. The TV next to the bedroll was on. It was some kind of Hollywood news show.

"Will it work?"

"I don't know." PJ sang softly to himself, protection words he had learned from his Shoshone grandfather.

"Put the crucifixes at the four corners," PJ said. Brian obeyed him. They stepped into the circle. "You got anything else? Any garlic? I'm all out."

Brian shook his head.

"Come in, Terry," PJ said.

And he was inside the room.

"How the fuck—"

"We can funnel through keyholes," Terry said. "We can turn into mists, we can turn into wild animals . . . we're awesome." He stood at the very edge of the circle drawn in holy water. "Oh, PJ, Brian, don't you trust me?" He had fangs all right.

Brian said, "Oh, Terry, why'd it have to happen to you?"

Terry laughed. His eyes sparkled. For a moment he seemed to be just Terry, but PJ knew the way they operated. "What do you think, my friend? You think I was sharing a needle with an undead junkie and I just caught the vampire bug from him like fucking AIDS or something? Fuck you."

"So you got bit . . . back at Junction . . . not enough to kill you . . . but enough to turn you . . . and it lay dormant . . . waiting for you to die." PJ couldn't believe that Brian was just sitting there on the futon calmly conversing with the undead. It must be the downers, he decided.

"Very logical," Terry said. "You ain't so dumb. But enough bullshit. I'm hungry and you've gotta help me. I need blood and I need a place to stay. Look, I brought my bed with me." He fished a Ziploc bag out of his tux. "Wyoming soil. I really come from Idaho but I was buried in Wyoming. So just let me spread this out in your closet or maybe like your bathtub—oh, but you only got one bathroom, never mind—and I'll just move in. I don't eat much, you'll hardly know I'm here—quiet as a mouse all day—gone all night."

"You've got to be fucking kidding," PJ said.

"I'm your best friend, PJ! Gimme a break, I don't bite. I mean, I don't bite my friends."

PJ looked into the dead boy's eyes. He remembered the video arcade in Junction . . . the old woman at the spook house suckling a wolfling at her breasts . . . Terry running so hard into the night shitting his pants he was so fucking afraid . . . where was this Terry?

"Jesus, PJ, I'm cold, I'm afraid . . . I don't want to be dead anymore." His breath smelled of meat that's been left out too long and of chemicals, formaldehyde, PJ thought. But behind the eyes that never blinked PJ thought he could see—

"Don't look into his eyes!" Brian shouted.

Too late. PJ reached out to his dead friend. Felt the deep-freeze fingers grip his arm. "Oh Jesus God I can feel your blood racing," Terry whispered. "Oh God, step over the line, come and be with me, dude, I'm the only one until *he* comes back. . . ." PJ felt himself being pulled across the barrier he had drawn. Felt the memory of Terry pulling him in through those dead eyes. He had always loved Terry. He had always been confused by Terry and that was why he had never tried to contact him after that parting at the bus station. Terry made him feel emotions that had only become clear to him after his vision quest.

"Who's coming back?" Brian said.

"Timmy's coming back," Terry said. His eyes narrowed. And he drew PJ toward himself and PJ felt the cold seep out of the dead flesh and shoot through his own veins, felt his blood stop still, felt his heart catch itself short, and still he couldn't help himself until—

Brian lunged forward with the thermos! Doused him and Terry with the holy water and then his friend was reeling backward with the smoke spiraling from his face and he was backing into the balcony and he could hear the glass shatter kind of in slow motion could see the glass shards piercing Terry's cheeks splintering glass slicing through his hands gashing his neck slashing at his trachea lancing his eyes but never any blood, no blood at all, only a viscous trickle of embalming fluid and—

"I wasn't gonna hurt you," Terry said softly. "I just needed a place to sleep." He shook the smashed glass off his face. Glass everywhere, on the shag, on the veranda, all over Terry's patent leather burial shoes.

PJ stepped back, behind the safe circle. Brian, behind him, brandished a silver crucifix.

"Wasn't gonna hurt you," Terry said, so so quietly, as he began to fade away. His voice could have been a tire squeal two blocks away. "My friends. I only wanted us to like be together again. For ever."

A few moments passed.

"He left his native earth behind," PJ said at last. The Ziploc bag lay on the floor on a pile of broken glass. Through the smashed panes came the sounds of rap and traffic. There was no wind. The outside air was thick with smog.

"Even dead the kid can't remember to clean up after himself," PJ said. "I guess he has to find someone to . . . you know. He's hungry. God, he can't do anything right. But I ain't scared of him. Not now that I've talked to him."

"He's got to come back for the earth," Brian said.

"It's okay I guess. As long as we stay behind the barrier. We can . . . stake him in the morning."

"I guess we'll stay up till he comes back."

"Yeah."

Brian laid his vampire killing tools carefully down next to the futon. "It doesn't seem like any time has passed at all."

"You're right. A few years went by and then we step right back into that old nightmare again." PJ realized that he had always known it would never be over. His years of seeking refuge at the reservation, his vision quest with its confusing messages from the spirit world, his decision to come to California . . . they had just been ways of escape. "Wonder what's on TV." PJ reached for the controller. "You like MTV?"

Brian shook his head.

"We don't have a lot in common, do we?"

A siren in the distance.

"Brian, since we're trapped here together for the night, I oughta tell you . . . maybe you'll feel weird about sleeping near me because . . . last year I went out on my vision quest, you know? the big fast, the sweat lodge, all that big-time tradition stuff . . . did it because I was supposed to, wasn't really expecting much . . . and most guys, they'll see like a bear or a wolf or an eagle and it gives them power . . . but I saw something else. I saw the sacred man-woman from when the world was young and he-she handed me this basket of corn but inside the basket there was a snake. My grandfather told me before he died, it means I'm a very holy thing, a *ma'aipots*." He wondered whether he should have told Brian, but he had the feeling he could trust him. "Sometimes this word also means—not that I'm gay exactly, but—"

Brian shrugged. "Doesn't bother me. I'm not your type." And fell asleep clutching the croquet mallet to his chest. One foot extended outside the charmed circle. PJ tucked it carefully back inside and threw a ragged old *Star Wars* sleeping bag over him as a comforter. The sleeping bag had once been Terry's or maybe David's.

PJ lay awake for a long time listening to the traffic. Come dawn Terry'll have to come back, he thought. Then we'll stake him good, while he's lying there helpless. It won't be so scary, not in the daylight like that. I'll wait for him. We always waited for each other before. I've always protected him. I guess I have to be the one to set him free now.

There was the MTV news coming on now. They were talking about the Timmy Valentine look-alike contest in Universal City tomorrow, about the massive search for a sultry pouting teenage boy to play the vanished idol in the fifty-million-dollar extravaganza the studio was making about him.

Brian stirred for a moment and looked at the image of one of the contestants—Angel Todd—some favored him to win—and murmured "Doesn't have a chance," and fell back asleep again.

Was that what Terry meant when he said *Timmy's coming back*? But hadn't they all burned up in the fire that consumed Vampire Junction—the boy, the chauffeur, the housekeeper, the Gishes and the Gallaghers, the Gods of Chaos, Mr. Kavaldjian the undertaker . . . the whole fucking town?

He closed his eyes for a moment. The sacred man-woman stood in the moonlight behind the veils of steam. In the distance came the howls of wolves and the wind shrilling across the prairie.

The sacred man-woman danced.

—Don't call my name . . . I don't want to be called.

—Why should I not call you? You have pleased me. You are a person who wants to see into the hearts of men and women. You are a person who can find pathways in the forest of men's souls. Take my gifts—

The snake's eyes reminded him of Timmy Valentine—

—*Don't call my name! I'm only half Indian anyway . . . it's all bullshit . . . bullshit. I'm gonna get out of this place and I'm gonna go to California and paint pictures.*

—But pictures are mirrors of the dark forest. You will take my gifts from me, even when you think you are casting them away.

The man-woman danced and the snake coiled over the hot stones. The snake twisted in and out of the pattern of stamping feet. It was a dance where every measure was death narrowly missed, where every step was the giving and taking of life.

It was starting all over again. Soon would come the nightmare. *Wake up! Wake up!* PJ told himself. But he could not. The eyes of the snake were Terry's eyes. Dead people's eyes.

LOST BOYS

At four in the morning there was nothing going on except around the Cahuenga newsstand where there were the usual all-nighters standing around the adult-magazine section and now and then a tourist slinking by. Hicks think that Hollywood at night is totally jumping but really it's like a cemetery. I used to think that until we came here, she thought, slipping a *Teen Beat* under her jacket and slinking into a side street.

She was a girl named Janey Rodriguez and about now every night she hung around next to the big dumpster behind the Mandarin Thai All-Night Pizza. Around four was when they usually trashed their no-shows. She'd called in an order only a couple of hours ago so she could count on it still being at least lukewarm. It was her favorite too—Peking duck and pepperoni—Dad didn't like nouvelle cuisine pizzas but he should've done his own ordering, shouldn't he, instead of squatting in the alley staring into space. Well, shit, in a day or two they'd get picked up and at least they could go back to the shelter, though it'd be a pain not to see Dad for a couple of weeks and have to bullshit the social workers one more time.

Suddenly there was someone standing next to her. He startled her—crept up on her like he'd been stalking her. "I ain't for sale," she said. "Fuck off." Turned around, saw him in the light from the back door of McDonald's. He was all in shadow. Seemed kinda young to be a john anyways. Not much older than she was. "Sorry," she said. "I guess you're on the street, same as me."

"Yeah." He was soft-spoken.

She moved nearer to him. It was about as chilly as it gets in Los Angeles, and she thought maybe she could eat up a little of his warmth, but he wasn't warm. He seemed to be standing in a pocket of cold air. She smiled at him. "You're new here."

"Yeah."

"From far away?"

"Far away."

"*¡Ay, mierditas!* So maybe you don't know the ropes too good yet. But I'll help you. Just this once anyways. You see that pile of garbage over there, kind of all squashed up behind that shopping cart? That's my Dad. We're from far away too. West Covina. Look, around here, when you're hungry, you find out what time the pizza places dump their no-shows, right? You call in your order, give a fake name and number, then you just stand around until they drop it in the trash . . . I saw it on a documentary . . . I rented the video when I found out we were gonna be homeless. My name's Janey."

"Terry."

"I like your voice."

"Yeah? Thanks."

"It reminds me of my brother. He's dead though—he OD'd." She thought she heard the latch on the back door of the pizza place and she leaned forward. "Watch this, Terry . . . you wanna live on the fucking street, you gotta be quick . . . you gotta be quiet . . . like a cat in the night . . . wait, don't breathe . . . then pounce."

"I'll remember that." Something about his voice . . . yeah, he really did sound a lot like Juanito. Especially after he got sprung from juvie. He had another year to live then, but they'd already sapped the life from him somehow. This guy was like that too. She didn't want to ask him why he was on the street—it wasn't good manners to ask people about their former lives—but she knew it had to be bad.

At that moment, the back door swung open. She grabbed Terry's hand and made him duck behind the dumpster with her. The boy's hand was freezing—maybe he had some kind of disease—but she didn't cry out because she didn't want to get caught. She just let go, left him standing. She heard something clanging against the dumpster, felt the reverberation of metal and garbage against her knotted stomach, felt her hunger howl. But she had to wait for seventeen footsteps and a slamming door before she bolted out, reached into the dumpster, pulled out her treasure from the goulash of offal, squatted back down to eat. She unrolled the *Teen Beat* and tilted it to catch the light from McDonald's.

"Have some pizza."

Terry didn't say anything at all. He was studying her or something. She couldn't even hear him breathe. Like Juanito at the embalming place. The dull feeling in the pit of her stomach may have been hunger but it tasted like fear. She turned to the centerfold poster which was like an old picture from Timmy Valentine's big victory tour seven years ago. Maybe this dude was dead but he was still a Clydesdale.

"You like Timmy Valentine?" she said. "If we go to the shelter tomorrow, we'll get to watch the look-alike contest on TV."

"He's coming back," Terry whispered. Something in the way he said it made her drop the magazine and look up at him. She could see his face for the first time. There were bits of glass sticking out of it. One jagged piece pierced his left cheek. His forehead was a mass of splinters. But there was no blood. Something else . . . a thin, yellow fluid . . . She knew that smell . . . a blend of bitter chemicals and sickly-sweet perfumes. . . .

It was the smell of dead Juanito. Embalming fluid. She could see him suddenly in the church standing next to the coffin with the incense billowing in his face and her Dad saying *Go on, kiss him, kiss him on the cheek,* and the reek of him choking her—

"You're *sick*," she said.

Terry said: *"You gotta be quick . . . you gotta be quiet . . . like a cat in the night . . . wait, don't breathe . . . then pounce."* He mimicked her voice perfectly.

She didn't have time to scream because he pounced. She fell face forward onto the lukewarm pizza. She tasted pepperoni before she choked on her own blood. She felt the cold hands driven into her flesh, felt the cold rush through her veins. She felt the fangs, hypodermic pin-pricks that found her jugular with the precision of instinct. There was no time for terror. It was over all at once.

LOST BOYS

When Brian woke it was almost noon. PJ was sitting up, staring at the balcony. Terry Gish lay on the shag, next to the broken glass door, clutching the Ziploc bag of native soil like a teddy bear. A smoggy half-light shone in from the street.

"What the fuck are we gonna do?" PJ said. "Look— he's come back—he's killed someone—"

On television, a beautiful woman was talking while an insert shot panned over the body of a dead girl. One of the homeless. Found next to a garbage dumpster by her junkie father.

"It's daylight," Brian said. "We can stake him."

"I just can't do it."

In his death-trance, Terry's face had a luminous tran-quillity that he'd never had in life. Could he really have killed some street person only two blocks from PJ's apartment? Brian knew it must be true. Terry wasn't even breathing. There were still glass splinters all over his face. A dribble of coagulating blood ran down the left side of his lips. It was broad daylight. It was no nightmare.

"Maybe we can—I don't know, call the police or something," Brian said.

"What'll we tell them? That this corpse walked all the way here from Wyoming?" PJ picked up the stake and the croquet mallet and stood up. "All right. I'll do it. You'll help me get rid of the body. But I don't want you to watch. He's my closest friend. I want to sing a special song for him. You know. Indian magic. Something I learned on my vision quest." Brian got up and started to walk through the bedroom door to the living room. "Wait a couple of minutes, man," PJ said. "The trash bags are on top of the fridge."

From the next room, Brian heard the wheezing falsetto of an Indian song. He heard the slow pounding of a drum. He went to look for a large garbage bag. He moved a few canvases aside. A television on the sofa cut abruptly to a shot of Timmy Valentine singing.

Just Timmy against a dark background, a lone spotlight on his face. Concert footage from the past. The look-alike contest was today. Somehow it was more than just a media exploitation of the Timmy Valentine myth, which had grown from a cottage industry to a multimillion-dollar business in only a few years—Valentine sightings only narrowly less frequent than Elvis sightings—T-shirts, mugs, videos, fanzines, books by putative experts— somehow this look-alike thing was more than a new moneymaking idea from the rapacious studios.

Timmy's voice filled the living room. God, how that kid could sing. There were centuries of pain in that voice . . . there was innocence violated . . . there was a dark lasciviousness behind that aching arc of sound. For a moment Brian simply stopped thinking.

Then he heard a *crack* from the next room. When he went into the bedroom with the largest trash bag he could find, PJ had already wrapped his friend's body in the *Star Wars* sleeping bag.

4

BURIAL GROUNDS

Out of the first rustlings of the forest leaves come whispered words, images, odors, memories in stark chiaroscuro.

. . . gutted, the Colosseum rears up over the makeshift shelters of the homeless . . . a full moon . . . Corinthian columns matted with decaying leaves . . . the heat heavy in the moist air, a rank perfume of cloves and rotting oranges and crushed rose petals and human sweat . . .

To the boy the place has a strange familiarity, yet he cannot quite place the meld of fragrances. The night is alive. Boys with torches race down steep cobbled streets to light the way for a cardinal in a litter. The accents are familiar, but the tongue is somehow no longer Latin. How many centuries has it been since Pompeii? The boy does not know. This time he has emerged from the forest with very little memory at all. He has slept for a hundred years or more. The dirt of centuries crusts his eyes. He is still of the night, of the forest.

He runs behind the chair as it weaves through unlit alleys. The litterbearers do not notice him. They see a dark creature, perhaps a cat, sniffing at their heels; they do not know he smells their very blood as it races in their veins. The night is humid and the cardinal heavy; the smell of age and sweat is ill disguised by perfume and incense, and his blood is sluggish. Curious, the vampire creeps closer. He springs into the litter, blending swiftly into the ermine fringe of the cardinal's cloak. The blood oozes in this man's veins. It does not tempt. It is tainted with alcohol and unwholesome diseases. Wine dribbles from his lips.

The cardinal closes the drapes of the litter. Leaning back against cushions of velvet and damask, he reaches into his cassock and masturbates. Catlike still, the vampire scurries behind folds of drapery. There is candlelight. Grotesque shadows against the curtains. The cardinal sighs and drinks more wine.

"Ah," says the cardinal, *"peccavi, peccavi, semper peccavi."*

Should he feed? the cat thinks. But the thirst is still dull in him.

The road is bumpy. The cardinal's silver goblet falls from his hand and grazes the cat. He remembers how silver once sapped his strength. Now it seems to have lost its power. A crucifix, studded with amethysts, dangles from a chain around the cardinal's neck. No magic emanates from it. A bible, silver-clasped, with a cruciform intaglio set into its spine, casts no spell either. Have the symbols of religion lost their ability to harm me? he thinks. There is something different about the world. He cannot tell whether it is himself—whether the unremembered trauma that sent him to seek refuge in the forest has inured him to the powers of light and darkness—or whether it is the world that has changed during the time he has spent in the womb of the forest—whether faith has been sucked from it, like blood from the throat of a beautiful woman.

Or it is both: the magic draining from the world, the light seeping into the forest of the soul.

They come to a stop.

The cardinal adjusts his clothing. He wipes away the last drops of semen with a fold of the cassock. He crosses himself. He kisses the crucifix. He places his hat on his head and whisks aside the drapes. The cat leaps out onto marble.

A forest of feet: the sandaled feet of the litterbearers, the dirt ground in, rank; the feet of attendants, stockinged and gartered; the feet of the cardinal, his boots fringed with dead animals' fur. Cold. The marble stealing the warmth from his paws. Row upon row of candles in the distance; an altar boy slouches past, swinging a censer. The legs are all stock still, standing to attention, except for two that shift neurotically from side to side. He darts between the feet. Whispers and murmurs everywhere. As his senses become attuned to the vastness of the chamber, he hears from somewhere far away the voice of a lone chorister, singing the same phrase over and over to himself: *Miserere mei, miserere mei.* The shuffling of feet and the rustling of vestments and the mutterings and coughs all meld into one cacophonous echo. It is a cathedral, but one so vast his head spins when he looks up.

"His Eminence," says one voice, piercing the hubbub, "Cardinal del Monte."

He sees the cardinal, bloated as the setting sun, making the sign of the cross through the incense mist. His eyes are smarting from the fragrance. He slips away, his paws sliding on the cold smooth marble. He follows the music.

Miserere mei. . . .

He focuses his mind on that musical phrase. Music is the one thing he can still grasp. Furtively he moves toward its source. There is an oak door, but it is simple enough for him to wriggle past the threshold where countless feet have worn a hollow in the stone.

He is in a vestry. Cassocks and surplices hang on pegs.

The room is drafty yet windowless. The smell of children's sweat pervades the air. The singing comes from a boy who is buttoning his cassock. The voice is a boy's yet not a boy's; the boy's face is smooth, yet the eyes betray some ancient pain. He is older than he looks, the vampire thinks. He too has had his manhood ripped away. In the service of music. We do have something in common, he thinks, though he is only mortal. How they strive to prolong the transient, these humans, though all must end in dust.

Perhaps I can show him my true shape, he thinks, and already he is resolving out of the incense and the dancing dust motes, naked as when he emerged from the forest. The dirt of death still clings to him, but he shakes it loose. Boldly he takes a cassock and surplice from one of the pegs and begins to put them on.

"Oh," says the other boy. "I didn't know there was someone here."

"People say I'm quiet," says the vampire.

"You must be new around here. I haven't seen you before, but if we don't hurry we'll both be late and we'll get whipped." For the first time the vampire notices a streak of dried blood on the back of the chorister's cassock. "My name is Guglielmo; who are you?"

He thinks quickly. What names has he overheard in the streets? "Ercole," he says, "Ercole Serafini."

"Hercules! What a name for such a pretty boy." Guglielmo laughs. "I'll call you Ercolino. You must have come with Cardinal del Monte."

"How did you know?"

"His Eminence always goes for looks before talent. I'll bet he bought you for twenty scudi from some old peasant in Naples . . . you've been freshly castrated too I should think . . . I can still see the pain of it in your eyes."

"Neapolis . . . yes, Naples." It is true, Ercolino thinks, that I once lived in that part of Italy. He does not tell

Guglielmo that it was fifteen hundred years ago, in a city long since buried beneath the brimstone of Vesuvio.

"Put on this ruff," Guglielmo says, tossing him one from a chest. It is heavily starched and presses too tight against his neck. "And hurry."

"Where are we going?"

"Vespers at the Capella Sistina . . . haven't they told you *anything?* Then a private party at the cardinal's in honor of the visiting Prince of Venosa—there's a pervert for you! We're to appear *travestiti* there—I hope they can find women's clothes to fit you. Do you sit on the *decani* side or the *cantores?*"

"Don't know."

"Decani then. That way you can stand next to me, on the south side of the nave. And you can avoid being noticed by Ser Caravaggio."

"Ser—"

"Michelangelo da Caravaggio. A mad painter who's the cardinal's pet monkey at the moment. If he catches sight of you he'll want you to pose. Something pornographic I'm sure, though there'll be some religious excuse for the subject matter. If he wants to paint you, you take his money but tell him to keep his poxy hands away from your delicate flesh." Guglielmo crosses himself.

"I'll remember," says Ercolino softly.

Guglielmo leans down and wipes a patch of dirt from his cheek with his finger. He snatches his hand away. *"Maledetto!* Cold!" he says, blowing on his finger. "You've been down into the mausoleum, all that marble, those freezing sculptures of dead popes, they have sucked the life from you. . . ."

Ercolino smiles sadly.

"Would you like to look in the mirror before we go?" Guglielmo says.

"No . . . thank you . . . I don't like mirrors."

"Come on then. There's over a mile of corridors to run down before we reach the chapel."

DISSOLVE: ROSES

Petra had intended to miss bereavement therapy that morning, but guilt had driven her there anyway. Not that she minded throwing away the hundred bucks—the insurance covered it—or the circle of yuppies pouring out their hearts to the bland Dr. Feinstein. It wasn't the guilt; it was the fear that had been feeding on her since her visit to Simone Arleta. The nightmare . . .

She reached Universal City before lunch, but the three-ring circus was already underway. In the lobby of the Sheraton, Simone was holding court, gesticulating extravagantly as photographers snapped pictures. She showed her press pass at a registration table and was handed a *Search for Timmy Valentine* press kit. TV camera crews hustled through crowds of onlookers. Here and there some of the great, near-great and would-be-great could be seen threading their way through the throng, each with a chain of hangers-on. Petra had her microcassette recorder in her purse. She was ready to interview anyone who seemed important.

It was lucky she'd already talked to Simone. Today she'd be lucky to get more than a soundbite or two. Nothing like the experience out at the Arleta estate . . . nothing like embracing the corpse of her son.

Black and white was fashionable that year. All the fashion plates were wearing it. Women walked by with high starched collars that looked almost Elizabethan. The producers swaggered past, their couture painstakingly casual, their cuffs hitched up just enough so that their Rolexes could catch the light from the postmodern chandeliers above. None of the contestants were anywhere to be seen. Probably getting last-minute pep talks from their agents, she thought.

Petra worked her way over to the coffee shop, found a table right next to the lobby so she wouldn't miss anything, and opened up the press kit.

It was nothing special: a few pictures of Timmy—a couple of the more sensational clippings, the sightings on Mars . . . an article by some academic, Dr. Joshua Levy, about the semiotic interpretation of the Timmy Valentine phenomenon . . . a pocket biography of Jonathan Burr, who was going to direct the forty-million-dollar picture *if* they could find a convincing Timmy Valentine lookalike. . . .

She had half an hour until the big "get acquainted" lunch. She sat and fiddled with her notes.

Suddenly the coffee shop swarmed with Valentine clones.

She couldn't concentrate. They must have just been released from some kind of briefing. She could hear their shrill voices as they complained to their agents and their mothers. They were swirling their capes and gesturing in that strange combination of Motown and Lugosi that Timmy Valentine had perfected. They were trying out their wide-eyed wounded-innocence expressions, sizing each other up, deliberately ignoring each other. Except for one.

She moved the flower vase to get a look at him. He looked up at her. Their eyes met only for a moment.

There's a winner, she thought. He's not even concerned about the competition. He's all wound up into himself, compacted, concentrated, like a cat getting ready to pounce. He's cute, but he doesn't really look like Timmy Valentine. Look at the way he looks at you—*hard,* masking his vulnerability. He doesn't have that sense of innocence that Timmy always had, even when he sang the most suggestive lyrics. It's something else. It's like he knows you . . . what you're feeling . . . down there.

And the boy was walking toward her. Oh, his mother was there, fretting and trying to flatten a cowlick, and his agent—a tall Hispanic woman—was talking to him, but he ignored them.

"Are you a reporter?" he said. The voice had a hint of

mountain talk in it. Nothing like the voice of Timmy Valentine.

"Yes."

"You want to interview me for a moment?" he said. "My name is Angel. Angel Todd." She started to demur, but then he winked at her as if to say, Help me, get them off my back. She laughed. He was a kid who knew how to get his own way. Like Jason.

"I'm Petra Shiloh," she said.

"Momma, I'm going to be with this reporter for a couple of hours," he said.

"But there's a photo op coming up," said the agent. He had clearly been driving her insane all morning. "You have to be there." The mother took out a compact and was trying to fix her lipstick. She had a beehive hairdo and too much costume jewelry.

"Leave me the fuck alone," he said to them, and made a dismissive gesture. Then he said to Petra, softly so they wouldn't hear, "This thing means so much to them, I don't know why. They just look at me and they see Porsches and Malibu beach houses and shit. You look at me, look at this stupid hair-dye job and these clothes. I'm blond."

"Want a Coke?" Petra said, flagging down the waitress.

"Sure." He sat down across from her. "You think you could slip in some of this without them noticing?" His hand touched hers under the table. It was warm. There was something not quite wholesome about the way he touched her. She retracted her hand and noticed he had slipped into it one of those miniature bourbon bottles you find on airplanes. "Come on, ma'am—like, I'm real nervous, I need something to chill me out."

She looked around. The mother and agent were nowhere to be seen. Perhaps they were relieved to have palmed him off on someone for a while. The Coke arrived and she spiked it.

"Thanks," he said, and drank the whole thing down.

"Actually," she said, "I can't really interview you for a couple of hours—I have to go somewhere right after lunch for a little while." The nightmare stirred at the back of her mind.

"Oh, where?"

"Forest Lawn." Why am I telling him all this? Am I going to tell him next that he reminds me of my dead son?

"Can I come too?" said Angel Todd.

Jason . . .

He plucked a rose from the vase she had moved, and brushed the tip of her nose with it. A petal fell onto her lap.

"You'll prick yourself."

"I already have." He dropped the rose and sucked the blood from his thumb.

He waited for her reply. His eyes laughed.

DISSOLVE: HIGHWAYS

They drove to Malibu. They turned south and drove to Pomona. They drove to Long Beach and then turned north, up the Sacramento Freeway, toward Antelope Valley. They didn't know where they were going. They were just hitting the road, Brian and PJ and the corpse that now and then shifted in the trunk.

Somewhere on Highway 14: just cruising, not talking, the dry wind searing.

"Maybe I should put up the top," Brian said at last.

"Maybe."

But Brian made no move to do so.

"The native earth—" Brian began.

"I vacuumed it all up," PJ said. "Put it down the disposal." They drove on. "Jesus Christ, Brian, where are we gonna dump the body?"

"I don't know," Brian said.

"Maybe we should go back to the ocean."

"No." Brian remembered his niece Lisa standing at the poolside door of a sleazy motel, the seaweed draped around her pipestem limbs, the ocean pouring from her thousand wounds. . . . "Not the ocean."

"We'll do an Indian burial then. Up in the mountains. No one ever goes there."

Brian turned at the next exit. Found a mountain road that wound up, higher and higher to the noonday sun. The wind was hot and he was sweating. He would have killed for a diet soda but PJ seemed untouched by the heat. He was sitting cross-legged in the passenger seat, heedless of the sweat that streamed down his forehead into his eyes . . . he seemed to be withdrawing into some private world. Brian thought: It's the world of vision quests and sweat lodges—the world that's convinced him he's some kind of androgynous shaman. He remembered reading about the sacred man-woman in some anthropology book when he was in college. . . .

Brian kept on driving. Occasionally PJ would open his eyes and murmur "Left here" or "S curve coming, careful." Brian had never ventured before into the wasteland that far east of Los Angeles, the barren mountains, the Mojave desert . . . but PJ seemed to know where they were going, and he was content to let him navigate. The air was thinning and the road narrowing and the hairpins ever more hair-raising.

At length the road dead-ended. They looked out over rust-colored mountains, cliff faces of naked rock, and in the distance more mountains capped with snow.

"I love L.A.," PJ said. "You can surf and ski right in the same county."

Brian didn't know whether to take him seriously. PJ had become strangely dissociated from his surroundings. "Where are we?" Brian said.

"I don't know," PJ said. "But I've been here many times. Behind that hill, yonder, there's an estate that belongs to Simone Arleta, world-famous psychic—you know, the one that's always quoted as being a 'top psychic' in the *Enquirer*. And way over on the other side"— Brian could make nothing out except a smudge of white against the side of the mountain—"that's going to be the fairy castle of some crazy movie director."

"I don't see anything."

"What you see around us is death and desolation, ain't it the truth? But my Shoshone mother and my Cheyenne grandfather taught me to see with other eyes. When I look with those other eyes I feel the scorpions wriggling along the sand and the coyotes prowling among the cactus and—"

"And the children of the night? Do you feel them too?"

PJ turned away. Brian got out and started to open the trunk. "I'll carry him! You leave him alone, you hear?" PJ said, before he could lift the body, still zipped up inside the sleeping bag. A foot dangled from the opening. It was peppered with splinters. PJ lifted his dead friend and slung him over his shoulder. There was no rigor mortis. Fresh blood seeped from the foot. Brian couldn't help wondering if—

They trudged uphill some more. It was chillier up here and Brian had to breathe in deep gasps. The way was steep, but there were flattened stones; Brian could almost see the outline of an ancient staircase carved into the rock. "This is one of the old sacred places, isn't it?"

"How should I know?" PJ said. "We all look alike to you guys, don't we? There were no Plains Indians in California, how the fuck should I know if it's sacred or not?" But he seemed to be concealing something, Brian thought. The way he found the place so easily, the way the whole place seemed vested with an aura of power. Perhaps Brian's encounters with vampires in the past had sensitized him to things and places that were somehow otherworldly . . . he could feel something here. But he wasn't comfortable with it, not the way PJ was. He was terrified. Even though the sun was shining and the sky cloudless and the terrain visible for miles around.

At length PJ found the place he was looking for. He built a makeshift platform out of boulders and placed the bundle that had been his friend on top. The wind howled. Blood seeped from the sleeping bag and soaked into the sandstone. Brian could not shake the terror.

"He never had blood before," he said. "It was all . . . embalming fluid."

"He killed last night," PJ said.

As Brian watched, transfixed, PJ took off his shirt and peeled down his jeans. Pulling a jar of pigment from his pocket, he painted his face white with the flat of a Swiss army knife. He drew a serpent on each cheek, using the blade as a mirror. He gashed his chest and belly with the knife and allowed the blood to run onto the *Star Wars* sleeping bag.

Then he began to sing in a wheezing falsetto, words with guttural consonants and drawn-out wailing vowels. Brian couldn't understand the words but he could sense their grief. As PJ sang he seemed to transform into another person. His hips moved sinuously. His hands gestured, caressing imaginary breasts. He was shifting into his man-woman persona. He began to ululate, his tongue darting in and out, fellating the wind. Though the movements were overtly sexual, Brian saw nothing lascivious in the dance; it was something solemn, invoking the union of earth and sky, life and death.

He danced until he fell, exhausted, over the body of his friend; Brian lifted him up. It was midafternoon by now.

He thought he saw the body shift, slump over, something moving inside that sleeping bag—surely not. The terror came back, swooping down on him like a hawk out of the sun.

He didn't want to stay there any longer. He hustled PJ down the slope, deposited him in the passenger seat, and began to drive furiously downhill. He had no idea where he was going.

It was a kind of magic; in only a few minutes he found himself back on the Antelope Freeway. It was as though the road had rearranged itself, and when he looked in the rearview mirror he could not be sure which mountain they had descended from. He didn't want to know. He drove.

After he turned back onto the San Diego Freeway he turned the radio on. It was the music that caused PJ to wake up. It was an old Timmy Valentine song:

Come into my coffin,
Don't wanna sleep alone.

PJ said, "He's ten times more popular now than he was when he was alive, he's like a fucking preteen James Dean now."

Brian said, "He killed Lisa." God, that still hurt so much. He wanted to be done driving so he could safely take a couple more Valium.

"And my mom, and my dad, and David and Terry, and Naomi, and . . ."

"Kitty Burns and Prince Prathna and . . ."

PJ began to weep like a little kid.

"It's over. You vacuumed up all the native earth, right? And you put it all down the disposal. Every speck."

"Yeah, yeah."

"So we're safe," said Brian.

"Yeah, safe," PJ said.

An announcer started talking about the big Timmy Valentine look-alike contest. Televised live—Simone Arleta planning to channel Timmy himself to be one of the judges—Joshua Levy, the controversial archaeologist, appearing on "Letterman" later to discuss Timmy Valentine "sightings" throughout history—"Fucking three-ring circus," PJ said. "You should write a book about it."

"Maybe I should," Brian said. "My *novels* are all on the two-dollar remainder shelf down at Crown. I've been jinxed by what happened in Junction. My books are terrible now. I tried to blame the sales force, the editors, the public, but shit, I might as well try nonfiction."

"Piece of cake."

"Wanna come down to the circus with me?"

"Nah, drop me off—I have to finish a bunch of paintings for tomorrow's swap meet. Hey, I know what you're gonna say but I gotta eat, and those Sitting Bulls and doe-eyed Indian maidens, they keep me in burgers."

"I never expected you to become a painter," said Brian, whose most vivid memory of PJ might well have been the boy playing Bloodsucker for an hour on a single quarter. "Who's your favorite artist?" He expected someone modern somehow—Picasso or Paul Klee.

PJ surprised him when he answered, "Caravaggio."

MEMORY: 1598

He stares upward from the *decani* choir stalls to the finger of God, the still center of the arc of the ceiling of the Capella Sistina, the moment of creation. Guglielmo whispers in his ear that eighty years ago a man named Buonarroti spent years painting that ceiling flat on his back. The boy continues to stare even though they are all kneeling, eyes downcast, murmuring the paternoster.

Our Father? he thinks. Surely not *my* father.

The boy gazes upward at the face of God. Is it only the painter's artifice, or has God changed so much during the time the vampire slept? Is that not a human God, who bears more than a passing family resemblance to Adam? Ercolino thinks: They are reflected in each other, God and man. This is a new thought for him. If even the highest, the most remote of supernatural beings has become a little human, has the same thing happened to him? For the spirit that breathes life into the boy who calls himself Ercolino Serafini itself draws life from the collective terror in men's hearts.

I have seen God so many times, he thinks. I saw him in the eruption of Vesuvius, in the eyes of the statue of Capitoline Jove, in Bluebeard's madness and in countless icons and crucifixes, a creature conceived in pain. Other people's father, not mine. How is this God different? Could I have been bewitched by the dead hand of Buonarroti?

The choir rises. The boys cluster around an illuminated part book that contains the notes for Prince Gesualdo's music. Ercolino is shorter than the others and squeezes in close to the parchment. A giant candle drips hot wax onto the page. He is unfamiliar with this method of notation, but it is not difficult for him to understand its principles. But as the music starts—it is the Magnificat—he gasps at its audacity. The melodic lines are twisted and fantastical. The harmonies are alien and abrupt. It is music that transforms itself before it can be grasped, and its eerie chords hang in the air, echoes clashing against echoes, like a series of unfinished sculptures. . . .

Who can have written such music? It is not a perfect music. It is a music of anguish and uncertainty . . . it is a *human* music. Again the vampire wonders whether it is he who has changed, or the world.

On their knees once more for a set of *responsoria,* he whispers to Guglielmo: "This Prince of Venosa, this Gesualdo—can you point him out to me?"

Guglielmo directs his gaze toward the altar, where there is a section reserved for the college of cardinals. Among the figures robed in crimson is a man dressed all in black. He seems sullen. He is fidgeting. Perhaps his own music has disturbed him. "They say he murdered his wife when he discovered her *in flagrante* with another man," Guglielmo says.

"Strangled her!" says another boy gleefully from the pew above.

"Nonsense—he ran her through with his sword—cut off the other man's balls, too," says Guglielmo. "And by the way, I'm sorry I said you had no talent. I'll never be a man, but I'm man enough to admit it when I'm wrong. You're well named, Serafini."

But Ercolino is not listening. His gaze has shifted to the man kneeling next to the mad composer. He is unkempt; he stares from side to side; his doublet does not match his cloak, and his left stocking is torn. He wonders who the man is, how he could be up there among the cardinals; he does not appear in the least bit embarrassed by his shabbiness.

"Don't look at *him!*" Guglielmo whispers urgently.

Too late. They have seen each other.

They rise for a reading from the Book of Revelation. It is a curious, stilted, ungrammatical Latin, he thinks, for he remembers well the severe cadence of that tongue as it was uttered by the pleasure seekers at Baiae and the doomed denizens of Pompeii and the courtiers from the palace of the Emperor Titus.

"Look away!" Guglielmo says. "Nothing good will come of your attracting the notice of Ser Caravaggio!"

They look into each other's eyes. The boy knows what the man sees: a child, malleable, a sheet of virgin parchment—mortals have always seen him this way. He does not look away. The music begins again—it is the hymn *"Ave Maris Stella."* Ercolino does not join in. He has smelled blood. Something has awakened the hunger, dormant so long. It is something about the man.

Suddenly he realizes why the man is so disheveled. He has come from a brawl. His arm is crudely bandaged with strips of linen torn from a shirt. The blood is fresh and pungent. The odor slices through the incense and the scented wax. It is irresistible. The paean to the virgin swells; the voices of the choristers tremble with that hopeless passion only eunuchs can muster. But the cardinals are nodding off and the altar boys are half-drugged by the incense; it seems to Ercolino that only he and Caravaggio are truly alive at the moment. No time passes between desire and its fulfillment. Ercolino transforms himself into a fine mist and is wafted toward the painter amid clouds of incense. The man continues to stare at where Ercolino stood. But he is already at Ser Caravaggio's side, ripping at the bandages with his cat claws, for all the painter can see is a dark furry creature lapping the lifeblood from his wounded arm. He closes his eyes. He smiles. He knows it's me, Ercolino thinks. He *knows!*

He feeds now. Blood spilled in violence tastes sweetest; sourest is the blood of the bedridden. This is an angry blood, a blood full of the spices of heightened emotions; it is the blood of an artist. The vampire exults. The warmth floods him. He drinks deep. He tears at the flesh, he thrusts his cat's tongue deep into riven muscle. Caravaggio murmurs. He utters a single sharp cry of pain or ecstasy and then snaps out of his reverie. He has ejaculated. He moves his hand to cover the stain on his codpiece. The incense masks the smell of semen, but the vampire can smell it even through the intoxicating fragrance of fresh blood. The painter glances shiftily about him. The cardinals are snoring; Gesualdo is scribbling on a scrap of parchment.

Caravaggio laughs out loud. The cat mews and leaps off his arm, nestling between the brocade of his jacket and the dark oiled wood.

"Who are you?" says the painter. There is wonder in his eyes. Has the illusion slipped? Has Caravaggio seen his true form? He wrenches himself back into the cat shape. He gazes up into the painter's eyes. He stares past those eyes into the eyes of God the Father.

I am a cat, he thinks. *I am a cat.* He does not think Caravaggio is convinced. How can that be? A few times, an innocent has been able to see through the illusion. A child who has not learned to separate the inner and the outer worlds—a village idiot perhaps—these are the only humans capable of seeing his true form. They, and the beasts of the forest in whose shapes he cloaks himself. He knows that the painter is not an innocent.

The cat retreats into the fog of incense. Panicking, he springs from the pew and swirls into the mist, resolving himself once more at the side of Guglielmo, picking up the *"Ave Maris Stella"* in midphrase, melding seamlessly into the arc of the music.

Without looking back he knows that the man is still staring at him.

I'm afraid, he thinks. I don't want to look back. When you drink someone's blood, there's a bond. It is the bond of hunter and prey, the love-death dance of the world. But with this man I don't know if I'm hunting or hunted. I'm afraid, he thinks.

But at last, with the borrowed life force racing in his veins and lending him the illusion of warmth, he gives himself up to the music. The music soars. It is the music that allows him to pretend he has not lost his soul.

He sings.

CEMETERIES

They stopped at Conroy's to pick up some roses. Then they drove to Forest Lawn. Angel left his cloak in the car but he was still dressed all in black. It must be hot for him, Petra thought.

It was a long walk from the parking lot to where Jason was buried. They trudged in silence past bombastic monuments, past marble mausoleums and replicas of Egyptian temples, past fairy castles and Cadillacs sculpted in granite. A lot of famous people are buried at Forest Lawn; Petra often wondered what had made her accept her father's offer to use the gravesite he had originally designated for himself. Her therapist had intimated it must be some kind of guilt, some feeling that she should give her son something or other that she hadn't given him in life; she was beginning to accept that there must be an element of truth in that, but it was also true that she'd been broke at the time and the plot was free.

At first she was irritated that the kid had managed to tag along. She was afraid that he'd be as grating and obnoxious as he had been to his mother and his agent; but the moment they left the hotel he seemed transformed. They were almost like mother and son on a weekend outing. They hadn't said much to each other, but she sensed that Angel was on the verge of telling her something important. He was sounding her out. It was difficult for him, and she didn't want to blow it by pressing him. She didn't want to fail. Not like she had with Jason.

"Oh, look," he said at last, pointing. A marble diplodocus reared up out of a sea of shrubbery.

"That must be O'Suilleabhain, that Irish palaeontologist," she said. "He died last year." She had written an article about him for the *Times;* he wasn't much of a scientist, more of a media personality, popularizing dinosaurs on the talk-show circuit—once he'd even been on with Simone Arleta, she recalled, with her trying to channel the souls of extinct animals by humming over bits of petrified bone—had it been "Letterman"? She wasn't sure.

"Jesus it's stupid-looking. I'm never going to be buried in a place like this. Rich folks just don't know what to do with all their money."

"You might just become one of those rich folks yourself, you know," Petra said, "if the judges like you."

"Don't give a shit about all that," he said. "I just like to sing."

He sang. The song was "Vampire Junction," which all the contestants were going to have to do; they could either sing themselves or elect to lip-synch, since the studio was more concerned about the look and the moves than about whether there was any actual musical talent. It was uncanny to hear this boy, who didn't look at all like Timmy Valentine and who hated the fact that they'd made him dye his hair, slip right into the Valentine persona. He aped the voice almost perfectly, though he strained at the high notes. The inflection was all there too, the accent that wasn't quite American or British. But it didn't have Valentine's inhuman quality . . . when you listened to the Valentine albums, it seemed as though the kid never even breathed, there was just this stream of pure, unbroken music . . . Angel had something different, just as appealing in its own way . . . a quality of violated innocence, an unaffected pathos that had to have been fed by genuine pain. His singing did not float above the world like Timmy Valentine's; it was of the world, and worldlier than any child's ought to be.

He noticed her watching him and stopped abruptly. He smiled. "I guess it's not really right for me to be rehearsing for the contest here, I mean, with all these dead people lying around."

They walked down the pathway toward Jason's grave. He was buried in a less affluent sector of the cemetery, in a sort of valley between two embankments. Memorials were crowded together rather than isolated. There wasn't a soul around, not even a tourist. There were rows of graves here, with the usual angels, crosses and headstones. Nothing outrageous. There were palm trees and evergreens.

Tactfully, Angel Todd stood a little way off while Petra laid the roses at the foot of the headstone. It was a simple grave, with only the words JASON SHILOH, and the dates, chiseled in simple lettering. Her father had wanted something monumental—a sheltering angel with outstretched wings, maybe—but that was where she had finally put her foot down.

The sunlight streamed down past the palm trees. The smog count was low today and the sky much bluer than usual.

She sat for a while, wondering whether this time she would finally be able to weep. She could not. She could only see the boy in her nightmare, rotting, climbing down from the lemon tree to draw her into his Oedipal embrace. She started to get the jitters and she fumbled in her handbag for an Advil.

Then she felt a hand on her shoulder.

"You okay?"

"Yeah, I guess so."

"He killed himself, didn't he? I can tell."

"Yeah." She looked up; Angel seemed to be looking straight past her, into the grave itself as if with some kind of X-ray vision. "He hanged himself. He had his headphones on and there was a Timmy Valentine song buzzing in his ears when I found him." Why was she telling him this? She'd had her dose of therapy for the day. Perhaps she was becoming addicted to therapy.

"So that's what we got in common. You and me, we're linked to this dead boy rock star somehow. He haunts us. You think he killed your son and I have to become him so I can get rich and famous."

"He didn't kill my son," Petra said. "I don't believe in Satanic messages. I don't believe that music can can kill . . . if I start to believe something like that, I'll go out of my mind."

"So what does this dead kid have that's got us so worked up?"

"You know you're right. Except we're not even sure he's dead . . . Simone Arleta says she's going to make some kind of dramatic revelation about him tonight."

"Mind if I smell one?" He knelt down beside her and picked out one of the roses, the reddest. "Nah, he's dead all right. Stone dead." He sniffed the rose. "Sure smells pretty," he said, "seeing as it's dead too." Then his mood seemed to change abruptly once more. "I love dead people," he said. "I wish I was dead. I wish I was your son."

"How can you say that, Angel?"

He was an unpleasant boy, imperious and unlovable, yet she felt a kind of protectiveness toward him . . . Jesus I'm just using him, projecting my guilt over Jason onto him, she thought. "Why do you say that?" she said.

He didn't answer her. Instead he said, "I love to spend time in cemeteries. You can listen to the grass growing out of the dead people when they start to dissolve into the ground." He seemed almost to be talking to himself. Then he turned to her and said, passionately, "Don't you come here when you're all burning up inside and there ain't nowhere left to go? When your mind's all twisted and wrung out because there's like a secret that you can't tell anyone and it's eating you up alive and there ain't no one to listen to you, because the only people who will listen are dead people?"

Petra stood up. "Yes," she said.

"I knew it," the boy whispered fiercely. "I knew I could trust you."

Tentatively Petra reached down to caress the boy's hair. He was crying. We're both so alone, she thought. People *are* islands. She wanted to embrace him, to comfort him, but she could not bring herself to; somehow, for her, this alienated boy was tainted with her nightmare . . . she dared not close her eyes, for she knew she would see Jason, decomposing, stretching out his arms to make love to his own mother.

5

SONGS OF INNOCENCE AND EXPERIENCE

ILLUSIONS

—Well, that was just the most *fascinating* thing we've ever seen here on our show—a woman who claims to have seen *Timmy Valentine on Mars*! And maybe next time Ms. Phelps will remember to bring her snapshots! That is, for those of us who don't happen to share her ability to fly throughout the Solar System in her *astral body*!

[LAUGHTER]

—Thanks again for sharing your unique vision with us tonight on the Timmy Valentine special, coming to you *live* from the Lennon Auditorium right here in dazzling *Universal City*!

[APPLAUSE]

—Well, we've got quite a show lined up for tonight— in just sixty minutes the judges will have tabulated their votes on the elimination round and we'll be able to see— *live from the Lennon Auditorium, Universal City*—the finalists in Stupendous Television Network's amazing

Timmy Valentine Look-Alike Contest! Later tonight we're going to meet Jonathan Burr, the *controversial* director who's signed to do *Timmy Valentine—The Motion Picture* . . . we're going to meet Dr. Joshua Levy—lotta famous folks tonight, folks!—who *hasn't* been to Mars but who just might have the goods on the *real* Timmy Valentine . . . we're going to get random impressions out of some of *you,* our very special studio audience . . . Queen of Psychics *Simone Arleta's* gonna be with us later and . . .

[APPLAUSE]

. . . oops, we've gotta take a commercial now but don't go away, folks . . .

[APPLAUSE]

COMMERCIAL

ONE HUNDRED DOLLARS A DAY IN HOSPI-TALIZATION BENEFITS

Coffin flies open. A Timmy Valentine look-alike pops up. He is dressed in black. He has vampire fangs. He has a cloak that flutters behind him as the mist swirls [A/B SMOKE MACHINE—ELECTRIC FAN]. *He sniffs a red rose and looks straight at the camera. He smiles an enigmatic smile. There's a twinkle in his eye* [OPTICAL EFFECT] *and he says:*

BECAUSE WE WANT *YOU* TO LIVE FOREVER.

His voice echoes in the cavernous castle . . . forever . . . forever . . . forever.

ANGEL

That look-alike on the TV spot doesn't look anything like Timmy Valentine. I know. He's inside me. Inside.

Fucking Jesus maybe I'll blow that A-flat. My voice is

gonna change. Just like that. Hair on my dick and my career flushed down the toilet. I'll crack on that A-flat and grow six inches in sixty minutes.

"Here, honey, let me put a little more gel in your hair, I sure do think that cowlick's gonna pop up when you least want it."

"Okay, Momma." Let her do want she wants. I'll be her Ken doll, I'll let her play with me, I'll be her anatomically correct Ken doll until she withers and dies, be her teddy bear, man of the house, little angel, God, I hate you, I hate you. "That hurts, Momma." Stop brushing my damn hair.

Glance across to another monitor. This one's panning across the studio audience. There's that Petra Shiloh woman. I wish she'd've been my momma and the dead boy got stuck with the bitch I got.

"Oh look, honey, it's Gabriela."

"How you feeling, Angel?"

"Like a million dollars." Which means that you feel like a hundred thousand, Gabriela Muñoz, ace agent and talent scout.

"I'm sorry I couldn't get you a big suite but we're not really in a position to make demands at this stage . . . still, with the in-house cable you get to see a lot of what's going on downstairs . . . you're practically in the control room."

"Gabriela? You know what? I need to get into *samadhi,* get the theta waves rolling." She likes it when I talk New Age to her. I've only been in California for a couple of weeks but I'm taking on protective coloring real fast. Sometimes I still sound like a hillbilly but mostly when I'm with Momma, 'cause I'm kinda like a chameleon that way. "Gotta channel all my inner vibes," I tell her, "gotta *resonate.*" Momma looks at me in a bewildered way. She doesn't get the way people talk here at all.

"Huh? Oh, sure. Your mom and I will go and—hint,

hint—powder our noses." And they're gone. You can manipulate them so easily. Now I'm alone in the room. Gabriela's right, it's raunchy . . . peeling paint and the toilet doesn't flush . . . we've seen worse, me and Momma, driving cross-country from Kentucky.

On the monitor, the camera tilts down a little and—there she is again. She's talking to some man now, five o'clock shadow, jeans, sloppy hair. Now she looks up at the camera almost like she knows I'm up here watching. I'm right. Somehow we belong together. Petra.

I was this close to telling her what was on my mind.

VISION SEEKER

After he dropped PJ off, Brian found himself cruising up the Hollywood Freeway toward Lankershim. If it was all to start happening again, he would have to be there. Otherwise vampires would haunt his nightmares for the rest of his life.

The Lennon Auditorium was a new building, psychedelia in concrete, that had sprouted up on the hill alongside the old Registry Hotel. Its central dome was covered with squiggles of outrageous color; its façade was a sixty-foot-high rendition of the album cover of *Imagine,* done entirely in jigsaw fragments of many-colored granite. Such a building would have been impressive rising in isolation out of the Mojave Desert, or maybe nestled in some nook of Forest Lawn Cemetery; here, in the company of such architectural marvels as Fung Lum's Chinese restaurant, with the flames of Universal Studios' "Miami Vice" tourist attraction towering up on the hilltop every few hours, it was just one of many temples to the artistic bankruptcy of Los Angeles.

Maybe I'm just bitter, Brian thought, as he pulled into the ten-story lot and waited for the elevator to the lobby, because I haven't been able to sell even a cartoon script, let alone a novel, since I moved here.

There was a line of fans stretching all the way out of the lobby down the hill toward Lankershim. Brian went toward a roped-off entrance marked PRESS ONLY. "I'm with the *Times,*" he said, flashing a business card that actually belonged to his old friend Ed Kramer, who had long since ceased to be on the editorial staff. The guard handed him a badge and waved him through. Brian had learned that in this town, you only had to act as though you were supposed to be there to be accepted as the real thing. The illusion was everything. He joined the throng of reporters and moved into an inner lobby, this one well stocked with alcohol and canapés which were being passed around by waitresses garbed in the New Wave fashions of the early eighties. It had taken less than a decade for those zipper-heavy sci-fi outfits to attain the status of "classic" couture. He had almost forgotten the existence of parachute pants, but several would-be fashion plates were parading around in them.

The lobby itself was a monument to *haute* bad taste such as would doubtless have caused Lennon to turn over in his grave—red carpets and opera-house chandeliers competed with neo-Giacometti sculptures of the Beatles, op-art wallpaper, and ushers dressed in garish quasi-*Sergeant Pepper* uniforms. There were recognizable faces—someone from *Rolling Stone,* whatshername from CNN—he'd met them at parties, but he wasn't important enough for them to have remembered his name. He'd have to look for someone from the sleazier media . . . over there, for instance, wasn't that Petra Shiloh from *Entertainment World?*

He waved to her; she wasn't looking; instead, a waitress brought him a canapé.

"Petra!" He hadn't seen her in some time—not since that business with her son killing himself—but surely Petra wouldn't snub him. She knew Brian was a starving-in-a-garret kind of writer. She'd known that one year ago, the night she told him she wasn't a one-night-stand kind of woman and then proceeded to walk out of his life.

At that moment, she spotted him and came over. "I never thought I'd see you again," she said softly. "Especially not at a place like this." God, she looked like she'd suffered. She had been crying and hadn't bothered to fix her makeup. There were lines around her eyes and mouth that hadn't been there last year. "Who are you stringing for?" she said.

"No one," he said. "But I had to come. I knew Timmy Valentine, you see. I was one of the last people to see him."

"No . . . really? But everyone has a story like that . . . come to think of it, you did mention him to me that night."

That night. . . .

"Who's going to win this idiotic contest?" Brian said.

"My money's on a kid named Angel Todd," she said. And looked away, into the distance. Jesus, she sounded like she was in love. Her kid's suicide must really have turned her into a flake, he thought.

"No one could replace Timmy Valentine," said Brian.

"Amen to that!" said a little bearded man in a tuxedo who had been working his way over to them. "I couldn't help overhear your saying that you *knew* Timmy Valentine and were close to him at the moment of his apotheosis. . . . My magazine, *Psychic Encounters Quarterly,* would be willing to pay handsomely for any physical proof of—"

"Let's go in," Petra said, taking Brian's arm. "They've been setting up this next segment for hours—it should be about ready to roll by now."

"Christ, thanks," Brian whispered in her ear.

ILLUSIONS

—Welcome back! And now I want to introduce a prominent archaeologist, anthropologist, and—most important!—Timmy Valentine-ologist . . . Dr. Joshua Levy! Welcome to the show!

[APPLAUSE]

—Thank you, Dave.

[APPLAUSE]

—So, Joshua, what's your insight into this whole Timmy Valentine phenomenon?

—Okay, Dave. I come at this from kind of a different perspective from most of the self-styled experts you've had on this show. I've had training in psychology as well as archaeology and phenomenology. I don't believe in magic and superstition. I'm a scientist.

—And yet you're going to be reading a paper at the—

—USC.

—Yes, USC annual conference on semiotics—whatever the hell that is!—in which you are going to claim that rock star *Timmy Valentine* has been sighted throughout history—has been depicted in art through the ages—and it's all connected with—I can barely believe what I'm reading on the teleprompter here!—angelology *and* UFOs? I mean, doesn't your theory have a little something for every crackpot in—I mean, you *were* hospitalized at Bellevue about three years back, isn't that true?

—Well, it's true that I'm a paranoid schizophrenic, but you know, that's quite irrelevant. That's a chemical imbalance, and I'm taking drugs to control it. It has nothing to do with my theory, which is—

—But you're a certified lunatic!

—Shut up and let me talk, Dave!

[WILD APPLAUSE]

—All right, all right.

—Let me explain. The noted psychoanalyst Carl Jung

believed that the sightings of angels in the Middle Ages, *and* the sightings of UFOs today, are manifestations of the collective unconscious. They come from *within* us, not from heaven or from other planets. They appear within the context of contemporaneous mythology—in an age of piety, men saw angels—in our age of *Star Wars,* we have close encounters. I believe that *Timmy Valentine* is such a phenomenon. He is a vision sent to us by the collective unconscious from which all human consciousness arises. It is my belief that the visitations occur at times of great artistic ferment—of despair—of cultural desolation and decadence—that the Timmy Valentine image is a kind of universal emblem of the death of art—

—Waitaminute, you're saying that whenever there's a major cultural crisis, *Timmy Valentine* will appear?

—Let's look at some slides, and you'll see what I mean.

—Okay, what's this one?

—Second century A.D. It's a silver coin that shows Antinous, the favorite of the Emperor Hadrian. Okay—the Roman Empire—the civilization was collapsing, art becoming decadent, the whole culture about to be subsumed into the ravening Leviathan of Christianity—

[TITTERS]

—There's a can of worms for you! Let him finish—what's this one here?

—A late Ming dynasty vase. There's a youth with a p'ip'a, a Chinese lute, in his hand. He's talking to a nightingale. Sometimes this vase is known as the *Saint Francis of Peking.* Look at the two of them—the Roman coin and the Ming vase—now look at a picture of Timmy Valentine—the album cover of *Vampire Junction.* Okay, here's a third example. It's a painting—late sixteenth century—called *The Martyrdom of Saint Matthew.* Very famous painting. Here's an X-ray of the painting. You'll see there's a nude figure of a youth that for some reason got painted over. He's standing right in the foreground. He's an angel of death, watching over Saint Matthew as he dies. An exquisite figure—his features are identical with the ones in the other slides we've seen. But for some reason, the artist covered him up completely with other figures—obliterated him. Why?

—Why indeed! Well, when we come back from these words, we'll hear Dr. Joshua Levy telling us more about why he thinks that the 1980s are another period of artistic crisis and that's why we're all suffering from a mass-hypnosis collective-unconscious *hallucination* of the figure of—

—I just call him the angel. The angel of death. Sometimes.

—Let's take another look at that X-rayed painting by—who was it now?—Cara—Cara—

—Caravaggio.

—*Caravaggio.* Of course. Who could forget a name like that?

MEMORY: 1598

The apartments of Cardinal del Monte: the announced entertainment is a masque penned by the celebrated poet Torquato Tasso. The boys are to appear only in the fourth act, as a chorus of odalisques, for the setting of the play is the seraglio of a Turkish pasha, and the plot, such as it is, concerns the efforts of Dionysus, a Greek mage, to rescue his beloved Francesca from concubinage and a fate worse than death. It slowly becomes clear that the performance is in fact a vicious parody of the poet's work, and that some wag has simply taken the noble Tasso's drama *Aminta* and cleverly turned it into a trivial tale by changing the names and bastardizing the rhymes. Double entendres abound, as do references to Cardinal del Monte's none too secret fondness for the Turkish vice of sodomy.

Guglielmo and Ercolino have donned some androgy-

nous tunics which bear little resemblance to the actual
dress of Turkish harem girls. They have wreaths in their
hair. They are there to mingle with the cardinal's guests.
There are few women. There are many princes of the
church, reclining on plump silken couches or sprawling
across the floor like scarlet tents. There are dandies.
There is a withered duchess whose face has been powdered to a marmoreal whiteness. The conversation is
carried on in whispers and titters. Now and then one of
the guests looks about him warily. They seem to live in
terror of some scandal.

The walls are covered with artwork, but all of it is
concealed with drapes. There are statues, but they too are
covered up. The apartment smells of the oranges stuffed
with cloves that the rich carry on their persons whenever
they must venture out into the streets, to sniff whenever
the stench of putrefaction becomes too suffocating.

Cardinal del Monte sits on an overstuffed throne, a
page boy on his lap. The boy is singing to the accompani-
ment of a theorbo. He cannot keep in tune because the
masque musicians, sawing away at their viols from the
next room, are in a different key. No one is watching
the masque anyway, except for Prince Gesualdo, who
squats on a stool with a bottle of wine in his hand.

"They'll be going on till dawn!" Guglielmo whispers in
Ercolino's ear. "But with any luck, after we muddle
through our little production number, we can slip away.
I know a good shortcut to the choristers' dormitory."

"I can't stay until dawn," Ercolino says. He hopes he
will not have to explain.

The cardinal is laughing. The throne's legs squeak
against the marble as he shifts his bulk. *"Per bacco,"* he
shouts, "the ancient Romans with their orgies were never
as decadent as we!" The audience claps as though his
utterance were a veritable pearl. But Ercolino thinks: If
only they had seen what I have seen. After fifteen hundred years, the past seems more present than ever. "More

wine!" the cardinal shrieks. "And after we have become very, very drunk, perhaps a peek at my secret paintings!"

Collective gasping in the audience. The secret paintings are what they have really all come to see. Ercolino sees Guglielmo chuckling to himself.

"Why, what is in those paintings?" Ercolino asks him.

"Street urchins masquerading as heroic figures of myth and scripture," says Guglielmo, "and all, of course, without a stitch of clothing. Oh, there are nymphs as well as shepherds; the cardinal knows his own tastes, but he has something for everybody."

Coyly Guglielmo adjusts the folds of his tunic so as to conceal as much as can be hidden with so skimpy a sheet of cloth. He straightens the wreath in his hair. He makes an attractive girl, Ercolino thinks, when he does not try to walk; his stride betrays him. Ercolino himself, though he has kohled his eyes and stuck a blood-red rose behind his ear, he feels no need to play the part of a woman. What is man or woman? he thinks. I am not even human.

Soon it will be dawn. The boy vampire has not yet slept since his emergence from the forest. He does not think the dawn will pain him as much as it used to. He is becoming inured to his own superstitions.

Cardinal del Monte has waddled off his throne. He has yanked the first curtain aside to reveal a startling Cupid, large as life. Attendants raise their candelabra. This is a brazen Cupid—one of the grubby children of the street, scrubbed clean and sporting a pair of ill-fitting wings. The child, still scrubbed, is right there—he is the one who has been sitting on the cardinal's lap. He giggles.

Another painting—the onlookers ooh and aah—depicts the blind prophet Tiresias as he gazes on the unholy coupling of serpents—the impiety, as the myth goes, causing him to sprout breasts and cursing him to live as a woman until the spell can be broken. Unable to control themselves at the sight, two of the cardinal's guests begin to couple themselves right there at the foot of the painting.

Cardinal del Monte trots off into the next chamber, where the depictions are still lewder. On a wall-sized canvas, an orgy is in progress; in one corner, a man in a flowing robe—an Israelite—views the scene with an expression of disgust; two *putti* hover around his shoulders, whispering into his ears. A muscular, winged youth stands beside him, brandishing a bejeweled sword.

"Ah," Guglielmo says, laughing, "the patriarch Lot and the Archangel Michael prophesying destruction to the Sodomites. The biblical subject justifies including the orgy."

"I see." He does not want to say that the orgy seems rather tame by comparison to what he witnessed during the heyday of the Empire. In fact, the proceedings at the cardinal's affair seem listless, the decadence self-conscious and contrived. He loses interest as del Monte moves on, whisking aside arrases, lifting draperies. He is like an overgrown child, Ercolino thinks, this prince of the church.

He remembers a scene from the circus at Pompeii—a Christian being crunched in the jaws of a lioness. Others burned alive, crucified, raped to death by jackasses . . . this is what they died for, he thinks. It is they who now rule in Rome . . . and this is what they have become.

Inwardly he laughs. Perhaps the world is not so changed as he thought. Perhaps it is only me after all, he thinks. His mind floats . . . he finds he has drifted unawares once more into the shape of the black cat.

It is good, he thinks. Good to forget being human, to partake once more of the forest.

The drunken laughter now comes from far overhead as he slinks across the costly Persian carpet stained with wine. In one room choirboys are giggling as they apply the feminine makeup of the odalisques. One room is empty save for a naked woman, pouting, in a copper bathtub. There is a corridor lined with busts and broken statues that seem to have been plundered from all the sacred places of the ancients. One room is hung with threadbare tapestries depicting the deeds of saints and sinners. A massive bronze Jupiter gazes down from a niche and he cannot help mewing a prayer in a half-forgotten language.

From behind a curtain he can hear a man singing softly to himself. *Miserere mei.* It is the same lilting strain he first heard from the lips of Guglielmo. He slithers past velvet into an inner room. Caravaggio is there. He is painting. A huge canvas dominates one end of the chamber, which is lit by row upon row of scented candles, like a church. The canvas is dark save for shafts of light that illumine the figures in the foreground. He sees Saint Matthew, thrown onto the ground and about to be slain. His killer hunkers above him. A boy shrieks out in terror, while overhead, riding a whirlwind, angels watch, their faces impassive. Other figures are crudely blocked out.

Caravaggio works with profound concentration. He is clearly in terrible pain. He does not hear the mangled verse of Torquato Tasso or the jangle of the theorbo and the off-key choirboy. He is absorbed. He paints with deft flicks of the wrist, working one tiny area—the flesh tones of a screaming child's face—over and over in infinitesimal gradations of color.

He still has not changed his clothes, and his blood is still dripping from his wound onto the marble. Blood runs onto his palette and streaks the pigments. He grimaces. Yet his wrist moves swiftly—it dances across the canvas to a music that the boy vampire can almost hear—the tortuous music of Carlo Gesualdo—the music of hell, the hell God made.

The hot blood wakes his hunger. Catlike he pounces. His paws slip along smooth marble till his tongue tastes blood again. Blood races through him like fire. Blood warms him into simulated life. He purrs.

As though in a dream the painter says: "Why do you stand over my shoulder? Have you come for me? Are you the angel of death?" Illusion is useless. The man has the power to see his true self. It is the same gift that has made him a painter, and the same gift that has made him mad.

"No, Ser Caravaggio, I am not the angel of death. I am Ercole Serafini, sir; I am a *decani* soprano of the papal choir." Only when he utters these words does he realize that this must be his new identity for a little while. The world has become more vast as well as more human. He must stay inside this microcosm until he has learned the new rules. "My friends call me Ercolino," he adds.

"Oh, beautiful and terrifying. Oh, but your eyes say so much more than do your lips. You are more than another one of del Monte's singing boys, bought from the slums, gelded by a cut-rate barber. I have seen you in dreams." He becomes animated. His eyes shine with passion and madness. "If I could only capture you on this canvas . . . perhaps I'd be less afraid then." And he has not even looked at Ercolino yet! He has only seen him . . . reflected in the oil of the painting, perhaps . . . a reflection of one who can cast no reflection! Unless he is speaking to a creature of his imagination, an angel of his dementia.

"Why are you afraid?" Ercolino says.

He puts down his paintbrush for a moment. "Oh, it is the fever," he says. Beneath the tangle of beard, Ercolino can see that the skin is soaked with sweat and cracked and caked with pus. Caravaggio is ill. His blood is almost at boiling point. It is a sweet blood, made tart by the ineffective possets of the cardinal's resident quack.

"So much darkness," the boy says, looking at the painting. "And the light, painfully bright."

"But life itself is chiaroscuro," says the painter, "a perpetual darkness leavened only by the lightning of love, inspiration, agony."

"You're not at the revels with all the other guests, Ser

Caravaggio? I've been told you're a lover of pleasure, a sensual man."

"Oh, no. They keep me here, the trained monkey, the caged artist. What would I do at the party? Oh, but they love my crude ways. I am so entertaining. Tell me, boy, when you sing, don't you feel like a whore?"

"I don't know."

"Well, just look at you!" He turns to the boy vampire. His blood stains the boy's lips. How strange I must look, the boy thinks, in my preposterous costume, a sexless creature radiating the sexuality of a borrowed gender. "Ah," Caravaggio says, "but you *are* the death angel I've been dreaming of. You must come to my studio in the morning; I'll pay you half a scudo a week for your pains, until the picture is done. And meals, of course; His Eminence has supplied me with an excellent cook until such time as the *Martyrdom* is done."

"I can only come at night," says Ercolino, "and I won't need food."

"No, of course not," says the painter. "But can man live on blood alone?" He does not smile, but his eyes hint of mirth and irony.

"I can."

"But soon my wound will heal."

"You will have other wounds."

"Yes."

He hears the strains of the ode of the odalisques from the cardinal's private theater. "I must go," he says. He backs away, unwilling to look away from the unfinished painting. Its beauty is yet unborn; it is a cadaver with no heart, no blood, like a hungry vampire on a dark street corner.

"Give me the rose," says the painter. "A pledge." Unasked, he plucks it from the boy's hair. A thorn jabs his finger. Blood spurts; he seems to relish the pinprick. If the boy does not go soon he will have to feed again. The hunger is always there.

· The boy escapes, transforms, darts through the mass of satiated flesh toward the candlelit theater to take his place with the choir of unmanned youths. The song of the odalisques is silly and though he has never rehearsed it it is simple enough for him to join in in the monotonous refrain:

Amor, amor, amor,
Vittorioso amor.

SHAMANESS

"You must go now," she told them, "because there are certain things that only *I* may know; you understand. Trade secrets, as it were. I must get ready. Communing with the dark forces; a few words in private between myself and my familiar." And they filed out one by one. The makeup person—("Give me a break, woman! Do I need makeup, I, born *centuries* before your time?")—she had the nervous laughter of a closet spiritualist—the director, a fey cliché—the show's researcher dashing off a few quick notes to be fed to the Great Dave by way of teleprompter.

After they all left, Simone Arleta was finally able to focus. She needed a moment of stillness before her performance. She had to admit to herself that she was becoming afraid. Perhaps she should not have agreed to come. Something was changing in the world within. Her victim was gathering power.

The dressing room was not her Mojave Desert estate. It would not do to decapitate any turtle or to spray chicken blood all over the monitors and computer terminals and the gray metal shelving stocked with props, mirrors, makeup, office supplies. Nothing messy here. Jacques was outside the room, guarding the door to prevent the uninitiated from learning her secrets.

Animal sacrifice is a metaphor, she thought. The turtle or the chicken is *pharmakos,* a scapegoat, a substitute for the self, magic directed outward. There were other means of purifying the human spirit to the point of being able to perceive the world within.

She removed her clothing and hung it carefully on three hangers alongside the costume she would be wearing on television, a billowing black robe embroidered with stars and moons, very show-biz-oriented—and stood naked in front of a wall-sized mirror, a paunchy, withered woman. She let down her hair and shook it this way and that. Now she was every inch the traditional witch, ready to anoint herself with levitating lotion and fly to the bosom of Satan on a broom on the sabbat. Perhaps she should fly on the television. But no—a cheap trick—and they would think it was done with wires or chroma key—audiences today, weaned on *Star Wars,* too sophisticated to deal with reality!

She practiced her theatrical cackle a few times. Then she reached for her purse and fumbled for the frog. There it was. Jumping up and down in its private little mason jar, breathing holes punched in the lid, just like something a little boy might have in his room. She placed the jar on the dressing table. Then she drew out a pin she had stuck in the lining of her purse.

Eternity, eternity, eternity.

She prayed to the gods of power: Xangó, Saint Barbara, the decapitated god—Isis, the Virgin Mary, the earth of death and rebirth—Xipe Totec, Jesus, the flayed god, bleeding life into the world.

She shrieked with laughter. (It enhances the mystique, she thought. The tech staff tiptoe past my door, wondering.) She was a sounding board for the laughter of the gods. Their glee vibrated in every jowl and every fold of flesh.

Eternity.

She opened the jar and grasped the frog firmly in her

left hand. Lifted the frog to her lips and kissed it seven times, each time gathering strength for the journey into the dark forest. Murmuring the Divine Name, she plunged the pin, with practiced precision, into the creature's brain. There was almost no blood. She shoved the pin in all the way. As soon as the pin found the right spot, the frog began a rhythmic twitching. She raised it up, looked into its eyes; whispered to it, "Listen to me, thou who art called the horned serpent, thou who art the phallic force of the sky. It is the earth who calls to thee, the earth, thy mother, thy lover." She spat three times on the frog's head and ran her tongue along its sides to lubricate it; then, sucking in her breath, she slowly pushed the creature into her vagina, crying, "Enter the cavern, dragon! Enter the womb that bore thee and be reborn."

The amphibian pulsed within her. She was racked with pain and ecstasy. She shuddered as her womb drank in the creature's life. She swayed to the rhythm of its dying. She closed her eyes. Oh, they were all one life, one force. Oh, she could see the portals of darkness open, could feel the dark wind on her naked skin. She could hear the shivering of dead leaves. The darkness sheathed her like a velvet shroud. It was cold.

Eternity!

"Come to me now . . . come to me . . . come to me now, my child," she said. "This will be the hardest journey of them all. I've brought blood to bring you forth, my lover, my son."

In the world within, she walked toward where the tree of the hanged boy stood, the oldest tree in the eternal forest, while in the world of forms and colors, Simone Arleta was squeezing herself into the gaudy garments of a television sorceress, relentlessly bringing herself to orgasm with the death throes of a frog.

VISION SEEKER

"So far," Petra said, "I think it's a pretty ludicrous show. I think the Timmy Valentine fad is—well, it's not entirely healthy, if you know what I mean. Some kind of malaise in our society or whatever. You think it's a good line to take? For my paper, I mean."

Since Petra had rescued Brian from the foyer, they had sat through several of the Great Dave's most preposterous guests: a woman who claimed to have seen statues of Timmy Valentine in photographs of Easter Island, the Himalayas, and the moon, as well as an informal poll of twelve-year-old Valley girls about the "Clydesdale Quotient" of the various contenders.

"What about that archaeologist or anthropologist or whatever he was? The one who claims to have seen Valentine on historical documents and works of art?" Brian said. "There was something . . . a bit uncanny about those slides, wasn't there?" Especially if you knew what Brian knew. If you'd stood, stake in hand, in the labyrinthine attic of a Hollywood Hills estate and seen a young girl draped in seaweed floating in a glass costume . . . if you'd stood in a burning mansion in Idaho and seen vampire after vampire writhing in the flames . . . yes. There was something to what this Joshua Levy was saying. The Caravaggio thing was uncanny. Looking into the eyes of the angel, even through the faded X ray, he had felt something. Goose bumps. A prickle of fear.

"Oh, just a crank with a wild theory," Petra said, though he had the impression she sounded uneasy. "This one's a good talker, though. College professors have an aura of distinction that lets them get away with a *lot* of bullshit."

Brian wondered how far he could trust her. If he started telling her the truth, would she just laugh in his face? He said, "I'm not so sure it's *all* bullshit."

"You're not?" said Petra. "But then again, you know something I don't know."

"I guess."

Brian looked down at the stage from the roped-off press section of the auditorium. It was crammed. The tourists had been waiting in line for days to get their free tickets to the taping. Timmy Valentine's audience didn't seem to have aged at all. There were the seventh graders in their neon outfits. Some had their mothers in tow, yuppies and aging Gidgets. There were a few clumps of punks, drawn to the Valentine legend by its necrophilic lyrics rather than its sugary melodies. In an overhead balcony sat various glitterati—Brian thought he could make out Shirley MacLaine, Prince, Stephen King, and even—scarcely to be credited—Woody Allen. In keeping with the Lennon theme, the ceiling was painted with assorted psychedelia: rainbows twisted around giant mushrooms which were actually high-tech chandeliers; the centerpiece of the ceiling fresco was a mandala containing a cruciform design made of four yellow submarines, each with the head of a different Beatle, like the prow of a Spanish galleon. "Pretty damn tacky," he said. Then, glimpsing a gaunt figure flitting across an aisle— "My God, is that William Burroughs?"

"Oh, you're just trying to change the subject," Petra said. "So what *is* it that you know?"

"You'd never believe me."

"You'd be surprised what I'm capable of believing. I was at Simone Arleta's this weekend. I've been through the fire." She leaned back in her seat, unfolded a pair of glasses from her purse. He was attracted to her. She was attractive in an off-Hollywood kind of way; younger than him, maybe thirty-seven, he guessed, just on the verge of fraying. There was something melancholy about her even when she smiled. She was not at all the pert and overstated woman he remembered. Perhaps it was the death that had changed her.

Jason—a wisp of a boy. A little glassy-eyed. Could have been on Ritalin. Or dope. Brian had met the kid once or twice; he hadn't made much of an impression; he was television cute, big eyes, blond hair in a skater cut, long on one side and shaved on the other. He would have loved tonight; every time Brian had ever seen him he'd been listening to a Timmy Valentine song on his CD Walkman.

"How about a late supper tonight? I know a little Thai dive that's open until five A.M. We'll be here till at least midnight. And by then the canapés will have wilted." He looked away. He had gotten into the habit of being rejected.

"Sounds intriguing, Brian," Petra said. "Shush now. Here comes the Queen of Psychics."

Suddenly Brian knew that they were going to spend the night together. Jesus, I hope it's her place, he thought. He hadn't cleaned his apartment in six months. She smiled at him, a smile that promised a new beginning. For Brian, whose life had ended seven years ago, with the burning of a hick mountain town and the harrowing of the snow, the idea of beginning had become strange. He wondered whether he would be capable of sharing again.

Petra was full of surprises. Her son's death had changed her into someone else, a deep woman, a renewing woman. This time, he thought, she is capable of commitment. It frightened and excited him.

ILLUSIONS

—Well, it's time for us to meet the last—and most notorious—of the panel of judges in tonight's *Timmy Valentine Look-Alike Contest*—and let me remind you that the winner will receive not only a cash prize of *ten thousand dollars* but will also be picked to play the role of *Timmy Valentine* in Stupendous Pictures' new *forty-*

million-dollar epic extravaganza *Valentine,* to be directed by Oscar-winning director of last year's comedy hit *Deaf in Venice,* Jonathan Burr!

[A bow from Burr. APPLAUSE.]

—Our final judge, ladies and gentlemen—the Queen of Psychic Phenomena—trance channeler extraordinaire— author of *The Year 2001—My Ten Most Harrowing Predictions*—a woman who claims to communicate daily with Cleopatra, Napoleon, Elvis, and—surprise— *Timmy Valentine!—Simone Arleta!*

[MUSIC: WEIRD CHORDS segue into THEME FROM THE EXORCIST.]

—This is getting weird, folks!

[WILD APPLAUSE. *SIMONE ARLETA* SWEEPS ONTO THE SET.]

—Just look at you. Will you just look at her, folks? What a cloak. What a hairdo. Where do you buy a cloak like that, Simone? Not at Neiman-Marcus, surely.

[LAUGHTER]

—A witches' supply store! No, really?

[LAUGHTER]

—Enough laughter, ladies and gentlemen. Simone Arleta, who actually turned a member of the audience into a toad on *live* television—

[GASPS]

—Well, Dave, there's really no need to go on and on about my accomplishments. I'm just a regular kind of woman, as psychics go. Every time I'm on your show, you keep announcing me as though I'm some kind of freak of nature who's coming on the air to do a geek act. But really, what I do is a gift of the gods.

—Did you say gods, Simone? Are you a pagan?

—I have an open mind—a *very* open mind.

—I suppose you'd have to to do channeling.

—Oh, I wish you'd stop calling it that. I was a medium long before Shirley MacLaine popularized this business

with New Agers—and I don't really believe in any of it.
It's what I do, that's all.

—And what are you going to do tonight?

—I am going to become Timmy Valentine.

—And who better to be the judge of his own look-alike
contest?

—Who indeed, Dave honey?

—We'll take a commercial now—and when we come
back—the moment you've been waiting for. The finalists!

COMMERCIAL

During the commercial break he left the dressing room
flanked by his mother and his agent. Angel could see the
others up close for the first time. There were four finalists, including himself. One of them was a girl, but she
had about mastered the swagger of a boy; no way you
could tell really, unless you waited a year or two for the
tits to start springing up. If she was to win, he thought,
I bet she'll have them cut off or something. For the good
of her career, and fuck the gender God made her. The
other two were boys. One of them was from New York
City, a snobby rich Jew boy he reckoned. The other one
had to be local—every other word that came out of his
mouth was "like." Both of them looked a lot more like
Timmy Valentine than Angel ever could. But the contest
wasn't going to be won on looks. They could make you
look like anyone they wanted to, those movie people.

There was a little room that opened up into the corridor that led right up to the set. The TV lights shone so
bright over there that it made the hallway seem right
shadowy, like a tunnel leading out of the bowels of the
earth up into the sunlight. The four look-alikes didn't
speak to each other, and their agents or whatever kept
pulling them back like they were greyhounds on leashes
or something.

Angel didn't glare at anyone. He tried smiling at one of them, the New York one, figuring him to be the toughest one to crack. The boy didn't exactly smile back, but he gave him a look as if to say, "We're both swimming in it, dude, might as well go with the flow." The California kid and the girl, they just looked at the floor.

He thought about the high A-flat and wished he had picked one of the easier songs.

Then this obsessively cheerful stacked blond woman came charging into the waiting room. "All right, kids! Are you all ready for your big moment? Let's have a big big smile now and—"

[FLASH FLASH FLASH FLASH]

Publicity stills.

The photographers scurried away and the cheerful stacked woman said, "All right now, here's *The Hat*." Which was an Oakland A's cap (but Angel had made fifty dollars by betting on Cincinnati) that contained four numbers. The singing order. "Don't all crowd around at once. And don't peek, Marie!" she said to the girl. Who backed off, embarrassed at having her gender noticed. Took one to know one, though, because Angel couldn't have known without them telling him to expect a girl and because the agent was holding two purses.

So it happened that Angel drew first and drew last place, the best place. Now if only he could only just not blow it. . . .

"My child's done and got himself last place!" His mother went and blurted it out loud. "Is that going to be all right, honey?"

"Of *course!*" he said. Why couldn't she just leave him alone?

Gabriela put a finger to her lips. His mother backed off like a scolded child.

They were calling for the first kid. It was Irving Bernstein, the one from New York. Irving sighed. "I've gotta change my name," he said, "first thing. My name sucks shit in spades. I wish I had a name like you, Angel Todd."

"Good luck," said Angel. The mothers glared at each other.

A woman rushed to powder down his face, and they hustled him off toward the dazzling light at the end of the corridor.

VISION SEEKER

She closed her eyes and saw the boy come down from the tree.

It was cold and she was shivering and she held on to the man's arm like a teenage girl watching a horror movie.

The boy's neck sagged and blood dripped from his shriveled eyes.

SHAMANESS

She stood before the tree to receive the crucified child. She pulled out the nails with her teeth. Her vulva throbbed with the power of the dying frog.

Somehow light had managed to filter in through the impenetrable canopy. She was afraid of him. He had become too powerful. How had he managed to achieve this? Were there others controlling him too?

"Mommy needs you," she whispered.

She thought: You're a butterfly with a pin through your heart, and I put it there, and only I can take it away. . . .

She wrapped the undead child in her cloak. Blood trickled from his palms onto the dry leaves. She hugged him to her; the two of them resembled an obscene *pietà*. From above she could hear the leaves rustling and the twigs clattering like dry bones.

Behind the dead wind keened a brighter wind. This was the thing she feared. There was another force at work, a force so vast and elemental that she was unsure she could control it. What power was there on this earth that could smash the barrier between the real and the dream, that could reach into the darkness she had made and cry out to a creature she held captive?

"Don't listen to them, my son," she said, kissing the desiccated lips. "They are shadows. Who are they to come between us? We are here together inside our private eternity."

I hope I can keep him chained up. I hope my powers are enough. Xangó, help me. Help me, ancient forces. Help me.

Who else is calling to you, my son? Who else? Oh, do not listen, fall into my arms, let my starry cloak wrap around your wounded body as the sky envelops the earth, listen to your mother who for your sake has yielded her body to ultimate pleasure and pain.

The frog twitched and she shuddered with delight.

MEMORY: 1598

A single swath of brightness sweeps across darkness. Ercolino stands half in and half out of the light. False wings sprout from his shoulders. He cannot see the painter's face. Only the rapid motion of the brush, shadow dancing against the far wall, the plaster peeling, a cockroach circling a wine bottle.

But now and then he hears Ser Caravaggio's voice, whispering to himself: *My love, my death.* He wonders what the painter means. The man will not let him see the canvas. The boy stands in the light and the shadow. He does not feel the cold because he is himself the source of the cold. It is high summer and a hot wind blows from Ostia and the stench hangs heavy over the sewer outside the window. But the room is cool. The boy holds a pose of marmoreal stillness; the feathers shiver, but he does not; he does not even breathe; a rancid sweetness hangs in the air; a dew has formed on his pearl-smooth skin; his eyes are innocent of feeling.

The shadow of the paintbrush moves feverishly back and forth along the wall. *My love, my death*—what do those things mean?

"Do you know why you cannot see me in mirrors?" says Ercole Serafini.

"No, tell me," says the painter from behind the canvas.

"Because I am myself a mirror. Of myself I am nothing. When you look at me, you see only yourself, your shadow-half, the part you do not wish to see."

"Philosophy," says Ser Caravaggio, "don't speak to me of philosophy. I get enough of that from those fucking cardinals. Philosophy is the handmaiden of sodomy." He flings his paintbrush across the floor. He downs a quarter of the flagon in a single gulp, cockroach and all.

The boy has not even breathed.

ANGEL

I can't even breathe because it's almost time and I know I'm going to fucking blow it and I'll never be able to go back to Paris Kentucky anymore but who the fuck wants to anyway it's hell there it's fucking hell and I wish they'd leave me alone those women parting my hair this way and that and retouching the creases on my cloak I'm just a Ken doll to them yeah an anatomically correct Ken doll and I have to win this so I can fucking be on top for a change but I can see the girl on the monitor and shit she's good she's got the moves and she ain't never going to miss that A-flat never going to get hair on her dick never going to have her voice turn into sandpaper on her 'cause she don't even got a dick and never will and anyways she didn't even pick the song that has the A-flat in it I just wasn't cautious like the others I just wanted to show them I could do it and now I'm gonna get fucked but that's nothing new they don't care about me never did I'm just their fucking meal ticket.

Right. Pop one of them pills. Better make sure it's the right one. Don't want to fall asleep in front of the hot lights, don't want to go over like some kind of hyperactive kid neither. The blue ones look right. I'll do it right in front of that producer woman. Maybe it'll enhance my Hollywood-ness or something. Here goes nothing. Here. Goes (I hope I won't shit myself). Nothing. She doesn't even bat an eyelid, in fact she's just ordered a flunky to go get me water from the cooler. Arrowhead brand. Like piss around here.

A line of TV monitors all the way down the corridor on my way toward the light. Monitor after monitor. There's a close-up of her face. She's staring down at me fifty times over, flashing a smile that spells triumph. I can't believe how much she looks like Timmy Valentine I don't know how he was able to look so much like a guy and a girl at the same time maybe he never had no balls neither. Timmy, Timmy. Maybe if I open up my mind I can let him come into me take me over just like that witch lady says she's gonna do she sure is fat enough to have a whole hundred-ten-pound kid inside of her ready to bust out.

OK so the pill is kicking in now. I'm calm. Calm. The blue pills always put me in mind of Hangman's Holler which is where I go to be alone where there's this cave there dark and quiet and always cool with a smell like Becky Slade's pussy I know because I took her there one time she has a lot of hair a whole forest of it even though she's only twelve and, and, and

Walk down the corridor of monitors now. Concentrate. Girl's fading out slowly from the monitors and they cut to a rainbow screen and there's the judges sitting in armchairs on one end of the stage now the camera's moving from one face to another there's that witch woman writing something down in a notebook the score maybe. Concentrate. Breathe. Regular. Breathe. Breathe. Like the coach tells you to. Breathe. Like Becky Slade tells me to, breathe, breathe, easy now, it ain't ever day you gets to touch a soft dark thing so beautiful like mine go on now push the button it's just like a elevator white boy gone take you higher higher higher breathe now don't get too excited yet you ain't seen nothing go on push that button Angel you cute like a angel Angel. You be so good for me 'cause you too young to come. Walking down the corridor is like coming out of the cave Jesus that light hurts.

—Our next contestant is a boy from Paris, Kentucky—twelve-year-old Angel Todd, a student at Col. Michael Sinclair Junior High—welcome to the Timmy Valentine Look-Alike Contest, Angel—*live* from the Lennon Auditorium in *Universal City, California*—tell us a little bit about yourself, Angel.

—Not much to tell, really, sir. I'm just your average seventh grader from the heartland.

[APPLAUSE]

—So what do you think you'll do with all the money you'll get, the fame, the movie offers—*if* you should happen to be the judges' favorite?

—I just want to see that my mother gets all the things she's always deserved—

[WILD APPLAUSE]

Like being torn to pieces by wild lions. Look at the judges and smile at them with your eyes, make eye contact. Gabriela's in the wings making signs at me, she's saying go for it the crowd loves you maybe they're sick of the California bullshit and the New York bullshit not to mention the cross-dressing bullshit they all just watched and before I get a chance to get it together the lights change and *boom* the band that's not a band but a

rack of sequenced synthesizers starts to kind of ease into
the intro, a swirling filigree of music waiting for the first
crack of percussion and my first words to fill the void
and—

[APPLAUSE]

They must like the way I look. Jesus I can't see them
at all because the lights are all on me, I've suddenly
become alone, even the three judges are just shadows,
moving pieces of darkness. Excepting the witch woman,
she's sitting in the middle and I can see her eyes like in a
cartoon, eyes of a wild animal floating in a black nothing,
shit she scares me, but I just open my mouth and the
notes come out one after the other breathe in, breathe
out, just like the vocal coach says, in, out, in, out, I think
I'm not here at all but floating overhead wandering
across the audience look there's that Petra Shiloh woman
she's sitting next to a man I don't know who's watching
me, really watching me, remembering something I don't
know about and the notes come pouring one after another all I have to do is hold on tight surfing the tide of
the music welling breaking. Breathe. Breathe. Breathe.
Just gots to breathe real regular let me put your hand
down there where it's warm there push the button watch
me fly like a elevator girl look look into my eyes don't
you like me? Did you think we was made different down
there, ain't you ever seen no nigger's pussy before white
boy? I bet you wants to put it in there don't you? Go on
it's dark no one ever has to know we alone now here in
Hangman's Holler just you and me ain't nobody ever
gone know. But leastways give me a quarter. Twenty-five
cents and you be flying too, out of the cave and out of the
forest and up to the blue sky. Listen to Becky, the onliest
black girl in the seventh grade in Col. Michael Sinclair
Junior High. Let me get that zipper. I know you going to
Hollywood to become famous so I wants to be first, I
wants to be the one you remembers rest of you life when
you a star. Look it free now it ready to fly like it singing.

Breathe. Breathe. That A-flat is lurking around the corner like a mad child killer with a candy bar. Try not to think about it. Breathe. What's happening to the witch woman? Her eyes are glowing. Breathe. Breathe. *We'll cross tracks at the vampire junction* breathe breathe *that sucks our souls away* breathe. Let Becky play with it now, Becky can make it stand up and breathe breathe and one day you gone get hair down there and talk in a deep voice one day you gone break girls' hearts 'cause you so cute you like a angel Angel. Go on now put it now I bet you never done that before *Yes I have* yeah sure *I have I have* who with then who did you do it with *I can't say* who who *everything is going black now everything's dark I'm in the forest I'm in the cave I can't get out I can't get out* breathe! breathe! the A-flat is sneaking up now sneaking up slow behind me breathing down my neck *no Becky I can't do it I can't I promised someone* is you a fag? *I can't I can't because* (Come on to bed honey, come to Momma, Momma's wore out, Momma wants you to touch her special place and) *I didn't know it was the same thing Becky I didn't know* you done fucked someone and you didn't even know it? *let me out let me run out of the forest let me breathe and* here it comes now that A-flat soaring out of me soaring out of the cave out of the dark forest up toward the blue heaven I can feel the air tingling I can feel the audience they're not breathing Jesus I made it through the phrase I made it I made it and, and, and

You come back and see Becky again one day you hear? When you be man enough.

My mother made me fuck her.

Suddenly the song's over.

[APPLAUSE]

steals up over the dying synthesizer riffs.

[APPLAUSE]

I'm standing alone in the spotlight riding the wave of clapping. The spot widens and there's light, more and more light.

Light.
Light.

The four of us, we're all standing up there in the light. Circling, jumping up and down. They have this huge fucking fan blowing to make our cloaks unfurl and billow and we're up here dancing to stupid music that goes bopbopbopbopbop, we're dancing, four weenie Draculas, swirling our capes and hopping and stepping up a storm.

The judges get up. That's when the witch woman starts staring into my eyes. She's all sweating and heaving like there's something inside her about fixing to burst. We're all supposed to be dancing up here and paying the judges no mind. I can't help thinking of Becky Slade all the time that I'm dancing because that was when I learned that it was sex, I mean that secret thing, that I learned it was secret because it was dirty and it belonged in the dark, and I knew I never wanted to grow up and look into people's faces and know they knew the secret too because I'd about die. Mothers breathe life into you but then it's like they become vampires and they suck the life from you over and over but you can't say nothing because it's the same life they breathed into you in the first place. She's standing next to Gabriela, they're both clapping hard, raising their hands and clapping, but behind her in the shadow I think I can see Becky's ghost because she's so dark and hard to see and she's always there, behind every curtain, behind every bathroom door, in every corner, under every bed, forever.

—And the winner is—but wait a minute!—something very mysterious is happening!—Simone Arleta is going into one of her famous convulsions! I believe we are about to be visited by one of *the inhabitants of the other side!*—hold on to your hats, ladies and gentlemen— could we have a drumroll please—better, a big fat juicy orchestra crescendo!—I think our *surprise celebrity judge* is about to make an appearance!

Oh my God she's stepping out into the middle of the platform you can tell this ain't how they rehearsed it because the cameramen are running around and the director dude has come onto the stage and he's waving his arms trying to get the lighting people to zero in on her and now she's center stage and she's shaking all over and her eyes have rolled up into their sockets and she's moaning and carrying on and, and

Oh my God she's splitting in two down the middle! We're not dancing no more. We're just standing on the side watching. It starts with her head which kind of unzips down the middle of the forehead, you see the skull and then it cracks and the brain comes spewing out and the blood is spattering all over the lights and the cameramen and her face falls apart and her chest rips open and the intestines are unraveling and pieces of bone are flying everywhere one of them whizzes past me grazes my cheek and I scream and try to back away against the flimsy stage flats and I'm sliding in a pool of blood and I fall facedown and I see one leg topple down next to me with the bloody stump splashing my eyes and I'm breathing blood. People aren't screaming that much just all kind of frozen in place like no, this has gotta be part of the show, we're too sophisticated to panic, better to just sit there because you don't want to look like the only fool.

She's a heap of body parts on the floor. Hands reaching up out of the pile, clawing at the air. Head in two pieces with the eyes popping out on stalks swiveling this way and that and there's smoke everywhere, scarlet vaporized blood and then when the blood starts to condense there's someone else there. Someone forming out of the writhing gore. Solidifying out of the bloody mist. It's a boy.

He's pale. He's slender. He has big eyes that make you think of a deer you've startled in the forest in hunting season wandering off the path somewhere in Hangman's Holler. He has no clothes on and that makes him look like those slides they were showing earlier, those ancient art slides. He's not buff but he's compact, all coiled up. He's got power. He gathers up the witch lady's cloak with the stars and moons and astrology signs all over it and he draws it up to cover up his nakedness. The fan is still going and the cloth swirls and billows around him but with him it looks real, it looks like he's come down from the sky riding the clouds with the wind of heaven still whirling around him.

He doesn't smile. He just looks solemnly around him like he's woken up from a long long sleep. He's so pale you'd think he was made of marble like the marble angels in Forest Lawn watching over the dead. I don't even know all this is really happening maybe it's a dream maybe I've lost the contest and I've run away into like some fantasy inside my head.

There's still no sound from the audience. They're bewitched. They're holding their breath. He ain't breathing either but I think it's because he doesn't have to breathe. There's no more gore, no more witch lady. He's sucked her up into himself. I guess he burst out of her stomach like you see in horror movies. Then he made her disappear.

He looks right at me. For me his bloodless lips twist into half a smile. He says to me, "You have a lot more passion than I did."

"Uh . . . I wouldn't say that, I mean, I studied your albums pretty good, you didn't make but two or three videos though, 'cause you went away before MTV really got big. . . ." Motor mouth! Don't you have anything better to do than yack his ear off, him a living legend and you just a mountain boy?

"Angel, Angel. You play me so well. Would you be me if you could?"

"I guess so. I want to have glory."

"If only you knew how much pain came with that glory, Angel." I realize this conversation's happening just between me and him I mean no mikes are picking it up we're speaking to each other in a private pocket of time, a hairline fracture between two split seconds, inner time. I can tell because everything's frozen. Everything. The scream on Irving Bernstein's mouth. The twitch in his cheek that ain't done twitching. The whole audience is turned into one still frame of a crowd scene. Time slowed to a crawl, to a full stop.

"Let me look at you," he says.

I step forward. I'm nervous but he has a hypnotic way with him.

"You look a lot like me," he says. "But you see, I have to stay the way I am. I'm not free like you. I tried to break the cycle once but they dragged me back. I'm an archetype. I'm a failure when it comes to growing and changing. You can be me for a little while but then you'll change. You'll become a man. I won't."

That's when I start crying I mean bawling my guts out because he's seen right through me right down to the thing I'm most terrified of I mean that dark thing, my mother and Becky Slade hovering in the shadow behind her, that secret that makes me never want to grow. "Jesus you understand, you totally fucking really understand," I say. "I don't never want to change. I'm so scared I could kill myself."

He touches my cheek. My tears turn to ice. His hand burns, I mean it's like being hit in the face by a snowball.

"Now I'll show you how's it's really done," he says. There's a bit of mischief in his eyes. Then he's all serious and when he turns from me I can see time wrenching itself back on course and the audience starting to come alive and this music starts playing all by itself and he just closes his eyes and plucks the melody out of the air and he starts to sing in mid-phrase, and he hasn't sung but two notes before I'm convinced I've just been talking to Timmy Valentine.

JUDGMENT

As the music dies away he speaks. They have been in awe of him. He has thrilled them. There has never been anyone like Timmy Valentine, a child who can imbue the banal detritus of the eighties' music with so much eternity, so much anguish, so much unfulfilled longing.

He speaks, knowing that they see and recognize him. The little girls with their pigtails done up in ribbons of neon pink, green, yellow. The aging punks who satirize him and borrow his imagery. The journalists. One or two of them he even knows by name. They come to his house in the hills, hungering for news. One was with him even at the end.

He speaks. There is a solemn music in his voice, even without instruments, without melody.

"You know who I am. I can't be with you long. Once, many years ago, I was with you in the flesh. You see me now, unchanged. I wanted to change. For two thousand years I searched for the missing portions of my soul. Many died to give me the life's blood to go on. It was a slow quest. It took fourteen hundred years for me to learn compassion, six hundred more to find the Sybil and the Mage, the two who created me in a sexual magic in the flames of a dying city."

He remembers Pompeii. Alexandria. Carthage. Castile. Rome. Tiffauges. Cathay. Thauberg. Oświęcim. Junction.

"I found them reincarnated in two people—a crazed musician and a healer of sick minds. We went up to the mountains in order to transform ourselves by fire. We should have become one being. We should have become whole. A town and all its inhabitants were burned up in the wake of our metamorphosis. The three of us began to fuse into one being. We rode the night train into the dark forest of renewal. But we were vulnerable. We were like a chrysalis. Anyone could step on the chrysalis and crush us before the transformation was complete. And someone did. A woman came, seeking to use the pent-up power of making in me. She made a great and terrible magic. The triad was destroyed and only I woke up from the dark dream a prisoner, nailed to a tree at the heart of the forest. Still in darkness."

Darkness. Darkness.

"The woman used me. She called and I obeyed. But then there came another magic. After I was gone, my name was on more lips than ever before. Children called to me in their dreams. The songs I sang drifted in the air. Each time my name was mentioned was a faint whisper in soundless night. And tonight, this night, with twenty million televisions concentrating on my image, the whisper has become the howling of a tempest. I can't stay long. I'm a prisoner. The woman still controls me. Tonight her control slipped a little."

Two thousand pairs of eyes, and beyond those eyes countless millions. He drinks in their attention. It is warmer even than blood. He thinks: Blood sustained me when I was among them. Now there's a kind of psychic blood, an invisible life force I can live on, even though I'm a shadow of a shadow, an imaginary creature nailed to a tree in the labyrinth of a madwoman's mind.

There is a frog at Timmy's feet, with a pin sticking out of its head. It twitches in a precise rhythm, soullessly. Timmy picks up the frog. It smells of a woman's lubricious fluids. It is beyond agony. Shaking his head, the boy withdraws the pin from its head. The frog's convulsions become arrhythmic. Gently the boy strokes it. It dies, choking on its own blood.

"One day," says the boy, "I'm going to come back. Someone out there has the key to my prison. Someone out there."

He looks out at the audience. He feeds on the tension in the air. There is terror, but there is also love; it is this concentrated outpouring of love that has been able to break the spell, though only for a short while. Who is it who possesses that key? Perhaps he has spoken prematurely. He turns to the one called Angel, the one who sang last. He is no longer sobbing. No one has seen his tears. The exchange between the two boys has taken place not in time but in the interstices of time, in the split nanosecond it took for him to travel here out of the dark place.

"But now I must render judgment," he says. "I have to choose the winner. I pick the only one who has seen me for what I am. The one who hasn't aped my mannerisms, but has sought out my soul. I choose the one called Angel."

And then he feels himself begin to dissolve. He sees the pieces of Simone Arleta fly together in a cloud of bloody steam. The pin drills down into the frog and the woman coalesces around the animal, which is twitching back to a semblance of life. He feels the chains tugging at him. He cannot stay. He is being siphoned back into her mind. He turns to Angel, tries to cry out to him as his shape attenuates, flattens, dissipates into the harsh studio lights: "Save me, Angel Todd! Save me!"

ANGEL

—and then the applause starts it just seems to go on and on and I'm standing staring like some yokel on his first trip to the big city thinking I've won I've fucking won I've won I've won.

VISION SEEKERS

"Why?" said Petra. "Why are you shaking, why do you look like you've just seen a ghost?"

"I have." She hadn't realized Brian had such a weak

stomach. He had changed. Somehow she knew they would end up spending the night together. She hoped it would not be like the last time, a year ago, when something about his hangdog demeanor had impelled her to go home with him. This time there was something different. There was something charged and magical about the way they had been thrown together, about the fact that he had known Timmy Valentine and that she had suddenly developed an almost maternal rapport with the boy who would play him in the motion picture.

"Jesus. Let's get out of here. There's something that— Jesus, you don't know, you don't realize what's happening, do you?"

"Oh, Brian, you fool . . . you haven't been to the movies lately, have you? Freddy Krueger, Michael Myers, you know who they are? If you did you wouldn't let a few animatronics get to you! It's all fake, I mean look at the Great Dave's great big gap-toothed grin. . . ."

[APPLAUSE]

"Brian, how about that Thai food you promised me?"

ILLUSIONS

—Simone, that has *got* to be the most stunning on-stage, no-mirrors transformation scene I've ever seen in my life! Maybe next time you'll give our production staff some warning you're going to do a big transformation number on us!

—Simone? Simone?

—Ladies and gentlemen, Simone Arleta's just had a very tiring evening. Going into a trance, exploding, turning into a twelve-year-old dead rock star and—hey, look, what's this?—a frog!—you know what, we've had tarantulas, chimpanzees, even an elephant on my show before, but I don't think we've ever had a frog—*ribbit, ribbit?*—

no, I'm *not* going to kiss you! It's nothing personal,
you're just not my type!

[WILD LAUGHTER]

—Simone?

—Let's take a commercial break, folks, and when we
come back we'll learn all about this kid from Paris, Kentucky, who's on his way toward being the teen heartthrob
of the 1990s!

ANGEL

It's me, Angel.

MEMORY: 1598

"Why do you call me the angel of death?" he asks the
painter. "I am no angel, and I am not death."

"Don't speak to me! I'm making the lightning dart
across your eyes. I'm making your glance arc over the
dying saint toward the portrait of myself I have put in,
peeking timorously from an alcove. No, don't say a
word. Don't move. Don't even breathe. Be. *Be.*"

6

CHIAROSCURO

SHAMANESS

"Jacques! *Jacques!*"

"You were magnificent, madame."

"No, no. I didn't address you just to have you flatter me, though I'm pleased you found time to watch the show on the limousine's television set. Something is afoot, Jacques. Things are happening that should never have happened. The enemy is abroad. The enemy could come even here, even into my stronghold, my oasis of magic in the heart of the desert. Stop the car. Stop. Stop."

"Yes, madame."

He halted the car and Simone Arleta stepped out into the cold night wind of the Mojave. They were still some miles from her estate. She did not mind the cold; it was welcome after the glaring television lights. Not just the lights either; when she traveled back and forth from the spirit world it always drove her body temperature up to fever level. Sometimes she thought her blood would just boil out from every fissure of her body.

Simone Arleta shed her cloak, her show-biz vestments, and she stood naked in the moonlight. The fresh creature that had twitched away its life lay cold and motionless inside her. She reached into her vagina and pried it loose. Then she pulled out the pin from its brain and laid it down on a flat stone, murmuring a prayer to pacify its spirit on its journey into the next hell. The air smelled of dust and distant burning.

Simone knelt down on the pile of her own robes. The wind whipped her hair into her face. She tasted sand. Coyotes howled in the distance. Looking around as though she were afraid of spies—though who could there be in such a wilderness?—she pulled her portable cellular phone out of a pocket of her shamaness's cloak and dialed an unlisted number in the small Kentucky town of Hangman's Holler.

"Damien," she said, "it's me. Simone."

"Jesus fucking Christ," came the voice that had never, in thirty years of televangelizing, uttered so much as a *darn* on the airwaves. "This better be good. It's goddamned three in the morning and I'm a-cussing up a storm."

She laughed. "Only your closest friends have this number, Damien. You know no one will be betray you."

"Don't be too sure. The IRS has picked up on it lately."

"Damien. We have to meet. Everything has changed. A new plan must be brought into effect. The channels of power have been altered. If we don't bend with the wind we will break."

"I watched you on the TV today, Simone. The kid that won that contest, why he's from my very own home town, did you know that? There could be a Satan-worship scandal right in my backyard, the way the people here feel about little boys that dress up as vampires and maybe have subliminal messages that tell other little boys to run around biting people on the neck and recoiling from the symbols of our savior."

"Forget him. The danger is to you and me." She felt the wind whistle through her very bones. "We must speak soon. I will come to you or you to me. We have to reconstitute the Gods of Chaos."

"And who in the name of hell and damnation are the Gods of Chaos?"

Wind was a powerful magic. Her body sang with it. Devour me! she thought. She whispered a word of power and the dead frog burst into flame. Cold blue flame, fanned by the desert wind.

"I will tell you," she said, "when next we meet."

VISION SEEKERS

The Café Ayudhya was a dive on Sherman Way, somewhere in the monotonous sequence of shopping plazas that went on for twenty miles all the way from Burbank to West Hills. Brian and Petra drove toward it in silence. What a dull street, Brian thought. He looked up at the rearview mirror and saw the car that had been tailgating them since the Lennon Auditorium.

"We're being followed," he said. "Do you know someone with a white Porsche?"

"Actually I do," she said. "But . . . she's at Mills College. She's a college student, a Thai girl . . . some kind of aristocrat."

Bingo! Prince Prathna was extending some kind of spectral hand toward them. Even though he'd seen the prince go up in flames, dying at the moment of orgasm when the beautiful Indian-woman-turned-vampire, Shannah Gallagher, bit off his penis and drank him dry. The prince who had been part of that unholy secret society, the Gods of Chaos, a dozen old men who had decided to give their lives a final burst of excitement by going on a spectacular safari, with the world for their veldt and a vampire for their quarry. How much did he dare tell Petra? How much could she be trusted?

Brian decided to turn north, up Coldwater Canyon. He turned abruptly without signaling. Petra gasped. "Sorry," she said. "I'm not used to it . . . anymore . . . I mean, to the way men drive."

He ducked through an alley, drove the wrong way through the drive-up window of a Jack in the Box, U-turned, sneaked through another alley. Presently he found himself heading back toward the Ayudhya. The Porsche was gone. "I think I've lost her," he said.

"Why are you so paranoid?"

"We're all paranoid." He fumbled along the dash-board for some pills. "Care for a downer or something?"

"I gave at the office," she said, laughing.

They laughed a lot. Too much. They were nervous. There was a sexual tension between them too, and they both knew how the evening would end. But first he would have to tell her what he knew. The air had to be cleared. Dark things had to be talked about so that they might lose some of their terror. So he started to talk about Timmy Valentine.

At 3 A.M. in the Valley, the streets were deserted. Doughnut houses, convenience stores and all-night supermarkets announced themselves to no one in particular in primal, primary neons. There were, of course, no stars.

"Timmy Valentine was a vampire," he said. "He was *really* a vampire. Not your garlic-and-crosses-fearing Bela Lugosi type, but a complex and tormented boy who happened to have been dead for almost two thousand years and who needed blood to maintain the semblance of life."

"You're not joking, are you?"

"No."

They didn't speak for a while. There was so much more he wanted to tell her, but when he opened his mouth to speak he was drowning in memories, incapable of making sense out of it. Hundreds had died. The Gods of Chaos, of course. His niece Lisa, transformed into a deadly naiad by the vampire who had visited her in the shape of a wereshark. Hollywood personalities like Blade Kendall. Psychiatrists like Dr. Carla Rubens. Musicians like Stephen Miles, the pyromaniac Wagnerian. The seductive Shannah Gallagher, all the inhabitants of Junction from the arcade manager to the undertaker, all of them burned to cinders and swallowed up by winter. David Gish and now Terry too . . . Terry who had come back to haunt his old friends. The drama of Timmy Valentine had had so many players that it was inconceivable to him that it could be played out one more time with a whole new cast and crew. Surely it was a nightmare, only a nightmare.

Pulling into the parking lot of the Café Ayudhya, he saw just how much of a nightmare it was. The white Porsche was already parked there. "Let's go somewhere else," he said. He pointed at the Porsche.

Petra said, "I know the girl, there's not an iota of evil in her, Brian . . . maybe they *have* unleashed the entire population of Dante's Inferno into the world tonight, but I don't think she's one of them. And anyway I'm hungry." Firmly she took hold of his hand and led him inside.

There was no escape. Lady Premchitra had already left her window seat and was walking toward them. Neon flashed, noveau "Miami Vice"-style, turquoise and pink, while a dusky Linda Ronstadt warbled in a corner in Thai to a desultory disco beat. "Petra . . . I was just at the Timmy Valentine show . . . I had to see it after what we talked about . . . can we talk?" She noticed Brian then, and eyed him suspiciously. "Oh, I'm sorry," she said. She was a slender creature, childlike; there was little of the dissipated Prathna in her features; she did not even have the British accent that her grandfather cultivated. Her English was pure Northern California . . . *I'm sawry.*

"I knew your grandfather," Brian said.

"Oh." Lady Chit looked at the ground. She didn't have the aura of evil either. What was going on here? "Why did you follow us?" he asked her, ignoring the hostess who was trying to find out if they wanted smoking or non-smoking. "How do you two know each other?"

"I wasn't following you," said Chit ingenuously. "I always come here late at night when I'm in the Valley. It's the only decent Thai restaurant that's open."

Petra looked at Brian with an "I told you so" expression. Then she said, "We all have to talk. Something's going on. Something I can't quite grasp. Something I'm not really prepared to believe yet."

MEMORY: 1598

He has come to the painter's apartments every night. Every night he has drawn a little blood, just enough to take the edge off his hunger; every night he has stood in the corner, half in, half out of the shadow, wearing nothing but the harness to which are attached two flightless wings. Sometimes he sings. Before dawn he returns to the dormitory where the choristers sleep, three or four to a bed; he lies, sleepless, next to the snoring Guglielmo, waiting for the bell that will summon them to breakfast and to matins; he is shunted from service to service, down dark hallways lined with ancient sculptures pilfered from the temples of pagan Greece and Rome; he never encounters the sun, though Rome in the summer is so sultry that the very stone of the walls sweats. Now and then a shaft of sunlight streams in through a chink in the ceiling, or into an atrium, or through an open window; the sunlight does not burn him anymore. He has ceased to believe in good and evil; light does not kill him, night does not nurture him. He has seen too much of the darkness in men's hearts to be affected by their folly, their superstition.

In the hour before the dawn he settles on the cold marble like dew; he resolves into his familiar shape, tiptoes toward the bed. The smell of eunuchs sleeping is different from the smell that rises from the beds of whole men. The air is innocent of the pheromones of arousal or the scent of drying semen. There is a sweetness to their slumber; their sleep is the limbo of the unbaptised. Ercolino stands for a moment in a pool of twilight, not yet quite substantial. It is at that moment that Guglielmo pounces on him. When the eunuch's hands touch the icy flesh they quickly let go.

"Ercolino, Ercolino!" says the chorister. "I've been spying on you at night. Cardinal del Monte pays me. He wants to know all about you."

"You shouldn't. Sometimes it's hard to follow me."

"I've seen you go to the painter's house, the one I warned you against. I've climbed up the wall and stood on tiptoe on the shingles and seen you drink the man's blood . . . what does it mean? I never see you eat or drink. Ercolino, you're not human, are you?"

"Caravaggio calls me his angel of death. But that is his own imagining. I am what people make me."

"I've heard about creatures like you. You are immortal. You were here before our Lord walked the earth. When you take enough blood from a man, he becomes immortal too."

"Half-truths," says Ercole Serafini, thinking of the painter grinding his very blood into the canvas, wringing his soul into the pigment.

"I want to be immortal too, Ercolino. Make me immortal."

"You don't know what you're asking."

"But I think I do. I think you are a vampire. I think I have seen you sucking the blood from the painter's fingers as he closes his eyes in ecstasy. There is something Satanic about you. Such beauty can only come from evil, put here to tempt men. Am I wrong?"

"You don't really believe that, Guglielmo." Though the room is dark, the boy can see with the clarity of one born from darkness. To him it is as though the chamber were awash with a soft sourceless light. Guglielmo only thinks that the shadow masks his emotions. The light that comes from the shunning of light shines so fiercely that it betrays every flicker of doubt in the chorister's face. Ercolino knows that his friend has seen something; he knows he does not understand what he has seen, and that for him all is confusion and terror and the yearning half-remembered from the time before he was unmanned. Ercolino says, "I can't give it back to you."

"I don't want that back," says Guglielmo, but the boy knows he lies. "I just want to be like you. And if I can't, then I will hurt you."

"I cannot be hurt," says the boy vampire. But that has not been true for over a century.

NIGHT CREATURES

Universal City, Studio City, Sherman Oaks, North Hollywood, Van Nuys, Reseda, Woodland Hills, West Hills, Mission Hills, Granada Hills, hills, hills, hills, hills, fucking fucking hills.

PJ hadn't been able to avoid the Timmy Valentine circus completely. After Brian left him at the apartment he had made a few stabs at finishing one of his large canvases, a commission from some foundation with money to burn if the artist came from one of the right minorities. It was a terrible painting but it contained all the correct icons of the liberal-guilt-laden artistic establishment. It showed a vast cliff riddled with pueblo dwellings, cracking under a monstrous, spectral jackhammer. In the foreground, a wolf howled. In the background, the sky was on fire. The painting seemed to fill up the whole bedroom.

There was not much left to do. A few brushstrokes . . . the whites of the wolf's eyes. But as PJ worked he became aware of another painting hidden behind his images . . . in the flickering of the flames, in the cracks in the cliffs, in the labyrinthine pattern of the pueblo caves . . . another image . . . a human face. The face of a boy, taunting . . . a boy with bloodlust in his eyes. You could only see the face when you leaned back, and then the lines of the rock and the dry-brush swirls of the fire resolved into the face. It was unmistakable. "Timmy, you're haunting me," PJ said.

He didn't want to have the painting in the house anymore. It wasn't finished, but it didn't matter. The client wasn't concerned about art, only about political correctness. PJ decided to spray the whole canvas with a high-gloss fixative and not to add another stroke to it. In fact, he wanted to get rid of it that very night. Why did he feel so strongly about it? He used up the whole can of spray and tossed it in the trash. He kept his eyes averted from the painting. It was an abomination of some kind. It did not come from himself but from some outside spirit.

PJ went into the living room. He could still feel the eyes of the painting on him. He had not been so afraid since the day he had experienced the terrible dream that had compelled him to take on the role of *ma'aipots,* the sacred hermaphrodite.

The gallery was open until midnight! He could take it there and leave it. It was a rash thing to do, throwing away this vision instead of confronting it and learning from it. But there was too much terror. His skin crawled. Maybe I should cut it up and put it down the garbage chute, he thought. But then he would lose the check. It was enough to cover the rent for five months. He went back into the bedroom. Usually the place smelled faintly of turpentine but there was another odor now . . . a fetid, choking odor . . . and the smell of something burning. Human flesh . . . boiling blood . . . gasoline fumes . . . the icy air of impending snowfall . . . it was the reek of Junction! The past was leaking into the present.

Oh, Jesus, Terry, he thought. I should have staked him. I should have made sure. They were crossing the snow again, him and Terry, dragging Brian along on a makeshift travois, with the burning town uphill behind them, with the stench of dead friends tainting the winter wind, with terror seeping into them like the slush in their shoes.

PJ threw a bedsheet over the canvas. The wet paint started to soak through but he didn't care. Most of it was dry anyway. The smudges would have some unpredictable effect, no doubt. A new texturing technique, he'd tell them. It beat selling portraits of Cochise and Sitting Bull at the swap meet.

He took the painting, went out to the van, threw it in the back. Plenty of time. He set off uphill, toward the Hollywood Freeway. The traffic was particularly bad tonight. After about half an hour of crawling he got off at the nearest exit. He was in the Valley, somewhere on Ventura Boulevard, a twenty-mile-long nightmare of art deco malls and nouvelle neon restaurants and palatial shopping plazas . . . the fucking Valley . . . God, he hated it . . . it all looked alike . . . he wished he were back on the reservation.

He found himself going in the wrong direction, not toward the art gallery in Sherman Oaks at all, but toward the Lennon Auditorium in Universal City. It was almost as though the van were moving of its own volition. He found himself pulling into the parking lot only to be told that tonight it was reserved for VIPs and that he couldn't use it without a special gold invitation; others had to use the lot on Lankershim, but they could get a three-dollar discount by mentioning the Timmy Valentine Look-Alike Contest.

The conversation with the security guard drew him out of his confusion a little. He realized he had been on automatic pilot, that part of him longed to complete the journey begun in his childhood, longed to relive it all, even the horror. He had to resist. He turned around and went back west on Ventura, and after a few disconcerting wrong turns found himself at last at the gallery.

It was a relentlessly trendy place. In the window was a neon re-creation of Picasso's *Demoiselles d'Avignon,* its cubist contours rendered in angular tubes of garish light, flickering on and off in time to a continuous-loop New Age score. Several other twentieth-century masterpieces were reproduced in neon—a Mondrian, a Braque, even one of those David Hockney swimming pool things. The neon pieces were amusing enough, but to PJ they underscored the cultural desolation of this place . . . it was a self-involved art, a masturbatory art, an art that had no anchor in reality.

He took the bedsheet-draped painting to a back office. Cheryl, one of the night staff, was entering addresses into a database. She was a platinum blonde with punked-out hair and nerd glasses. Encino born and bred.

He leaned the picture against one wall and said, "Cheryl, I'm leaving this here for Roscoe. Do you mind?"

"Does the bedsheet come with it?" she said, looking up from the computer keyboard and fluttering her eyelashes.

"No," he said.

"Looks good with it on it though."

He turned and saw what had happened. Paint had seeped through the linen and highlighted the outlines of a human face. Especially the eyes. The eyes had soaked right through. They were imprinted on the cloth. Yellow eyes of a demon. More details were coming through. The crack-veins in the cliff wall were emerging as strands of long black hair. Lips were forming, lips fringed with blood.

"Awesome," Cheryl said, and turned back to her data entry.

"Don't look at it! Cover your eyes!" But he couldn't look away. Timmy Valentine was in the picture . . . was in his mind . . . trying to claw his way out from some supernatural limbo.

"Hey, mellow out! You artists are all so . . . so . . . I don't know. You need some help relaxing? I've got condoms."

He had to get out of there. He started for the door.

"Don't you have to fill out some forms or something?"

"Tomorrow. Next week. Whatever. Enjoy the picture." And he was in the main gallery, swimming in New Age muzak and blinking neon lights.

He got in the van and started driving.

Driving.

Universal City, Studio City, Sherman Oaks, North Hollywood, Van Nuys, Reseda, Woodland Hills, West Hills, Mission Hills, Granada Hills, hills, hills, hills, hills, fucking fucking hills.

He didn't know where he was now. Maybe Pacoima, maybe San Fernando. He was running low on gas and he didn't have any cash. He pulled in beside an ATM machine and got out of the van. It was a seedy street. Only a few cars around, and the all-night supermarket had letters missing from its neon sign:

A　NIGHT MAR E

Coincidence, he told himself.

It was what passes for cold in Southern California; a sandy wind blew trash around; the air smelled faintly of malathion. Although PJ was used to the sleaze of Hollywood, he found the Valley's sleaze unnerving. Quickly he put in his card, praying that last week's checks had cleared so he could squeeze a twenty out of his account. He drummed his fingers waiting for the money. Then he heard a voice: "Mister, could you spare some change?"

He turned. It was a woman with a shopping cart. She

wasn't a stereotypical bag lady at all. She had tried to make herself presentable; there were traces of lipstick on her mouth; she hadn't been homeless long. She had come right at him out of the shadow of the bank; he hadn't even noticed her there before.

"Wish I could help," PJ said.

The ATM beeped. He reached for his twenty dollars.

"Please, mister—"

"Hey, I'm in bad shape myself. And if I don't get gas, I won't be able to get home."

"At least you have a home." She stood half in shadow and half in a pool of yellow light from the only lamp on the street.

PJ didn't know what to say to her. I've been on the street too, he thought. But he couldn't break the twenty and he couldn't get any more money from the machine. The way she looked at him, not reproaching him but not forgiving him . . . it was how his mother looked at white people sometimes. "Lady, I—" He didn't know what he was about to say. He never got to say it anyway, because in the next moment, the homeless woman came apart.

At first it was just a trickle of blood from her lips and nostrils. Then a pair of thumbs poking through her neck, ripping out her trachea. An eerie sound, half whistle, half gurgle, issued from her ruptured larynx. The flesh ripped with a sound like Velcro. Gore oozed onto the shopping cart piled with dirty blankets. Two bloody hands clawed their way down her chest. The sternum snapped. Her head rolled forward. PJ could hear a slurping sound, like an uncouth kid wolfing down an ice-cream soda. The body cavity was split down the middle. Framed in the flesh was a face. The face of a pale redheaded youth who was gorging on the gushing blood. PJ wanted to look away but he couldn't because he knew that he brought this scene about. He could have prevented it. He could have driven the stake through Terry's heart.

"Terry. . . ."

The body slumped forward onto the cart. Terry had done a thorough job. The face was bloodless, the skin pale, jaundiced-looking in the sodium glare. Terry gave the shopping cart a kick and it went skidding across the street, down toward the parking lot of the all-night market.

"You sure did a half-assed job of killing me dead, PJ," Terry said softly.

"How could I kill you? You're my—"

"Friend." Terry laughed bitterly. He reeked of decay. "My friend who wouldn't even let me sleep in his closet . . . who shoved my native earth down the disposal . . . who laid me to rest in the mountains with a lot of singing and dancing and voodoo bullshit and hoped I'd never come back. Well, fuck you, I'm back, because you couldn't vacuum every speck of dirt . . . and you never looked inside my socks."

The shopping cart was still rolling. It came to a stop beside the handicapped-parking spaces. A few shoppers came out of the market with grocery bags, but they didn't notice the pieces of dead woman strewn in their path. People only see what they expect to see, PJ thought.

"You asshole," said PJ. "She was homeless."

"The homeless are our friends," Terry said, "they're just like us, wandering the night, raiding the garbage of the daylight world. Yesterday I had a teenage girl who was standing by the dumpster of a pizza place waiting for them to throw out the cold pizzas. It's cool."

"I guess you'd better come back to the apartment," PJ said.

"Damn straight."

Terry held out a bloody hand. And PJ took it in his. It was cold, but it wasn't hard. It felt more like those packs of gel they put in coolers. The blood was congealing fast. PJ snatched his hand away quickly and Terry licked his fingers clean. "It's not so bad to be a vampire," he said. "I mean, look at *you*. You're totally confused, buddy. You ain't a white boy and you ain't an Injun. It confused you so much that you decided to like go on this vision question, and you had a dream and now you ain't a woman and you ain't a man. You're a big intellectual artist and you paint tacky pictures of Cochise for middle-class living rooms. PJ, you're just one big old bundle of confusion. But I can fix that. Uh, uh, I know you're going to turn me down and you're my friend so I'm not gonna force you, but PJ, Peeeeejaaaaaay, listen up good, I can make it better for you. I can take it all away, everything that's fucking up your mind, better than any shrink, better than any medicine man. Do you believe me?"

"Jesus, Terry." PJ found himself weeping. God it was strange to be like this, crying in the middle of the street somewhere in darkest Pacoima, between an all-night market and an ATM machine, watching a shopping cart with a shredded bag lady go bump bump bump against the bike rack next to the handicapped parking, in the chill night air that stank of smog and malathion.

"You're gonna need me, PJ," Terry said. "I'm stuck between two worlds now and I can see things human beings can't. Like for instance I can see Timmy Valentine . . . I can see him smashing his fists against his coffin . . . I can see the black train pull into the junction in the middle of the night."

The neon of the market flashed unevenly:

    A   NIGHT MAR E

    A   NIGHT MAR E

    A   NIGHT MAR E

Then it went out altogether.

"At least you didn't have to give her any change," Terry said. In the pool of light his eyes were bloodshot and his lips were full and red.

ANGEL

Angel. Come on to bed, honey.

Just a moment, Momma.

How long was it going to take the goddamn Valium to kick in? It'd been an hour since Angel had ground it up and dissolved it in his mother's nightcap. God I need to think tonight, I need to be alone with myself.

I ain't finished yet, Momma. I think maybe there's a zit coming, I gotta fix it. You know I have to look perfect for tomorrow. When the people from *People* come. You know I—

She's snoring now. Yeah. Easy . . . easy . . . she's snoring, definitely snoring.

It was a better suite than last night. The studio had moved them across town to this hotel. They said it was the hotel Eddie Murphy checked into in *Beverly Hills Cop,* but Angel didn't care if it had been in a movie or not. They hadn't really gone to the movies much, not in Hangman's Holler. Most folks just had their TV tuned to the Damien Peters channel permanent, so all they ever heard was talk of God.

But God it was a lovely hotel. It was pink and it had palm trees that seemed to reach all the way to the moon. It wasn't owned by Americans, though. It belonged to the Sultan of Brunei. Everything in L.A. belonged to some other country, like the movie studios were all owned by Japs and stuff.

The hotel had these individual bungalows and their bungalow had a bathroom that was as big as some of the motel rooms they'd stayed in on their way cross-country. The bathroom opened out into a patio that had a private Jacuzzi. There were two bedrooms and the beds were as wide as baseball fields.

Angel was in the bathroom now. He was folding his clothes. The bathroom was all pink marble. It was still hard for him to believe he'd won. Especially since as soon as they got back to the hotel it was like nothing had changed. His mother hadn't even told him, "You done good," seemed like she'd expected him to win all along, but that was the way she always was. The agent had praised him, but he could see the dollar signs in her eyes, didn't trust her one goddamn moment. Anyways, he wasn't fixing to pop no zits, no sir, his face was still as perfect as perfect could be, the face of an angel, just like Becky told him. It was the only thing he could think of that would get his momma to stop hollering after him though. He had to look perfect.

Angel was scrubbing the last flakes of that makeup off his face. There was nothing he could do about the hair. He wished it was just spray-on dye, like that glitter stuff you put in your hair to go to parties with, but it wasn't going to wash out in a long long while and then they'd just put more of the same stuff on. They'd even done his eyebrows and his eyelashes. They'd of done the rest of him too excepting there wasn't no hair anywhere else on him. But he'd overheard them joking about it.

Was that a snore? No. Maybe. Then . . . *Angel* . . .

She was still awake. He'd have to stay in the bathroom a little bit longer. He brushed the gel from his hair with deliberate, painful strokes. Studied his own face in the mirror for a long time.

This is how they're going to see me.

Timmy Two.

Nothing is green in L.A., not green the way the hills are green beside Hangman's Holler, the green has a sandy look to it, like it's always craving water. The streets run round and round like spaghetti and the buildings have signs in Japanese and there's homeless people hiding in the cracks. I hate L.A. *Brush. Brush.* L.A., home of Timmy Two, the latest teen sensation.

I was perfect!

But I wasn't Angel Todd.

In the mirror: the hair and the eyebrows were wrong,

of course. Timmy's hair was so black it seemed streaked with blue. The black dye accentuated the pallor of Angel's skin and gave it an anemic sheen. But surely it could not have thinned his lips or edged them with a brighter crimson. He scrubbed at them with a sponge. He didn't want even a trace of rouge left. But the lips became more red. And his cheekbones seemed to have moved up a notch.

Angel became afraid. He covered his mouth with one hand and looked into his own eyes. They were not his eyes. There was something in them that could not have come from inside himself. It was a kind of hunger. A desolation. An ancientness.

He stared down at the water as it swirled down the drain of the sink. Braced himself. Looked back up. Pried his hand away from his lips and uncovered a different mouth altogether. He tried to scream but his lips were clamped shut. But the boy in the mirror smiled. And the teeth in the smile were fangs.

He slammed his fists against the mirror but there were no fists in the mirror, only the face of a vanished rock star. Timmy's smile faded and Angel could see that his eyes had never smiled; the smiled had been a false smile, a twisting of the corners of the mouth, and that the singer's true feelings were in his eyes, which held the sadness of savaged innocence. They were a child's eyes but the creature that possessed them was no child, could never be a child.

"Who are you?" Angel said. "Are you what I think you are?"

His terror was beginning to dissipate. Somehow he sensed that Timmy was trapped inside the mirror and could not come into his world.

The boy in the mirror said, "Help me, Angel Todd."

And began to weep tears of blood.

"How can I help you?" Angel said. "You ain't even real, you're a dream or something that I'm seeing in a mirror because I've been thinking about you day in and day out and trying to make myself become you so I could win the contest."

"Angel, I want to get out of here. I want to come back."

"Come back?" said Angel. "Folks say you're already dead. They've seen you on Mars and Venus and in their dreams. I think I'm dreaming now. It's the only way I could be seeing you, because you ain't a thing from this world at all, you're maybe what the preacher's talking about when he tells about being tempted by demons and evil spirits."

"Preachers? Demons? Do you really believe in God, Angel Todd?"

He thought about that for a long time. "I guess not. Not really."

"I'm not an evil spirit, Angel. But I've seen evil. I'm not a demon. But there are people who are trying to make me into a demon. I want you to see something. Take my hand. Reach into the mirror."

This can't be happening, Angel thought. He put one hand out against the glass and he could feel it softening, he could feel someone grab hold of his hand, and Timmy Valentine's hand was more cold than you could ever imagine, colder than a snowball on a winter's day, and the hand was tugging him into the mirror, his arm was elbow-deep now, and Timmy was saying, "Slowly, slowly, don't come all the way in, or I'll never be able to get you out of here. . . ."

His face touched glass now . . . the surface of the mirror was blurry, like gauze, and it hugged his face like elastic . . . then, all at once, he was through . . . half in, half out. He felt a foul-smelling wind on his face, heard the distant wuthering of wind through thick foliage and far caverns. At first he couldn't see at all, not even the hand whose icy grip he did not dare relinquish. But there was a kind of light. Cold light. It's like looking into hell, he thought, not the Damien Peters hellfire brimstone hell but the real thing, a cold hell, feelingless, cut off, without hope. Brambles along the stony earth, twisted trees, the sky churning with dark clouds. The wind on his skin was sharp, sandy. "Why are you here?" Angel said. His own voice echoed and reechoed in the voice of the wind.

They seemed to be moving, but Angel still had one foot firmly anchored in the world beyond this world. With his bare right foot he could feel the slippery texture of the marble floor, while his left was gouged by pebbles and pierced by thorns.

And then it seemed to Angel that they stood at the very heart of this world inside the mirror. At the center was an ash tree that reached far out of sight and whose roots were gnarled and knotty, and in the trunk of the tree was a depression shaped like a young boy with his arms out-stretched, and where the palms of the hands would have been two massive nails had been pounded into the wood, and shreds of flesh still clung to the nails, and the tree itself was bleeding, its sap was blood where the nails had riven the bark and struck living tissue. And Angel looked down at Timmy Valentine's hand, the hand that clutched his hand, and he saw that the palm was pierced.

Timmy Valentine bore the stigmata of Jesus. Fucking Jesus, what would the preacher make of that, the boy who was beautiful as sin and whose songs they claimed were full of Satan's messages and whose television appearances were full of splattering gore effects?

"This is where I live," Timmy said. "Until a few hours ago, I was nailed to that tree. Now I can move a little. I can speak to you. If it makes you feel less crazy you can think that I come to you in your dreams. That doesn't make me any less real."

"You must have done something to be put into a place like this."

"I've done many things, Angel. Terrible things. Dark things. But they were long ago, before I understood what

I was doing. I had turned away from the dark things, because when I lost my innocence I also lost my capacity for evil."

"You ain't making much sense. Evil and innocence don't go together."

"Oh, but they do."

"Are they punishing you?" Angel knew that a place like this could only be hell, no matter that there wasn't any fire and brimstone.

"I was on my way to becoming something new. I was vulnerable, like a chrysalis before it has metamorphosed into a butterfly. And a woman captured me with magic and nailed me to this tree and began to sap me. There is a glamour in me, a power to seduce mortal creatures and make their hearts beat faster, and she needed a potent source of this charismatic power. I don't know how long I would have remained here, bound and isolated . . . but there were other voices too . . . people who had loved my music . . . people who remembered my face. In time light came to this lightless place. But there was no hope, not until you came."

"Me?"

"Tonight there was more power focused on me than ever before. You were the focus, Angel Todd. The world was watching you and saying my name. A name is the most potent of all magics. *You* called me out of the dark places, not the witch woman who enslaved me."

"Me?"

"You were the catalyst, Angel Todd."

"Why me?"

"I don't know, Angel. It's just how it turned out."

And the wind howled.

"I want to be free, Angel. Can you blame me for wanting to taste the flavor of the world again? I want to come out of the looking-glass world, to step through the mirror as you have stepped. But I can't yet."

"I ain't changing places with you," Angel said. The

chill crept from Timmy's hand into his own. He could
feel its numbness steal into his flesh, crawl up his arm,
work its way toward his heart. The leaves of the forest
whispered to him: *angel, angel, angel.* "If you think I'm
going to stay here and let you go out into the world—"

Timmy shook his head. "I would never do that to you.
But you have the power to free me by awakening the
memory of me in men's hearts. Don't you see? That's
why I need you. My name on the lips of millions can
counteract the magic that has enthralled me. And you
can make it happen, I know it."

"But—"

"Don't you want to be immortal? To be a child forever?"

Angel remembered how he'd been thinking, My voice
is going to change and I'll grow hair and I'll lose everything, I'll fail, I'll fuck up my whole life. "I understand
now," he said. "We're kind of like twins."

"Darkness and light."

"I had a real twin brother once. He died when I was
three. They called him Errol." It was after Errol died that
Momma had become different . . . had turned into a
monster kind of.

"You could have a twin again."

God he could feel what was inside Timmy, the rage
and the aloneness. The hell that they stood in was inside
Timmy. The screaming wind was the voice of his despair.
Or was it his own? I'm trapped too, he thought, I'm
trapped in a hotel room waiting for the dope to knock
out my momma so I can be alone with myself for a few
hours and lie tossing and turning and choking on the
smell of her dime-store perfume. God when he looked
into Timmy's eyes he was starting to see himself. God it
scared him and he wanted to twist his hand free of him,
he wanted to run away out of this hell back into his own
hell, Timmy's eyes weren't even human, they glowed in

the dark like the eyes of a jaguar in a jungle, God God God and—

"If you were like me," Timmy said, "you'd be able to change shape. You could take the form of a wild beast. Any wild beast, even—"

Ain't you ever seen no no! his face was contorting itself into the shape of *nigger's pussy before white boy?* Becky the black girl who'd led him by the hand into the secret cavern in the hillside near Hangman's Holler and *I know you wants to put it there* and the voice was *her* voice, taunting and seductive, and *you beautiful like a angel Angel.* And then the girl's face dissolved into thin air and there was Timmy with a big grin on his face as if to say you ain't got no secrets from me, mountain boy, I can see just as far into your soul as you can see into mine.

Angel was full of stark blind terror and he couldn't hold on anymore and he near tore his hand off when he yanked it free and stepped backward through the mirror, just two short steps, back to the pink marble floor that was so cool to his bare feet, back to the suite in the fine hotel that belonged to that Sultan dude. He threw a towel over the mirror and went back to the bedroom.

She was snoring loudly and rhythmically. Usually when she snored like this she was too plain wore out to reach over in the darkness and play with him. Angel thought he could risk stepping out into the bedroom.

There was another mirror over the dresser, with a fancy gold frame, all curlicues. It was in shadow. His mother lay on the bed, a mound under the bedclothes. The cheap scent filled the room.

Angel was too jumpy to go to bed. Maybe I should check out that private Jacuzzi, he thought. I could take a few pills but I'm sick of pills.

He slipped out the French doors into the private patio. He turned on the timer, shucked his clothes and slid into the water. God it felt good. He let one of the nozzles gush against his tailbone. God how relaxing. He closed his eyes. It must have been some kind of bad dream. I've been taking too many pills lately. I'm going to stop. Pills will kill you, and if I get rich how am I going to enjoy it if I'm dead? But Momma will enjoy it. Momma's like the witch woman who has Timmy nailed to a tree in the dream. Maybe that's what the dream's really about, maybe it's a warning that I gotta get out before it's too late, before I get myself swallowed up.

God what a dream though! The wind that whined like a child being tortured. The sharp stones rasping against the sole of his foot. The darkness.

He let the warmth of the water soak into him, breathed in the steam, waited for it to dissolve away all the horror. He tried to think only of music. Music could take away the pain. He wanted to remember the kind of songs he used to sing before he'd been forced to saturate his brain with Timmy Valentine. Songs that smelled of the mountain air. He tried to remember a folk song his mother'd used to sing to him, in the good times before she turned strange, after his twin brother died.

'Tis the gift to be simple.

He could hear her voice now, and him huddled in her arms with his head lolling on the firm breast that strained against the bloodstained cotton shift—

'Tis the gift to be free.

and her arm tied around him and the smell of her sweat mingling with the fragrance of the summer grass and the wind kicking up the moist earth, and there was blood on her fingers and Errol was quite, quite still, resting on a tree stump, not even breathing, and then she stopped singing and her eyes darted from side to side and she said, "Let's bury him now, you and me together," and he'd stood leaning against the porch post watching her digging with the tears streaming down her face. That's the only memory he had of Errol, him lying on the tree stump, him rolling into the hole Momma dug. It was like the place where all the memories were had been ripped

out of his mind and there was this yawning nothing there
and that was why he filled it with music and why he could
never take the pain out of his music even when the song
was supposed to be happy.

I don't know why I'm seeing all this again. I never
think about Errol. I never talk about him. Momma never
mentions his name. We have photographs where we're
together, the three of us, outside the shack, but his face
has been cut out of all of them, I don't even know if we
were what they call identical twins, maybe we didn't look
anything alike.

He tried to push away the memory. Forget, forget. The
water churned and frothed around him and he fell into
almost a trance because he could hear that old Appalachian song in his head. God that water felt good. He'd
felt so dirty somehow, dirty inside.

Then, abruptly, it stopped. You had to reset the timer
every twenty minutes or something. He opened his eyes.
The water was blue-green and softly lit. The bubbles were
settling. The surface became mirror-still. That was when
he saw Timmy again. Timmy's face, his own face. The
hand reaching out to clutch his own. The smile. Come
down, come drown in the watery depths. . . .

'Tis the gift to be free. . . .

"Leave me alone!" Angel whispered.

"Oh, I can't do that. I will always be with you now.
Can you not learn to love me, Angel Todd?"

"You ain't . . . you ain't Errol? Come back from the
dead, wanting us to change places so you can get a taste
of what it's like to be alive?"

Timmy shook his head slowly. "People always think
that I am someone else," he said. "Don't do that to me.
I can't be your brother, but perhaps you can learn to love
me, in your own fashion, somehow."

"Get the fuck out of my life! You're a dead thing, a
thing the witch woman made! You can't give me anything!"

But as he slammed his fist against the timer to set it off, as the foam began to agitate and the bubbles began swirling, driving the phantom ever further into oblivion, he heard the boy say, above the gurgling of the water, *I can give you eternity.*

Angel scrambled out of the Jacuzzi and got into bed, naked and shivering, beside his mother. He put his arms around her and let the rhythm of her snoring rock him into an uneasy sleep.

NIGHT CREATURES

Universal City, Studio City, Sherman Oaks, North Hollywood, Van Nuys, Reseda, Woodland Hills, West Hills, Mission Hills, Granada Hills, hills, hills, hills, hills, fucking fucking hills.

"I'm hungry."

Fucking hills, hills, hills.

"I'm—*hungry!*"

What are you gonna do, drink my blood now? PJ thought. He was sweating. He was lost again. Always got lost whenever he came to the fucking Valley. He thought he was somewhere in the Hollywood hills now but he could have gotten all the way turned around for all he knew.

"Hungry!"

"Can't it wait?" Terry Gish sat beside him in the front seat of the van. Even though he had killed a lot of vampires, even though the best friend of his childhood was now a vampire, he didn't really understand their feeding habits. Why sometimes it seemed they could go without, why sometimes it seemed they'd about blow up if they couldn't get blood that minute.

Looked like Terry was that way now. He was trembling all over and he was even more pale than before. Even the red from his hair seemed to be draining away.

"You just ate," PJ told him, wondering to himself how much he sounded like Naomi, Terry's mother, dead now, like everyone else from the town of Junction, Idaho.

"I'm new to this," Terry said. "I don't know anybody else. I'm . . . I'm . . . I got like this *hole* inside me and I gotta fill it up with blood and it don't matter how much I pour down I just feel more and more empty, it's like pouring it down the toilet and flushing with the other hand . . . I feel so damn alone and like I'm the only one around and I need someone . . . I need more vampires . . . God you don't what it's like holding back from sinking my teeth into your thin brown neck, I can see one blue vein throbbing in your wrist when you grip that steering wheel and it makes me crazy PJ, crazy crazy."

PJ stopped the van. "All right. Get out and feed."

Terry looked at him. PJ saw fear fleck his eyes. Terry said, "Oh Jesus, can a vampire have bulimia?" And there wasn't even a hint of humor in what he said.

"I'll see you at the apartment," PJ said.

"By dawn."

"Yeah."

"Oh, PJ, stop by the cathedral and pick up some more of that holy water and get out your crosses . . . oh, I'm so . . . suddenly I'm . . . I thought I could trust myself with you but suddenly I feel . . ."

He was gone. He hadn't opened the door. He had just siphoned out through a crack in the window. Vampires could do things like that, turn into vapors and just float away. But they had to figure out how it was done. PJ didn't think Terry really knew how; he'd just done it by accident, out of anxiety. It was just like Terry to be Mr. Macho one minute and suddenly go all woozy with wimpiness the next.

"I'll see you at the apartment," PJ repeated to the empty passenger seat.

MEMORY: 1598

The death angel rears up from the shaft of radiance, his arm upraised, one finger pointing up to the sky. He is impassioned; there is a lasciviousness about his smile; the paintbrush has imbued his boyish musculature with a silky, sensuous sheen, as though it were kissed by moonlight. A line leftward from the crook of the painting touches the upraised weapon that will strike the doomed evangelist. A woman pleads, her arms reaching out toward the angels' knees; and old men look on, lugubrious and morose. To the far left, surfacing in abrupt chiaroscuro, is the face of a somber woman, her hand against her chin. Her emotions are unfathomable. Perhaps she is awed at the mystery of martyrdom; perhaps she is a little aroused at the sight of blood; perhaps, perhaps . . . it is the angel she sees. Perhaps it is he who stirs, within her, longings dark and profane. For the street-urchin curl of his lip, the insolent forwardness of his demeanor, the tantalizing *vade mecum* of his gaze, surely these do not spring from the divine in him, but from the earthly; perhaps the woman is perplexed that the eunuch of heaven is imbued with such sensuality.

The boy vampire hears the pause in the nervous rhythm of brushstrokes. Caravaggio has put down his brush and steps back to admire his handiwork. The room is full of dancing, flickering light; there are candles and oil lamps everywhere. Ercolino steps away from the wings, which have been attached to a free-standing metal frame against which he has been leaning, holding the same languorous gesture for about an hour.

A heavy arras has been drawn over the chamber's bay windows, blocking the moonlight. The air in the room is stifling. The dust that dances in the dense and sodden air is peppered with powdered pigments. It is oppressive, but Caravaggio is oblivious of everything except the painting and the boy vampire.

"It is close to completion," the painter says, and drains the third wine bottle of the evening. The wine is sour and its vinegary odor pervasive. "Come, Ercolino, look at how I've immortalized you."

"But I already am immortal."

"My love, my death," Ser Caravaggio says. He always says this. Over and over he says it. "Yes, you are immortal, you beautiful child; you are immortality made flesh. Oh, it is a sin for you to be so beautiful; how can I dare to imprison such beauty in a cage of canvas, pigment, linseed oil?"

The boy laughs. "I am not imprisoned," he says.

He stands there, his expression a perfect vacuousness. He knows what the painter sees: a creature maddeningly erotic yet strangely inviolable. He sees the painter's gaze move downward from his unblinking eyes to his unsmiling lips, the undefined musculature, the inhuman pallor of his skin, the flat and hairless pubis, the white scars of castration, the penis that cannot stiffen. Caravaggio's eyes are glazed from drunkenness and sleepless nights. The blood will be sour tonight from the alcohol, and sweet from the burning up of body fat; Ercolino smells the blood, and knows its composition intimately, as a wine-taster knows his vineyards and his vintages.

"Oh, Ercolino, I long to possess your body and yet . . . why do I find myself unable even to try? . . . Cardinal del Monte sends over the pick of the choirboys all the time; he hired me, you know, because I . . . understand his tastes . . . I've had every homeless urchin in the street for the price of an evening meal . . . you, you, you . . . who come here willingly . . . not in fear of the cardinal's wrath, not driven by greed or hunger . . . you I dare not have. Why do I fear you so much, my angel of death?"

"I have told you, Ser Caravaggio, I'm not an angel and I'm not death."

The painter's blood is racing. Yes, he can hear its music, joyous, like the rustling of mighty wings. The hunger wakened in him is akin to passion. I must feed, he thinks. I have stood here, motionless, playing at being his dark angel, creature of his fantasies. I have told him time and again that I am not what he wants me to be. It is always this way. Always I fulfil the dream wishes of men, sometimes even their death wishes; I can never be perceived as anything else. Perhaps I do not even have an independent existence apart from these mortal passions, the self-destructive yearnings, that men project on to me.

Oh, that music! It is the blood, responding to the hunger; that rhapsodic and chromatic surge of life's essence, driven by the rhythm of heart; oh, I am hunger, thinks the boy vampire, hunger is all I am. Oh, I must feed, I must feed.

Caravaggio says, "I am ready. Take me, dark angel of my passion. Is that not why you've come to me . . . to carry me to hell in some ecstatic transport of forbidden lust? You have already drunk my blood . . . now drink my soul!"

"I don't want your soul. I only want the blood itself."

"I demand that you take my soul!" the painter screams. He turns to void his bladder into a chamber pot. "My soul!" he cries again.

And he flings himself upon the boy, whose flesh is colder than marble. The boy reflects: To him, life and art are one; both are chiaroscuro, fragments of brilliance set against vast canvases of shadow. They are at cross-purposes, and yet each feeds on the other.

Ser Caravaggio tears away at his own clothing, hugs the cool flesh with an ardor that cannot be quenched; he strokes and caresses, trying to waken a response that cannot come; he is on his knees before his dark angel, who is no spirit at all but the very opposite of the spiritual, carrion imbued with the illusion of life, carrion that thirsts so much for the life force that it drinks and drinks again and yet is never sated; oh, oh, I am carrion, Ercolino thinks, and bends down to sink his canines into

the painter's shoulder, making him cry out with pain that
is also lust. Ser Caravaggio sweats and moans but there
is that about me which prevents him from becoming
hard. What does it matter? Why should it concern me,
the illusion that this poor mortal has fashioned for himself? Is he not prey? Is he not just a warm teat from which
to suck the life force? Oh, but the boy vampire is troubled
where he was never troubled before. The encounter with
Bluebeard has changed him utterly. Not long ago, he
remembers, in England, I watched Kit Marlowe bleed to
death in a Deptford tavern, and I did not even feel the
hunger, not in the same way as before . . . the hunger was
tinged with bitterness.

But here comes blood. Blood. Oh, oh, the blood . . . oh,
it is warm, warm, warm . . . oh, it is a drug that feeds its
own addiction. Oh, yes, the bitterness that he has begun
to feel is there too, but perhaps he is more used to it now.
He tongues that gushing warmth. It tingles. It shoots into
him and leaves him wanting more. . . . I could kill him,
he thinks to himself. I could suck all of it out and still not
be fulfilled. But I would kill his genius.

Caravaggio weeps. "I love you," he whispers.

What kind of love can this be? the vampire thinks. It
is a pavane in which each partner dances alone. He sinks
his teeth deeper into the painter's neck. His canines rend
flesh now. The blood comes spurting. I must not take too
much . . . I must conserve . . . gently . . . gently . . . the
painter's body shudders with a terror that is like ecstasy.

They hear a tearing sound. It is the arras. It is ripped
down, and two figures stand framed in the open window,
one bulky and big-howled, the other a slim and cowering.

"Shame, shame, shame, shame," says the voice of Cardinal del Monte.

"I told you, Your Eminence," says the voice of Guglielmo, "that the two of them were up to some vile
perversion."

The boy looks up. His lips are blotched with crimson.

"Satanic blood rituals," says the cardinal. "I tend to turn a blind eye at the vices of the flesh—ah, for is not flesh weak?—but heresy is another matter, isn't it, Guglielmo?" Guglielmo nods. "He has been a good spy, and well deserving of the extra scudi I have lavished on him." And the cardinal tosses him a purse, which the chorister pockets, never taking his eyes off Ercolino.

Who slowly licks from his lips the last traces of blood.

The cardinal and Guglielmo step forward. Del Monte, robed in crimson, each finger ringed with a different jewel, is shaking with hypocritical indignation; the eunuch Guglielmo looks at Ercole Serafini with trepidation and desire. Caravaggio sobs.

"You have drunk each other's blood, in savage mockery of the holy sacrament of the eucharist," the cardinal continues. "I witnessed it, and so did this boy. You're at my mercy."

Defiantly, Ercolino says, "He did not drink my blood, Your Eminence; I was the only one who drank. And not to mock the Scriptures, but to fulfill a terrible need which is the curse of all my kind."

"And what *kind* might that be, boy?" says the cardinal.

Guglielmo crosses himself and looks away at last. "He promised me immortality if I would follow his dark ways . . . if I would sell my soul," he says. "He is a demon." The lie does not come easily; it is wrenched from him; Ercolino feels a certain compassion for him in his confusion.

"He is an angel," Caravaggio says. "He has come to foreshadow my death."

"Vanity, vanity, all is vanity," says the cardinal. He comes forward. His blood smells of cloves and garlic.

The cardinal glares at the painting. Caravaggio steps back. Somehow he seems lost.

Ercolino sees himself. Am I really this beautiful? he asks himself. He has never seen himself since his transformation, of course, since his world contains no mirrors.

He cannot even see himself reflected in Caravaggio's eyes. The cardinal pulls a little hand mirror from his capacious vestments and holds it up to Ercolino's face. He sees nothing, of course. He throws the mirror on the ground and the glass shatters. Then, turning to the table, covered with candles and with mixed pigments, he seizes the largest of the brushes, dips it in carmine, and proceeds to desecrate the figure of angel of death.

Caravaggio watches, stony-faced. An artist is little more than a liveried servant. He does not look away as the cardinal covers the angel's features with smears of red, as he daubs the crimson over the slender body. He takes particular pleasure in bloodying its genitalia. He laughs. He is as drunk as Caravaggio. He is as drunk with power as he is with wine. He laughs and laughs until Ercolino is afraid he will collapse in a stupor. But before he can do that, Guglielmo comes, supports him as he staggers back to the window; there is a basket and a pulley there. It must have been constructed just so the cardinal could spy on Caravaggio and play his little joke on him.

Just before he disappears, Cardinal del Monte says to Ercolino, "Go back to the gutter, *ragazzo;* we don't want any devil children in the house of God."

Gugliemo does not look into his eyes; Ercolino knows that he fears his silent reproach. If he were only to look, he thinks, he will see that I do not reproach him. They all grasp at me; when they not hold on to me, when they find me insubstantial as the air, they become angry; they turn their anger on me; even the cardinal.

The night air, muggy and oppressive, blows into the chamber. The candle flames waver and flare up.

"It is just as well," says Ercole Serafini to the painter. "I am not what you think me. Paint me out of the picture. Forget me. Let me step back into the *oscuro,* out of the beam of light."

Caravaggio seems stone sober now. He seems to be

looking at the boy vampire in a completely different light. "You're right," he says. "You are no angel. You're just another one of those children of the streets, kinkier than the others, perhaps; you tricked me. I tricked myself. Go back to the gutter, boy."

"Addio, mio signore," says the boy vampire softly. Then he funnels into shadow and drifts down into the street below.

ILLUSION AND REALITY

It was three in the morning in Los Angeles, but in Hangman's Holler, Kentucky, it was already sunrise. Damien Peters had been awakened early by that mysterious phone call from the witch woman. The talk of the Gods of Chaos disturbed him. Perhaps she had finally gone completely insane. But of course, there was nothing wrong with that, he reflected. The prophet Isaiah was probably certifiable; indeed, even Our Lord himself, were he to be judged by the standards of modern psychiatry, might be in an asylum today, a victim of the ever-popular Christ complex.

Blasphemy! he told himself, and chuckled. That Simone Arleta woman might well be mad, might well be a creature of Satan; but she had power. Power was the single most important thing in the universe. Even God understood that.

A quick cup of black coffee, then into one of those tailored, spangled suits and down the velour-lined subterranean corridors that linked every building in the Peters domain.

He betrayed no sign of tiredness or irritation as he walked into the cathedral set of his television station to begin taping the first of the day's inspirational messages, which were repeated during each commercial break. He took his accustomed place on the set, behind a gilded lectern. The stage itself was bare, the backdrop a blue screen; by the magic of chroma key, he would be seen, on television, to be standing against a simulation of one of the great cathedrals of the world. At a flick of a switch, the setting could be transformed into the Blue Ridge Mountains or some other natural wonder, God's own cathedrals.

The taping was completely automated. Three robot cameras tracked his every movement; a complex, MIDI-driven computer program linked close-ups, medium shots, pans and zooms with surges and harmonic frissons in the accompanying music, a strange cross between synth New Age and country and western. The staff would not even be in until nine o'clock.

Damien loved these tapings best of all the duties of his ministry. There was no one to watch, to criticize. Even when he preached to those huge live audiences, sheep, every last one of them, even when he stirred them up to a very storm of *amens* and *hallelujahs,* he knew that there'd be one or two among them he wasn't reaching. Doubters. People cursing him in their hearts. People who only came because they'd read about the scandal in the newspaper, or seen the ridiculous "confession" of that cheap, painted harlot that the television people had sicced on him just so they could bring down the ministry, so they could gloat over him in their jealousy and pride.

The robot cameras never doubted.

They moved with eerie precision. There was a music to it.

Damien Peters smiled confidently at the cameras and opened the good book at random. It was not, of course, really the Book; it was a prop, and he didn't open it at random, but to the only page that contained any writing at all, and that writing just random Olde English lettering that looked impressive from a distance.

"My faithful flock," he began, "my friends, my gentle, loyal, generous, reverent congregation . . . today I'm

...lking to you about one of the most im-
...ul God's commandments. It's important be-
...ny people just think it's so blame obvious that
...on't even realize it when they break it. They think
it just goes without saying that 'thou shalt have no other
gods before me.' But today I want you to search your
hearts and I want you to try to answer this question:
What does Our Lord mean when he talks about 'other
gods'? Is he a-talking about Baal, or Zeus, or Allah? Is he
a-talking about the kind of gods where you go out and
you butcher a lamb or a bull or even your firstborn
child—the gods of heathens and idolaters? Or is there
another kind of god we should be mindful of, a god
closer to home, a god that's as close as . . . a credit card?
A Dungeons and Dragons monster manual?—a teenage
rock idol?"

Damien Peters smiled as he lifted his arms outward in
his famous "crucified" posture that the newspaper car-
toonists had had so much fun with in recent months. He
looked up at the monitor and saw the projected backdrop today, a sweeping vista of the Grand Canyon. As he
brought his palms back together in the folded position
common to many paintings of the martyrs, the background dissolved into a montage: Elvis thrusting ob-
scenely, Michael Jackson humping the air; each image
chosen for maximum sexual suggestiveness, for Peters
knew that one must appeal to the prurient interest in
order to interest the audience long enough to turn them
toward Jesus.

Finally there was Timmy Valentine.

"Now take a good look at this critter, my brothers and
sisters. Not quite male and not quite female. Not quite a
boy and yet not quite a man. Look at the way he seduces
with his eyes. Look at the way he dresses . . . he has
borrowed the form of the prince o' darkness himself.
Have you listened to the words of his songs? Do they not
incite our children to devil worship and even suicide, a

sin which is punishable by eternity in the everlastin' fire? Is this boy not dead, and yet has arisen more powerful than before, in a filthy parody of the birth and resurrection of Our Savior? I say unto you, my faithful congregation, do not follow false gods. . . ."

He shook his head sadly. The camera seemed to close in, for a moment, on the image of Satan's child. Casually, Damien Peters drifted into the plea for operating funds which was the other requirement of each five-minute sermonette.

It was a perfect solution, he thought, to the problems Simone Arleta had been having squeezing the last drops of charismatic energy from the spirit she had imprisoned. While seeming to condemn the vanished rock star, he was increasing his influence over the consciousness of his audience, thus increasing the power that Simone had to draw on.

Besides, images of Timmy Valentine always brought in big checks. His market research had proved that conclusively. If not the son of Satan, this boy was surely the very incarnation of Mammon.

And later, around lunchtime, he put in a call to the Arleta woman again. He was more collected now, more ready to deal with her ravings. He was eating, in the twelve-person dining room of the estate, alone with a maid and a cordless phone.

"And who," he asked her, "are the Gods of Chaos?"

Simone said, "Take your Learjet and come in tonight, and I'll tell you."

"I can't leave today! Don't you realize what today is? Today is the big blockbuster heal-a-thon that will bring millions into my coffers. I can't just drop it and run over to the Mojave Desert, not even for you, Simone."

"Millions, indeed. You certainly live in a world of illusions, Damien. You should know by now that your ratings will probably never recover from that sex scandal."

"Bullshit, ma'am! Pardon my French."

"You and your schedule! I believe the Almighty Himself would have to talk to your social secretary before you'd condescend to give him an audience."

"Well, but you know that ain't true, Simone. I take my duties as pastor of the Cosmic Love Church very, very seriously. Oh, sure, I falter, I covet, I make compromises with . . . dark forces . . . but I'm just a human being, honey, just a poor miserable sinner like anybody else."

"And the prince of darkness . . . does *he* have to make an appointment to see you, my dear Damien?"

"I do not have intercourse with devils."

"Intercourse is the least of it, Damien darling. Perhaps I should let it be known to the right magazines the true nature of the woman with whom you were caught in a compromising position. She was an incubus, wasn't she? Or are the female ones called succubi? I always get them muddled up."

Damn that woman. Damn her and damn her enigmatic airs. But Damien Peters, who once held a congregation of millions in his thrall, was losing more and more of his audience every day. And the witch woman held him in thrall, and would not release him.

"And what is the position of the Cosmic Love Church on vampirism, by the way?" Simone added. "Garlic and crosses? Surely not holy water, since you reject that as being a product of the Whore of Rome."

Damn that woman!

Oh, what does it matter damning her to hell? he thought. She's already damned a million times over.

And so am I, he thought, as he idly spread a generous spoonful of beluga caviar over a toast point and rehearsed tonight's big sermon and heal-a-thon in his head.

7

AND THE EVENING AND THE
MORNING WERE THE FIRST DAY

♣ ♣

VISION SEEKERS

Muriel Hykes-Bailey.
Prince Prathna.
Sir Francis Locke.
Owlswick.
Terrence.
Strathon.
Stephen Miles.

"The names don't mean anything to me," Petra said. "Except . . . Miles, Miles . . . wasn't he some kind of concert pianist?"

"Conductor," Brian said. "It doesn't matter anyway. They're all dead now. They weren't hunting vampires for the good of humanity. They were hunting them for kicks."

They had been at the Café Ayudhya for over an hour now. They were the only customers. The waitresses were clustered around a private table, playing cards. A television, on the counter, showed images of the Timmy Val-

entine look-alike contest—it looked like CNN or some
other news channel, rerunning the tape on the entertainment news. Timmy was everywhere. The media had
found a new obsession.

Lady Chit had been doing the ordering, and they
ended up with a far more exotic repast than Brian would
usually have ordered. There was a fiery salad with bizarre
shellfish, an even more fiery curry with lumps of squishy
meat and turnips, and a weird, still more fiery crab soup
flavored with lemongrass. Brian didn't much care for it;
at this place he always tended to order the one or two
dishes whose names he could pronounce. He only picked
at the dishes, but Petra and Premchitra ate with gusto.
Perhaps, he reflected, it was because the things he had to
tell them were so outlandish, so disturbing, that they had
to be drowned in the gut-wrenching spices of Thai food.

The pieces were coming together. Lady Chit confirmed
much of what Brian said and filled in many of the pieces.
Brian could tell that Petra didn't want to believe, didn't
dare believe; but how else could such an unlikely story be
corroborated by two people who had hitherto been total
strangers to one another? There was something else he
could see in Petra's eyes, too. Curiosity. The need to
know. The killer instinct of the journalist.

"My grandfather," Chit said, "I don't think he *is* quite
dead. When I went to see that spiritualist—"

"Simone Arleta," Petra explained to Brian.

"She made me see a vision . . . my grandfather . . .
crawling around in the snow . . . transformed into a *phii
krasue!*" Lady Chit laughed nervously when she said the
word, but Brian could tell that she was more upset than
she wanted to appear. "It's a mythological monster," she
explained. "A decapitated head creeping around with its
guts trailing behind, using its tongue as a sort of pseudopod. You know, we learned about them in anthropology
at Mills College; otherwise I wouldn't even have heard of

them, even though I was born in Thailand. I guess I just don't know much about my native country."

He could tell she was talking too much, trying to cover up her terror.

"It's all right," Brian said softly. "We're all afraid." He added, "I've been through all this once before. I know it all goes against everything you've ever believed in . . . but it's all true. I've seen dead people get up and drink the blood of people they once loved. I think that sometimes the world of myths and illusions can spill out into our world. That's what brought Timmy Valentine to us. He went away once but now he wants to come back. I know. A vampire told me. That's right. I saw a vampire last night. I talked to a vampire. A vampire who used to be just a kid, until Timmy Valentine moved into Junction. The kid played video games and rode his bike in that small town in Idaho. He and I, together, we helped burn down the town. I watched him stake his own twin brother in the heart. He harrowed hell, that kid. And then he became one of them. Last night his best friend drove a stake through his heart, and today we gave him an Indian burial up in the mountains."

I'm sounding frantic, hysterical, he told himself. No one will believe me, no one. Lady Chit was staring into her Thai iced tea. Petra wouldn't meet his eyes. They think I've gone insane, he thought.

"I believe," Petra said at last.

"I'm afraid," said Chit. "How will he come back? What will he do?"

"I don't know," Brian said. "But I do know one thing. Timmy Valentine himself is not evil . . . not as such. Good and evil don't even apply to him, they're not part of his universe. But he leaves a trail of evil in his path. He can't help himself. In a way, he's a complete innocent."

A burst of chattering from the waitresses. They were all pointing at the television. Brian, Petra and Premchitra looked up at the same time. There was a murky videotape. At first, all it seemed to show was a shopping cart outside an all-night market somewhere in Pacoima. The camera was hand-held and it was zooming jerkily toward the cart—the video of an amateur newshound.

Suddenly it became a lot brighter. Someone was shining a flashlight on what was inside the cart. At first it seemed to be a pile of clothes, but as the camera focused it became clear that it was the remains of a bag lady. This was a *Texas Chainsaw Massacre* sort of a corpse: an arm here, a leg here, and the head resting atop the whole pile, crowned with a wreath of intestines. One eye was missing and the other dangled. There was no gore. The body parts were pale. The blood had all been drained.

One of the waitresses turned up the sound just in time to hear ". . . uncanny similarities to yesterday's murder of a homeless girl, Janey Rodriguez . . . torn apart with his bare hands . . . barely a trace of blood to be found . . ."

Cut to a forensic expert who started to give a dry and droning "personality profile" of the serial killer. . . .

"It's no serial killer," Brian said. "It's Terry Gish. We must not have killed him. We must not have . . . oh, Jesus, Jesus." He was losing control of himself. The fire in Junction . . . fucking Jesus it was still blazing in his memory, it was never going to be put out . . . he remembered the look on Terry's face when he'd staked his brother . . . could it be that PJ hadn't had the heart to drive it into Terry's heart? They'd been best friends, PJ Gallagher and the Gish twins. Best friends.

"Can he be stopped?" Petra said.

"How? He's not even human." But Brian knew where Terry would be after dawn. And this time *he'd* have to do it himself. Just as he'd staked his niece Lisa.

The television news story segued to footage of yesterday's killing, the girl by the dumpster by the pizza place. It was sordid, too sordid.

Lady Chit said, "I suppose I ought to go back. I'm staying at my parents' condo in West Hollywood . . . they never use it . . . I'm planning to drive back up to Mills College in the morning . . . even though it's almost morning already. I'm kind of, well, reluctant to stay there alone though . . . I guess . . . I guess I'm, I'm scared shitless. Shitless! I still have to call my parents in Thailand to tell them about what I saw at Simone's; they're going to insist on a formal exorcism, they're kind of old-fashioned that way. Am I talking too much?"

"We all are," Brian said. The sound of our voices is the only thing that keeps us in one piece, he thought. "Why don't we all go back to my place for coffee or something? It's the closest; it's just over the hill."

"Yeah," Petra said. "We can wait for morning."

"Things won't look so frightening in the morning," Chit said dubiously.

"No," said Brian. He was thinking of how, only an hour before, he had been anticipating spending the rest of the night having sex with Petra—for old times' sake as much as anything. Then the Thai girl had shown up and . . . God, she was beautiful, he thought. And she had such poise. Even now, afraid as she was, there wasn't a strand of hair out of place. She was a woman used to being looked at. He wondered whether there was a subtle flirtation in Lady Chit's unwillingness to spend the night alone.

The nearness of the two women, the known and the unknown, was arousing but disturbing too, because of the images of death and dismemberment on the television screen.

"My house is a pigsty," he began.

"Oh, I'll pick up for you," Lady Chit said. "I know how to do all that stuff. Even though we always had servants at home, of course." She was eager, very eager. Brian saw how vulnerable she was, and his heart went out to her. And when he glanced at Petra he saw that her eyes held no jealousy. There was a bond between those two, maybe because they'd both been through one of Simone Arleta's notorious séances.

LOST BOYS

Four in the fucking morning, Matt Lewis thought. Freedom! Lock up the kitchen, toss the leftover pizzas in the trash, drive home and crawl into fucking bed.

He folded up his apron with the stupid *Mandarin Thai All-Night Pizza* logo, peeled off his uniform shirt to reveal a Danzig T-shirt underneath. Then he carefully removed his pizza parlor cap, squeezed some gel into his hair from a tube, and stuck it all back up into its proper shape in a sort of pseudo-mohawk. It was stupid to do his hair only an hour before going to bed but shit, at least it made him feel human again.

Sunday 4 A.M. was the only time the Mandarin Thai ever closed down, and then it was only for like six hours; they were open for business by ten on Monday. There was a lot of sweeping up to do, a week's worth of shit to dispose of, but Matt didn't care. He loved being there and he loved the graveyard shift.

Thank God for having a night job in Hollywood. He never had to be home to listen to his parents complaining about his hair, his clothes, his music. They were always asleep when he got home, and when he woke up they were always gone. And they trusted him here, trusted him alone with the till, trusted him to lock the fucking place up. His parents didn't even trust him to take the garbage out by himself. They'd stand over him and watch him. Jesus, he had to move out of there. That'd mean holding down two jobs as well as working on his high school equivalency test, but at least he wouldn't have to hear the phrase "lazy bum" again.

Matt snapped off the lights, gathered up all the uncollected pizzas—there were fewer than usual, which meant that there were fewer street people out tonight—did the last-minute check of the outlets, the till, the phones. Then he started to let himself out the back. He'd toss the pizzas on his way to the car, which was parked two blocks away.

He made extra sure of the deadbolt. That weird sex murder had happened in the alley last night and his boss had been kind of jumpy. God knows why. People get fucking wasted every day around here, he thought. I mean, there was that one tonight, that bag lady over in the Valley. Jesus! Looked like she'd been through a paper shredder.

He stepped outside and slammed the back door shut.

The alley was empty. From the dumpster there came the ripe smell of rotting pizza. Strange. Usually they didn't stay there long enough to rot. There wasn't a single bag lady to be seen. Not even that drunk dude, the girl's father, who was usually crashed out behind the dumpster.

There wasn't a sound. It was totally fucking dark except for this one shaft of light from the back of McDonald's that made a yellow circle over against a far wall where you could see that some dude had tagged "Sun Valley Locos Rule" in crimson spray paint. This was miles away from their turf. They must be getting powerful, he thought. This part of town's a danger zone all right. If only the parents really knew, shit, they'd be fucking shitting themselves about their precious little Mattie getting his ass carved up.

No homeless at all. Weird. Usually they hovered nearby around pizza-dumping time. Like scavenger rats. Like vampires.

Fuck the homeless, Matt thought.

He felt nervous for some reason. Maybe it was just seeing that Janey Rodriguez bitch on television, all drained of blood. Man, whoever killed her had to be a fucking pervert. The thought of it made him shiver. If only there was some kind of sound, like the snoring of drunks or the distant throb of a ghettoblaster! But no. Silence. Dead silence.

Softly he whispered, "Come and get your pizza now, all you street dudes. Come on, come and get it. Just smell that pepperoni and anchovy. Mm-mm-mm-mm. Come and get it."

Silence.

Matt shrugged and lifted up the lid of the dumpster.

That was when he heard someone crying. At first he didn't even think it was a human kind of sound, more like the sound the wind makes up around Mulholland or in one of the canyons. Where was it coming from? Seemed like it was like totally inside the dumpster. Fuck. There was someone in there. Trying to protect themselves from the night chill, maybe, cushioning themselves against the air with garbage. This world sure is a fucked-up place, he thought.

A kid. A fucking kid. Sobbing its guts out. He wished he had a flashlight because it was totally dark inside the dumpster. But a grownup couldn't be squatting in there. It sounded like a young girl.

"Hey," he said softly. "It's okay. Don't be scared. Want some pizza?"

"*¡Mierditas!* Leave me alone." A girl all right. A Mexican accent. Not East L.A. though; Valley probably.

"Hey, take it easy."

"Go fuck yourself."

"Fuck," said Matt, "I know how it is. Come on. I'm not gonna do anything to you. I'm not gonna rape you or nothing."

He didn't want to feel around inside the garbage, but as he stretched his hand out something grasped his wrist. Something cold and clammy. He pulled back but the hand wouldn't let go. He yanked and the girl stood up, still clinging to him.

In the light of the distant McDonald's her skin was white as paper. It looked like she didn't have any blood at all. She had dark hair and her eyes didn't focus. They were almost like a blind person's staring into some dark inner mystery.

"Are you sick or something? You shouldn't be out on

the street." Probably a fucking preteen prostitute. Where was her pimp? Maybe he shouldn't be seen helping her out. You never knew if they'd thank you or waste you. He looked around. "Did you run away or something?"

"Kind of." She was attractive in an anemic kind of way. He'd never seen a spic that looked so pale. She was wearing a stained T-shirt. She was probably one of the pizza vampires that hung out every night. She looked familiar. Maybe he'd seen her haunting the back door on some other night.

"I have some pizza. But you're probably pretty sick of nouvelle cuisine pizza by now . . . hey, here's a good one . . . shrimp, avocado, white clam sauce . . . cool, huh."

"Jeeze, I sure could use a good meal," she said softly. "You smell so . . . so warm."

You smell warm? What did that mean? God her hand was cold, and she still wouldn't let go. She must really be sick. Maybe she was OD'ing on coke. But she wasn't shivering or sweating. She was just cold. Cold as death.

"Come on out of there," he said, gingerly putting down the pizzas on the concrete and then pulling her out of the dumpster. She didn't seem to weigh anything at all. "Now, what the fuck are you doing here anyway? I can drive you somewhere if you want."

"I can drive you somewhere too."

"Is that some kind of a come-on?" Maybe she was a whore after all. Well, I don't want to get no AIDS, he thought. And besides, she's so fucking young. Like fourteen or something. Junior high, Jesus. Course, he'd never made it out of ninth grade himself.

"I can make it good for you." She smiled. Suddenly she seemed a thousand years old. "Feel me."

There were just the two of them. The McDonald's light flickered. She took his hand in both of hers. Cold, so cold. Girl just came up to about his lips, even though he was only maybe two, three years older than her.

She pushed his hand up her T-shirt toward where her

breasts would have been if she'd been old enough to have
them. Her flesh was cold, so cold, and it didn't even seem
to breathe. His fingers ran lightly over her navel, up her
firm, flat abdomen. He caressed her. It felt like kneading
a fish. She must really be sick, dying maybe, he thought.
I have to keep her warm somehow. Oh Jesus she stank.
Like day-old meat. Fucking Jesus.

"Touch me," she whispered.

His fingers continued roving. They rested for a moment on one nipple and then they moved across to touch
. . . something else. An opening. Something squishy.
Flaps of flesh against his skin. He tried to snatch away his
hand but she held him there. He felt a strange detachment as his fingers probed what had to be some kind of
wound. He felt his hand slide deeper into her, touched
bone, touched something softer. There was fluid inside
her but it was sticky and viscous, like Karo syrup.

"Yeah, baby," she said, "touch me right there, inside,
go right through my skin. Jesus I'm scared, it's only been
a day since I've been like this and I don't know what to
do, I only know I need something warm, something red
and spurting—"

Suddenly he knew where he'd seen her before.

Television. Lying in the alley. Drained of blood.

"Oh, oh," she moaned, "oh, I'm so hungry. You gotta
feed me, dude. I need what you got." She never loosened
her grip. "We can do stuff together, dude, after you
change. I mean, like, it's so goddamn lonely, I never felt
lonelier before in my life, not even at the children's shelter."

"Janey Rodriguez," he whispered. "Son of a bitch.
You're supposed to be dead."

"Do I feel dead to you?"

"Yes."

Cold. Cold. But his hand moved deeper to explore
more viscera. He touched a bulbous mass of fatty tissue.
Unaccountably, he found himself getting an erection. He

stroked the rib bones, brittle as icicles. It sure was a lot different from watching this shit on *Re-Animator*. It was fucking real. Real. The not-quite-clotting blood oozing between his fingers. Her guts sucking all the warmth from him. He could feel the racing of his own blood, he could hear its pounding. Jesus, I'm scamming with a dead chick and I fucking *like* it, he thought.

She kissed him. Her tongue was soft and cold . . . like a liver-flavored frozen yogurt bar. It didn't feel bad, just . . . different. Suddenly he realized that his hand had shoved its way all the way through her, that it was sticking into the back of her T-shirt.

Now he remembered. The body of Janey Rodriguez had had a gaping hole in it. As though her killer had torn into her with his bare hands and ripped her all the way open. If only my parents could see me now, he thought. That'd show the fuckers.

She pulled away from him for a moment. His hand was still inside her body cavity. She looked at him at last, long and seriously. "Do you like me?" she said.

"Sure I do."

"I mean really, really, like me? Enough to come over to the other side?"

"The other side . . ."

"Things ain't so bad here. It's strange at first. You feel all empty inside. You feel so hungry you wanna eat the whole world. You feel like you're on the outside looking in. But then you start to understand that this is forever. There's time to heal. There's eternity."

"Forever . . ." Suddenly Matt realized that he already felt empty inside. He already felt the hunger, the aloneness. The emptiness came from never having had someone to love.

"There's a place we can go to," she said. "A place where no one screams at you, where you don't have to fill out forms, where they never lock you up for your own protection."

"I'll go," he said. "What do I have to lose?" He felt the coldness seep into him. The coldness climbed up his forearm, slid through his veins. He could feel his blood turn sluggish.

"Okay, dude," she said, "kiss me then. This time it's forever."

And they kissed.

And then she crushed him to her and bit down hard on his neck. His heart was pumping like crazy. The blood gushed out and she gorged herself. He could see the red flushing her cheeks. Red filling out the irises of her eyes. Red dripping down the side of her lip. Red smearing her cheeks, her neck, her T-shirt. She whimpered like a lost girl, but her eyes were tearless. Dead people don't cry, I guess, he thought.

His hand delved deep into her. He touched intestine, sternum, heart, the heart still and rubbery. But as his blood infused her he could feel the heart go flip-flop in the palm of his hand . . . beating to a rhythmless music . . . beating . . . cold and beating. He could feel the ooze liquefy as the fresh blood gushed down her esophagus and into the dry pit of her stomach. I'm really inside you, he thought. He wasn't afraid.

This wasn't like any of the other times he'd screwed some tenth-grade gum-chewing Valley girl in the backseat of his battered Civic. This was important, dude. It was filling up that yawning chasm inside. It was giving him what his parents never gave him.

With her free hand she unzipped his jeans. He could feel his cock slide into something cold and slippery. It tightened around him and squeezed and he cried out; he couldn't tell if it was pain or orgasm, couldn't tell if it was his come or his life's blood spurting into her lifeless body. He didn't care. He didn't care because he felt big and powerful and full of awe. It was fucking worth dying for.

He was already changing from within. He was so eager to slough off his past. He wanted it all now. He didn't feel any pain. He was numb from the cold of her. He didn't care. It wouldn't be so cold on the other side. He didn't care because at least he was in touch with something bigger than himself, with the mystery of life and death.

VISION SEEKERS

Lady Chit was the last person to enter Brian Zottoli's apartment. She flicked on the light; Brian was listening to his phone messages; Petra had already gone into the kitchen and was starting to make coffee.

There were some old messages. Then there was a longer beep, and Chit heard the agitated voice of a young man.

"He ain't dead, Brian. I can't bring myself to do it. I can't. Call me."

Brian turned to Lady Chit and said, "It's started. I've got to go." Chit did not know what to say, and she began nervously to straighten up some of the papers that were piled up on every surface in the living room. "I'm sorry about the mess," Brian said. "God, I'm sorry, but . . ." He picked up the phone and started to dial a number. "Shit, they've cut off my phone."

Lady Chit said: "Surely not . . . maybe it's just unplugged from the jack or something. . . ."

"I haven't paid them in three months." He slammed it down. "Goddamn it, why at four in the morning?"

"I hate the phone company," Petra said from the kitchen.

Lady Chit, who didn't really understand the idea of not having money, who thought of writers as living a Bohemian and somewhat enviable existence, sat down on the sofa and digested this concept for a few moments. Who was this man who knew so much about her grandfather, who declined to laugh at the occult experience she'd had at Simone Arleta's? It was all most confusing.

"Look," Brian said, "I really have to go over to PJ's."

He turned from the phone just as Petra came in from the kitchen with coffee.

"Something wrong over there?" she said.

Chit noticed immediately the electricity between them. At the Café Ayudhya she had been too preoccupied with her own confusion to notice that she was intruding on the beginning of a new relationship—or the resumption of an old one. Now she realized that she might be stepping on their toes. She didn't know how to back away gracefully, but she did know that she would be terrified if she was left alone in that big apartment of her family's. It was absurd, she thought, to be weighing the social ramifications of the alternatives, to worry about losing face and saving face . . . sometimes, she reflected, I'm just so Thai. Where do I get it from? . . . surely not from the years in Europe and America . . . surely my culture couldn't be genetic.

She realized that thinking of these things was helping to distract her from her terror. This was good. Good. She took a cup of coffee from Petra, smiled that all-concealing smile that was also part of her cultural heritage, and said, "We could all go to my place if you'd like. The telephone works and"—she tried not to sound too knowing—"it has two bedrooms."

Petra mouthed a silent *thank you* at her.

"I'll be gone for a little while," Brian said. "Why don't you two go over to Chit's and . . . and I'll meet you there." He rooted around in a cupboard and produced three crucifixes—cheap ones you could buy at one of the tourist shops on Olvera Street—and pressed one into Chit's hand. He stuck another in his pocket.

"Why do you have to go?" Lady Chit said.

"I have to go and take care of someone. A friend. I'm the only person who can—"

"A vampire?" Petra said.

"Yes." He handed her the third crucifix.

Petra nodded. She was having difficulty, Chit could see

that, but she was trying to accept it all as it came, however weird it was. Because she needed to believe Brian. Because she was already falling in love with him. Perhaps she didn't even know that yet. But Chit could tell.

NIGHT CREATURES

Still dark. Who was banging at the damn door? Clara Lewis woke up from a bad dream. God it was dark. And Mitch lying next to her, snoring like a pig. The door . . . so damn loud! . . . Clara thought, It's gotta be something to do with Matt. That damn kid. Probably in trouble again. Wouldn't be surprised if he was in trouble with the law. Maybe the cops were with him now, maybe they'd picked him up lying drunk in an alley or . . . Clara tried to remember whether she'd flushed those pills down the toilet yet, the way she'd promised herself to last week.

Dark. She didn't dare turn on the light because Mitch would wake up, and Mitch, awakened before dawn, was an ogre. She slipped out of the bed, fumbled for a robe, and felt along the wall until she reached the door.

"Aw, shuddup," she mumbled, but the pounding wouldn't stop. It was regular, mechanical almost. It was almost like it wasn't a human being knocking. "I'm coming already," she said.

Found the lamp beside the living room sofa. Dim light cascaded over red velour. A huge plaster Jesus stood above the lamp, his arms projecting a shadowy cross upon the drapes. Clara sighed and went to the front door.

"What is it?" she said. She put on the safety chain and peered through the crack. A dank, dead smell flooded her nostrils. She saw her son. Slouching, with his hair stacked up to a sharp point, like a rhinoceros horn. There was a girl standing beside him. Red was dripping from her lips. The smell was coming from both of them. "Don't you have your own key, Matthew?" she said. "And who's the girl? I just want to get back to bed."

"I have the key, Mom," Matt said. He dangled it in front of her nose. He leered at her. Something about that leer . . . there was something obscene about the way he looked at her. Like he was hungry. "But the key doesn't work no more. Now you have to ask me in."

"You and your games, Matthew." She undid the chain, but he still stood there, one arm over the girl—she was just a slip of a thing, no more than fourteen years old—and he stared straight into his mother's eyes. Disquieting. He never used to look her in the eye before.

"Invite us in," Matthew said. A hint of menace in his tone.

"Suit yourself," Clara said, shrugging. She started to go back to the bedroom. She leaned over and kissed the top of Jesus's head for luck and started down the corridor.

"Goddamn it, Mother, fucking invite us in!" It was an animal shriek. What was wrong with the boy? Ever since he'd gotten that job in Hollywood, he'd become increasingly bizarre. She didn't know how to reach him. She'd never been able to.

"Come in," she said. Almost inaudibly.

And suddenly they were inside and the door was shut. There had been no crossing of the threshold. Just like that they were there. Special effects almost.

"I want you to meet a very special girl, Mom. Very, very, very, very special. Someone you're dying to meet. My permanent new girlfriend, Janey Rodriguez."

"She's not moving in here." Rodriguez, Rodriguez . . . where had Clara heard the name Janey Rodriguez before? Surely Matt hadn't mentioned her. He never talked about girls. He never talked about anything on the rare occasions when they encountered each other, facing each other off over breakfast, she bound for her dreary job at Pac Bell and he for bed. "Isn't she a bit young? Did she run away or something?"

"I ran away from life, Mrs. Lewis." The girl's voice was clear, high-pitched. "I don't even think about it anymore."

"This is a strange girl you picked up, Matthew Lewis."

"You don't know how strange, Mommy dearest! By the time you get to know her, you'll fucking understand *strange.*"

He gave the girl a little peck on the cheek. The girl giggled.

"I always wanted to be a Valley girl," she said softly. Clara could sense the wistfulness in her voice and she almost relented. But it would be no good to have her here. She would probably steal. Matt's friends were often criminals. Or they ran in gangs.

Matthew snapped his fingers.

Suddenly the girl was behind her. Just like that. Special effects again. I must be dreaming, she thought, and then she felt cold hands seizing her wrists, twisting them together . . . God this girl was strong, she was bending her wrists back and back and . . . sweet Jesus, Clara could hear the bone cracking, could feel the wet blood trickling from the wrenched joint . . . she screamed. Then her son was there. Gagging her with a hand. An ice-cold hand. Ice. Ice.

"I've always hated you, Mother," Matt said. "But now I'm hungry for you." She tried to move her hands and she could feel bone ripping through flesh. The pain, oh God, the pain made the tears spurt from her eyes but she couldn't cry out, she was paralyzed, she kept thinking Oh Jesus Jesus I'm going to wake up soon Jesus Jesus, and Jesus stood there looking at her, the plaster Jesus with the outstretched arms. . . .

Just then Mitch came lumbering in. "Heard the fucking noise," he said. He had a shotgun, the one he always kept under the bed.

Clara moaned.

"Let go of your mother!" Mitch shouted.

Slowly, deliberately, Matt ripped off his mother's nightdress. God, Clara thought, I'm so ashamed, my son is going to rape me . . . she looked down at herself, worried about the age spots that flecked her sagging breasts, started to scream again, but before she could, Matt had wadded up a piece of the night dress and shoved it into her mouth. It was all so dreamlike. Except for the pain. God, the pain. And now she couldn't breathe and she could feel the vomit crawling up her throat and seeping into the gag.

Mitch stared and stared.

"A little bit of domestic violence," Matt said softly, "adds spice to life. Don't it, Mom?"

Janey ripped a piece of electric cord from the vacuum cleaner and began slowly, methodically, to tie Clara up.

Mitch fired. Clara saw holes tear open in Matt's cheek. Then the flesh knit itself back together. "My, that was a close shave," Matt said. As Janey threw Clara onto the sofa, Matt turned around, pulled his father toward him, and casually ripped off his head. He tossed the head aside. Blood spewed up from the neck stump like a geyser, and Matt bent down to lap at it like a child at a water fountain. Mitch's body was still jerking. A headless epileptic. Clara tried to scream and began to choke on her own vomit.

"Be still, my heart," Matt said softly as he clawed into his father's body and yanked out his heart. The spasms stopped.

"Cardiac arrest," said Matt, dropping the body and sucking on the heart as though it were an orange.

Janey sat down next to Clara on the sofa. She was peering at her intently. Now and then she touched her lightly with a finger. The nipple. Ice brushing against her clitoris. Staring. Staring. The staring seemed to violate the most secret parts of her. She was raping her with her eyes.

"Catch," Matt said. He tossed Janey the heart. Janey giggled. The heart missed and landed between Clara's legs. Blood oozed over her vulva. Blood crawled along her vagina's wrinkled lips. "I guess he's not going to be coming back, is he?" Matt said. He dribbled his father's head into the corridor and kicked it into his parents' bedroom. Coming back, he muttered, "He deserves this. Fucking asshole. He didn't love me." For a moment Clara thought he was going to weep. But he didn't. He just stood there, the scarlet drooling from his lips, his eyes darting from side to side. God, she thought, could it be true that we didn't love him, didn't understand him, and this is some kind of crazy revenge for some childhood thing we didn't even know about? "What are you staring at?" he said to Janey.

"Hungry," Janey said. "You're hogging the prey."

"What do you mean? I left you a whole . . . a whole . . . aw, Mommy, it's just gonna be for a while, the pain . . . soon it'll all be different."

Seizing one of Clara's broken hands, Janey pried off one of the fingernails and began lapping up the blood the welled up from the wound. Her saliva burned like brine. It was more pain that she imagined possible. She couldn't run away from it. And her son was hulking over her. His eyes were bloodshot. "So what do you think, huh, huh?" he said. "I'm coming to save you, Mommy. Oh, you've lived a fucked-up life with that man, slapping you around, hitting the booze, prowling around with that fucking shotgun and scaring the shit out of you. It's all gonna be better soon. Yeah. Yeah. What do you think, Mommy dearest? I wanna hear what you think!" He bent down and ripped off the gag.

"Jesus!" she screamed.

Jesus looked on, his doe-eyes brimming with compassion.

She screamed.

"It's Jesus you want, ain't it?" said Matt. Screams tore from her again and again as Janey continued to rip off her fingernails one by one and to tease the tender flesh with her tongue. "Well, you can have him." He picked up the statue. Pried her legs apart and began shoving it into her headfirst. The outstretched arms clasped her waist in an agonizing embrace. She screamed and screamed. He pushed harder and she felt her consciousness slipping away at last. She shrank back into herself. Jesus was hard and cold and jagged, tearing at her womb. "Thank God he ain't wearing no cross," Matt said. "I never liked crosses. I never liked religion." He smiled at her. She retreated into some far place within. The pain receded. It was almost like watching a movie. It was happening to someone else. She was losing consciousness fast. I'm dying, she thought, I'm dying.

"Get it over with," Janey said. "Kill the bitch. Like I'm totally hungry." Clara could hear her from an immeasurable distance. She could feel her life force draining away, but she was too weak to struggle. The cold was waiting for her, but it was better than the anguish.

"This is getting me horny," Matt said.

"Horny. Hungry."

"I'm not gonna kill her all the way," Matt said. "Eternity's a long time to be without a mother."

Janey laughed. She wriggled out of her jeans. She pulled her T-shirt over her head. "Horny. Hungry."

"Bet you didn't know we can still fuck after death, Mom," Matt said softly. "I've had it up to here with religion—and now so have you."

Through a fog of pain Clara could hear a whimper escape her own throat. She saw the girl—as though from infinitely far away—a tiny thing, underdeveloped, undernourished—her fangs glistened. She leaped onto Clara like a kitten, clawing, licking, rubbing herself up and down against the plaster Jesus. Matt shed his clothes too. He was so thin. Stooping. Still so adolescent.

"Horny. Hungry," Janey whispered.

"We can do both."

"Coolness."

"You think she'll turn before sunrise?"

"Nah. Give her a night's rest. I'm surprised you came through in the same night. You were barely dead for like a second."

"There wasn't any resistance. It's what I've always wanted."

They kissed. They coupled. They fed as Clara drifted into the death of transformation. . . .

DISSOLVE: WAITING

When Brian arrived at PJ's apartment he could see that everything was in disarray. The television was blasting away and the stereo was on at the same time. Paintings were scattered all over the floor of the living room. An easel was upturned. A half-eaten hamburger sat on the kitchenette counter. The furniture had been pushed against the wall, and PJ sat, cross-legged, in the middle of the room. Around him was a circle of bizarre votive objects: sacred stones, the skull of a buffalo, an arrow, a pipe, some sheaves of dried corn, and many crucifixes. Smoke from incense burners filled the room. A flute and a several unidentifiable fetishes lay in front of PJ. Candles were burning. There were a couple of pitchers of what Brian realized must be holy water.

PJ was dressed—well, it wasn't exactly cross-dressing, but it seemed pretty close—in a knee-length buckskin gown. His hair was braided and he wore a heavily embroidered neckpiece from which hung a turquoise cross. There were Catholic symbols, Indian symbols, voodoo and pagan symbols. As an example of cultural syncretism PJ seemed implausible, grotesque.

Then he began to sing. It was a curious yodeling, full of drawn-out high notes and sudden, wild melismas. It wasn't like any kind of Indian music Brian had ever heard. Although PJ had told Brian about the vision that had turned him into a Shoshone *ma'aipots* or androgynous shaman, he couldn't reconcile this image with that of the grungily handsome teenager he'd known years before.

He didn't want to interrupt PJ. He didn't know how important these rituals were to PJ. Presently PJ seemed to come awake, and he said, "Brian."

"Yeah." Brian crawled inside the sacred circle. He didn't know if it would really provide any kind of protection. But somehow he did feel safer behind the barrier of religious objects.

"Brian, I just couldn't bring myself to stake him that night. I—I'm sorry. I guess I failed."

"I understand. I miss Terry too. But the thing that comes to us and speaks to us in Terry's voice . . . that's not Terry. That's just animated flesh . . . Terry's soul is gone."

"I wish I could believe that."

"So do I," said Brian softly.

DISSOLVE: MORGUE

"Dr. Goldberg . . . Dr. Goldberg . . ."

"What?"

"Come here. Come right down. I'm here in the morgue. Quickly. Quickly! You've got to see this."

"I'm having coffee."

"Please. . . ."

Elevator. Corridor. Double-lock. Security. Password. Chill.

Corpse.

"Yes, Nurse Raitt. I haven't got all night, you know. I was just about to get back on the road. You know I like to hit the freeway before the morning rush hour. Yes, yes, all right. Let's have a look."

Sheet. Blood. Corpse.

"Oh, for heaven's sake, Nurse Raitt! I do wish you wouldn't tremble and shake so. My coffee is getting colder by the minute, and you drag me down here to the morgue, where it's freezing cold and you know I'm not dressed for it . . . I do hope this isn't some kind of sexual advance. I am not in the business of granting promotions for favors, sexual or otherwise."

"I'm scared."

"Oh, oh, oh. Now who is this we're looking at . . . oh, that Jane Doe bag lady? The one that was hacked to pieces and stuck in a shopping cart in Pacoima?"

"Yes."

"Well, let's take a look, shall we? Take off the sheet."

"But Dr. Goldberg, you don't understand . . . it was moving. Something . . . somehow . . . under the sheet . . . fibrillating . . . not quite dead."

"Oh, nonsense, Nurse Raitt; you've been reading too many of those doorstop horror novels. Take off the sheet. You see . . . there's nothing. Nothing that would occasion any . . . supernatural suspicions."

Head. Arms. Torso. The head neatly severed. The hands placed in such a way that they seemed to burst from her chest like breaching dolphins. The legs stuck, stump down, into a shopping bag, with the feet sticking up into the stomach.

"Whoever arranged the pieces must have had quite a sense of humor, Nurse Raitt . . . oh, my . . . you really must learn to control your opprobrium, nurse; you really must. . . ."

Scream.

And then the movement. In the head. The eyes. Swiveling slowly. Slowly. The lips slowly starting to part. As if they were on the verge of speaking. And the fingers . . . clawing at the air . . . wiggling . . . the toes twitching . . . and then the whole torso racked with spasms.

"Nurse Raitt, I really must insist that you—"

"Dr. Goldberg it's moving it's moving it's—"

And then it was still.

Quite, quite still.

Dead.

Somewhere, far away, a clock was striking.

Quite, quite dead.

"It must be almost dawn, Nurse Raitt . . . really, there was no reason to interrupt my coffee. I'll have a few cultures taken, do a few tests . . . all in good time. For God's sake, don't we have an empty drawer for that thing? It's a terrible idea to have loose body parts lying around . . . oh, don't be hysterical, nurse, you can see very well that it's stopped those palpitations or spasms or whatever they were . . . get it all taken care of by tomorrow."

"Yes, Dr. Goldberg."

"And now, if you'll excuse me, it's not my habit to greet the sun when I'm on night shift." .

Turn. Start walking. Unlock double lock. Security. Elevator.

Up.

"Dr. Goldberg, come back, please, come back, it's moving again, it's—oh my God, it's grabbing hold of me pulling me down it's drooling oh God I think it's trying to bite me and—"

Screams. Screams.

The morgue: not a soul was stirring.

Not a soul.

DISSOLVE: TWILIGHT

They did not have long to wait.

The ruse had been Brian's idea. It was a cowardly way out, but PJ had to admit that he didn't think he could bring himself to kill his friend himself. It had to be done in an impersonal way, even if that way smacked of an episode of *The Little Rascals*.

He had sat in the sacred circle, and he had prayed for some great flash of illumination, some guidance from the universal spirit. But nothing had come. Things had changed so much since that first vision quest. Things had been clear and certain. Now they were blurred, and the spirit that had guided him before would not appear to him. Was it because he had left the reservation and gone back to the life of white men? But I am white, he thought, fifty percent at least. PJ was torn. Perhaps it was true that a great evil had been unleashed into the world—but how could that evil take the shape of Terry Gish, his friend?

And now he and Brian Zottoli were resorting to a childish booby trap in order to bring down this supposed great evil. Somehow he just couldn't reconcile the two images—two shining knights battling creatures of hell— two confused men tilting at windmills. I am plagued by doubts, he thought as he watched Brian fill the trash can with holy water and set it in place.

"How much longer until dawn?" he asked Brian.

Brian said, "No more than a half hour."

"Better get back inside the sacred circle."

"Yeah."

Brian crawled back inside. He had a rubber mallet— the kind used to flatten the brads on film scripts—and a stake he'd made from a mop handle. "I'll do that part," he said. "I know you can't stomach it. . . ."

The two of them sat together. PJ closed his eyes and waited. He was conscious of Brian's presence, conscious of all they'd gone through in the far past. He tried to stir his soul from its hiding place. I want you to go out on a spirit journey, he told it, I want you to hover over the city until you see Terry, and I want you to guide him here. He knew that Brian was looking at him curiously because, although Brian had experienced the supernatural first hand, he was still suspicious of things that smelled like New Age mumbo jumbo.

He called out to Terry in his mind. Would Terry hear him? He could not tell. He did not know if the body that had been Terry contained any remnant of Terry's soul. But he believed there must be a piece of it still there.

He could feel his own soul shifting. The numbness of the little death was seeping into his body. His soul was struggling to free itself. His soul was like a she-eagle. His soul came loose now. He could see himself in the center of the circle, could see the puzzled Brian staring strangely at him, marveling perhaps at how still he was, how chill his flesh.

He hovered over the circle for a moment and then he soared up, up, through the ceiling, over the wall, past stucco apartments in nouveau-"Miami Vice" pastels, down the hill now toward Hollywood Boulevard. There was almost no one out. A wino or two slumped against a bench. An RTD bus lurched past, passengerless. Neon pornshop signs winked. He could feel a million souls in slumber, pinpricks of color against the cosmic gray . . . Terry . . . where was Terry? . . . yes. A knot of concentrated blackness. Evil. And here and there more evil. It was already replicating itself.

There it was! Heading home. Heading toward PJ's place. Trusting in their old friendship. The creature that was slinking through the back alleys did not wear a human shape, but PJ knew it right away. Terry had taken the form of a black kitten. He was darting from shadow to shadow. Soon would come dawn. I let this happen, PJ said to himself. I let him live, and set in motion the cycle of blood. In horror he retreated back into the circle.

"He'll be here any minute," he told Brian. "Listen. Listen."

At the doorway, a plaintive mewing.

A scratching sound. Another mew, louder, more mournful.

"He's waiting to be invited," Brian said.

"Come in," PJ said softly.

The door was pushed open, upsetting the bucket of holy water Brian had balanced between the top rail and the jamb. There was a heartrending scream. Then came Terry's voice. The voice of their childhood.

"How could you do this to me, PJ?"

"I—"

"Don't talk to him!" Brian cried out. "He'll try to trick you!" He grabbed the sharpened stake and the rubber hammer and started to leave the circle. "Don't even look at him! Close your eyes!"

He did. He squeezed them shut and put his hands over them for good measure. Like a frightened teenage girl at a horror movie. But in his mind's eye he could see Terry even more clearly than before. Terry in the video arcade. Terry sleeping over, drifting into dreamland while PJ talked about moving away from Junction, about burning away the Indian in him and making it in the concrete world of white people. Terry driving a stake into his brother David's heart.

"PJ—how can you hurt me like this?—you fucking loved me, dude—don't you think I didn't know that?— You're the only person in the world who I'd trust with my life—my *un*life."

PJ opened his eyes. He saw his friend, his skin scarred by the holy water, peeling away to the raw meat and bone beneath . . . a sour stench came from the burning flesh . . . through the blood-tinged fumes he saw Terry's eyes, gorged with gore, saw the lips half eaten away in a permanent sneer . . . and still there came the childish voice, an obscene parody of their childhood memories . . . "You couldn't do it to me. Look at you in that dress. You say an Indian vision makes you dress that way but like, I think it's just because you're a fag and you won't fucking admit it."

"Don't listen to him," Brian said. "He's preying on your fears, your self-doubts."

"You ain't man enough to drive that stake into me. You couldn't handle a phallic symbol if it was sticking up from your crotch."

"You're not Terry Gish," PJ said softly. He said to Brian, "I can do it now. I have to do it." He seized the stake and mallet from Brian's hand. "Stay inside the circle! Be safe!" he cried, and he left the circle and charged at the man-thing that was standing in the door-way.

Blue flames were spurting where the holy water had soaked into Terry's pores. The cheeks were charring. Blood and pus welled up. Viscous bile spewed from his nostrils, his mouth, from which issued a cacophonous cackling, a mad-scientist laugh that went on and on like a stuck record.

"Asshole," PJ said softly. "You fucking asshole."

He rammed the stake into Terry's heart and pounded it in with the mallet. The blood that oozed out was black and sluggish. PJ pounded. He didn't know he had so much hatred in him. He pounded. And Terry screamed, and in between the screams came that hideous laughter ... and Terry slumped down onto the floor of the apart-ment as the first rays of morning sluiced in through the blinds, and a cold blue flame enveloped him, and in the last moments before he shriveled and charred and turned to dust PJ saw him once again the way he used to be when they rode their bikes downhill with the autumn wind in their faces and ran the only stop sign in the whole town of Junction, hollering with glee, the three friends. But the child-Terry faded away and there was only dust. Dust and suppurating stains and a pool of frothing dark red ooze. All PJ could feel was a terrible emptiness—no sadness, no joy.

"I've killed him," he said. "I've really killed him this time."

"Don't waste your grief," Brian said. "It wasn't him. You've set him free."

"Guess I have." Even the blood was fading from the carpet.

PJ knew that Brian was struggling to convince himself that there was purpose to all this, that they had won a small victory in the timeless war between the light and the dark; it was hard for Brian, who saw things in grays and mixed-up colors, not in the pure, stark primary hues of myth. PJ had been that way himself, before his vision quest.

DISSOLVE: ANGEL

Angel went back to the mirror. It was almost morning. Momma was in a Valium stupor. It felt better in the bathroom—cool, with the lemony fragrance of air freshener, and the air more humid than in the bedroom with its air-conditioning sucking out the moisture from it.

Angel sat down in front of the mirror and splashed cold water on his face. He started to go through his zit-hunting ritual. There were never any zits to speak of but he hunted all the same, obsessively. He was afraid of zits. Zits meant his voice was going to change. Zits meant the end of his career. He was convinced of that.

Had it been a dream last night, the twin-thing pulling him into the world behind the glass, sucking him into the mirror image of the hot tub?

No. He stared hard into that mirror. Stared hard into his own eyes. There were someone else's eyes there. The thing that claimed to be Timmy Valentine himself. Trapped behind the glass and desperate to be free.

"Maybe we can be friends," he said softly.

The thing behind the mirror smiled.

He saw a hand extend toward him. He couldn't help moving his own hand toward the mirror. For a split second he felt flesh—death-cold, but spongy, not stiff like the mirror glass.

"You're there, aren't you?" he said. "Jesus, you're really there. And I can't tell anyone or I'd be locked up in a loony bin."

Their palms touched. They were perfect mirror-twins. No one could have guessed they were not each other's reflection.

"It's weird," said Timmy. "When I'm on *your* side of the glass, I cast no reflection at all."

"So you really are a vampire."

"We don't choose who we are."

"And you want to be born again. You want to escape from the witch woman. And I'm the only one who can help you."

"Do we have a bargain?"

"What will I get in return?"

"Anything you want."

Timmy Valentine looked completely serious. "What do you mean, anything I want?" Angel said. "Seems like I could want a whole lot and you ain't a genie in a lamp."

"Anything," said Timmy. "But you have to *really* want it."

"Well I do have something you can do for me." And Angel leaned over the sink and whispered into Timmy's ear. Timmy smiled a wry smile.

DISSOLVE: NIGHT CREATURES

The dawn light stole into the Lewises' living room. It oozed along the mottled carpet. It touched the edge of the floral couch where the night's carnage had occurred.

The Lewises had been new to vampirism. They had not drawn the curtains.

In the brightening morning, the headless corpse of Mitch Lewis seemed absurdly incongruous with the bourgeois surroundings. The head, propped against the edge of the bedspread, remained in darkness, linked to the torso in the living room by a long thin bloodstain that stretched, curled, twisted, warped over the corridor like yarn.

On the couch, Matt and his mother and Janey Rodriguez were melting in the morning sun. Their flesh was liquefying, melding into a Cuisinart-like consistency. Blood running into bile, digestive juices eating away at the oversized flowers of the upholstery. Bones becoming porous, rib cages crumbling into sprinkles of dust that were carried away on rivulets of rheum.

By midmorning there would be nothing left of them but a few smears and, of course, the putrefying carcass of Matt's father.

They had not been very good vampires after all. They had not understood how to survive. They had not taken the long view.

DISSOLVE: ANGEL

After he had confided in Timmy Valentine, Angel tiptoed out to the bedroom and tugged at his mother's arm. Fitfully she stirred.

"Come into the bathroom, Momma. I want you to see something."

"—tired—"

"Come on, Ma. Come on. It's something wonderful. Something you've always wanted."

He led her by the hand. He stayed by the door so that the mirror wouldn't accidentally reflect him. That would only confuse her.

"Look in the mirror, Mom. Go on. Look."

He knew what she would see in the mirror. Not the shiny white tile of the bathroom wall but the green hills of Kentucky. The mirror would become a television screen for her memories. That's what Timmy promised him. And he knew it was true. He saw her standing there, pudgy and dissipated and groggy, and he could see how the wall behind his mother had picked up the green sheen from the image in the mirror.

Angel knew what his mother would see in the TV of the soul. She'd see the hills behind their old shack and she'd just about smell the grass and maybe even hear it growing. And she'd see the spot where Errol was buried. She'd be carried back to the moment in time when everything changed for their family.

"What is this, honey? What are you doing to me, baby?" his mother said. "You're making me see things. Where my face oughta be, I can see the hills over Hangman's Holler. Them's the trees used to stand behind our house. Did I take the wrong kind of pills? Shit, Hollywood . . . they probably spiked my nightcap with one of them shrooms."

Angel kept out of the way. He could see Momma's face, knew what she was seeing from the way it changed . . . startled . . . disbelieving at first . . . then finally mesmerized.

"Look into that mirror, Momma. Look at that big old hole in the ground you dug. The hole which you and me rolled him into. The ground is opening up, Momma. There's a hand bursting up out of the mud. It's grasping at hanks of grass now, trying to pull up the rest of him. You know who it is, Momma? You know?"

His mother nodded. Her lips parted as though she were about to say something, but instead a tear came rolling down one cheek. . . . "I'm drunk," she said softly. "I'm dreaming."

"Just keep on looking, Momma. Look. It's him all

right. The one that died. It's Errol. I spirited him back from the dead for you."

He heard a child's piping voice from behind the mirror:

> 'Tis the gift to be simple,
> 'Tis the gift to be free.

"Christ Almighty have mercy on my soul," said his mother. She was weeping copiously now.

He knew exactly what she was seeing. Timmy had plucked the memories from his brain, had mimicked Errol's voice so perfectly that it brought Errol to mind so goddamn vividly he started to cry himself, mourning his brother and mourning the childhood his brother had stolen from him on the day he died. Errol had clawed his way back up from the grave and now he was standing there, the waves of grass maybe halfway up to his knees, no blood on him at all.

How had Errol died? What had happened between the mother and son? Angel didn't know. He'd been outside when it happened. All he remembered was the way she carried him out into the meadow. Singing all the while. And her eyes, shifting, peering, afraid of something. Angel didn't know, didn't want to know what went on between his mother and his brother. He only knew one thing for certain. "You loved him a lot more than you loved me, didn't you Momma?" he said. "Well, he's yours again now. He can always be yours if you want."

I think you loved him to death, he thought, the way you try to love me, the way you crush me in your folds of fat. I'm glad I can't see him, he told himself. I hate Errol. I can't even remember what he looked like. Jesus I hate him.

He heard Errol's voice: "Mommy . . . I've been waiting for you a long time . . . it's so cold down here down in the ground so cold so scary oh I've been afraid I've been lonesome . . . Mommy won't you reach out your hand to me, won't you reach through the glass and hold me and make me warm?"

Angel saw his mother reach out toward the mirror. Both arms. Like a sleepwalker. Slowly her lips wrenched themselves into a kind of smile . . . the smile of a crazy woman. "You can have him forever, Momma," Angel said. "You can follow him right back into the past. You can live in the mirror and never have to lose him again."

Her eyes shone with an eerie light. Angel knew she was tempted. Angel knew that she had loved Errol more than him, that she had always hated the way he had lived and Errol had died, that somehow she was the one who had caused the death, and that was why she wanted to clutch Angel to her, squeeze him, suck him into her, suffocate him with twisted love that was drenched with the scent of dime-store perfume. He wasn't sure how far he'd wanted to go when he whispered his plan to the spirit of the mirror. He knew that his mother might step into the mirror and be lost forever. He didn't know if he really wanted that to happen. He didn't know what he wanted except that it had to be something different from what he had now.

His mother began singing softly. Her voice was raspy from too much smoking and drinking. It wasn't the way it used to sound, sweet as the mountain wind.

'Tis the gift to be free, she sang. And began to step toward the mirror. "Can I really be with you forever, Errol?" she said. And took another step. And another. And another.

"Be with him, Momma," Angel said. "You'll be happy. And you won't never have to touch me no more. I want my freedom." The vehemence in his voice surprised him. Jesus. I hate her, he thought. And I can live without her now. I'm going to be making the money, I'm going to be running the show. Things are going to be different.

She stepped closer and closer to the mirror. She was just going to sink into it and disappear. Suddenly Angel panicked. Did this mean she really didn't love him after all? "Don't do it!" he screamed. "Don't do it or you'll be damned! That mirror leads straight down into hell!"

His mother stopped short. The wind stopped whispering. The green reflection was gone from the wall. She was breathing heavily, as though she had been fleeing the bogeyman. The life was stealing back into her eyes.

I've blown it, he thought. There's something in me that can't see her walk away from me. We're tied together for all time.

His mother said, as though awakening from a dream, "What am I doing here?" Then she turned, saw Angel, looked back at the mirror as though to catch some fleeting image . . . looked at Angel again . . . turned pale. "My mind's playing tricks on me," she said.

"No it ain't," Angel said. "You saw what you saw. Things are gonna be different from now on, Momma. There's three of us now. He's come back and he's standing between us. I made him come back to take away your pain. Because he knows how to love you better than I do."

In that moment, the balance of power in their family shifted, and Angel felt the first stirrings of freedom; it was not a comforting feeling; it was like a vague anxiety, a dull hunger; it frightened him more than he could say.

DISSOLVE: VISION SEEKERS

When Brian came to Lady Chit's apartment that morning he brought a young man with him. He had long dark hair and penetrating eyes. There was an almost feminine beauty about him. Chit had been making coffee and watching the late, late show, a Bela Lugosi film that did little to mitigate her unease; but she did not have the energy to turn it off. Petra was sleeping in the spare bedroom.

It was a spartan apartment in some ways, although there was nothing in it that was not of the finest quality, from the Italian marble floor tiles to the gold votive image of the Four-faced Brahma that sat serenely in its niche above the coordinated, black-matte audiovisual components, to the original Turner in its understated frame above the white leather sofa and loveseat.

Brian murmured something that Chit couldn't hear, and then went in to look for Petra; but the young man stood there, taking in the furnishings, gazing with particular attention at the Turner.

"I love Turner," he said at last. "I can never make my colors dance that way, no matter how hard I try."

"You're an artist?" Chit said.

"Yeah. PJ Gallagher."

"You're something else, too. . . ." The Thai word *katoey* sprang to mind. One of the maids at Prince Prathna's estate had been a *katoey,* a man who mimicked a woman to perfection. "Something about you . . . something ambiguous."

PJ smiled. "Americans can't see it. It must be something about your culture. I'm a shaman, kind of. Not that good of a shaman, but I'm getting better. And when I'm doing my shaman thing, I become the sacred man-woman, a holy transvestite. That must be what you see in me. In Shoshone it's called *ma'aipots.*"

She could see that this wasn't something that he could talk easily about with *farang,* the white people. But he seemed to be part white. That was another ambiguity in him. He was caught between worlds, between white and red, between man and woman, between the inner and the outer realities. She decided she liked him a good deal.

"And you're also a painter," she said. "I can tell by the way you talk about Turner."

"It's just a hobby," he said. But she could tell it was far more than that. "I paint famous Indian chiefs and sell them at swap meets. Sitting Bulls and Red Clouds."

"And ravishing Indian maidens?"

"Minnehaha. Pocahontas. Sacajawea. Two hundred bucks a pop."

"But some of those aren't Shoshone," Chit said. "I remember them from cultural anthropology one-oh-one."

"Thanks for noticing," PJ said.

Brian shut the door of the spare bedroom. Chit and PJ were alone together. She could feel an awkward tension between them. She was attracted to him; she had never met anyone like him in the rarefied social circle of her father's diplomatic friends or among the kind of men who liked to go out with Mills College women. She knew he was drawn to her too.

"I knew your grandfather," PJ said.

"Strange," she said. "I hardly knew him at all. And now that he's gone I know him less than ever. I'm always finding out new things about him, terrible things that I can't reconcile with my memories."

Still gazing into each other's faces, still filled with a kind of wonder at their discovery of each other, they sat down on the sofa together, and Chit tried to pour him a cup of coffee. He smelled like the crushed herbs the cook used in her mother's kitchen. He was as earthy as she was ethereal. She spilled the coffee and they both laughed, a little nervously.

"I'm in kind of a state of shock or something, I guess," said PJ.

"I know. You just killed your best friend." She tried to imagine how that must feel. "I mean, he was already dead, but—"

"I *killed* him."

He seemed so forlorn that she could not help embracing him. Suddenly they were in each other's arms, devouring each other with a desperate passion she had never known in herself. If only her mother could see her now, she thought, consorting with one of *them,* a Red Indian no less, instead of keeping herself pure for a man of the correct social status! . . . But she hungered for him, she loved the little-boyness of him; she was excited by where he'd come from and what he'd experienced. He possessed, as her grandfather Prince Prathna would undoubtedly have phrased it, the "mysteries of the West." So powerfully did her emotions overwhelm her that she found herself in tears.

"Don't cry," said PJ. "You're kind of a special person."

She laughed, thinking to herself, He probably sees me as a kind of "mysteries of the East" thing himself.

"So much has happened," she said. "I went to see this medium, or whatever she is, and she showed me my grandfather transformed into a monster, trapped between worlds, in a place called Idaho, and now there are vampires everywhere and it's all because of a dead rock star I used to idolize when I was just a teenybopper myself. . . ."

"Yeah," he said. "It's hard to believe." He kissed her again. "You're hard to believe too." He smoothed back her hair, and she didn't even mind that he had unknowingly violated a social taboo of her culture.

The phone rang.

It was the operator: a call from Thailand. Chit found herself talking to her mother. It was almost as though her mother had been in telepathic contact with her and knew that she was about to yield to the advances of a person of the wrong social background. . . . *"Khun mae,"* Chit said, "are you calling about Grandfather?"

"Yes, *thun hua,"* said her mother. "I went to see our shaman earlier today. After she went into her trance, she told me that you'd seen the truth, that it was too horrible to contemplate . . . she went into convulsions . . . I had to have the chauffeur take her to Dr. Dickson's surgery."

"Mother, we're going have to do the exorcism in Idaho."

"Heavens . . . where is that?" *Khunying* Saluei, Chit's mother, affected the ignorance of American geography common to the British-educated.

"It's in the mountains," she said. "Mother, I think Grandfather's spirit is very troubled."

"I daresay it is," her mother said. She sounded distracted, distanced; perhaps it was just the fuzzy connection, or perhaps the *khunying* was really more concerned about the latest round of extravagant Bangkok parties than about the soul of her princely father-in-law. "Well, you'll take care of it, won't you? Hire the best exorcist you can find. We'll wire you the money."

"It's not that easy," Chit said. "Mother, you know they don't grow on trees here."

"Ah, those unenlightened Americans; even a major city only has one or two exorcists," her mother sighed. "How can they bear it? They live in the Dark Ages—no servants—why, they don't even have a king." Such sentiments were commonplace platitudes among the Thai aristocracy; Chit had been hearing them all her life. It was true that life was much more convenient in Thailand, where one never had to lift a finger to do anything; but Chit loved America. Here you could be anonymous. Here nobody judged you by who your parents were. She listened to her mother babbling on a while longer, and, as soon as was polite, reminded her mother that this was a long-distance call, and during peak hours, too.

"Heavens! I'd better get off," her mother said. "Give me a ring when it's taken care of, will you? We can't delay your grandfather's cremation much longer . . . people will talk."

"Yes, *khun mae.*"

"Oh, and that Viravong boy sent a marriage broker to see us last week; are you interested? They're part Chinese, unfortunately, but *very* well connected."

"Oh, don't worry, Mother; I'll find a husband in due course—*after* I graduate!"

After a few more pleasantries, she hung up the phone and noticed that PJ was still staring at her. He hadn't moved since the phone rang. "Jesus, you're beautiful," he said. "I wish I could paint you."

"Could I pass for an Indian maiden?" said Chit, laughing.

"A *ravishing* Indian maiden."

"God, I'm afraid. Do you think that your friend . . . that he made a lot of new . . . you know, that there are more of them out there now?"

PJ closed his eyes for a moment. He became utterly still. She had seen the family shaman do this before; when it happened, she would say that she had sent her soul on a journey, sometimes halfway around the world, to spy on some distant happening. Perhaps this was what he was doing now. She saw his lips move, as though he were speaking to someone far away.

At length he opened his eyes. He said, "Last night I was convinced he'd made more vampires. There were two, three, maybe four creatures out there . . . little blips of darkness . . ."

"It sounds like radar," she said.

"Yeah, it kind of is. But right now I don't feel anything. Maybe the sunlight killed them."

"Maybe."

She kissed him. They didn't make love; she was afraid Brian might come bursting out of the other bedroom, or the phone might ring again with some terrible new development. Although the California morning was streaming in through the windows that overlooked the mid-Wilshire district, the daylight could not dispel the foreboding she felt, the sickness in the pit of her stomach. *Maybe the sunlight killed them.* What if it hadn't?

She was convinced that the evil was bigger than PJ's dead friend, than her grandfather, maybe even than the vanished teenybopper idol Timmy Valentine. What they'd seen so far was just the warm-up act for the main attraction. They were gearing up for some kind of cosmic battle between the light and the darkness.

The terror of it made her tingle all over, but that tingling was also something akin to desire. She clung to PJ. Somehow he represented hope. She doubted he was the kind of shaman her mother had in mind, but he had known Prince Prathna before his metamorphosis.

He must have read her mind, because he said, "I don't do exorcisms."

She said, "Maybe I don't need a witch doctor who charges by the hour. Maybe I need a reluctant shaman."

"I'm reluctant," he said. "But every good shaman is reluctant. I could be the little shaman that could." And kissed her one more time.

MEMORY: 1600

For many years he has haunted the back alleys of the Eternal City. The city is rich in prey. It has been easy for him to hide in the squalor, in the shadows; like Caravaggio's chiaroscuro, it is a city where the bright places shine with the brilliance of the sun, and the dark places are utterly dark; where the marble still gleams on the walls of the Michelangelo's Basilica of Saint Peter, where prostitutes ply their trade in the shadow of the grime-crusted walls of the Colosseum, where the marble gleams no more.

He has had many names in the intervening years. Ercolino, Andrea, Sebastian, Gualtier, Orlando. He has lured countless travelers to their death, offering to show them the ruins of the Forum Romanum or Nero's Golden House, giving them instead surcease of feeling. He has been careful to kill cleanly and permanently. He needs no companions in the twilight world that he inhabits. He contemplates eternity alone.

One evening, strolling through the marketplace, he overhears the name Caravaggio. Pausing to listen to the chatter of apprentice artists, he realizes that the *Martyrdom of Saint Matthew* has finally been completed; that tomorrow it will be unveiled at the Chiesa di San Luigi die Francesi. It is not far from the market. He is seized by a need to see what has become of the painting, which he last saw blotched by the cardinal's wrath.

His form blurs, shimmers, condenses into the familiar black cat. He races through the alley. His senses are made keen by the nature of the animal; the smell of blood is heightened. In a doorway a wounded soldier is bleeding. Inside a seedy apartment, a girl is menstruating. A child trips, skins his knee against the cobblestones. All these give off the sensual scent of blood. There is time for that later. Tonight he must see what has happened to the angel of death.

He leaps; he springs; his feet pad softly on the stones; soon he is at the Palazzo Madama, across the street from the massive portals of the church. How well he remembers that place; it housed the studio where he drank the painter's blood. Soon he has made himself into a mist and is funneling through the keyhole into the house of God. Incense and candlelight. Stillness. And there is the painting, still draped, still unseen, in a side chapel dedicated by the Contarelli family.

He has become a cat again. He sidles up to the altar, insinuates himself through the wooden railings. The shadow of the great crucifix dances in the flames of a hundred novena candles. The pain is but a pinprick as he slips in and out of the crucifix's penumbra; he has become more and more inured to it, understanding now that even the devices of the divine are stained with corruption. He leaps onto the altar. There is as yet no altarpiece. The *Martyrdom* hangs on a lateral wall. He leaps again, he scurries down the nave, he crouches at the foot of Caravaggio's painting.

He is close to the drapery; he could perhaps whisk it away with a flick of his paws, or return to human shape and simply pull down the eleven-foot-square velvet covering. But before he can make up his mind, he hears footsteps on the stone floor, echoing; he slides into a fold of the drapery; torchlight fills the chamber. It is Cardinal del Monte. He has put on weight; he leans on the shoulder of a young man . . . Guglielmo.

He is glad Caravaggio is not with them.

Guglielmo has changed. Because he is a eunuch, he does not seem to have aged that much; but there is a deadness in his eyes, like that of one whose mind has been dulled by opiates. The vampire watches.

"Pull down the veil, Guglielmo! I want to see." The cardinal manages to stuff himself into a front pew. Guglielmo opens the railing and pulls aside the velvet.

At first the vampire sees nothing but a jumble. Light and darkness jigsaw across the eleven-foot-square canvas. Out of the kaleidoscope emerge faces, arms with taut musculature, wings, a plumed hat; all flicker in the candlelight; all seem in constant motion.

This is the *Martyrdom of Saint Matthew*. The angel of death no longer stands in the foreground, lit up in all his grim beauty. The painting is full of darkness. Where the angel once stood, a boy is recoiling from the scene of the saint's assassination. Here and there in the front stand naked penitents, readying themselves for baptism. There is an angel on a cloud above; the angel's face is hidden; he hands the dying saint the palm of martyrdom; all that can be seen of the angel is the crook of the arm, the taut curve of a buttock jutting from the obscure ether around the cloud, a boyish leg with its foot pointing skyward, perhaps to the face of God.

Where the woman was sitting, on the far left, there are now other figures. In the middle distance, peering from the gloom, is the face of Caravaggio himself, an observer, within yet perpetually outside the world he has created.

It is beautiful, the boy vampire thinks.

Cardinal del Monte is speaking to Guglielmo, who squats obsequiously at his feet. "That devil-child is gone from the picture now," he says. "Pity."

"Why, Your Eminence?" Guglielmo says.

"It was a pretty thing, and I like to come to churches in the middle of the night and gaze at these . . . divine manifestations of beauty and . . . enjoy their profane aspects. If you know what I mean."

Still in his feline shape, the vampire slithers from darkness to darkness along the cold stone floor of the *chiesa*. He sits in the cardinal's shadow. The cardinal has loosened his cassock and allowed his penis to rear up from the folds of red fabric. Mechanically, his eyes devoid of feeling, Guglielmo begins to fellate him. The cardinal gazes at the painting and sighs. "That devil-child—such a pretty thing, with such a fine voice; a pity. A pity. He could no doubt have been trained to perform your function, Guglielmo, and he might have put a little more ardor into it than you."

Guglielmo does not answer. The black cat peers into his eyes. He remembers it all now: how the young eunuch begged him to give him immortality, not understanding its dreadful consequences; how, thwarted in his plea, he told the cardinal stories of blood rites and devil worship; how they had parted, with the cardinal angrily defacing the canvas, with Guglielmo unable to look his old friend in the eye. . . . How low he has sunk now! the vampire thinks. He is an empty thing. His betrayal of me haunts him; it has made him into the cardinal's whore.

It is not so the much the casual sacrilege of it that

appalls him—is he not himself, after all, a sacrilegious thing to these people, a very concretization of the demonic?—but the vacuousness he sees in Guglielmo. It is as though he were already dead.

An uncontrollable anger rips through him. He cannot stop himself. He is changing from black cat to ferocious panther. He springs at the cardinal's throat. He claws his cheeks. He befouls the incense-laden air with his spoor. His hind paws strike Guglielmo in the chest and dislodge him, sending him reeling back against the neat rows of novena candles. Confused, Guglielmo tries to stem the blaze by throwing his cloak over the flames. They are plunged into darkness. The cardinal rises to his feet. His penis dangles flaccidly from his vestments as, making the sign of the cross, he cries out, *"Retro me, Satanas!* I adjure thee and conjure thee, spirit of darkness, to depart from this holy place!"

The vampire laughs bitterly. Through the larynx of the panther, the laugh becomes a roar. The cardinal slinks away toward the vestry. Should he pursue? Should he snuff out this bloated monster? The boy vampire feels only revulsion. The anger was a momentary thing; as it leaves him, he abandons the shape of rage and resolves into the form of the young boy once again.

"Guglielmo," he says softly.

"You came back!" the eunuch whispers. He turns to face him. He has retrieved his cloak from where the molten wax continues to burn a little. Once more there is candlelight, more subdued than before, throwing the chiaroscuro of the painting into even greater relief. "How I longed for you to come back," Guglielmo says. "I've hurt you, and it was only because of envy. I don't want to be immortal anymore. I only want to die."

"I can bring that about," says the boy who was once known as Ercolino, chorister in the Sistine Chapel. "If it's what you really want."

For a fleeting moment the deadness leaves Guglielmo's

eyes. He is remembering something; what, the boy vampire cannot fathom.

"Yes," he says at last, "I do want it."

He comes forward. He has become pitifully thin. He does not even possess a ghost of his old arrogance, his love of mischief and intrigue. Cardinal del Monte too is a vampire, the boy thinks. They are all vampires, these humans; they feed off one another in ways I cannot even conceive of. If I take his life, what will I give him? Freedom? Is there a hell beyond this hell? The boy vampire cannot know. To endure the torments of hell, it is necessary to have a soul; by his very nature, he is soulless.

Guglielmo loosens his ruff collar and tosses it against the railings. The boy vampire approaches him.

"I'm sorry," he tells him.

Guglielmo is weeping as the fangs, with a pitiless tenderness, pierce through his skin and into his jugular vein. The blood is sour; truly it is laced with opiates and other drugs to numb the awareness of life's bitterness. The boy drinks deep. Blood is blood. His body begins to tingle with the memory of having once lived. The color drains from Guglielmo's face. He grows limp and cold. The boy vampire lays him down upon the altar, beneath the glowering visage of a marble effigy of Saint Matthew.

Then he hears a voice from the shadows. "So it was not for me you came, angel of death," says Michelangelo da Caravaggio. He steps out from behind a stone pillar.

"Let me finish my work," he says softly. "I don't want him to awaken to eternal loneliness."

Gently, lovingly almost, he rips open the dead eunuch's chest and pulls out his still fibrillating heart. He licks a few last droplets from it as it grows still, and then he places it on the altar cloth, watching the red veins radiate outward from it. He breaks Guglielmo's neck for good measure. He does not want his friend to have to face what he has faced.

Then, wiping the blood from his lips, he turns to Caravaggio. "Thank you for removing me from the painting," he said. "I never belonged there."

"Ah, but I didn't remove you," says the painter. "Look." He points. "You are still there. I only concealed your face. In art, what is not seen is the most beautiful of all."

And the boy looks up, following the curve of the painter's hand, and he sees at last what he should have seen all along; the angel with his face concealed in shadow, leaning down from the sky to bestow on the saint the symbols of his martyrdom.

"There," Caravaggio says, "concealed in the shadow of the crook of your own arm, unreflected in the surface of the cloud, the perfection of your features only hinted at; there you are."

The candlelight flickers. The shadows dance. The shapes of dark and light seem to revolve, to flit across one another. There is life in the picture. Perhaps, in a moment, the angel will look up.

"No," says the boy vampire. "Until we see his face, he has no face. You only think he has my face because once, lost in the labyrinth of your own imagination, you saw me and thought me someone else."

It is true. The angel's face belongs to everyman now. Each man is free to picture it as a reflection of his own yearnings, his secret self. In that sense, it *is* my portrait, thinks the boy. In obeying the cardinal's forbiddance, he has painted me more truly than he himself can know.

"I must go now," he tells Caravaggio.

"Wait! Will you not—for old times' sake—a few quick drops of my blood?"

But the painter speaks to the empty air. Only the art remains.

In the distance, the painter can hear a soft voice, inhumanly sweet and pure, soaring above the music of night: *Miserere mei, miserere mei.*

Only the art . . .

ILLUSION AND REALITY

In her private inner chamber, surrounded by thousands of scented candles, Simone Arleta watched Damien's sermon gleefully on the pop-up television window of her Macintosh computer. Seeing Damien this way—a little man in a two-inch square, surrounded by her occult computations with their dozens of astrological figures, alchemical symbols, and arcane formulae—really cut him down to size.

The man's hypocrisy was so deliciously outrageous that it had the quality of an Andy Warhol Campbell's soup can painting. How clever of him to exploit the image of Timmy Valentine—at once calling him the devil incarnate and using his sex appeal to bring in cash!—and Timmy Valentine was a subject so close to all their hearts.

"Jacques!" she cried out in the empty room. "Get me Damien Peters on the telephone."

A minute later: "Damn it, woman, I can't make it out there till Friday. Can't it wait?"

Simone smiled. "Damien," she said, with venomous sweetness, "you want to be powerful again, don't you? You are in league with me, aren't you? With me, the conduit of the forces of Satan?" She giggled a little, wondering if he felt any discomfiture at her casual invoking of the Adversary's thrice-cursed name. "Well, there is a plan now, and I want your cooperation."

"Count me in."

"The Gods of Chaos are to be reconstituted. The only member that survives—in a manner of speaking—is Prince Prathna, who has turned into some kind of Oriental demon; not surprising, considering what he was playing with when he died. The Gods of Chaos were a bunch of silly, decadent old people who were pursuing something a lot bigger than they could handle . . . the soul that is my prisoner, the source of my power. They knew nothing about the dark forces that control the universe; they were amateurs. But my captive is getting away, Damien Peters—do you understand?—Timmy Valentine is seeking to reconstitute himself in the concrete world—to make himself flesh!—as though he were the word of God."

"Of Satan!" Damien growled, so loudly that the speakerphone crackled with distortion.

"You yourself helped him a little today by showing him in your sermon. Don't you know that every time his name is uttered, every time his image appears in the mind of one of those mindless fans, he gets a little bit more real, he slips a little bit from my grasp? You fool."

"Well, I don't know nothing about how this mumbo jumbo of yours works."

"Time you learned, Damien."

"So what can I do for you?" said Damien, and she could sense his anxiety. He knew she was his ticket to whatever it was he wanted—some bizarre kind of world domination, no doubt!—men were always the same, when they became power-hungry they metamorphosed into little Hitlers, every one of them.

"Timmy is rapidly reaching the apex of his charismatic power. There's a big studio picture planned. People will be reading about it, watching it on television, thinking all the time, *Timmy Timmy Timmy,* and a boy is going to take on all his attributes, absorb him into himself . . . become him. It is the Holy Incarnation, you see, all over again."

"The Antichrist!" said Damien. There was a certain relish in his voice. He was already smelling the money.

"Paradoxically, Damien—his moment of greatest power—the moment when I have the highest risk of losing him—is also the moment when we are most likely to be able to recapture him, chain him once more, control him—regain all our sources of power—redouble them!"

The two-inch image of Damien raised his arms in benediction. It was the heal-a-thon, taped an hour or so before. A line of cripples, cancer victims, epileptics and leprous suppliants had formed as the camera pulled back. The diseased were not actually in the same shot as Damien, of course; they were in another studio altogether, and seemed to be in the same cathedral only through the magic of chroma key. The medium of healing was a television image. Why not? she thought. Image *is* truth. That is the very root of sympathetic magic.

On the phone, the aural image of Damien Peters was far from the Apollonian healer of the video. "Fuck, fuck, and double motherfucking fuck," said the world's saintliest television preacher. "Will it work? We have to make it work."

"With the latest Playboy bunny scandal about to hit the news, with the IRS breathing down your neck, I would very much agree with you," she said.

"Whore!"

"My, my, Damien, the pot is certainly calling the kettle black today."

Damien sputtered.

"Get on that Learjet, Damien. You may think that the center of the world is Hangman's Holler, Kentucky, but it's not. It's not even Washington, or New York, the Vatican, or even Jerusalem. That's not where the great battle for the possession of the world is going to be fought." She chose her words with great care, for the carrot had to be just right for this particular donkey. "Soon, the center is going to move to a burnt-out ghost down in a remote part of Idaho."

"A ghost town in Idaho? Are you out of your cotton-picking . . . What town?"

VISION SEEKER

And they made love, as Petra knew they would, with an urgency that was almost like pain; they made love the way they had not done in the brief days of their old relationship; they made love laughing, shrieking, once coming close to tears. Their lovemaking was an end and a beginning. She knew now that the nightmares that had been with her since Jason's suicide would one day be exorcised. She knew also that with today's dawn a new nightmare had been born.

The phone rang.

"Let it ring," she said, and kissed Brian one more time. "It's not our phone anyway."

"I thought you'd had your calls forwarded."

"Who'd call?"

"Who knows?"

They started to make love again, but presently there came a light tapping at the door and Chit's voice: "Petra . . . it's Angel Todd."

She picked up the bedroom phone then. This was it, the beginning of the nightmare. She could feel her heartbeat pounding. Her head, too. If only she could find another Advil in her purse.

"Petra . . . my agent says I need a publicist. We're going on location in a week. Can you come?"

"Location?"

"Jesus, Petra, I need you. My mother . . . she does bad things to me . . . I can't think straight . . . I can't talk about it over the phone, but . . . but . . . God, I need you."

The things Jason had never said to her.

Brian sat up now. She felt his hands around her waist. He cupped one of her breasts in one hand and kissed it. The unshaved whiskers stung her a little. She moaned.

"Petra . . ."

She wanted to say to the kid, You have something I need, too—I need to feel that there is a child who needs me, who doesn't want to throw away my love. . . . "I don't know," she said slowly, but she couldn't get her voice to sound noncommittal.

"Is it that friend of yours, that guy I saw sitting with you in the theater last night? You could bring him with you. I ain't the jealous type." The boy laughed; through the laughter she sensed his insecurity.

"Where's the location?" she asked him. There was Brian's war to think of, the battle against the vampires. She didn't want to abandon Brian, although she was still having trouble believing his version of the Timmy Valentine story.

"Oh, they want to shoot in the place where Timmy was last seen," said Angel. "They've gone and bought the whole town. It was cheap, too—it's been abandoned."

"The whole town?"

"Yeah. It's a place called . . ." The boy paused for a moment. But Brian, listening over her shoulder, was already mouthing the name of the town to her.

SHAMANESS

"Junction," said Simone Arleta.

DISSOLVE

"Junction?" said Lady Chit.

DISSOLVE

"Junction," Angel said, hanging up the phone.

PART TWO

❬ ❬ ❬ ❬ ❬ ❬

JUNCTION

Y la luz que se iba dió una broma.
Separó al niño loco de su sombra.

Departing, jesting, the light
Parted the mad little boy
from his shadow.

LORCA

8

MORE IMPRESSIONS

MOSAIC STONES

Sissy Robinson, age 12:
So like the next time I see him it's on TV and it seems like he's always belonged there. The *unrealness* of him when I saw him step out of the elevator at the lobby of the Sheraton Universal, well that's like gone. He's totally real now.

But I still love him.

Jonathan Burr, director:
I think that the idea of method acting can also be extended to the process of directing, you see. You might say that I'm a "method" director. That's why I made the decision to take everything, lock, stock, and barrel, to what's left of the town of Junction, Idaho. I wanted to see the new Timmy Valentine against the wreckage of the old. I wanted to blur the interface between reality and illusion. Which is what the cinema means to me anyway.

The boy we hired to play Timmy Valentine really went

for my way of looking at things. Jesus, he was so real he scared me shitless sometimes. But what could I do? You have to go with the flow. And if *you're* not prepared to be scared, how can you demand it of your audience?

Not that *Valentine* is supposed to be a horror movie, you understand. But Timmy's life is scary. His death is scary. We made up the death, of course. Timmy Valentine isn't known to have died. But in the world of illusion, in the fragile false reality that we have to put up on the screen for two short hours, we must have a beginning, a middle, and an end. I think you'll like the way we kill him. It has a bittersweet quality. It's very nineties. Yes, it is has the sensitivity of the sixties, but it also has the cynicism of the eighties. That's what nineties-ness means to me. Yes, you'll like the way he dies and you'll wish that life could imitate art so neatly and so seamlessly.

But we don't know that he died at all, of course. Nothing is known about him at all after the blaze that burned down Junction, Idaho. In fact, we sent an invitation to him to attend the première, care of his agent, care of his estate, which is run by someone named Rudy Lydick, an ancient old Polish man—Auschwitz survivor—an enigma. He won't say why he's the executor.

Angel Todd really took to it all. It was as if he was born to play Timmy Valentine, even though we had to change his hair and work on his hillbilly accent. When the transformation was complete, his own mother wouldn't have been able to tell the difference.

Well, that's not really saying very much. Angel's mother floated in a Valium-induced fog. Pretty tragic really. Kid had so much going for him. She was the domineering type. Mrs. Bates in spades. Creepy. They used to sleep in the same bed together. There's a lot of juicier stuff than that, too, but I don't think I should allow you to quote me. After all, this is a very litigious business.

I've already said too much.

PJ Gallagher, artist; Native American activist:
Brian, Petra, they'd all seen him in Los Angeles, but I didn't lay eyes on him until I was back in Junction. Seeing him brought back all the confusion I'd felt when I was a boy. I began to doubt my own visions. That's how powerful he was. I knew that he was more than Angel Todd, a kid who'd won a look-alike contest and was starring in a movie that exploited the myth of Timmy Valentine. Somehow, Timmy had managed to possess him.

Somehow, he had become Timmy Valentine.

I knew no one would believe me, but it was the only explanation for everything that followed.

But how does one person turn into another? Stranger yet, how does one person change into a creature who's seen more as a myth than as someone real? I should know the answer to that. I've been through the vision quest and I've become another person. I am always in the process of becoming another person. Even though I don't want to. Personhood is an illusion. We shift in and out like shadows trying to gain substance, but shadows are all we can ever be. Only in the dream world can things be called by their true names. Only behind the mirror can we confront our real selves, without illusion.

This is what my visions have told me. This is what my heart tells me.

Petra Shiloh, journalist:
The studio treated us like lower-class camp followers. They didn't answer our calls. They didn't want us. But they did what Angel told them. He had become a star.

It was changing him.

Gabriela Muñoz, agent:
It was really the day after the television special that I realized that I was onto something really big, bigger than

I'd ever dreamed. First the mother shows up at my office in tears. She's going on about witchcraft and satanism and magic mirrors and making wild accusations about her son making a pact with the demonic spirit of Timmy Valentine.

Maybe she had a bad dream or something. Anyone would after seeing that Simone Arleta woman going through that fucking special effects extravaganza last night. That sure took all of us by surprise.

She's a borderline schizo or something, I'm convinced of it. You know those sordid allegations that were made about Elvis and his mother? You know, in that biography by . . . oh, I don't remember. Didn't really believe it about Elvis, but you could fucking believe it about Mrs. Todd. And it's not just the way she talks, straight out of "The Beverly Hillbillies" . . . she's *disturbing,* man. Takes too many pills, too. Pink bills, blue pills, striped pills, dotted pills. So now she has a paranoid delusion that her kid's in league with the devil.

I've had a *lot* of experience with child stars, okay? and I know it's just the usual adolescent hormones and the inevitable snipping of the apron strings. But I wasn't going to tell her that. No way.

Feed the delusion.

Gain power.

Jonathan Burr:
That mother of his is insane. I would keep her off the set if she weren't the designated guardian.

Gabriela Muñoz:
My first move is going to be to get someone else designated as the set guardian. I have to pry him loose. Maybe that Shiloh woman . . . he sees her as a kind of surrogate mother.

Brian Zottoli:

PJ promises that the vampire problem in Los Angeles has abated for now. He's traveled the streets in some kind of astral body projection thing and he doesn't get vampire vibes anymore.

I don't know whether to believe him, but we're talking an Alice-in-Wonderland world where *anything* can happen. The rules have a kind of logic but it's the logic of a bad dream. So I'll accept that and I'll agree with him that the next step is to go back to Junction.

Back to where we left off.

Back to the past.

Timmy Valentine:

I'm standing at the mirror's edge. The mirror is the boundary. Angel is on the other side, looking at me. He's not afraid of me. He is the only one who knows I am not his dark self. Not yet at least. In time, we could become each other.

He is as beautiful as I once was.

He is the Angel of Life.

9

HELL OR HIGHWATER

❧ ❧

DISSOLVE: LOBBY

Highwater, Idaho: the Highwater Inn was a dilapidated high rise in a high-altitude city, a hotel that had been owned by Hyatt, by Hilton, by Ramada, by just about every one of the big chains before being found unprofitable by all of them. Shannon Beets was lucky to have kept her job after the last big takeover. It was one of the only places in town where anything ever happened. One of the only places in the whole county, truth to tell. It was either the hotel, get married, or ship out to the big city . . . to Boise, anyway, which passed for a big city she guessed.

Summer was about started. It was a couple of weeks after Memorial Day when things really started happening. The circus came to town.

Well, not the circus, exactly, but even weirder—*Holly*-weirder to be exact—the location shoot for that Timmy Valentine movie. Course, the location manager and some crew had been there all spring, building the sets, driving down to Junction to scout out exteriors. But the excitement didn't start until the stars showed up, of course. Shannon and her friends'd been talking about it all through April and May.

She wanted to make sure she was at the reception desk when that Angel Todd kid showed up. She'd circled the date in her calendar, traded shifts with crabby old Verna Holbein, and she'd spent an extra hour putting on her makeup that morning. Everybody'd noticed and teased her about it. But she didn't care.

Only Angel didn't show up at the scheduled time. Nobody showed up at all. Oh, there was the director of photography storming through the lobby in a huff, cussing and smoking up a storm. There was an associate producer walking around taking notes in a legal pad. All sorts of production assistants running around . . . it didn't take Shannon long to realize that their job was really no different from hers, a kind of glorified gofer.

There hadn't been this much bustle in Highwater since the day Junction burned to the ground. And Shannon'd been just a girl then. Daddy was still alive in those days.

She liked the commotion. She wondered what it was like where these people came from. They didn't talk like normal people, didn't dress like them, didn't think like them at all. The questions they'd ask at the reception desk weren't normal kinds of questions. Like where to get a nice meal at two in the morning. Like where could you find a gay bar. (The way they asked, it might just as well have been where you could find the nearest church.) Like where you could find decent snow. The last one seemed obvious until she figured it was the kind of snow that came in small packets, like Sweet'n Low. They talked about colonic cleansing and gerbil sex and other exotic practices which Shannon didn't even want to think about. She was sure they were sins. Mortals sins at that. She didn't know there were so many sins she hadn't heard of before. She wondered if these people were all going straight to hell, like Damien Peters claimed in his daily "Hour of Heavenly Love." Sheesh, what would Mom have said about people like this?

Still, they didn't mind paying a dollar for a can of pop (the management had jacked up the price on the pop machines a week before they were slated to arrive) and they tipped very well. The director, Mr. Burr, even gave her ten bucks just for calling the bell captain over to take care of the luggage. Seedy-looking guy, sunglasses, hair pointing every which way, and an earring in the shape of a dangling dick. Hard to believe he was anything but a punk, until you saw his credit card, his Rolex, and his wad of C notes. Lord, *that* made her eyes pop out of her head.

She'd wangled the night shift because the stars were supposed to be coming in at two in the morning. At one or so, the lobby was still full of people—they were like vampires—they loved the night. The manager gave the kitchen staff time and a half. They totally cleaned up because the nearest other places to eat in the middle of the night were a Denny's in the next town and a truck stop forty-five miles away.

At one-thirty, a call came in saying there'd been a day's delay. Don't bother to cancel the rooms. They were all paid for anyway.

She couldn't conceal her disappointment. She'd told all her friends she'd be catching a glimpse of the stars, maybe even get their autographs, even if only on a credit card slip. She put down the phone—she was the only one at the desk—and turned to sorting a stack of preregistration cards. They didn't even have a computer at this hotel. They didn't even have one of those Visa card authorizing machines. Sheesh, they were so darn primitive sometimes it embarrassed her.

Shannon sat back down. She picked at a tear in the vinyl of her seat and gulped down half a cup of black coffee. Should never have taken the dark graveyard shift, she told herself.

Getting on toward three, the lobby was emptying finally. Shannon suddenly realized she was alone. She looked up from the desk and saw herself reflected a dozen times over in the mirror-lined walls. She wished it weren't so bright. The coffee was cold but she couldn't leave the desk to get a fresh cup because there'd be no one to watch the lobby. Everyone else on duty was up in the control room changing the Muzak tapes because the manager had this idea that for the duration of shooting they'd turn off the easy listening and run a continuous tape of all Timmy Valentine's old albums. They were having some trouble with the machinery—the Muzak man was a three-hour drive away, so they were trying to mess with it themselves—and so there was an eerie silence in the lobby. In the glaring light she felt unnerved, exposed. She poured the rest of the coffee down her throat. It was cold and sour-tasting and didn't make her feel any more awake.

"Shannon."

Must've dozed off. Someone's hands on the counter, clasping hers . . . rough hands. She blinked, saw slender pale fingers and chewed fingernails.

"Shannon Beets. I never thought I'd see you again."

"PJ?"

It *was* him. He was a lot taller now but he still had that long, dark hair, Indian hair crowning an Irish face. She'd known him only briefly in her sophomore year at Highwater High.

"Glad you didn't forget me, Shannon."

How could she forget? He had popped her cherry.

Now he stood there wearing a tailored suit, with an Oriental girl on his arm, the kind of woman you had to look twice at before you'd believe she was real, like a Dresden china doll. She'd heard that PJ had moved to Hollywood, after going through a bunch of weird rituals

on the reservation, and that he was some kind of artist—
but weren't all artists funny bunnies? Her mother had
always said there was somethng wrong with a man who
wanted to be an artist—but he sure didn't look like a
funny bunny now. He was handsome. The way he smiled
was something special. The way the corners of his eyes
crinkled up. Shannon was so jealous of the Oriental girl
that she couldn't speak for a moment. Those clothes!
They were plain, but even a country girl could tell they
cost hundreds of dollars.

"This is Premchitra," PJ said. "We've got a reservation."

Shannon's hand was trembling as she got out the stack
of file cards. She couldn't find anything under Gallagher.

"We're with the movie," PJ said softly.

"Holy Mother of God," Shannon said. "Who'd have
ever thought it?"

"Well, it's kind of a long story. I had a friend who had
a friend, and well, *his* friend found out I knew this area
and that I'd once had an encounter with . . . with, you
know."

As if to underscore his words, the music kicked in.
There was a lot of wow on the tape, but the song was so
familiar she could've almost sung it herself:

> I'm scared to sleep alone
> It chills me to the bone
> The coffin's big, I'm just a kid,
> Too young to sleep alone

A wry smile played on the Oriental girl's lips. *"Sleeping Alone,"* she whispered. It was the name of Timmy
Valentine's first album.

Shannon got out the special reservations folder and
found PJ's name quickly enough. Strange she'd never
noticed it before. "Oh, you're in the Queen Elizabeth

suite," she said. The half-breed sophomore from High-water High was certainly coming home in style. "Look, the bell captain's not here, you might have to take your stuff up to the suite yourself . . . you don't have to show me your credit card, it's prepaid."

"Let's just—" the Oriental girl began.

"I think I'll—" PJ said.

They looked at each other and laughed. They seemed nervous.

"Look, Shannon," he said at least. "We're just gonna leave our shit by the bell captain's desk. We want to take a quick drive on up to Junction."

"You mean right now? At three A.M.?"

The girl made an impatient gesture. They both seemed driven, desperate somehow. I guess it's true what they say, Shannon thought, all that glamour doesn't make you happy.

In fact, those clothes of his look kind of too new. And his eyes are haunted. He stares past you, like he's looking right through you into something you can't even see, something scary.

That time in the drive-in back in high school, looking up from the back seat of Herb Philpotts's Mustang where they were squashed together against two bags of grocer-ies and she had her jeans peeled down to her ankles and she could feel the chafing parachute silk of his brand-new pants against her thighs and then he finally did it and she let out a kind of whimper because it hurt more than she thought it would because she wasn't quite wet enough yet and she closed her eyes and tried to relax feeling him fill her up and then opening her eyes and seeing his eyes, yes, just like they were now, staring, staring, as though he wasn't even there. . . .

"Shannon?"

"Uh. Yeah. Sure. Sign this card, sir." She slid it across the reception desk with an automatic hand. God it was strange to see him. It was like reality was slipping away.

He touched her hand again. "Gotta go." Smiled that curiously forlorn smile, whispered for her alone, "I haven't forgotten."

Then he went out into the night with the Oriental girl, with a black backpack slung over his shoulder. A couple more hours and Shannon could crawl into bed, in time to see her mother creep away to morning mass. . . .

She started to nod off again.

Was she dreaming? She was staring at her face in the mirror. The mirror across the lobby. Between her and her reflection, a potted fig tree in a *faux* Ming dynasty planter. Me. Myself. A girl who's going to go nowhere. Look at me. Cheap makeup. Who'd I think I was going to impress? A girl who dropped out in her junior year, a girl with no talents; did I really think I was going to sit here at the reception desk of a third-rate hotel and snare me a Hollywood movie star?

The image looked back at herself. I'm kind of pretty, she thought. It's about all I got going for me. A pretty girl with a too-too Catholic mother. But my eyes are nice. Blue as the sky on a clear winter's day, like the day that Junction burned down.

Tears ran down the mirror-Shannon's cheeks. Tears of blood. Blood! And she was aging. Wrinkles breaking out. Burrowing like groundhogs, tearing up the skin, age spots, mottled patches of discoloration, blood torrents popping up from volcanic pimples—

I'm dreaming! she thought—

The mirror shattered! Behind the mirror . . . fire . . . fire . . . the Junction town hall crashing into the snow . . . a woman on fire rolling down the slick iced downhill street toward the town's lone stop sign . . . but I don't remember this, I wasn't in Junction that night, I was sleeping in my bed in Highwater listening to "The Star-Spangled Banner" as Channel 17 faded away after Damien Peters's sermonette . . . wasn't I? Or was I with Dad?

And suddenly she remembered Dad's funeral.

In the snow.

It was all there. Behind the broken mirror. Monsters out of the past.

Daddy! she cried out.

They were lowering him into the earth.

Ashes to ashes . . .

Her face was an aged woman's face. Splintering. The mirror cracking in slow motion with chalk-on-blackboard screeching. Blood welled up from empty eye sockets. Maggots crawled from dead nostrils. Nausea seized her.

She screamed again, screamed with the taste of old coffee in her throat, screamed as the angel voice of Timmy Valentine crescendoed over hidden speakers.

The illusion faded.

The potted fig tree trembled. Someone had opened the front door and let in the night wind. A man and a woman. She was draped in a sable coat and her eyes were framed in mascara. She was old. The man wore a camel-hair overcoat. They both looked familiar. She'd seen them before somewhere. They were actors maybe. She was sure it had something to do with television.

Paul had come back down from the control room and was helping with their luggage. There was another man standing behind them: weasel-eyed, dark-haired, thin-lipped; she could tell that he was some kind of underling.

Her throat felt raw. She must really have screamed, but if she did, no one seemed to have noticed. She was disoriented, drifting in and out. It was more than just lack of sleep. There was something in the air. When you looked at that old woman's eyes you could sense it.

Those eyes . . . "Do you have a reservation, ma'am?" She assumed they must be with the movie people.

"We don't need reservations."

Those eyes . . .

"Ma'am—" A credit card was being dropped onto the desk. But she couldn't read the name. It was all blurry.

It was a gold card. She picked it up. Heavy. Like *solid* gold. The Visa hologram spinning above the churning sea of gold light. "Oh," Shannon said, "I see."

What was that noise? A croaking frog?

"Sign here."

Croaking . . . croaking . . . there was something reptilian about the woman's face . . . "You're doing very well, my dear. Jacques will take care of the rest. Now, if you'll just hold on to the illusion until we've checked into our room . . ."

"It's a sin . . ." she murmured. *What* was a sin?

"The Lord forgives all sins," said the man in the camel-hair coat. That voice was so familiar! Deep, liquid, resonant . . . as from the altar of a cathedral . . . as from a cave behind a rushing waterfall . . . she *knew* that voice. It was someone she could trust. A friend.

The party drifted toward the elevators. The croaking of frogs poured out of the PA system. Battered at her eardrums. Cacophony. Madness.

She looked at the signature card. The signature was illegible. She wondered what letter she was going to file it under.

MONSTER

Off the Highwater state highway, which wasn't much of a road to start off with, a winding uphill road, barely wide enough for two cars, not completely paved in places. A sign read:

JUNCTION—27 MILES

but underneath it someone had scrawled the words:

blood doners well cum

PJ drove steadily. He thought he'd never have to drive this road again, but the memory of it was still in his fingers. "Bump coming up," he said. There was a full moon. The road was lined with conifers and the moonlight made the needle clusters glimmer like tarnishing silver. He and Lady Chit didn't talk much.

It was hard to believe everything that had happened in the last month. Angel Todd insisting that Petra be brought on board as publicity director. Petra insisting on Brian's involvement as a creative consultant because of his knowledge of Timmy Valentine. Brian bringing PJ on board as a local expert. Suddenly they were all out of debt.

PJ did not believe in coincidences. He had lived too close to the edge of the supernatural world to believe that things ever happened by chance. The world was a mirror of the greater world. Events were moving toward some cosmic confrontation. The world was out of kilter; there would have to be a great wrenching before the light and the dark were brought back into balance. Once more the world would reenact the story of the first *ma'aipots,* the sacred man-woman who was all possibilities in one.

"Are you scared?" he asked Lady Chit.

"Should I be?" she said. She was masking some profound inner emotion; he knew that her people thought it improper to make a public display of their feelings.

"You should be a little bit afraid, Chit. But the spirit still has something of your grandfather in him. I doubt that he would harm you."

In the backpack in the backseat of the car were the tools for this ecumenical exorcism: the medicine pouch that he had possessed ever since his vision quest; an image of the Buddha to turn the cursed prince back toward the eightfold path and the cycle of karma; holy water and crucifixes in case there were vampires still present.

He drove in silence. Presently he became aware of

Chit's hand on his shoulder. Though her face was still an image of utmost serenity, the hand trembled as though palsied.

He looked in the rearview mirror. Two lights, golden, slitty, like the eyes of a mountain lion.

What would anyone be doing driving to Junction at three in the morning? The set construction crew were all on days. Filming was still a week off. There was nothing left in Junction but hulks. He shifted into second as the way grew steeper. There was a turnoff that led down to Dead Dog Creek, but the car behind didn't take it. They were about a car length behind. And honking. Like they had to get somewhere fast. It made PJ nervous, but he didn't want to get Chit even more upset than she was now. He gunned the accelerator and downshifted.

Rounding a curve. Didn't see them for a mile or so. Then they were there again. He could make out license plates. California. Why am I so worried? It's irrational. But there was something there. A disturbance in the psychic balance. He didn't know if it was just the turbulent aura that still hung over Junction or whether it radiated from the car behind.

"You look fidgety all of a sudden," Chit said.

"I'm beginning to think we're being followed."

Without any warning, they were in fog.

"Don't worry," he said, more to calm himself than her, "I know this road like the back of my hand."

He couldn't see a thing. The headlights illuminated a few feet of road stripes, then oblivion. The mist kept rolling in. Something wasn't right about the mist. It was tinged with red. As though it were blood, condensing out of the night air. PJ thought: We are in the visionary realm now. Somehow we've sidestepped the road and gone straight into the dream country. I don't know how it happened. I haven't been fasting and I haven't been doing peyote or shrooms. And I've never gone there with another person before.

He glanced at Chit, who had moved closer to him in the front seat. Yes. She was seeing what he was seeing all right.

In the rearview mirror, the cougar-car still followed. It was losing its hard metallic lines now. Its fenders were pulsing with animal musculature. Its headlights were definitely eyes. It was bounding uphill. There were fangs where the grille would have been.

Chit could sense his unease, he knew. He jammed his foot down on the accelerator. The mountain lion was not his totem. It was an interloper in the dream world. It was a sending from an adversary.

"Hold on tight. Someone's following us. Don't look back, Chit."

He should never have said that. Instinctively she turned. "It's a panther or something," she said. "They don't have panthers in Idaho, do they?"

"Don't look. This is dream country. The territory of the soul. Just look straight ahead. It's safer. Otherwise you might see . . . the thing you fear most."

Lady Chit screamed.

"Don't look!" He reached across and shielded her eyes. It was impossible to imagine what she had seen. We all have our own secret terrors. Better to keep his eye on the tiny strip of road ahead and—

The mountain lion leapt! A dark flash and a thudding crunch on the roof and then the crack of buckling steel and—

Chit said, "I'm all right now. I'm telling myself it's not real."

Car was skidding now, veering to the right where sheer mountain plummeted into pine forest and—

Chit's face, set into that expression of timeless serenity and—

Faces in the fog. Dark spirits. The Corn Woman cradling the World Serpent in her arms.

In the air now. No road. The cow jumped over the

moon. Somersaulting, the mountain lion over the rent-a-car, fireballs whirling through dull space. In the fog, Timmy Valentine stood with his arms outstretched, his lips slightly parted, about to receive the breath of life, and then—

Stillness.

The fog had dissipated as suddenly as it had come.

The car had plowed full tilt into a tree trunk. Branches crisscrossed the windshield. Moonlight streamed in from a cloudless sky.

Chit opened her eyes. It seemed to PJ that she was awakening from a dream. "I saw my grandfather," she said softly. "He was snaking his way along the forest floor. Something's calling to him."

"Yes." He didn't want to tell her it was something so powerful and single-minded it had driven them off the road. "Someone else knows about your grandfather . . . wants him for some reason . . . but who else is there who knows about him?"

"Only my family. And the medium, Simone Arleta."

"Simone . . ."

"Yes. She was the one who first showed him to me. At a séance."

SHAMANESS

"Slow down now, Damien. We've overtaken them."

"What did you do to them?"

"Never you mind."

The fog cleared all at once. They were parked on a ledge just off the mountain road, overlooking what had once been the town of Junction. Deep forest was not far off. They started to get out of the car.

"Now listen, Simone, if you'd just stop the hocus-pocus for a moment to tell me what the hell's going on—"

"They were after what we're after. Now they've been delayed. By the time they get here it'll be too late."

Rev. Damien Peters unloaded his leather Samsonite suitcase from the trunk and rooted around for his church vestments. It wasn't too hard to see because the moon was full. The air was crisp and cold and you could hear an owl hooting somewhere. Just below them, where Junction began, were the burnt-out hulks of houses, a cemetery, a church and, farther downhill, ugly, rectangular concrete structures that housed the interior sets the movie people had been putting up all month. He took out the dark blue cassock blazoned with the insignia of universal love, designed by his ex-wife in the days when they were still a team, working on figuring out the most lucrative religion to throw in with. It had an ecumenical look, as did the surplice and stole he wore over it, owing a little to every major denomination. It was his deliberately noncommittal attitude to certain issues of dogma that had allowed him to steal as many converts away from the mainline churches as those rah-rah fundamentalists.

In the moonlight, Damien Peters admired himself in a hand mirror, almost as though he were about to go on the air. After all, there was always an audience. God is everywhere, he sighed to himself. Just look at those blazing stars and you know there's a divinity of some kind. What kind exactly, Damien would rather not have contemplated.

That moonlight with its blood-tinged halo put him in mind of the Book of Revelation, which says that the moon will be as blood.

Jacques was now opening one of the witch woman's magic trunks. It was big and painted with suns, moons and cabalistic sigils. He began to dress his mistress in a series of increasingly gaudy robes, each one fitting neatly over the other like those dolls-within-dolls they sell in third-world souvenir shops. Simone stood uncomplaining as she was dressed, her face indecipherable. He had to admit that her sense of the theater was as good as his own, better even perhaps. But why, indeed, were they bothering with theater, out here, with only God for an audience? He was about to frame the question when she answered it for him.

"Damien, Damien," she said. "You've served Mammon so long that you've lost your way. You don't even really believe in the forces of light and darkness, do you?"

He had no answer. He thought he'd come to an accommodation with faith, and lack of faith, long ago. Faith, after all, was a gift. If the Lord had not seen fit to give him this gift, what use was it to try to attain it by mortal means? He had not always doubted.

"Nevertheless, Damien, you must believe me when I say that there is a being out here, and that tonight we must trap that being and make it serve our purposes. The being was once known as Prince Prathna. He was, apparently, killed when an attractive female vampire bit off his penis and drained his blood. He has now become a *phii krasue,* a monstrous apparition trapped between lives, unable, because of the circumstances of his death, to be properly reborn in the world of men."

"You believe this bullcrap, Simone?"

"I have seen it."

"But not really. In some visionary trance, maybe . . . but not . . . in the flesh, as it were."

"As you wish," Simone said. "Now, did you do the thing I asked you to do earlier? Bring me the jar."

Damien shrugged, then got the mason jar out of the suitcase. As he'd been instructed to do, he had defecated in it earlier and sealed the jar with his left hand, murmuring a ritual formula. "I feel like a fool," he said, "clambering around on mountaintops in the middle of the night, shitting in jars, consorting with witches."

"Just hand me the jar. *Phii krasues* live on human ordure. There is an imprinting process, you see. It has something you want . . . you have something it wants. Black magic does not turn its back on bodily functions and excretions the way your into-denial eat-my-body Christian rituals do."

She strode toward him and seized the jar. The wind made his vestments flap in his face. "This creature we are about to trap," she continued, "died while hunting down Timmy Valentine. Do you understand that? Its humanity is gone. All that remains is its rage. Its rage must be put under your control, and for that you must feed that rage. Ergo, shitting in jars." The theory was outlandish, yet she acted as though she were explaining the ABCs to a small child. He could feel the absurdity of it, but in her eyes he could detect no sense of humor about all this at all. Only a kind of madness. In the bloody moonlight her eyes glittered.

"Still, it goes against everything we know about the afterlife that—" he began, but she interrupted him with a peal of witchlike laughter.

"When will you people ever learn," she said, "to tell the difference between reality and metaphor? Do you think we can truly understand the supernatural world on our own terms? What nonsense. We all carry our own cultures with us, you know, even beyond the grave. Shit-eating monsters, vampires, even your own angels and demons—all these things are spun from the fabric of our own unconscious, are they not? Or will you accuse me of the heresy of secular humanism?"

The wind sighed. Twigs and pinecones skittered past.

Simone drew a circle on the ground with quicklime. She wrote the four letters of the unspeakable name of God,   , around the circle, and inscribed a pentagram within it.

"Blasphemy," Damien murmured. She ignored him, but presently Jacques directed him into a spot in the magic circle with a perfunctory wave, like an usher at a concert. When he started to say something, Jacques put a finger to his lips. He then placed a paper crown on his head and stepped into his own designated place.

All the while, Simone mumbled to herself, nonsense words of which Damien could only catch one or two. It was much like speaking in tongues, he thought to himself. Her voice crescendoed and the wind began to die. Presently there came fingers of blood-tinged mist, tendriling toward them from the forest depths. Damien became aware of a presence . . . it was akin to the feeling he'd had as a child, in church, touched by the power of the Lord . . . but there was an obscene quality to this manifestation. His arms and legs began to tingle. There were words in the whispering of the wind. The wind smelled like an unflushed toilet. He wrapped the sleeve of his surplice around his nose but the wind battered at his face. What were the words that the wind was whispering? *Shit shit shit shit motherfucking shit shit shit.*

I'm hearing things.

The Lord thy God eats shit shit shit shit shit motherfucking shit shit shit. Come to me Damien come to me come eat shit eat shit shit shit.

Was this all there was to Simone's magic? Giving the wind an advanced case of Tourette's syndrome? The wind gusted. Simone placed the turd jar in a hatbox and placed it just outside the circle; then she began to sprinkle it with a foul-smelling oil. "The oil will addict it," she said. "It must know its master."

Jacques set a brazier in its own little circle. He lit the coals, threw incense over the flames, lit two tapers, and handed one to Damien. To his dismay, Damien realized he was actually getting scared.

"Don't panic now!" Simone whipped around. "Think of the IRS! Think of the government investigation and the sex scandal and *do as I tell you!*"

Damien's hand shook as he held the taper. The wind shrieked more obscenities. The wind's voice was the voice of an old man, raspy and raging. *Give me shit give me shit give me shit give me shit shit shit shit . . .*

"Prathna!" Simone screamed, raising her arms aloft. "Creature between worlds . . . enslaved by your own base lust . . . come to me . . . come to Mother."

And then Damien heard the creature. As the wind died down he heard a faint gurgling sound . . . a slurping, smacking sound . . . the sound a snail would make if it were man-sized, sliming the asphalt as it crawled toward the magic circle. But it wasn't a snail. It was a human head. The flesh was gangrenous, the lips half ripped away, the nostrils dribbling a greenish pus onto the road. Its tongue, like a pseudopod, propelled the creature forward, rippling as it gripped the pavement. From the neck stump, a mass of entrails writhed. Intestines wriggled like a nest of snakes. The esophagus coiled upward and darted to and fro like a periscope. A stream of fecal invective issued from the creature's mouth, uttered in an upper-class British accent that belied its Southeast Asian features.

Why have you summoned me you shit shit shit shit shit do you not know me shit shit shit who are you that dare call me out of the dark places shit shit shit have you no terror of me shit shit shit do you not fear retribution shit shit shit shit

"This is the Reverend Damien Peters," Simone said in a businesslike tone. "I am Simone Arleta. Come toward the circle. You will find food."

Shit shit shit shit shit

The *phii krasue*'s tongue was surprisingly nimble. It snaked along the road, across the grass, toward the jar of excrement. Damien stood, transfixed by its eyes . . . depraved eyes . . . desolate eyes. The tongue anchored itself on something in the hatbox and began dragging in the rest of the creature.

"Say the words," Simone hissed.

Damien cleared his throat and began to speak as he

had been schooled. "Creature of the dark! I offer you my excrement in exchange for your help. We seek to bind one Timmy Valentine, a spirit, like yourself, trapped between worlds. We offer you an unlimited supply of that which you hunger for."

Feed me feed me feed me

"Now!" cried Simone.

She shed the topmost of her ritual cloaks and flung it over the hatbox and reeled it into the circle. A bloodcurdling howl rent the air—so human, so like a soul in torment—and Damien could see the serpentine forms twisting and writhing under the cloth, trying in vain to escape. Simone knelt down and tied the cloak tight with a *saisin,* a sacred cord from Thailand. She then removed a mouse from one of her pockets and, holding it over the box with both hands, squeezed its juices over it as though it were nothing more than an orange.

"Shit to attract you, blood to bind you fast," she said. "Like constrains like, vermin commands vermin."

She tossed the used mouse into the brazier. Blue flames sprang up and engulfed it.

Muffled howls came from the box. The wind began to rise again. The stench assailed his nostrils and he could feel his gorge rising.

You've tricked me shit shit shit you've poisoned me let me go or I'll devour you I'll rip you apart limb from limb yes yes I'll suck the shit right out of your ruptured colon shit shit shit shit shit

"All right," Simone said, "let's get out of here."

She handed the box—its occupant was still struggling to free itself from its physical and magical restraints—to Jacques, who, after tossing it onto the backseat of the car, began methodically to collect the magical paraphernalia and load it piece by piece into the trunk.

ANGEL

. . . and then he was there.

She was sure it was him. He was just a little boy, really; somehow, on music videos, he seemed larger than life. He was surrounded by people, running around, signing slips, brandishing credit cards, hefting a dozen designer bags. And then they were gone and there was just him.

Shannon said, "They sent word you wouldn't be coming until tomorrow."

Angel Todd said: "I like surprises." He smiled at her.

"Something I can do for you?" I must be dreaming, she thought. There's something not quite right about him. Was it the mist roiling at his feet, or the red glow of his eyes? I have to be dreaming.

"Shannon."

I never told him my name . . . did I?

"You waited for me. All night. Pity it's almost dawn."

She left her desk. Lifted the flap and went to him. His lips were lined with crimson. She walked toward him slowly, slowly . . . the carpet was woven cloud.

"Why did you wait for me, Shannon?"

"I don't know. It's the excitement, I guess." She thought she would be nervous at seeing such a celebrity close up, but he was different from the others who had passed through the lobby, all puffed up with their own importance, treating her like dirt under their feet. "There's just so little glamour in Highwater." Oh, she ached. She'd seen all her friends move away, lured by brighter horizons; she lived alone with her cranky mother who spoke only of mortal sins . . . oh, she couldn't even remember the last time she had touched a boy . . . not since high school . . . maybe not since PJ Gallagher.

"Oh Shannon," said the boy, "if only you knew what it means to me to be waited for . . . to be invited into a person's heart . . ."

She smiled. "So young, so good at breaking hearts already."

"Hold my hand."

The hand was cold. She rubbed it between her hands. The hand sucked all the warmth out of her and yet stayed cold, like an ingot of precious metal, she felt the coldness even in her blood, slowing the circulation, retarding the beating of her heart.

"Angel," she said.

"Oh, but I'm not Angel. Angel is outside. In the real world. On the other side of the mirror."

On the wall was a sign that read:

The Highwater Inn

and she thought, wondering, to herself, that sign is backwards, that sign is the wrong way round, and she looked down at her hands and thought, Funny, my watch is on the wrong wrist, now I *know* I'm only dreaming and it must be true that they're not coming till tomorrow. . . .

"Quickly," he said. "Before you have to go back to the other world."

He embraced her. She had to bend down. His lips brushed the nape of her neck. She felt a pinprick of pain. She tingled.

"I'm sorry," the boy said. "Truly I'm sorry. If only you knew how lonely I am . . . if only you knew how much my appetite still holds me in thrall . . . oh, soon, soon you will know."

Delicately his tongue probed the little wound in her neck. The wound widened. She stiffened. Pain lanced her. But it was followed by . . . not pleasure exactly, but a kind of comfort. He was drawing her blood now, ounce by ounce, and she did not mind that her life was ebbing from her . . . Highwater is a dead end anyway, she was thinking . . . a dead end . . . Highwater is hell, she thought. Her friends in high school always used to say that.

Shannon relaxed now. She felt light-headed, dizzy. She was flying through the night sky, skirting the moon, skimming the treetops, sucking in the cold mountain air.

"Sleep now, my angel," the boy whispered. "Sleep. Sleep."

She could no longer hear him.

10

MIRRORS

❦ ❦

Back! back! back into the mirror!

He had only let go for a second. Hadn't he? And then he'd found himself behind the looking-glass. And Timmy was out there. Somewhere, Simone Arleta was working a magic so powerful it had caused her to lose her grip on Timmy for a moment. They'd changed places.

It had just been a second, hadn't it? A second inside that inner world was torment enough. Who knows what Timmy could have done in a second. But they were still in the lobby. There was the counter girl—Shannon her name was—and there was the pile of luggage waiting for the bell captain to materialize. The rest of the entourage had already gone upstairs.

On Shannon's neck, a tiny smear of blood.

"Oh, Shannon," Angel said softly, "did I do something to you? Did I hurt you?"

"Hell, no," said Shannon. "You're somethin' else. You could never hurt me now. Before, I was hurting. Not anymore." So Angel knew that Timmy had slaked his thirst.

Or is it *me?* he thought. Maybe I'm doing it all, and blacking out, and blaming it on my invisible companion—like one of them multiple personalities.

He didn't know what to say to her, so he just smiled and said, "I'm going to my room now." And left her in the lobby, gazing raptly into the mirrored wall, waiting for something. If only she knew the hell behind that mirror.

If only she knew she was dead.

SHAMANESS

In a suite in the hotel, Simone sat and Damien paced, and a hatbox with a prince's head in it lay on the bed.

"And just what do you hope to achieve with that . . . that creature, Simone?" Damien was railing. "It's unholy . . . ungodly . . . and it stinks." He sprayed more air freshener over the room. It fogged in the dense, muggy air, the air-conditioning barely alleviating the oppressiveness of it. God, he looked stupid. He was a man who only seemed real on television. In the flesh, he was a shell. Though Simone could feel souls in the very air, throbbing and pulsing and shrieking their despair at being cut off from the sources of life . . . she could barely sense anything inside this living man. Of course, she thought, chuckling to herself, he could be said to have lost his soul long ago . . . sold it to the devil, if one wanted to indulge in so antiquated a metaphor.

"If it makes you feel any better . . ." She scooped up the hatbox and tossed it to the back of the hotel closet. Then, methodically and passionlessly, she began to remove her clothing.

"What the hell are you doing now, Simone?"

All bluster and no substance.

"I'm going to fuck you now, Damien."

"That wasn't in the agreement, was it?" he said. "You're a woman, to be sure . . . but you ain't no beautiful young church secretary raring to be ravished. In fact, you're considerably over the hill, if you don't mind my saying so . . . and if spending the evening summoning up shit-eating monsters has aroused your lusts, I can't allow as it's done the same for mine."

"Oh, be quiet. You're no spring chicken yourself, if the truth were known. Sex scandals indeed! But this is not lovemaking, Damien; this is fucking. By the rules, there may be no love at all in this coupling. And it is not for ourselves, but to fulfill the requirements of magic."

"Oh," said Damien Peters. "The requirements of magic."

Simone smiled. From the closet she could hear the *rat-tat-tat* of the captive spirit as it battered its intestinal pseudopods against the physical and supernatural restraints that made it her prisoner.

"Yes," she said. "We must cloak ourselves with the magic of dark places. Of loveless couplings. Of despair."

Later, thrashing in the televangelist's arms, Simone found his unschooled and mechanical attempts at copulation rather charming, in a way. She wondered whether he'd been so lacking in ardor when he seduced—if CNN was to be believed—three Playmates of the Month at a wild party at a senator's mansion in Atlanta to which he had been invited as a token cleric. Or the time he was rumored to have paid a pair of Girl Scouts to perform mutual masturbation in the Imperial suite of the Milwaukee Regency Hotel. Those newspaper reports must, she decided, have been greatly exaggerated. She was having trouble concentrating on him; she was sure that the word *cunnilingus* was not in his vocabulary. Nevertheless, it was necessary for the magic.

She had to have his seed within her—to anoint the axolotl she had slid into her vaginal passage earlier that evening. The life essence to warm the death-cold fire creature. Death inside her birth canal. The little drama played inside her body was the most powerful of sympathetic magics. By fomenting confusion between the elemental forces, she was simulating the chaos she planned to unleash. That was theory. As for practice . . . she shifted, she heaved, she undulated. I am the ocean. I am the world. Plough me, seed me, reap me. Softly she whispered to herself the empowering words of the god Xangó:

Oba kòso
oníbanté owó jìnwìnnìn.

"What are you talking about, woman?" The man was tiresome, so tiresome. What did men matter? The world, from Neolithic times until only a few millennia ago, until that time of aggression and disturbance that *men* called, arrogantly, *civilization,* had been ruled by women.

Civilization!

Civilization had produced Damien Peters and reduced the women of power to the status of chattel. *Civilization* had stolen the magic from the world and driven the gods into the embrace of darkness. And forced such as herself into the shadowlands of a man's world. But from the shadows one could still rule. Watching this pathetic man grunting and moaning in a lackluster parody of a Z-grade porno, Simone Arleta thought: At least I'm not one of them.

MEMORY: A.D. 119

Out of the cage of ash and stone—

Dark. He knows only dark. Night is good. Night is comforting. Night is the mother that feeds the hunger.

Pompeii: there is nothing there now. He does not want to think of the day and night of fire, but the flames lick at edges of memory and he feels the *spatter spatter spatter* of blood on red-hot stone. I was alive once. I served the Sybil. She and the Mage made me what I am somehow.

The city has died. Beneath the sea of twisted lava the boy hears the soundless music that only the dead can sing. They are buried there in their multitudes. Even the Mage and the Sybil, for they have purchased mortality with the boy's virginal manhood, ripped from him as brimstone rained from the sky. They have bought death and cursed him with their immortality. They have forced on him the gift of night.

Eternal night. Eternal desolation.

Released from the rock, he is barely human; his form feels fluid; sometimes, as he scurries along the pavement of the straight road to Neapolis, his feet are the paws of some forest beast, a panther perhaps, a wolf. It is midsummer and the night is short. Already he feels the noisome day creep up on him, though the sky is dark and the stars are shimmering in the haze. He runs. He springs. His feet thud on the cobblestones. He is hungry. All he can feel is the hunger. The other emotions are not yet born in him. There is only the hunger, all-consuming, elemental. He still does not know what it is he hungers for. He runs.

Vesuvius, behind him, smolders a little. A taint of sulphur in the air. He runs.

Ahead is Neapolis. He tastes salt in the air. The air has a reek of sweat, of human suffering, of semen, of blood. He remembers the town vaguely. He has seen so little of the world in the twelve years of his human life; for eleven of them he has lived in the cave of the Sybil of Cumae, the old woman hanging in a bottle, breathing the vapors of the underworld and uttering incomprehensible prophecies; for the last year of his life he has been a slave in Pompeii, knowing only the way to such places as the *dominus* wished him to know, sausage vendors, wine merchants, purveyors of the exotic ingredients the mage

used in his magic. This is the first time, he realizes, that
he has ever journeyed alone. It has taken death to make
him master of himself.

At the outskirts of the city there is a crucified man. The
cross is not one of those towering display crosses such as
will one day become traditional in depictions of the passion of the *christos;* the criminal's feet are barely off the
ground, and there are no nails to hasten the slow death
by asphyxiation. Doubtless by day there were onlookers;
by night, the man is dying all alone.

Pantherlike, the boy vampire growls and paws the sod
at the foot of the cross. The man is still conscious. Flies
are buzzing where the cords have chafed him. The blood
that oozes from the sores is old and gangrenous; it moves
sluggishly; there is bitterness in its smell, and it takes the
vampire a few long moments to realize that this is what
he hungers for, this enervated life force. The sour stench
permeates his senses. He is getting drunk from the smell
alone. In his confusion he cannot hold the shape of the
beast any longer and he shifts; he is human now; he is a
frail boy, naked, the scars of his castration barely healed
despite the forty years of hibernation.

"Water," says the criminal softly. "Give me water."

"Why have they done this to you?" the boy says.

"Water, water."

There is no water. The boy spits on his hand and
brushes the saliva against parched lips.

"It burns," says the criminal, "it's not real water; it
burns." Thus it is that the boy knows that this physical
shape, so precise a simulacrum of his earthly self, is but
an illusion, as the wolf and the panther were illusions; he
has become undead; he is a reflection without substance.
Knowing that he is not real, he is filled with despair.

"Tell me what you did," he says to the crucified man.

"I was a slave. A page boy poisoned the *dominus.* We
were all condemned to death. I didn't do anything—I
was only the janitor—I loved the *dominus.* I had almost

my whole peculium saved up—would have bought my freedom in a year's time." Although each breath causes him pain, the criminal seems to want to talk. The night is long and lonely and he craves companionship; he does not mind suffering for it.

The boy has heard of the law whereby, if a slave were to kill his master, every slave in the household must be put to death; it is a law much criticized for its harshness yet unlikely ever to be repealed. Rome has learned its lesson from the servile rebellion of a century ago.

"And you . . . are you a slave?" the criminal says.

"Yes."

"You are very beautiful—some rich man's cata-mite—"

"No. My master employed me to . . . sing to him."

"Sing to me now, boy," says the man. His eyes are cloudy; perhaps he is already blind, and sees the boy vampire only in a dream.

The boy sings:

> Love shook my heart
> As a mountain wind that swoops upon an
>   oak tree. . . .

"Sappho," says the dying man. "Sappho." And closes his eyes.

He sings for a while longer. His voice was beautiful when it was alive; now that he is dead, freed from the need for breathing, it has become more than beautiful. The twisty melismas of the song intertwine with the wind as it whispers on the walls of Neapolis. He sings. The archaic accents of Sappho's Aeolic dialect are almost a thousand years old; the boy thinks of his own future, a thousand years hence, two thousand, thinking: I too will become like a classical poem, changeless, cold. Only the singing can make him forget the hunger for a moment.

For him as well as for the dying man, music comes as a gift of the gods.

"No human could sing like you," says the dying man. "You are Mercury, messenger of death. Come closer. Drink the life from me."

The boy touches chill flesh. "I am not Mercury," he says. "I don't even have a name yet. I don't know what I am. All I know is hunger. Forgive me."

He knows that he must feed. He is not yet quite sure what to do. Behind the perfume of decay, the sour blood sings to him as it courses through the dying man's veins. He cannot stop himself. Catlike he springs up the cross. The man moans. He claws at the open sores. He purrs as his jaws rend flesh now and loose the flow of blood. The man makes no complaint as the feline shadow leaps onto his shoulder. Clinging to the crosspiece with his hind paws, the cat gouges out the scabs of scourge wounds and laps at them. But fresh blood is more sweet. It maddens him; he cannot hold his shape; he is a carrion wind, he is Sappho's wind of love transformed into a wind of death; oh, oh, he feeds; he feeds; he feeds.

And the man, opening his eyes for the last time, says only a whispered *"Gratias."* At these words, the boy tears open his chest and plunges himself into the sanguinary torrent. Oh, the blood. Oh, the heart, bursting, warming, pumping its life into the empty air.

This man does not fear death, the boy thinks; he welcomes it. He thinks I am his savior, because I have released him from the pain of his existence. Perhaps it is on such as these that I am destined to feed.

But now that death has come, the blood is losing its flavor. The hunger stirs again. He must find others. It will not be hard. He remembers: they are always crucifying people, these Romans.

ILLUSIONS

Aaron Maguire had no illusions about the film biz after twelve years. He knew why they'd given him the job as dialogue rewriter on *Valentine*. His predecessor had been willing to go very far indeed to work on this show; but he had drawn the line at allowing Beatrix ben David, the executive producer, to insert live gerbils into his ass-hole. "Creative differences" had ensued. Aaron had once screwed the director's sister. A mercy fuck at a boring party in Malibu. Mousy little Jenny Burr, simultaneously blizted on acid, dope, and cocaine, had somehow remembered Aaron's act of kindness when she blackmailed someone into making her an associate producer on her brother's picture.

Aaron knew he probably wouldn't even get credit on the show; they'd already hired and fired eleven other writers. And a month in Idaho was hardly his idea of a fun-filled summer. But it was work, and there were a lot of house payments on the summer cottage in Malibu, the house on Mulholland, the two alimonies and three child supports, not to mention the tab for Lucille's AZT. He wished the girl would fucking die. Running away like that, sharing needles in some Hollywood alley, when she already had every toy that a generous court-ordered child support could buy.

If life wasn't such a bitch, he thought, I'd be sitting in some small New England town typing two-fingered on a battered manual working on a novel. A labor of love. Not some megabuck megahit designed to charm the drug and Nintendo money out of kids' pockets.

He'd gotten into Highwater late—four in the morning. Screamed into the parking lot in his third-hand Porsche, swaggered into the lobby of this dump as if he owned the place. The writer's the low man on the totem pole in Hollywood, he thought, but this for sure ain't Hollywood. He thought about the old joke about the starlet who was so dumb she'd tried to climb the ladder by fucking the writer.

Maybe things would be different here. You could have respect here. People wouldn't know any better. At least, not until filming started and they sent him back to the back of the bus.

That babe at the reception desk for example . . . not bad-looking in a redneck sort of way. He'd made sure to ask her name. It was Shannon. Quaint. She had a Saint Christopher medallion around her neck. A Catholic yet! But Catholicism was rampant in Indian country, he remembered. Something to do with French missionaries.

"I'm the, uh, *writer* on the show," he'd told her in an aw-shucks way that was bound to pique her interest.

"You mean you know all the stars and everything?" She smiled at him. He couldn't tell if the stars in her eyes were over his revelation or whether she was staring, glassy-eyed, past him at something in the wall-to-wall lobby mirrors.

"Sure do," he said.

"So do I. At least, I know one of them. The main one. He . . . touched me. Know what I mean?"

He did not. He did not care to pry either. Probably a hopeless fanatic who'd managed to convince herself that a handshake and a glance constituted an earthshaking romance. He hadn't realized that the Todd kid was already here. It was good. He hadn't had a chance to meet him and he wanted to know what the boy was like before he started rewriting his dialogue.

"Say," he said, "I sure could use a guide around here—show me the sights, the dives, the places with the best punk bands."

"You're kidding around, aren't you?" Shannon said. "There's only one kind of music around here and that's country."

"Yeah. I'm kidding around. But not about needing a guide. It's lonely at the top," he added, winking.

"You must have a really big house. In Hollywood and all."

"Right in the middle of Hollywood," he told her. Why fuck with her illusions? "A huge gigantic monster of a house." And a huge motherfucking mortgage to go with it. "So—Room 805—private Jacuzzi? Phone in the bathroom? Xerox machine with massage attachment?"

She laughed. Then she looked at him in a strange kind of way. A *hungry* kind of way. For a moment he thought he'd wandered onto the set of *Deliverance*. But no.

He slept for three hours, and then his internal alarm woke him. Six in the morning, Sunday morning. He always went to mass on Sunday morning. It was his way of atoning for the life of dissipation he led for the other six days and twenty-three hours of the week. He'd never missed it in his whole life except once when he'd been laid up with chicken pox back in the fourth grade. It was the one thing from his childhood he still clung to. Silly, really, no more than a security blanket. He didn't even believe anymore, not really. He just needed the ritual. Groggily he threw on a halfway decent suit and staggered down one flight of steps back to the lobby.

Saint Clement's was a little brick church a few blocks from the hotel. There was hardly anyone at all at the early-morning service. He was late; the host was already being elevated. The priest looked like Homer Simpson on Quaaludes. A pug-nosed altar boy stood dozing; he almost forgot to ring the bell. Incense wafted down the nave and made him feel like a little kid again. What a shame it wasn't in Latin anymore. He let the feeling of security wash over him. Sure it was hocus-pocus, but it was the only thing that kept him sane.

He was zoning out, listening to the organist's botched rendition of a chorale prelude as one by one the scattered celebrants got up to go to the altar rail. Then something made him sit up. It was Shannon, the woman from the hotel, making a distraught and belated entrance. She wasn't exactly dressed for church. Her hair was wild and she glanced furtively from side to side. She genuflected hurriedly and elbowed her way past two old ladies to the railing. What was wrong with her?

Aaron moved along the empty pew toward the aisle. He got up and started to get in line to take communion. Shannon was kneeling now. She was very agitated. She clutched the railings and she was shaking and shimmying like a voodoo priestess. The other members of the congregation stood there like statues. This was too appalling for their bourgeois sensibilities. They stared steadfastly at the floor. Aaron pushed some of them out of the way and made it to the front of the line. She was writhing. He crept closer; the others were backing away. Her eyes had rolled up into their sockets. Blood spurted from her nostrils. The priest looked confused. Probably wondering if the church's insurance covered women with weird seizures. Demonic manifestations. My God, he thought, she's spewing pea soup now . . . what do you fucking know, an live-action replay of *The Exorcist*.

"Spit it out, my dear," the priest was murmuring.

She retched. The altar boys, wide awake now, were prodding each other and probably making prurient remarks. There was something in her throat . . . throbbing . . . like a goiter with a mind of its own.

Aaron felt a strange detachment as he watched what happened next. It was so improbable that it was more like watching a screening of a grade-Z horror movie than anything real. There was the girl he'd seen at the counter only a few hours ago, thrashing and carrying on; there was the priest, wringing his hands; there was the congregation, standing around shiftily eyeing the nearest exits and wondering whether they could tactfully disappear.

At length Shannon seemed to dislodge something from her throat. It flew out of her mouth and landed in the aisle at Aaron's feet. Something fleshy and fibrillating and soaked with gore.

He blinked. The organist came to the end of the prelude. He could hear one of the altar boys giggling.

When he looked again he saw that it was a communion wafer. I'm going crazy! he thought. Could the lyrics of all those Timmy Valentine songs finally have been getting to him? Raw meat one second, the next—

Shannon had been choking on the consecrated host. How strange—how mythic. Like she was some kind of unholy being. A werewolf or a vampire. Too many goddamned Timmy Valentine songs . . .

"Oh, Jesus, oh, Jesus," Shannon was saying softly. "It's true, there's no turning back, oh, Jesus."

Aaron crept up to the railing next to her. There were bags under her eyes and her makeup was streaked from her crying. There was a smear of blood on her lips. "Shannon," he whispered. "Remember me?"

"The body of Christ," the priest intoned. Aaron crossed himself quickly, ingested the wafer, and led Shannon by the hand, away from the altar. Astoundingly, the priest had fully recovered and the service was proceeding as though nothing had occurred. It was almost as though the psychodrama that had just transpired had occurred in a private reality, witnessed only by the two of them.

"What's happening to me?" Shannon said. She was speaking half to herself. "Last night . . . he came out of the mirrors . . . he did something to me."

"You're having some kind of hysterical reaction," Aaron said, hoping his faked air of omniscience would calm her down. "Come back to the room with me . . . I've got some Valium . . . that ought to mellow you out some."

"Are you inviting me?" she said in a very small voice, unsure. "I have to be invited, you know. It's in the rules." He didn't know how the hotel could enforce such tyrannical rules when their staff were off-duty.

"I'm inviting you."

"I had to make sure, you see." She wouldn't look at his eyes.

"Don't worry, I'm not going to seduce you," he said, although that was exactly what he had in mind.

"I'm sorry about that spectacle. You see, I've been having a very . . . um . . . upset stomach lately."

They had reached the west end of the nave. The organ music started up again. Aaron automatically dipped his hand in the holy water and made the sign of the cross. When he reached for her hand again, she flinched and went around to his left; she didn't mind holding on to his left hand.

Holy Mother of—he thought. The woman's nuts! She thinks she's some kind of vampire or something.

Highwater, Idaho, wasn't such a backwater after all, if it had a few good-looking schizos. Maybe there was something here he could work into a spec script . . . the one he never got around to writing, the one that was going to net him a million bucks and finally let him pay off the IRS.

Well, he thought, as they emerged into daylight, that's my quota of religion for another week. And at least I know I'm going to get laid.

MEMORY: A.D. 130

The God is dead. The emperor is in mourning. Egypt is stricken. Rome is desolated. By the banks of the Nile, beneath a silken pavilion dyed in purple, the emperor Hadrian has broken his journey and rests the night. The barges are moored and the guards are posted and the slaves are all asleep, all save one, a scribe, kneeling beside the imperial lectus with a wax tablet and a stylus in case the divinity should be moved to issue some command, weighty or trivial, serious or whimsical; but even the scribe is nodding off, and Hadrian reclines alone, contemplating, by lamplight, a basket of fruit and the ceaseless whisper of the wind from the desert. A child with a lyre snores softly at Caesar's feet. . . .

The boy vampire has come out of the desert. Again it is music that has called him from the wilderness. He has crossed the Mediterranean in the hold of a warship, hidden in a gold-chased marble casket lined with Neapolitan soil. He does not know for whom the sarcophagus is intended, but it is clearly that of a patrician. The casket lid portrays in sculpted relief Zeus' pursuit of Ganymede, swooping down on the young boy on the Phrygian shore in the form of an eagle; it is a realistic depiction, not idealized in the Greek fashion; the terror in the stone boy's eyes is all too real.

The trireme has been at sea for a month. The boy remembers little since he broke free from the ashes of Pompeii. He has been a wild creature knowing only night, feeding on the crucified. At times he has avoided inhabited places altogether. But not now. Egypt, the granary of the world, is teeming. Alexandria's air sizzles with the commingled scents of many races' blood: Greeks, Romans, Jews, Egyptians, Nubians, Numidians, Parthians. And outside the city gates there are plenty of crucifixions. But somehow it is not enough. He is starting to remember music. His life was music before they stole him from the oracle and made him serve the darkness, and finally made him part of the darkness.

The music in Alexandria is a jangle. There are kithara players in the whorehouses. In the agora each hawker has his own refrain. In the palaces are orchestras of drum, aulos, and psaltery. In the circuses, massive water-organs drown the screams of men as wild beasts rend their flesh. So much dissonance . . . his hearing attenuates as the days pass. So many strands of sound, and the skein so tangled, so jarring.

But on the seventh day he hears, in the chaos, a frag-

ment of a melody. It comes from far away, upstream. He
knows the song and the words:

> Call no man happy
> Till he has crossed the bourn of life;
> Only the dead are free from pain.

They are the final lines of *Oedipus Rex,* composed by
a poet who has been dead for over half a century; often,
when he was alive, he has sung those lines in the Sybil's
cave, when words of such import were called for to ac-
company the oracle's darker prophecies.

It is the familiar words and the archaic melody that
have drawn him out of the city. The song has called to
him across the deserts and oases, carried on the wind and
the downstream current of the river, flush with the yearly
tears of Isis. There are cries and lamentations all along
the Nile. Someone important has died; he cannot figure
out who; this ancient play of Sophocles', which shows the
inexorable workings of fate, has been revived and is in
rehearsal; it will be performed as part of the dead one's
funeral rites. This much he has gathered from the pieces
of conversations he has caught from the wind.

The melody haunts him. He hears it every dusk, as he
emerges from the deathlike sleep of day. As the barge he
has stowed away on gets farther south, the melody comes
ever more clearly. At last he reaches a city of tents beside
the river. A dozen barges are moored there. A pavilion of
purple rises behind a clump of palm trees. It is the same
color as the twilight that hangs in the sky long after the
sun has set.

Beside the river, professional mourners, their faces
whitened with gypsum, beat their breasts and tear their
hair and cry out: "O Adonis, O Tammuz, O Antinous."
The first two names are gods worshipped in the east, gods
who die in the spring, are mourned, and come to life

again on the third day. The last name is unfamiliar to him. He too seems to be a god.

Or is he?

He follows the voice he has followed since Alexandria, and reaches the tent where the chorus master is instructing the boys who will play the female citizens of Thebes in Sophocles' drama. They are young boys, freeborn he imagines; they do not have the passive look of slaves. They stand in the lamplight in their woolen chitons. Their master, a bald man with a flagellum in his hand to enforce discipline, seems, paradoxically, to be a slave. One can always tell a slave from a free man however elaborately he is dressed, however costly his jewels and perfumery.

Unnoticed, the boy vampire stands in the shadows.

"Don't mouth the words like a goldfish, Pertinax!" says the chorus master. "And you, Ariston, you're flat. Don't glide in and out of the notes; hit them squarely, and hold them for their full value; you've an entire theater to fill with your puny little voices."

They begin again.

> I will no more go visit and revere
> The navel of the earth. . . .

They sing of the oracle at Delphi. The fragrance of frankincense hangs in the air. One voice in particular stands out. It is the voice he heard in Alexandria, carried on the wind from the desert. The boy who sings it is young. How can he know of these dark truths? The child has not crossed the bourn of life, as has this dweller in the shadowland. The antique melody soars, swells, dies. I was once like him. I sang of destiny and sorrow, of loss and love and lust, and never knew those things. I sang to awaken memories in others which I could never share. I was the vessel and not the wine, the voice and not the music.

The boy vampire stands in the shadows. He remembers the past. There was a time when he still knew how to weep. But vampires do not weep.

At last, the music, which speaks of human pain, dulls the inhuman pain inside him. Even his thirst seems less overpowering.

At last the rehearsal ends. The slave who is master says, "And we remember Antinous." The children bow. There is a moment of solemnity, but it evaporates as they run from the pavilion, chattering, telling jokes.

The boy who has crossed the bourn goes among them unnoticed. The child with the most beautiful voice walks alone. He does not need friends. He carries a lyre under one arm. As he walks he sings softly to himself. It is some Celtic language, eerie and barbaric.

The young singer is walking toward Caesar's tent. The vampire knows it from its size, its canopy of Tyrian purple, and the ceremonial guards who stand watch. He follows.

And now he is in the tent. He is swathed in shadow. The Celtish boy, sitting at the Emperor's feet, begins unbidden to sing. But presently he falls asleep, like the scribe, nodding over his wax tablet; there is only Caesar, leaning against a silken cushion on his lectus, a bearded man in Greek clothing. He has shorn his hair. He is in mourning. His chiton and himation are torn with the traditional rips of bereavement.

The vampire moves closer. Though he makes no sound, Caesar hears him. His grief has made him sensitive to things that cannot be sensed. He looks up. He says, "Antinous. I knew you would return. It is true. You are the god."

"I am not who you think I am," says the vampire. "Antinous is dead. I passed the mourners by the riverside. I am . . ." His mind gropes for a name. "I am called Lysander. And you?"

"You slip unnoticed through my guards; you spiral

into being out of the shadows; you do not know my name. How can these things be, if you are not some supernatural creature, newly awakened from the world beyond, who has unlearned all that he once knew? I am P. Aelius Hadrianus, emperor of the world; and you, who call yourself by another name, are Antinous, the boy whom the emperor loved; out of love for me you drowned yourself in the Nile to buy me life; now you have returned from the realm of Hades; it is the evening of the third day since your death, and here you are—just like Tammuz, just like Adonis, just like this Jesus whom the Christianoi worship. Now I know you're a god. I'm going to build a city here and name it Antinoöpolis. And people will worship you."

There is joy in the emperor's face. He thinks I'm someone else, the boy vampire thinks. He looks at me, creature of darkness, and he sees light. He sees a god.

"What do you want of me, Antinous?" said the emperor Hadrian.

"I'm thirsty," says the boy.

"Then drink," says Hadrian, and holds out both his wrists . . . wrists that have been tightly bound to stanch the wounds of an attempted suicide. "Here are the remnants of the life I owe you. . . ."

And the boy kneels at the emperor's feet, tears at the linen bandages, laps up the blood that wells up from the severed veins, the blood intended as a love gift for someone else, someone who will never return. . . .

MIRRORS

As soon as Aaron and Shannon got back to the hotel she had fallen into a deep sleep. She lay on his bed, on her back, her arms crossed over her chest, like a corpse at a funeral. She was beautiful. She'd become more beautiful the longer he sat beside her and looked at her. Her skin seemed almost to become translucent. He had the inexplicable feeling that the light would damage her skin, and so he drew the curtains and turned off the lights; he only left on the light in the bathroom, cracked the door a little so that her face lay caged in a swath of yellow radiance. The chiaroscuro enhanced her beauty even more. Of course, she wouldn't know what that word meant, he thought. It didn't matter. It was good to look at her. And he did.

All day long she lay there. He peeled away her clothes and looked at her some more. He wondered if she was faking it. Her breathing was so slow and shallow that she could almost have been dead. And when he touched her skin it was cold as marble. It made his flesh crawl. Until he got used to it, and then it became kind of exciting. He wondered if she would wake up if he fucked her. He looked at her, wondering and wondering, prodding her now and then, guzzling straight bourbon and smoking like a chimney because she made him so nervous, because her body was so . . . open and vulnerable and desirable . . . maybe she suffered from some kind of narcolepsy. If that was true he'd be able to do almost anything and she wouldn't wake up until some hormone or enzyme or something kicked in. Jesus, he liked what he saw. Aaron, he told himself, you really lucked out this time. She won't even know what hit her.

He tried stroking one of her breasts. Gently, like a kid with a brand-new train set. Not wanting her to shatter under his fingers. Then more boldly. Teased the aureola with the edge of his tongue. The nipple stiffened the minute his tongue touched it. She was like a well-tuned piano. She wasn't dead at all. She had to be playing some kind of kinky mind game! He got out of his clothes in haste—ripped out a shirt button, for God's sake, but who gave a shit—and flung himself on her.

She didn't even moan. Until he plunged into her and felt the liquidescence of incipient arousal . . . felt the slow pulsating of her vaginal muscle . . . then there came a tiny moan from somewhere inside her . . . it didn't sound like it was coming from her throat . . . she moved. Slowly. Slowly. God but it was exciting in a necrophilic kind of way. She was cold . . . so cold . . . but somehow it didn't turn him off, it only increased his desire to squeeze some warmth out of her.

He became bolder. He slammed hard into her. She didn't wake up. He ploughed her in sharp, angry, rhythmical movements. She whimpered once or twice, then fell silent. He made love to her. Her body was as unresisting as a Barbie doll; whatever way he folded her arms or arranged her legs she held the position until he moved her again. It was uncanny. Like one of those yoga trance things. Maybe she'd had some kind of sex trauma when she was a kid and she'd developed this way of zoning out so she could deal with it.

Or maybe it's just my writer's mind, trying to manufacture all these complex backgrounds for every character I run into, he thought. Maybe I should just keep pumping away and not think about it too much. It's sex, isn't it? Sex is sex, and I'm horny from all the fucking frustration of dealing with the Hollywood bullshit.

He made love to her all afternoon, and when he got tired he showered, went down to the coffee shop for a burger (only $2.95! He couldn't believe it) and a quick conference with Burr on some dialogue changes for tomorrow's shoot, which was mostly Timmy Valentine arriving in Junction to hide out from the press and the fans after that scandalous multiple-fatality concert in Boca Blanca, Florida, the one where they'd found the old woman's head in the piano. Something about the special effects backfiring and the fake gore turning real—not too much had been pieced together about what really happened—a *lot* of money had gone into the cover-up.

The dialogue changes were cosmetic, really—that was the kind of bullshit you had to cope with, with all the ego-tripping busybodies that have to have a hand in every big-budget production. He talked to the star and his wicked-witch mother too. Never any harm in licking the asses of the up and coming. Then he went upstairs again. They were playing Muzak Valentine songs in the fucking elevator, for God's sake. One line kept running through his head:

I'll be waiting at Vampire Junction
To suck your soul away. . . .

The sun was starting to set outside. Twilight was leaking in through a gap in the closed curtains. She was lying exactly where he'd left her. She hadn't so much as moved a finger. He couldn't wait to go to it again. He slipped out of his clothes and got back on the bed. He started to stroke her again. But it didn't feel the same. This time there was something uncomfortable about it. Her flesh resisted him. It was cold. There was a faint whiff of decay about her. He suddenly wondered if she had any diseases. Diseases could make you smell strange, couldn't they. Like cancer. And cancer could be a by-product of . . . Jesus! I didn't use a fucking condom earlier, he thought. He was shaking. But they couldn't have AIDS in Highwater, Idaho. They probably didn't even have sex that often there, except to procreate, that is. Still . . .

Nervously, Aaron got out of bed and went over to the closet. His condoms were in a jacket pocket. He got one out and shut the mirror door. He started peeling it over his penis. That was when, looking in the mirror, he saw that the bed was empty.

He turned. She was still there.

Looked back again.

In the mirror, she wasn't in the bed. There were only the shards of sunset, a mottled pattern, scab-brown against blood-red.

I'll be waiting at Vampire Junction
To suck your soul away. . . .

He took a deep breath. His pulse was pounding. I'm
scared shitless, he realized. Shitless. The condom hung on
his limp dick. He turned to look at her again. Slowly, as
the sun died, her eyes opened.

She said—in a voice curiously devoid of emotion—"I
feel your come inside me, Aaron. What did you do to me?
I've been dead all day and you've been fucking me."

"I—"

"It's all right. I'm still dead. I'm dead and what was
you that's in me's gonna be dead too. But I can still feel
it. A blob of fire hugging the stone cold wall of my dead
vagina."

"Shannon, quit playing mind games." He didn't want
to turn to look back at the mirror. His eyes had to have
been playing tricks. Timmy Valentine wasn't really a
vampire . . . he was a kid with a brilliant PR shtick. That
was all!

"I'm beyond mind games." She smiled. Funny how he
hadn't noticed before how sharp her canines were. "I'm
dead and I'm lonely and I'm cut off from God forever
. . . I knew that when I choked on the communion
wafer."

"Jesus fucking—"

"It's funny. I liked you from the first time I saw you.
I never dreamed I'd see you in church this morning. You
a Hollywood big shot and all, and you weren't all talking
about cocaine or gerbil sex. But I'm not afraid of you
anymore. I felt you making love to me even though I was
in the dreamless sleep of the dead. I think every dead
thing feels this way when a living person makes love to
them. They can touch a shadow of life. Oh, Aaron, I
want to drink your blood."

"You've got to be shitting me." That was it. She'd

gone off the deep end, needed a fucking shrink. He backed away, feeling for the door.

"Don't you walk away from me."

He grabbed at the doorknob, couldn't find it.

"Don't you walk away from me!" She was up from the bed in a single bound. Like a cat. Her eyes were yellow slits. "I don't want to do this . . . you gotta understand . . . but I have to . . . I have to." And she was upon him. She moved faster than a human. Her arms pinned him against the door. He was still fumbling. Got it! He pulled the handle. It caught on the chain.

"Help," he said. But it wasn't much more than a squawk. This couldn't be happening to me. I go to mass every Sunday for God's sake. Six days a week I'm as corrupt as they come but Sundays I'm still my mommy's little goldenhaired altar boy ringing the bell that says the bread is flesh now and the wine is blood . . . blood . . . blood . . .

The arms closed around him. "Come on, baby," Shannon said in a robotic parody of a sexy voice, "you've spent all day fucking a dead body . . . now it's the corpse's turn . . . the night is mine . . . and I'm lonely, I'm lonely . . . I need someone to be with me . . . my mother says she wants me to be with a nice Catholic boy and you're the first one I've found who really cares about me. . . ."

Aaron ducked. Slid from her grasp. There was nowhere to go. He stumbled toward the middle of the room. She whipped around, grabbed him, hurled him face forward against the mirror doors of the closet. In the mirror he saw only himself, being smashed against an image of himself by an invisible force.

"Do you want to run away?" she said. "There's a place you can still run to, you know. Do you know where it is? Look ahead of you—look, look, look—you can see where he came from—where he stepped out of—"

There was a gash on his forehead. Blood filmed his

eyes. He could feel her fingernails drive deep into his back. Blood and sweat were running down it.

"Jesus!" he cried out. "Jesus, Jesus . . ."

And then he saw Jesus.

Or someone like him. Through the veil of his own blood, deep inside the mirror, beyond the glint of reflected twilight . . . he saw a young boy nailed to a cross, on a promontory silhouetted against a sun that was just emerging from total eclipse.

The mirror was melting . . . turning into a fine mist . . . he could feel himself tread on damp earth and human skulls . . . Shannon's arms enfolded him and he knew she was drawing the life out of him . . .

"Jesus . . ." he said.

And the boy came down from the cross and opened his arms to receive him, bleeding from the five sacred wounds. The boy had the face of Timmy Valentine. On his tremulous lip was a smear of blood, and in his eyes was the light of eternal undeath.

Aaron fell toward his savior, he fell fell fell and never reached the ground.

DISSOLVE

In their room, PJ and Chit heard something thudding at the base of the door. A foul stench drifted in through the crack. They looked at each other, and then each moved, in the way dictated by divergent cultures, to protect the other. Chit took a *saisin* cord out of her purse and stretched it across the door with Scotch tape. PJ took sacred pebbles from his bag and arranged them in a circle around the two of them.

The thudding went on. They waited.

"Premchitra." The voice of an ancient man.

"Not yet," PJ told Chit. "He's malevolent. We gotta trick him somehow. He's been sent to get us."

"But he's my grandfather. . . ."

"Yes." He held her hand and led her to the couch. "But we still have to wait."

DISSOLVE: MIRRORS

In the hotel coffee shop, Brian and Petra sat and didn't speak to one another. They were waiting. They didn't know what for. Presently Angel came in and joined them at their crimson vinyl booth, sliding in next to Petra. Brian said, "Where's your mother, Angel?"

He said, "Lost in a fog somewhere."

The waitress came by and Angel ordered a hot fudge sundae.

"Real food first, Angel," Petra said. He started to protest but meekly changed his order to a chicken salad. Brian was astonished at how quickly Petra had become Angel's surrogate mother. They needed each other. He wasn't quite sure how he himself fit in. He wasn't really prepared to be the daddy in this ménage. Not yet. He wasn't the fatherly type.

Presently he saw Jonathan Burr, the director, come sauntering in. Jonathan came up to their booth. "Angel," he said.

"Dude," said Angel.

"This that writer friend of yours?"

"Yeah."

"Zottoli. Right? Look. Have you ever written a screenplay before?"

"I've flirted with it, but I've never had anything made," Brian said, wondering whether schmoozing with Jonathan would have any effect on his future career.

Angel said, "You didn't fire the writer *again,* did you?"

"Worse."

Petra looked at Brian. Suddenly he knew. "He's dead, isn't he?" He looked at Angel. Angel was crying. Like a

little boy. He must have known already somehow.
"What room's he in?"

"Eight-oh-five. Police are on their way," said Jonathan. "Be a while though. They have to come from the
next town. Go cop a look. It's the weirdest thing you've
ever seen. Some kind of suicide or something."

They got up. They didn't wait for their food. The
waitress stared at them. Brian hollered as they rushed
into the lobby, "Save it, we'll be back." Then they dashed
for the elevator.

There were a few people milling around outside Room
805. Mostly they seemed to be hotel staff. One of the
producers was there; he was calling someone on his
hand-held cellular. Brian had expected to find people
screaming, weeping; instead, they stood and stared vacantly like extras from *Dawn of the Dead.* The door was
wide open and no one seemed to want to stop him. He
and Petra and Angel walked right inside. Angel flicked
on the light by the door.

They'd never let us walk right in here back home, he
thought. But out here, where these things never happen,
where people leave their cars unlocked . . .

"Oh, God," Petra said softly. Angel didn't say anything at all.

It wasn't what Brian expected. First there was the bed.
It was unmade and it smelled of sex. There were clothes
strewn across the floor—women's clothes. They were
good clothes, the kind you might wear to church. But
there was no woman. Next to the bed, between the bed
and the closet, there was a pool of blood. Aaron Maguire
was in the closet door. *In* it.

His body was half-buried in the mirror, as though he
had been trying to walk through it. His elbows were
sticking out. He was naked. There were bloodstains all
over the mirror. It looked as though the glass had melted
to admit him, and then hardened right back again . . .
fused solid around him.

"He was going to find Timmy," Angel said softly.

It was an insane idea but it had a kind of logic to it. Lewis Carroll and all that. Brian said, "Who was the woman?"

"And where is she?" said Petra.

Then they heard footsteps. A tall, balding policeman came in. "All right," he was saying, "calm down, everyone, we're taking over now." He glanced at Brian, Petra and Angel. "Name's David Carson. You people know anything?"

"No," Brian said.

Carson took a look at the body. "Holy shit," he said. "Rest of him must be on the other side of this." He opened the closet door. Brian saw that there was nothing in the closet except clothes. The back of the door was just the back of a door. The front of Aaron Maguire hadn't gone through the mirror. It was just not there at all. "I'll be damned," Carson said. "This ain't some kind of special-effects trick you movie people are playing on me, is it?"

Angel turned to Petra and Brian. He held on to their hands. He whispered, "He must have died on the way in. That's why he didn't make it through."

"On the way into where?" Petra said softly.

"Into the mirror. The other place. The place where Timmy's still alive."

There were other officers in the room now and the three of them slipped away. They went down the corridor toward the elevator. Cameras were flashing behind them.

They pushed the Up button. Obviously none of them were going back down to eat. The elevator door opened and two people stepped out, a man and a woman. The woman was carrying a hatbox. They were wearing scarves wrapped tightly about their faces, so that only their eyes could be seen. There was a terrible odor, like a stagnant swamp, like an unflushed toilet.

Brian watched them slink down the corridor as the elevator door slid shut.

"I know those two," Brian said. "I've seen them before."

"Who are they?" Petra said.

"Bad news," Brian said.

"Petra?" Angel said shyly. "Can I sleep in you guys' room tonight? I just don't want to go back to . . . you know."

Brian wasn't thrilled at the idea. There was a kind of Oedipal rivalry between him and Angel.

It's silly, he told himself. Angel Todd's just a kid . . . a vulnerable kid who needs us . . . even though he's making a hundred times as much money as we are. We've got to stick together. We've each of us got a little piece of the truth—Angel, Petra, Chit, PJ and me—and we need all the pieces.

Because when the shit starts, no one is going to believe any of it, except us.

11

SPECIAL EFFECTS

SHAMANESS

Breakfast in bed came with a copy of the Highwater *Gazette*. When she saw the headline she began to laugh. Jacques withdrew and Simone's laughter crescendoed until it became the full-blown cackle of a Shakespearean witch. She prodded Damien awake.

"Look at this!" she exclaimed. "Look! Sleight of hand . . . the art of illusion . . . we've pulled the wool right over their eyes."

There it was in black and white:

FILM MAKERS' EFX FOOL LOCAL POLICE
Corpse in mirror has forensic experts baffled; hoax exposed

"They didn't suspect a thing," she said, digging into her bacon and eggs with gusto.

Damien came to slowly. "I've gotta call in my sermonette," he mumbled, and he crawled out of bed, got his all that power, and more. Have you ever thought of ruling the world, Damien Peters?"

"I've been tempted."

"You shall. Do you know about sleight of hand?"

"Magic tricks, you mean? Throw the handkerchief, distract the audience, lo and behold—the rabbit's gone? Sure I know about it. My whole ministry's one big magic trick."

"We're going to distract not a few hundred thousand television viewers—we're going to distract the fabric of the cosmos. And we're going to do it at a place and a time when illusion and reality are so blended that the universe itself goes blind . . . sort of an eclipse . . . an eclipse of reality."

"A movie set."

"Yes. Real death, false death, the world and its mirror image . . . everything will begin to unravel . . . and then, you see, *we* will seize the last strand of the last thread of reality, and *we* will know the way out of the labyrinth, we alone."

"I don't know about all this. I'm a right down-to-earth sort of a guy."

"Good. I'm not going to tell you any more about the plan. You might screw it up, with your down-to-earth sort of attitude. Just shut up and fuck me again. We need more sex magic. Don't listen to the thing in the hatbox rattling away in the closet. Fuck me and think dark thoughts."

She wondered what he'd say if he knew about the live salamander crawling at the mouth of her womb.

ANGEL

The first day of shooting. The location was outside the façade they'd built into the side of the mountain. Wrought-iron gates, a spooky house, the perfect residence for a vampire. Behind the façade, nothing but steep sheer rock and a pavilion for craft services—where all the snacks were laid out for the crew, continually consumed and replenished. Angel was amazed at how much caffeine and sugar it took to make a picture.

This was nothing like the couple of videos he'd done for the Nashville Network. This was intense. Up at the crack, breakfast burrito over makeup and wardrobe, and four lines to say, over and over and over, from every conceivable angle, before lunch. And talk about shooting out of sequence—this scene was almost the last scene in the movie.

No one knew what had happened that night in the town of Junction. Only that somehow the house had burned down. Followed by the whole town. It could have been sabotage; it could have been an accident. Several solutions to the mystery had been proposed and thrown out. In the most recent version, written by Aaron Maguire, the fire had been set by a crazed fundamentalist preacher who thought that Timmy Valentine was the Antichrist and that his coming signaled the start of Armageddon. And was trying to hurry it all along. Couldn't wait for the rapture to seize him and take him into the bosom of the Lord. The whole emphasis of the script was on innocence betrayed—manipulated by agents, a scheming stage mother (though Timmy Valentine had, as far as could be determined, no mother at all), crooked record producers—and finally destroyed by a madman. The madman—the big star, the top-billed actor—wasn't due to arrive until next week, which was just as well since they had been rethinking his whole part.

Right now, Angel knew, Brian Zottoli was sitting in the trailer—Angel's, that is—rewriting the ending, toning it down because someone in the legal department thought the character of the fundamentalist preacher was too close to one of the real-life televangelists, Bakker or maybe Damien Peters, the one from his own hometown.

The new ending wouldn't have any effect on today's scene, though.

Weird circumstances, Angel thought. Wasn't more'n a few weeks ago that Brian Zottoli was just another starving writer in a Hollywood garret. Then this dude vanishes into a mirror and all of a sudden Brian's the writer—because he happened to be there.

Scene 94: Timmy is standing outside the mansion in Junction. A strange presentiment takes hold of him. His past flashes by in a series of quick, sepia-tone cuts as Timmy starts to sing the song Vampire Junction. *Slowly, Timmy walks into the house. In slow motion, the house explodes as the final bars of the song fade away.*

Angel stood behind the railings. This was a master shot—they might only use a few seconds of it in the final cut—but he had to stand and lip-synch the entire song as the camera, with agonizing slowness, dollied away from a close-up of his eyes into a wide-angle shot of the entire house with him, a tiny figure, walking up the steps. Since he was lip-synching, the whole shot would be MOS—no sound. That meant that there were noises going on all around him—people didn't bother to be that quiet—and it was hard for him to concentrate. Especially since he wasn't really singing.

Action.

The director was far away. In another world. Angel thought about Timmy, trapped in the mirror, nailed to the tree, waiting to be freed. Angel knew he had the key. Every time he acted the part of Timmy, he focused a little more of the world's cognitive attention on the real Timmy. Reality and illusion were a dog chasing its own tail, a yin and a yang.

The intro to the song played over speakers concealed behind a rock and a stone lamp.

It was getting on lunchtime and the sun streamed

down, but in the illusion it was winter. The ground was blanketed with bleached cornflakes. Another kind of artificial snow blew down from an overhead window. Electric fans directed the snow into the shot in an elegant spiral pattern. Another fan stirred Angel's hair so that it whipped against his face. Angel closed his eyes and tried to drift into the rhythm of the song. Somehow his timing was off. But it didn't matter because the focus puller had screwed up *his* timing too, and they hadn't laid the dolly track right after all.

"Take a break, Angel," Jonathan said from his godlike seat a ways off, in the shade of a clump of pines, where winter ended and summer began.

Angel was grateful; he went off to find craft services and let the stand-in take his place while the technicians redesigned the setup. After he'd found himself a Coke and a candy bar he went back to the trailer to wait it out.

He found Brian hard at work.

"Where's Petra?" he said.

"She went down to see the interior sets. Preparing your PR package."

"And PJ and Chit?"

"I don't know."

"Brian?" Brian was hunched over a laptop. There were papers everywhere. The script pages were color-coded according to which version they were—pink for second draft, blue for third and so on—but there'd been so many drafts that they'd run out of officially sanctioned colors. Aaron's pages had been a kind of indigo; Brian's was going to be neon pink. "Brian, I was thinking . . . you think we maybe imagined it? I mean, like I read the paper this morning and it said it was some kind of special-effects gag."

Brian looked up from his typing. "I think it was real, Angel."

Angel said, "Brian, I've been through the mirror before. I know what it's like in there. It's hell, Brian.

Fire-and-brimstone hell I mean. Could be that he's alive in there. Could be we could get him out of there. I hear they got that closet door down at the police station somewhere, next town over."

"We can't think about people who're already gone, Angel." Angel could tell that Brian was thinking about Lisa, his niece. Brian had told him how he'd had to drive a stake through her heart . . . in Timmy Valentine's Encino attic. Angel could feel Brian's pain. He knew Brian didn't trust him totally, and he wished there was something he could do to smooth things out between them. It was something to do with Petra, he knew that.

"Brian? Are you mad at me because of Petra?" Angel didn't know any other way of asking these embarrassing questions, except for blurting them straight out like a fool.

"Of course not," said Brian. But Angel thought he seemed uncomfortable. "Petra loves you the way a mother does. But she and I, you know, we, well, we're lovers. You're a kid; you can't have an adult as a girl-friend."

"Sometimes that ain't exactly true," Angel said.

Brian turned back to his typing. I've upset him again, Angel thought. I wish I could tell about Momma. About the things she makes me do. I wish I could tell *someone*. I started to tell Petra that time and then I kind of chickened out. But maybe she knows. Maybe everyone knows. I'm scared to look people in the eye sometimes.

Where is Momma anyway? he thought. Isn't she supposed to be the designated guardian? Probably zoned out in the back somewhere . . .

There was a knock on the door.

"They need you back on the set, Mr. Todd—" It was one of the production assistants.

"Gotta go, Brian. Is my hair okay?"

"Sure, Angel. Why don't you use a mirror?"

"I don't like mirrors anymore."

VISION SEEKER

PJ was looking for Shannon. He'd had a bad feeling about her since he saw the dress lying on the floor of Room 805. Shannon used to wear those sorts of dresses to church. Her mother made them. He remembered. It hadn't been that long ago, their sophomore year at Highwater. Even though so much had changed it seemed as though an eon had passed.

At first he hadn't wanted Chit to come with him—he was embarrassed to show her just how humble his past had been. He knew intellectually that it was only because he'd grown up half believing the prejudice against halfbreeds. It felt weird, driving Chit's white Porsche through the white-trash neighborhood where he'd once lived. He kept looking over his shoulder to see if a cop car was going to pull up and ask him if the car was stolen.

They turned off Main Street. He was sure that Shannon's house would be where it had always been . . . across the railway tracks that went nowhere . . . past the ruined post office . . . right at the general store that had had a sale on lawn mowers for the last twenty years . . . uphill a ways, on a street named Maplecrest Circle.

There it was. The front yard was landscaped in nouveau Munsters style, with weeds running riot. A plaster Madonna peered from a sea of knee-high grass. He parked. Chit got out; she seemed a little intimidated by her surroundings. "This isn't any palace," PJ said. "Come on; you'll see how I used to live before I moved to the land of fruits and nuts."

"Are you sure it's okay?" she said. She sounded like a little girl suddenly. "Would I be intruding?"

"You can wait outside if you want. I won't be long. I just want to know if Shannon's . . . you know. Alive."

He couldn't see into any of the windows of the wooden A-frame house; the drapes were all drawn. He could see the back of old Mama Beets's head though; she was sitting in a rocker in the screened-in front porch. Maybe he wouldn't even have to go inside.

"I'll wait in the car," Lady Chit said. "I'll listen to the radio or something."

"Not the radio. Nothing but country. You'll hate it."

"I'll dig out one of my CDs." She walked meekly back to the Porsche. He heard her start up the engine, heard, through the closed windows, faint strains of a Mahler symphony. She must really have it cranked up for him to hear it at all through all that soundproofing. I guess she's frightened after all, PJ thought.

It was so quiet here. There was no wind. "Mrs. Beets?" He tapped at the screen door. She didn't answer. It was like a scene from *Psycho*. I mean, he thought, Mrs. Beets . . . Mrs. *Bates*. He opened it up and went inside, half expecting the chair to swivel round and reveal the rotting skull face of a long-dead crone . . . but no. She was there all right. Old, but alive. Probably a bit hard of hearing by now.

But she remembered him. "Oh, you're the Gallagher boy," she said, and started, with a tremulous hand, to pour him a cup of tea from a thermos. "I thought you'd never come back to Highwater. Eh? Speak into my good ear, boy; age ain't been so kind to me."

"I just came to see Shannon," he said, vigorously working his lips in case she needed to lip-read. "Is she home?"

"Fancy that!" She clapped her hands, then wiped a tear from a mottled cheek. "You remembering her after all them years. They say Injuns have long memories."

"Yes'm." He couldn't be bothered to argue. "Is Shannon inside?"

"She's in her room, resting; but I imagine she'd be glad enough to see you. She's being wayward though, moody; been that way ever since she came home from church. When you come out, bring me some of them Doan's pills, will you? My back's hurting real bad." She fingered the crucifix around her neck. "I sure hope the Lord takes me soon. I'm in pain all the time."

"Yes, Mrs. Beets."

She turned away from him and started reciting the Lord's Prayer to herself in Latin.

Inside the house: garbage piled up in heaps on the floor. A painting on the wall: young Jesus instructing the elders at the Temple. Another over the fireplace: the Last Supper—one of those black velvet paintings. And then, turning toward the kitchen, he was surprised to see something of his own: a charcoal sketch of the teenage Shannon, with a big broad smile and without her retainer, and bangs down over her eyes. The picture was in a cracked Woolworth's frame and hung over the kitchen lintel. The only light came from a kerosene lamp. He remembered that the Beetses used to get the electricity cut off pretty regularly.

"Shannon?" he said. Then he remembered where her bedroom was—to the right of the fireplace—no door, just a bead curtain. Jade-colored beads. No light came from the room, so he picked up the kerosene lamp and took it with him.

All the curtains were drawn. He put the lamp on the nightstand. The orange flame danced. She was lying on the bed in the nude, half-covered by a patchwork quilt. "Shannon, Shannon, are you okay?" Abruptly he knew that it was useless. Her sleep was the sleep of the undead. He could tell. She wasn't breathing. The perfume of putrefaction was in the air. He sat down next to her. He wasn't afraid, not yet; it was afternoon; she wasn't going to wake up until the start of the brief summer night.

He touched her cheek. Her lips. Blood was caking at the edge of her mouth. He wondered why she hadn't already killed her mother, but then he recalled the crucifix old Mama Beets wore around her neck. There was a stand-up crucifix on the dresser table, too. A scarf had been thrown over it, but a crossbeam and a nailed-down hand poked out of the gray wool.

The vampire vibes were there all right. The way she never moved. The bloodstains—there were more on her fingertips. The covered crucifix. The darkness.

I'm going to have to kill you, he thought.

He remembered the last time he'd been in this room. It was here, wasn't it? Or was it the back of Herb Philpotts's Mustang? God, he wasn't sure anymore. Hadn't he snuck in through the window? Yeah, and Mama Beets was out of town, at the bingo parlor down in Oaksville. He hadn't been prepared and nor had she. Lucky she hadn't gotten pregnant. He remembered: she was just lying there, not moving much, and the room was awash with the light of a full moon reflected on acres and fresh-fallen snow; he working so hard to arouse her, caressing, tickling, licking, teasing, and finally, the hormones getting the better of him, he'd eased his penis into her even though she wasn't really wet enough, and he'd started to move his pelvis thinking I hope I'm not hurting you and then finally he looked at her face and saw she was squeezing one tear after another from clenched eyelids, drop by drop, and he couldn't help himself but came, all at once, too early, withdrew, too quickly, saw the blood, silver-black in the moonlight; whispered an embarrassed "I'm sorry," and sat up, hunched, staring at the floor; and then she'd reached up and touched him lightly on the thigh and said, "I wanted you to. I'm sick of hearing about sin all the time and not knowing what sin tastes like." And then she nuzzled her head in his lap and started to taste his sin, so so so so slowly playing the head of his penis with her tongue; she wasn't an expert; bit him a couple of times until he showed her to suck her lips back over her teeth; oh, then she made him feel like a master of the world, and not the fatherless breed from the burnt-up town that none of the kids in school would talk to. . . .

Or had it been the back of the Mustang?

He would have loved to have asked her. So much in those years was murky. As though it had all happened to somebody else . . .

I'm gonna have to kill you.

He looked around for something sharp that he could use as a stake. Nothing came to mind except the crucifix itself. He went to the dresser and shook it free of the scarf. Not too sharp, but it might be able to shatter the rib cage and penetrate through to the heart. If he could find something to drive it with. He went out to the living room. Maybe there was a toolbox somewhere. He found Mrs. Beets sitting on the living room sofa.

"You got a hammer, Mrs. Beets?" he asked her. *I need it to send your daughter into the next world,* he thought.

"Look in the kitchen," she said, "and do bring me a glass of water for them pills. I had to get them myself. Don't be all day getting rid of Shannon."

Was that some kind of Freudian slip? he thought. Or does she know? Did Shannon come home just before dawn, and try to attack her mother, only to be repelled by the crucifix? He went into the kitchen, poured Mrs. Beets a glass of water—the refrigerator was off—and noticed the garlic bulbs in the sink. He came out and gave Mrs. Beets the water. He found the hammer on the counter.

"You be a good boy, now," she said. "I ain't gone tell."

Sure now that she had some inkling of what had happened to her daughter, PJ said, "But what if people come calling? What are you going to say when the hotel asks why she hasn't been in to work?"

"Burn down the house," she said. "They don't like fire. My grandma told me." She crossed herself, and then she pulled a plastic rosary out of her blouse and began counting off Hail Marys.

He went back into the bedroom. He took the crucifix and hammered it, head first, into Shannon's chest.

At the first blow she opened her eyes.

At the second she started weeping. Like the time when they'd made love. And she spoke to him. Her voice didn't seem to have changed since those high school days. It was the voice of a girl who had yet to taste sin. "PJ, why'd you come in through the window like that? You know I'm a good Catholic girl and I can't do anything nasty."

He pounded. Blood welled up, thick, dark as molasses, sour-smelling.

"I'm not ready for this yet, PJ . . . don't take me yet . . . I want to be a little girl a while longer. . . ."

"You're all confused. That was a long time ago. You're dead now. Be dead." He pounded again. Blood fountained up to his face. He wiped it off with the back of his hand. Something cracked. His next blow struck home. Jesus' head had pierced her heart. She screamed. He pounded again, harder, harder, like the time they'd made love even though he'd known she wasn't ready for him yet, and she screamed and screamed and the tears that spurted from her eyes were blood and blood and . . .

"I loved you!" she whimpered.

He saw her thrashing, saw the upturned crucifix bob up and down in her chest like a buoy in a hurricane.

He smashed the kerosene lamp on the bed. The flames ran along the headboard and up the bedposts. She screamed. It wasn't a human scream; it was the firewind whistling through her trachea and her ripped lungs.

Plenty of kindling here with all the garbage strewn about the house. There was a lot of smoke. He was choking. He wanted to make sure the fire would consume her but he had to get out before he suffocated. He dashed into the living room. Mrs. Beets was still sitting, staring into space.

"C'mon, Mrs. Beets, we'd better get out of here!"

"She's all I had, you know."

"Yes . . . yes . . . c'mon!" He lifted her up. She weighed almost nothing.

"Let me down! I got nothing but my back pain left . . . I don't want to go on!"

"Mrs. Beets . . ." Smoke was pouring into the living room now. She coughed. She struggled to free herself.

"Don't you Mrs. Beets me, you savage Injun child . . . I know you deflowered my daughter years ago . . . I've always knowed. You get your hands off me. You younger generation is all alike. You sass your elders and you try to bite the hand that feeds you."

"Mrs. Beets . . ." What would it take to get her out of the house? "Mrs. Beets, suicide's a mortal sin! You'll burn in hell if you don't allow me to save your life!" She seemed afraid for the first time. She put her arms around him and let him carry her outside. The flames were devouring the living room furniture now, ripping down the flimsy walls. He ran to the car, flung the door open and flipped the seat so that Mrs. Beets could slide in. Mahler's Ninth Symphony—music about death and resignation—blared from the car stereo. Lady Chit had been sitting, eyes closed, meditating.

She opened her eyes. "Was she—is this—"

"Dead now. This is her mother."

"Had she turned into—"

"Yes."

"Please . . . take me out of here. Please."

"The house is going to burn down," PJ said. "We're gonna drive down to the general store and call the fire department, but they'll probably take a while to get here from down in Oaksville."

He turned the key in the ignition, slammed into first, and they headed downhill. He didn't look back. But in the rearview mirror he could see the flames reflected. He could see Mrs. Beets, numb, rocking to and fro.

He wondered where she could go and whether he should have just let her die the way she wanted to. That would have been the Indian way . . . when the aged were allowed to select the time of their passing . . . but Mrs.

Beets would not have understood that. Hellfire and damnation she could understand. It was just as well.

They tore down the steep slope. He turned the music up louder.

And louder.

MIRRORS

The soundstages began just a couple of hundred yards from the last burnt house in Junction. There was the edge of town . . . Petra could see it quite clearly as she pulled into the parking lot . . . on one side the ground charred and covered with rubble, on the other lush; it was almost as if the land that had once been Junction had willed itself not to bear fruit again, as if the ground had been sown with salt, as the Romans had once done to ancient Carthage, vowing that it would never rise again. It was uncanny to stand between the two worlds. On the one hand, the real Junction, forever dead; on the other, the illusion of Junction, about to be brought to life on celluloid.

The stages themselves were ugly, concrete things. A security guard checked her name against a list and waved her on through. She stepped inside. The hall was cavernous and echoed with the sound of hammering and drilling. A woman with a punk hairdo and leather pants called out to her: "Petra Shiloh! You're Petra Shiloh, aren't you?" The New York accent was unmistakable.

"Yes." She smiled a little. Workmen bustled past. A crew of three were busy painting a plywood wall to resemble stone. Above, crew members negotiated a maze of catwalks and platforms. Ahead, carpenters were constructing scaffolding around which two women were wrapping yards and yards of tinfoil. "What's with the tinfoil?"

"It's going to be a cave of nightmares or something. Scene Twenty-six—inside Timmy's mind—I don't know exactly." She removed a wad of gum from her mouth and chucked it at a trash bin that was being wheeled past. "I'm Trish Vandermeer. I'm, you know, the P.D. Production designer." She turned to scream at some passing workmen. "No, no, no, that armchair goes in the attic set, not the office set—jeeze, some people—shit, you're gonna drop the toilet!" The object in question was a toilet with a pseudo-gold-plated seat.

"You look like you're going crazy around here."

"Sure thing. Want some nose candy?" She waved what looked like a sachet of Sweet'n Low at Petra's face.

"Thanks but no thanks."

"Well, lemme show you around. Loved your piece in *Vogue,* by the way. Or was it *People?* The one where you interviewed that serial killer."

"Vanity Fair. You read it? Thanks. Not many people remember bylines." She couldn't help warming to the woman after that.

"This way." Trish led her through a narrow passageway—they had to squeeze through it sideways—between two sets. They stopped at a craft services table to stoke up on coffee. Then, through a canvas flap, they stepped through to what looked like the interior of a cave. "It's all tinfoil," Trish said. "Tinfoil and spray paint—and later we're gonna use glycerine to make it drippy and nasty."

"This is part of the dream sequence too?" At the end of the cave, the two women she'd seen earlier were busy spraying the tinfoil in earth tones.

"Uh-huh. Actually we salvaged the tinfoil from this other movie, *Angels in Leather.* Fifty million dollars doesn't go as far as it used to. I think Jason Sirota is getting a million himself. He's playing, you know, the preacher guy. Timmy's nemesis. But now they're thinking of writing him out of the picture because some real-life preacher's threatening to sue them, except that they've already paid him and there's no money-back guarantee—a million down the drain! Sheesh!"

They went through the caves in short order. They were all back-to-back and wound around in such a way that a few yards could appear to stretch forever. Petra had to admire the illusion.

"You want to see something *really* amazing?"

"Sure."

The next set was Timmy Valentine's model-train layout. It was more than just a tabletop with a few yards of track and a choo-choo train. This thing was huge. There were two or three towns. A mountain range. Tracks that split up and coalesced and snaked up hills and across streams and through bridges and tunnels. There was a Bavarian castle. There was a river of Plexiglas. And in the center of the layout was a couch and an armchair; a Southwestern-style floor lamp; a Navajo rug. "One of the writers had the idea that Timmy Valentine might go to see a therapist," Trish said. "One of those strict Freudians. We know he used to collect model trains, so the analyst tells him to build a train layout that goes through his whole life. He's trying to root out some trauma in Timmy's past. You know. The usual bullshit."

Trish took Petra by the hand and led her to another room on which there was an exact copy of the train layout in a smaller scale, shrunk to the size of a tabletop. "We made two of 'em," Trish said, "one of them in HO—the one you just saw—and the other one in Z scale. A miniature of a miniature. That's because we're going to blow it up and we need a couple of good high-angle shots of it and—oh, but I'm boring you with this technical shit." She turned to bark a few orders at the ubiquitous workmen. "Careful with that carpet, you idiots—that thing cost some Iranian peasant three years of his life! Sorry we're so damn disorganized," she said to Petra. "You want to see something—something wonderful?"

"Sure." It was all very overwhelming; she had to admit that she could barely make head or tail of what was going on.

"C'mon then."

More corridors; more pounding; then up a makeshift ramp and into a large, square room. The floor was Plexiglas. The walls and ceiling were mirrors. A couple of feet beneath the transparent floor was a subfloor, also made completely of sheet mirrors. The light sources were all hidden. Petra experienced an utter disorientation. She saw herself infinitely replicated as her image bounced back and forth from mirror to mirror.

"This is weird," she said.

"Truly demented."

"What's it for?"

"Oh, it's in the script—a room in Timmy's house— where he communes with the mirrors of the soul. Whoever cobbled up this script doesn't have a clue about story structure but he sure comes up with popping images. Look!"

Trish clapped her hands. As Petra stared at herself in the ceiling, she suddenly found her image lurching . . . stretching . . . distorting . . . crisscrossing herself.

"How—what—"

"All done by moving the walls," Trish said. "They're on servos. Shift the angle by a hair, shift all the images, kaleidoscope city." She yelled to an invisible operator. "Enough already!"

Petra saw her myriad selves coalesce back into one. She caught her breath. In the split second before the images flew together, she thought she saw something else . . . fire. Yes. Flames spurting from a dead man's eyes. A naked man trying to burst out of a closet door. The man's eyes glazing over, staring at something incomprehensible, terrible. Only a split second. Then just herself again. No fire.

She found herself shaking. I'm going crazy, she thought. It's all done with mirrors. Just mirrors.

"Oh," said Trish, "and the walls fly, too."

She clapped three times. One of the walls slid aside and Petra saw that they were only a few feet from the craft services table.

"I think a need another cup of coffee," she said.

"It gets to me, too," said Trish. "I've never built anything this—this—elemental before. It—well—it gets to me, it gets to me."

DISSOLVE

Mrs. Beets was sitting in the lobby of the Highwater Inn because nobody knew what to do with her. She was sitting by herself because nobody knew quite what to say to her. People never knew what to say when you were going through tragedy. There she was, her house burned down, her daughter dead and more than likely burning in hell, owing her life to the boy from Junction. . . .

That boy was talking to a police officer now.

"Yessir, I'm the Gallagher boy; it's been a long time since I came back to Idaho, though. It was amazing I got this job. . . . Yessir, I pulled Mrs. Beets out of the fire. . . . I don't know how it came about. . . . They were using kerosene lamps, their electricity'd been cut off, I guess. . . ."

"What a terrible thing." Policeman was taking notes. If only they'd managed to get those Doan's pills out of the house. Her back was killing her. Where was she to go now? She had a sister in Florida somewhere . . . hadn't seen her in twenty years . . . the seaside town of Boca Blanca.

The site of Timmy Valentine's last concert.

Those rock music people were behind this thing somehow. That's what Shannon'd been babbling on about when she stumbled home last night. *I'm with Timmy now and I'm going to live forever,* she'd said.

Damn Satanists.

I look a sight, too. Look at me in that mirror. I look a heck of a lot older than sixty-two. I should've never hit the booze after Dan died.

Damn Satanists must have gotten to her. It was a mistake to let Shannon come and work at the hotel. It was a mistake to have stayed on in Highwater after the disaster at Junction . . . anyone could've seen it would only be downhill from then on. Towns burning up for no reason, horror stories, people clamming up about what they'd seen . . . and now this moviemaking business come to town, that'd only stir up the old ghosts . . . the old ghosts were back. They'd taken her Shannon . . . delivered her up into the arms of darkness. There was a curse on Junction and the curse was spreading to Highwater. We're all steeped in it and we can't get away, she thought, all of us that remembers the night of fire. . . .

She found herself crying softly to herself. No one was paying her any mind; she was an old woman, wasn't she? She'd a right to cry if she felt like it. She cried and the Indian boy and the policeman went on talking about her as though she weren't there, right there in the same lobby she was sitting in, talking, talking, talking. She covered her face with her hands.

She became aware of someone else's hands on hers.

"Now don't you cry, ma'am," said a soft voice. So gentle. So familiar.

He pried away her hands and she gazed up at the gentleman who had voiced such concern. It was a miracle. She couldn't believe her eyes.

Standing in front of her, in the flesh, was Damien Peters.

"I've seen you on television," she said. "Oh, you've been sent to me, like an angel of the Lord."

Peters chuckled. "There's some that calls me that," he

said. "Though personally I try to sidestep the sin of pride."

"Oh, Lord, is it really you? You ain't come to fetch me up to heaven?"

"Oh, to be the angel of death, Mrs. . . . ah . . ."

"Beets."

"What an honor that would be. But no, I'm just a poor itinerant preacher. Charmed to meet you, and I'm sorry you seem in such dire straits."

"I'm feeling better already," she said.

"Perhaps you would care to come up to my suite for, ah"—and he actually winked at her, that special wink that he loved to do on his show—"a glass of refreshment? Quite chastely, I assure you, since there will be, ah, another lady present. And I will minister to you in your sorrow." ·

Mrs. Beets smiled at him. The Reverend Peters was a television personality. Maybe she had lost everything she'd ever owned and loved, but she knew that television could work miracles. She had felt its power many times, reaching her hands out to touch the screen when Peters whispered to her of heavenly love. . . .

ANGEL

Angel sang. He didn't have to, but he couldn't help himself. The voice from the hidden speakers drowned him out anyway. He was just singing for himself. It gave him something to concentrate on while the camera brooded over his face.

Once, just once, he looked into the camera by mistake, breaking one of the most stringent rules of filmmaking. He'd caught sight of himself in the lens. Only it wasn't him. It was Timmy stretching out his arms to him, Timmy calling out his name from behind a wall of fire. . . .

"The moment is coming," said Timmy. "We're both going to be free."

At once he looked away. But it was too late; the director had already called *cut* and made them all go back to their marks.

Roll camera. Rolling. Speed. Speed. Take twelve. *Action.*

Angel sang. He let the music take hold of him completely. He closed his eyes and plucked the melody from the air, a thin, sweet thread of sound.

Beautiful. Beautiful. They were talking the whole time because it was all MOS anyway but he didn't care, he was in his own world, he was letting Timmy ease himself into his soul.

He didn't look at the camera again. He didn't have to. He knew that Timmy would always be there for him.

Beautiful. Beautiful.

SHAMANESS

She heard Damien's key in the lock. She heard Damien whistle "Amazing Grace." That was the signal.

She positioned herself behind the door. It swung open, someone stepped through, and Simone immediately thrust the chloroform-drenched handkerchief over the woman's nose and mouth. Damien held her arms. Simone felt only a momentary resistance. This was an old woman without any fight in her. The victim collapsed, fell back into Damien's arms; the two of them carried her to the coffee table and laid her out. Simone couldn't help shuddering at the ugliness of the coffee table—its fake early-American sculpted mahogany legs and its tacky mirror top—bad taste was rampant in this town. She wanted to go back to the desert. Her mind could roam at will over the empty spaces, and there weren't all these throngs of dirty little minds to sully her grand visions.

In the background, the television was playing an episode of "Chip 'n' Dale's Rescue Rangers."

Mrs. Beets moaned. Simone said, "Was this the best you could do?"

"The easiest," said Damien. "A fan. And she appears to be the mother of . . . that victim, you know. I thought I'd best keep it in the family."

"All right," Simone said. She started to lay out the candles. Black candles in the shape of naked men and women, five of them, arrayed at the points of a pentagram that she had drawn on the carpet with talcum powder, with the coffee table at its center. "Now take off her clothes and masturbate over her. Make sure you asperge her *thoroughly* with semen, you understand. I don't want to have to go through this twice."

She took the hatbox out of the closet.

"How now, my prince," she said softly. "Soon you shall feed."

The hatbox rattled. She placed it next to the coffee table. She ignored Damien as he hunkered over the old woman's prostrate body and, with his left hand, methodically manipulated himself until he reached orgasm; his wheezing and moaning seemed to her both unnecessary and distracting. When the subject had been anointed to her satisfaction, Simone selected an obsidian knife from her bag of tricks—it was one she had obtained from Mexico, and she had ascertained from its aura that it had actually been used in human sacrifices in pre-Columbian times—shooed Damien out of the way, consecrated the knife with a quick prayer to the forces above and below, and performed the necessary excisions as quickly as she could, betraying no emotion. She had long learned to suppress her natural compassion for the ritual subjects; in her line of work such qualms only got in one's way. Turtles and chickens were one thing, but people had a tendency to talk back.

She was glad she had used chloroform; there was nothing more disconcerting than an unwilling sacrifice. This one would never know what hit her.

After she extracted the necessary parts for her own private rites, she made one last cut in the abdomen, insuring that the colon and its contents were clearly exposed. She bent down, whispered the spell that unsealed the hatbox, and let the *phii krasue* out.

"Is that really necessary?" asked Damien, revolted.

"Better this than to have it lapping incessantly at your asshole, Reverend," Simone said dryly as she stepped out of the circle. It was not a pleasant sight to see the creature wrapping its entrails around the old woman in a slithering embrace, raking its tongue up and down the carved torso, slurping up the contents of the intestines. She averted her eyes, but could not turn down the volume on the slurping sounds, nor stem the stench that arose from the creature's arousal and its hunger. "There's no need to stay, unless you simply *have* to gawk," she said. "The magic circle will keep our friend from escaping. We might as well go down and get a bite to eat at the hotel coffee shop."

On television, the chipmunks were jabbering away. Damien was staring fixedly at the screen, zoning out.

"Come on," she said. "You've seen that one. It's a rerun."

At that moment they both heard a noise. The voice of Prince Prathna shrieked out: *"Curse you curse you chasing me even in death you monster you apparition you shit shit shit shit shit—"*

Simone turned around. A hand was emerging from the mirror surface of the coffee table. The pale hand of an undead boy. "How dare you!" she screamed at the spirit in the mirror. The hand seized a hank of Mrs. Beets's white hair and began to pull her into the tabletop.

"Curse you!" Simone shrieked. She did not dare enter the circle. She was too vulnerable there. She watched impotently as the body was slowly pulled down into looking-glass country. The Prathna-creature thrashed about, coiling its tongue about the torso, tying its own intestines into knots around Mrs. Beets's exposed colon, pulling. The body was sucked down with such force that torsoless monster was thrown from the coffee table.

"Shit shit shit shit shit shit shit shit shit—" It cried, in grief and hunger as much as in rage. It writhed. Sputum dribbled from its lips. Its bulging eyes rolled. The tip of its tongue was caught inside the mirror. It howled. It battered its neck stump against the side of the table.

Only Mrs. Beets's left foot remained, pointing at the ceiling, blue-veined and filthy-toenailed.

"Cut me loose!" screamed the *phii krasue*.

Damien Peters had backed up against the door. He was shaking. A man who dealt daily with the supernatural shouldn't be so frightened of a little thing like this, she thought. She was pleased he was going to be in Hangman's Holler for the weekend, working on his major Sunday sermon; all men were like him; they were good in spurts, but they didn't have endurance. She was going to have to groom him a little better. He would have to learn how to be a dignified consort for the mistress of the universe. Assuming that she decided to keep him on, that is. Her patience was wearing thin.

Murmuring a prayer to Xangó and the seven African powers, she crawled back into the circle and slashed off the tip of the Prathna-creature's tongue.

"Hungry," it said.

She stepped out again before it had a chance to importune her more. She would have to be more careful about mirrors. Timmy Valentine was loose, and getting looser by the hour. She had to be careful.

"Aren't you afraid?" said Damien Peters, as he straightened his tie.

"I thank the powers of darkness," she said, "that for once they've given me a worthy adversary."

12

CIRCLES OF LIGHT AND DARKNESS

SHAMANESS

Twelve trailers were lined up in the parking lot next to the soundstages. The thirteenth was invisible. Not through magic—although Simone Arleta had placed a defensive ring of powerful objects around it—but because the parking lot backed into the forest that covered most of the mountain save for the bald and snowy peaks in the far distance.

The thirteenth trailer was camouflaged behind a row of pine trees. Even in broad daylight, it was enveloped in shadow. It felt good to sit in the shadow, surrounded by the tools of her trade. Sometimes the more sordid aspects of witchcraft did get to her. Such as last night, sawing the coffee table into pieces so they could heave it into the trash bag, keeping watch for passersby while Jacques dragged it out through the lobby, concealed by a spell of masking so that he seemed to be some garbage collector or hotel staff person, if the guests didn't look at him too closely . . . sordid, sordid, sordid.

So far, the maid hadn't noticed that the table was gone; why should she? It wasn't something that would occur to someone, a piece of furniture missing from a hotel room . . . not unless one had made a point of memorizing it. Besides, the maids spent as little time as possible in her suite. They didn't like the smell.

Jacques served tea and slipped quietly away so that she could meditate.

She sipped her tea. It was a delicious situation. Her trailer was stealing power from the movie people's generator, and they didn't even suspect. She was going to devour them from within. She was the canker worm in the apple's core. And it was a beautiful thing, this apple.

She meditated. She sent her spirit out of herself, felt it darting from soul to soul. How she despised them. There was the director, dreaming of cocaine as he offhandedly oversaw the setting up of the next shot. The writer, who yesterday had just been a hanger-on, agonizing about how he should reconcile the preposterous script with what he really knew of Timmy Valentine. There was the publicist, hopelessly lost in self-recrimination over her son's suicide, desperately seeking a substitute in the bumpkin from Hangman's Holler.

And the bumpkin himself . . . an innocent, a pawn. He was beautiful and he had a beautiful voice . . . he had intensity. His intensity sprang from the fact that he was abused by his mother. To cure him might deprive him of his presence, of the emotional wellspring of his art. What a tragedy. What a pity he would end up being consumed by forces far, far, far beyond his understanding or control.

Simone sent her mind out farther now. She caught glimpses of former lives. That's what they had to be, so vivid were the images. Here she was a Celtic priestess, preparing warriors to be burned alive inside a monstrous wicker man. Here she was a sibyline oracle, a wizened crone hanging in a bottle, longing for death. Here she was a shamaness dressed in furs, beheading the king of spring with a double-headed axe so that his blood could fertilize the earth and make it bring forth fruit and grain. Always she was a woman of power. The power had been growing for a thousand years, ten thousand, fifty thousand. The dark powers were the true powers.

How foolish men were to think of what she did as evil! Was the goddess Kali evil, though she devoured men's hearts? There is no evil, she thought. There is only the dance of the light and the shadow, the ancient dance that holds the world in balance. I am a sacred thing.

She felt her spirit soaring now as she meditated on the cosmic underpinnings of her art. She touched the edge of a transcendent joy. It had a beauty that was like pain. She could not bear it and send her spirit plummeting back to earth. And now she emptied her mind of intellect and she ran in the cool forest with her nose close to the dirt and the wet earth between her toes and the scent of prey in her nostrils and the twigs cracking beneath her, her belly to the muck, her eyes darting, darting . . . following the blood-spoor of a wounded animal. She was free of reason. She knew only instinct. She ran.

She came to the trunk of the tree. The blood still clung to the bark. The chains were still there. The nails dug deep into the living wood. But the boy was gone. Like an animal that willingly gnaws off its own foot to escape the hunter's trap, the creature who fed her powers had slipped free.

No matter. She was still queen of the wood.

She remembered:

By the banks of the Tigris and Euphrates, the women were weeping for Tammuz, the god-king, dead and ploughed into the earth. By the shores of the Nile, Isis was weeping for her consort Osiris, cut into pieces and strewn across the earth. At Golgotha the two Marys were mourning the heaven-sent king; in the north, the ravens hovered over the bog of the hanged god, waiting for resurrection. She had stood in all those places. But those who worshipped these sons of the gods had forgotten the crucial thing: it was woman who was the slayer, and it was woman who gave life anew.

Woman the earth.

And I the woman.

Slowly she eased herself out of her reverie. It was the axolotl she felt first, symbol of rebirth, wiggling and twisting in a sea of menstrual blood. It was good to feel the little life within her. It was as good to nurture as it was to destroy.

Simone downed the rest of her tea. She nibbled on a chocolate chip cookie as she lit the candles for the afternoon invocation. She would need seven candles—red, she thought to herself, the color of passion. She finished the cookie and sat very still, plotting the death of the world and its rebirth in her own image.

DISSOLVE: VISION SEEKERS

PJ and Chit were in the forest scattering stones. At least, PJ was scattering them; Chit held a bag of the small, flat pebbles, and watched, fascinated, as PJ felt in the bag for just the right one, held it in cupped palms, knelt by some gnarled stump or some towering pine, and laid it down so that it seemed to blend perfectly with the pattern of undergrowth.

Then he would move on. She followed. He seemed to know the forest so well he did not need to pause to sniff the wind or glance upward, seeking the sun through the canopy of green. She had never been in a forest before; all the trees looked alike; she did not even know their names. But sometimes PJ would pause to speak to one, and sometimes he would caress a tree trunk and whisper to it, words in an Indian tongue, words so alien she could not tell if they were words of love or of despair.

She wondered what her mother would think of all this. "Wandering about in the wilderness with a half-savage Red Indian!" she'd probably say. "Good heavens! And a dozen of the richest, most eligible bachelors clamoring for your hand!" Lady Chit decided that she did not care. There was enchantment in this forest; it was Sherwood, it was Arden, all the forests in those endless works of literature that she'd been forced to slog through in her teenage years in private school in New England, suddenly brought to life. In a strange way, this time of terror was a magic time.

She watched PJ, marveling at the way he moved; in his breechclout, with his dark hair half covering his eyes, crouching, darting, borrowing the movements of some forest creature . . . he was beautiful to her. He became the forest, pausing now and then to mimic the call of a distant bird. "Oh, God," she said, "you're beautiful."

"Are you calling me God now?" PJ said, laughing. He turned away from her to drop a stone into its place in a thin shaft of sunlight.

"Oh, don't make jokes," she said. "Make love."

"Here? Now?"

"Yes. In the dirt. Sully me. Soil me. I've never done it this way before. Only in bed, with two-hundred-dollar designer sheets, in condominiums in front of a fire on the skins of animals I didn't kill myself." She'd never talked this way before; she'd always played the role of the demure aristocrat even when she was seething inside.

"Sully you? Soil you? But you're practically royalty!"

"Bullshit. And you're practically a noble savage."

"I'll get a blanket from the car and we can spread it out."

"No. No." They weren't touching, weren't even close. But there was something about the forest that made her feel they were joined together, immersed in the same amniotic fluid, sharing a single womb. She sloughed her clothes and moved toward him with her arms spread wide. She kissed him. He smelled of wet leaves, of soil; her tongue teased his chapped lips; his fingers explored her skin, her hardening nipples; she knelt in front of him, unclasped the breechclout with her teeth, breathed in his manhood's musk, licked at the uncut penis; then, her arms about his hips, she felt him slide into her, thinking if only my mother could see me now, if only she could know the wind on the bare flesh, not some air conditioner shielding the tropic air and shutting out the scent of night-blooming jasmine; if only she could smell the moist earth and the moistness of an earthy man, hard and urgent and elemental. Oh America, she thought, so savage, so far from the civilized order of a hierarchical society . . . so pure, so young. That was what PJ meant to her. She thought of how one day she might enter a loveless, dynastic marriage and sit in an air-conditioned mansion overseeing the servants, and she knew that she would always remember this, the forest of ancient magic.

"Yes, it's magic," PJ said softly, seeming to read her thoughts; "it's a strong medicine we're making, and we have to make it with love. But sometimes I'm scared because I don't think you can be serious." She could not protest because just then a sexual climax rent him and she drank the bitter honey of his love, and later, like a doll, she let herself be laid down on the ground, felt the twigs crack against her naked back, closed her eyes, felt his lips against her breasts, her abdomen, felt his tongue fleck her clitoris and send a joyful shudder through her; closed her eyes and saw fantastical images that seemed to be plucked from his mind; saw the forest with the eyes of a soaring eagle; saw the great sacred circle of protection that he was laying down, stone by stone, a circle whose circumference encompassed the entire peak of the mountain they were on, all of Junction, all of Highwater, all the people involved in the making of the film, all the bystanders whose lives the film would affect . . . hawklike she plummeted with the sun behind her, plummeted as he plunged deeper into the inner warmth of her; now she was a fish that rived the watery depths of a swift-coursing stream, and the stream was part of the circle of waters that the circle of stones circumscribed; now, springing onto land, she was the rabbit, breathing in the sharp smell of fresh-torn vegetation; she was the wolf, dancing the dance of life and death with the leaping deer; she was earth before thunder, waiting for rain.

And the rain started to fall.

"Shit," PJ said, laughing, "I wasn't trying to do no rain dance."

"It feels good." The rain was warm and turned the ground soft around her.

"Yeah," said PJ. He enveloped her completely. She opened her mouth and drank the sweet water from the sky. His slick limbs slid across hers. The water tickled. They laughed as they made love. She knew then that this lovemaking was a part of PJ's spell; the circle was drawn with stones but drew its power from their act of love.

The rain sluiced down now. Thunder threshed the twigs from the treetops. As she climaxed she left her body once again, found herself soaring higher than before, thrusting through the nimbus clouds into a realm of light. They danced at the eye of the storm, wrapped and raptured in an inner radiance. She saw the circle they were drawing, saw the image of it in PJ's mind as well as the necklace of stones with which they were encircling the stage where the great conflict was about to occur. And then she saw something else.

Someone was drawing another circle.

As fast as they could lay the stones, someone else was blotting them out. Someone whose magic was fueled as much by lovelessness as PJ's was driven by love. Her spirit swooped down. She had to see the face of the enemy. The enemy was driving uphill—no, being driven —in a car that was also a cat-creature—the cougar that had chased them that night!—she could almost see her face—it was the person she had always suspected—the old woman with the piercing eyes, who had first shown her her grandfather slithering along snowy mountain trails—it was Simone! Plunging through the sunwind, back into the storm, she hovered above the car roof. She darted across the windshield and saw Jacques, Simone's assistant, clenching the wheel, grim-faced; she saw a hatbox on the empty seat beside him; and behind—there was only Simone, but she knew she carried another creature inside her, one that writhed in agony but would not see relief until the spell was woven—a tiny creature—she could feel the pinpricks of its pain—and there was another creature too—a supernatural one—inside the hatbox.

The creature's soul cried out to her. She knew him.

"Grandfather!" she screamed. Her scream was lost in the scream of the wind, in the crash of the thunder, the pelting of the rain. And then, all at once, she fell back into herself. The rain was receding. She was leaning against the trunk of a tree. PJ was wiping the tears from her eyes with a callused finger.

"Did you—was I dreaming?—" she said.

"No," he said. "I was the hawk, I was the rain. Those were my eyes you saw with."

"We're being followed," she said. "That woman—"

"Yeah." The rain had moved on; she could hear its patter in the distance. He was wiping her face with his breechclout. The mansmell clung to her nostrils. "She thinks she's fighting you and me. She doesn't know she's fighting Mother Earth herself. She thinks she *is* the mother. It's true that the earth can destroy us, the way she can, but she's the healer too. That's what I learned long ago, when I had the vision that sometimes makes me see the world the way a woman sees it."

"But she's trying to neutralize your circle."

"Marking territory on my territory doesn't make it

her territory." PJ laughed, a dry, bitter laugh. "Let's go on. . . ."

Lady Chit ran behind him with her bag of stones. Wet mud squished between her toenails. The wood was a patchwork of dark and breaking sunlight. PJ cast his stones, murmured his words of power, walked on, unhurried, each step an echoed step of the grand cosmic dance; behind them, she knew, came the shadow, always approaching, always at bay. And she danced alongside him, naked and unashamed of her nakedness.

SHAMANESS

She too stood naked in the forest. She too held stones in her hand, small flat pebbles; her stones, too, were anointed. She had taken the axolotl from her vagina; with a certain regret, she had placed it in the blender along with certain other herbs and reagents. A drop of resultant liquid was smeared on each of her stones. She knew that an enemy had gone before her and was drawing up his own circle of power.

My circle will swallow his circle up and spit it out, she thought grimly. No two-bit magician's going to stand in my way. . . .

DISSOLVE: THUNDER

Distant thunder.

Angel waited in Brian's trailer; he didn't like going to his own. Because there was always the reek of alcohol from his mother's compartment.

Brian typed away on his portable PC.

"Are you doing some new sides for tomorrow?" Angel said.

"No." Brian grinned. "Actually I'm kind of . . . working on a novel."

"What's it about?"

"Oh, I don't know . . . well, there's a boy, you see, and he's growing up in a suburban neighborhood in the nineteen-sixties, you see . . . and he feels alienated . . . until one day these aliens show up at his window."

"It's a sci-fi story?"

"Nah . . . the aliens are like . . . well, you know, a metaphor for his alienation. They're not real. Like reflections in a mirror. They're two-dimensional images of himself."

"Cool. Except . . ."

"What?"

"Mirror images *are* real."

"I know," said Brian. Angel saw that every mirror in the trailer had been turned to face the wall.

Angel said, almost inaudibly, "My mother does terrible things to me. I think she's sucking my soul away." He was a bit self-conscious about accidentally slipping into Timmy's lyrics, but there wasn't much he could do; Timmy Valentine's music was always running through his head now.

"What terrible things, Angel?" Brian snapped his laptop shut. He turned to Angel and looked straight at him in a way that adults rarely did. Like he might be worth taking seriously.

"You know." Angel looked down at the floor. Then he got up to get a pop from the cooler. "Terrible things. But she says it's because she loves me. She needs me. I know she really needs me. I'm the only one who knows what pills to give her and how many and what time of day."

"But you're very close to her."

"Sometimes I can hear her all the way from another room. Another building. I had a twin brother once. We buried him in the hillside. His name was Errol. As in Flynn."

"No shit? You just buried him? How'd he die?"

"I don't really know," Angel said edgily.

"It's strange the way you talk about him. Maybe he's like an imaginary companion or something."

"Get outta here. Imaginary companions're for little kids."

"Okay."

"Tell me about the new scene."

"Okay." Brian opened up the laptop once more, pushed a few keys, pressed Enter with a flourish. "It's a dream sequence. You're helping mad scientist's beautiful daughter take care of a gorilla in a cage. She's beautiful and she's dressed all in red. The gorilla escapes. He pursues you and the woman up a long flight of steps into an L-shaped apartment house. The woman runs into the bathroom and locks the door. You go to the piano—a white piano—mists are rising from the floorboards—and you start playing. But the ape is pounding at the door—in slow motion—and you're playing in this really remote, detached way, as though you were trying to leave the whole world behind—and meanwhile, the woman in the bathroom is still screaming—and we pull into a close-up on the pool of yellow light leaking from the threshold—and your music plays on, more and more ethereal, more and more heartless."

Angel was quite for a long time, thinking: I had a dream like that once. I was playing in F-sharp which is a key that pop songs are never written in because it's so far away from the chords people know how to play; you bend and twist your fingers around those guitar frets and you skitter over those black keys like a crab; it's music of the mind, not of the heart. And I remember the woman in the bathroom but I think that she was Momma. And the monkey that clambered up the steps, big as King King. He had the face of Errol, my face . . . and then came other bits and pieces of the dream to the surface of his consciousness . . . a dog yapping by a piss-stained fire hydrant . . . a refrigerator flung open to reveal a decapitated head . . . a girl with gaping wounds, floating in a

Hollywood swimming pool . . . *These aren't my memories! Angel thought. They're someone else's!*

"Angel?"

. . . an emperor weeping beside the statue of a dead youth . . . a painter opening his veins to the lapping tongue of a black cat . . . and then . . . *fire fire fire fire* . . .

Those weren't in my dream either. There's someone tearing at my mind. But I won't let him get to me because I'm still me, I'm still me.

THUNDER

Thunder rolled again. The voice of darkness. That was good. Simone stepped out of the forest into the parking lot with its rows of trailers. She passed unnoticed among the hordes of carpenters, production assistants, extras and assorted lackeys. Some were milling about; others clustered around a table piled with junk food; yet others pored over paperwork or sat in small groups gossiping. If they saw her at all there was no reason to assume she was not meant to be there; she had cloaked herself in an illusion. She was a corner of a trailer's shadow; a shadow cast by the gathering nimbus clouds; a shadow of one of their shadows.

She stood and watched. There was a trailer marked MR. TODD. But she knew that Angel was not to be found there. A Hispanic woman, overdressed and overcoiffured, was knocking at the door.

"It's Gabriela," she was saying. "Marjorie, Marjorie . . ."

Staying in the trailer's penumbra, she crept closer. The door opened. There was Angel's mother. She was in a see-through nightdress through which Simone could see sagging breasts; her face was lined before its time; her hair, stringy and straggly, showed traces of artificial coloring.

"Yes?" she said. She sounded like a ghost.

"It's me. Gabriela Muñoz. You know? Your son's agent." The contempt in the agent's face was unmistakable. "There's trouble. They don't want you on the set anymore; you're embarrassing people with your white-trash ways."

"Leave me alone. Did you bring me some of them blue pills? I'm all out of blue ones."

"Anyway, in the interests of smoother sailing—"

"Just get the hell out, Gabriela, unless you got some of them pills."

"Listen. You're going to lose everything—the pills, the Porsche, the hotel room, the big fat twenty-five percent of Angel's income that the Jackie Coogan law allows you to skim off the top—if you don't listen to what I say."

"Everything?"

"Yes."

Simone saw the woman gulp. Avarice was what motivated her, that was certain; but there was something darker too; she was a woman who had never been able to bring herself to cut the umbilical cord between herself and her son. And it was eating them both alive. She was weak.

"Look," Gabriela said. "We can compromise. You can stay at the hotel and you can sign this paper authorizing me to be the set guardian."

"But you're the agent, too . . . don't that sound fishy?" She took the paper that Gabriela waved in her face. "Make it someone else. . . ."

"Who else?"

"I don't know."

"Here . . . I do have your blue pills, actually," said the agent, brandishing them for a moment before whisking them back into her purse. "Just sign the damn thing."

Simone saw the longing in the woman's eyes. She

would not be difficult to seduce over to her side. She could tell. Marjorie Todd scrawled her name in spidery print across the bottom of the proffered sheet.

"All right now." Gabriela yanked away the paper and tossed her the bottle; then she stalked away. Angel's mother slammed the door.

Simone prepared herself for a moment, murmuring a prayer to Xipe Totec, the flayed god, whom Christians call Jesus. She called upon the power that comes from self-inflicted pain. Pulling a thorn from her purse, she carefully jabbed it into the flesh part of her left palm and worked it through the cartilage to the back of her hand. Then she drew it out, did the same to her right hand, and put it back in her purse. She climbed the three steps to the door of Angel's trailer and, palms outstretched, imprinted the stigmata on the door. *Blood to blood,* she thought.

Then she whispered, very softly, in a sweet high voice that mimicked that of a child, "Mrs. Todd . . . Mrs. Todd . . ."

She drew contrary circles on the door with her bloody hands.

She repeated words of power in five dead languages and five living ones, five being the number of dark magic. She leaned into the door, willing it to open until it finally did.

Mrs. Todd was reclining on a red vinyl bunk. She stirred a blood-colored drink with a swizzle stick topped with a cherry-red plastic heart. A television set blared out an episode of "Days of Our Lives." A radio played country-and-western music in jarring counterpoint. Mrs. Todd was paying attention to neither.

"Who are you?" she said. But then, as Simone moved silently to sit beside her, she seemed to recognize her. "Oh yeah. I know you from somewhere."

Simone touched her hand, making sure a smear of

blood would linger on it. "How's your son treating you these days?"

Marjorie Todd began to weep. It was a repulsive sight. The puffy eyes, the runny nose . . . there was more strength in one of Simone's sacrificial turtles than there was in this creature.

"Go on," Simone said. "Tell me about it."

"It's like . . . he doesn't have no respect no more. Like he's listening to someone else's voice and not minding me. Oh, we're so close, you know. Times, we used to be more like one person than two, always knowing what the other one craved. And now . . . him being the breadwinner and all . . . he sasses me. He mocks me and calls me a drug addict. It just ain't right."

"I don't suppose it is," Simone said. She held her stigmatized left hand over Marjorie's drink. She tensed the muscles of her palm. Three drops of blood fell into the bloody Mary.

"And that agent just orders me around like I was garbage . . . me, his mother, who brought him into this world."

"Wouldn't you like to be back in control?" said Simone. She reached out and cupped Marjorie's face between her hands. The blood was caking but it was still powerful. She gazed into the woman's eyes and wouldn't let her look away.

"Sure," said Marjorie wistfully, "but—"

"Everything's going to be better soon. I promise." Simone stroked the woman's prickly hair. "You'll have your son back. He'll be more than a son to you. I promise. I promise."

"That feels good. Soothing. Don't stop."

"You can talk to me. We're both women, aren't we? We've got to stick together. There's power in womanhood, ancient power that men can't tap."

"What do you mean?"

"Reach over and turn your television to the Damien

Peters show," Simone said. "Damien has an important message for you in today's sermon."

Marjorie's eyes darted from side to side like a frightened squirrel's. "You ain't . . . from the devil or nothing like that?" she said.

Simone smiled. "How could I be? I'm coming to you from Damien Peters. I'm a messenger of the Lord."

"An angel," Angel's mother said. "No wonder your face seems so . . . so bright." She still didn't want to look into her eyes, but Simone chanted a mantra of petrification to give her the qualities of stone—motionlessness, sculptability.

"Yes," Simone crooned, "I am an angel, I am, I am."

THUNDER

Brian and Angel listened to the thunder.

THUNDER

PJ and Chit listened to the thunder.

THUNDER

Petra, listening to the thunder, thought of Jason. He'd always been scared of thunder when he was little. As she pulled into the main parking lot of the set, she glanced up at the rearview mirror and saw him—

—reach out to her out of the lemon tree, the maggots boring through his palms like nails and—

Petra braked.

Took several deep breaths.

She pulled into the first available space, although it was far from Brian's trailer, and started walking.

In the far distance, there were thunderclouds; but the thunder sounded close—too close.

DISSOLVE: THUNDER: MIRRORS

Gabriela Muñoz went right up to her room at the Highwater Inn. She had a raging headache and she wanted something stronger than Ibuprofen. Where were the damn Fiorinals? She pulled the tweed garment bag out of the closet, sat down on the bed, and swallowed three of them without water.

Then she reached for the phone so she could call her office in Los Angeles. Her head was still throbbing but she couldn't stop now.

"Yeah," she told the secretary, "I got the bitch to sign. Of course I can't be the set guardian, I'll write up a power of attorney for someone else . . . maybe that PR woman, Shiloh, can handle it. The sooner we get the mother off the set, the better; just the sight of her makes Burr want to vomit. I'll be back in town Monday; set up that Orion meeting for me, but no earlier than three o'clock, all right?"

She was scribbling her signature on a standard form even as she spoke. "Oh, and delay everyone's checks for seven days," she added. She was worried about the mortgage payments on the condo in Palm Springs. Shouldn't have bought it in the first place, of course, but you had to have somewhere to stash your parents when they started getting too . . . too damn *Hispanic* on you.

She glanced up at the closet and saw someone in the mirror.

Aaron Maguire . . . the writer who disappeared? . . . bullshit. Eyes playing tricks.

She reached for the phone again.

"No—cancel that contract. Absolutely not."

—trapped in the mirror—but his hands reaching out

to her—blood everywhere—oh, Jesus, those eyes, what could a man have seen for his eyes to look like that?—

. . . side effects. She shouldn't have had the three Fiorinals. Maybe there was something in her suitcase that could cancel it out. She rummaged. Damn it, Mom had packed, she'd been at the house that weekend and she'd *insisted,* and what was a goddamn *rosary* doing there, twined like a serpent around that medicine box? . . .

—behind the man there were flames—the smell of burning sulphur—charring—the sizzling of blood on hot stones—

Maybe a couple of ludes would do the trick. She gulped them down. Took a swig of last night's champagne, a flat *demi-bouteuil* of Bollinger still sitting by the nightstand. That was better. Fog was closing in on her. But that was good. It would shut out unpleasant thoughts. She toyed with the rosary and it got tangled up in the phone cord. Cheap plastic thing. So what if they'd bought it at Saint Peter's, if the Pope had blessed it? Tacky. So damn superstitious, that's how Mom and Papa were.

Another phone call. "Oh, Flora, honey . . . don't forget to take your medication. Magic Mountain? Well . . . next week maybe. I just don't have time . . . call the office and make an appointment . . . yes, yes, I know I'm your mother but make an appointment. Love you. Bye."

—the eyes—

"Who the fuck are you?"

"Don't you recognize me, Gabby? We did lunch only four months ago. . . ."

The eyes. The flesh, hanging in ripped ribbons on his torso. His hands gripped her hands now. They were cold. Ice-cold. As though he'd stepped out of the meat locker at an abattoir.

"Let go of the fucking telephone and look at me."

"You can't be in the mirror. You're—you're—"

"One half of me is in here. The other half is dead. Look!" And he shrieked with soulless laughter . . . and abruptly turned around so that she could see him from behind . . . there was no behind . . . he had been sheared in two . . . she could see, as though the mirror were a glass front over a cross section of a man, the heart pumping, the half-lungs inflating and deflating like blood-gorged balloons. Where the buttocks should have been, muscles rippled as they dripped dark rheum over the mirror glass.

She screamed. "Go away! I'm imagining you, this is a bad trip—" Could it really be a flashback, now, maybe twenty-five years since those thrill-seeking times?

The creature turned around. The eyes held her. She barely noticed that he was naked, and that a gnarled erection was among the body parts that protruded from the mirror, that the hands had gripped her wrists so tightly she could feel the blood seize up and refuse to flow, could feel her knuckles whitening . . . oh, but the eyes impelled her, without knowing what she was doing she found herself rising from the bed, pulled as much by an eerie longing as by the force of the half-man's hands. . . .

—distant thunder and—

"Gabriela . . . I've always kind of liked you." Behind the voice was the whisper of a firewind and the breath held the stench of brimstone. The hands moved down to her waist, tore cloth now, ripping through denim and pantyhose . . . she could feel his cock, ice-cold, rock-hard . . . riving the fabric and the flesh like an iron speartip.

She screamed.

The mirror was melting into a fine mist. Two realities were intersecting. And where the two worlds met, he was raping her. His pelvis was thrusting in and out of the mirror. Oh God, he was cold, cold. The cold exploded through her veins. Jesus it felt like a fucking Freon enema or something. "Gabby," he sighed, "Gabby, Gabby," his voice gusting like an arctic wind. "God, I'm so thirsty and you're so warm, so full of life."

"Please . . ."

He was pulling her in now. The lower half of her body had vanished into the mirror as though it were a pool of mercury. She couldn't see where her body ended, only the reflection of her upper torso.

"Help!" she shrieked. He was dragging her into the mirror!

His grip didn't loosen. He's a vampire, she thought. I'm stuck in a low-budget hammer movie without a crucifix. Her mind moved sluggishly through the fog of ludes and painkillers. His hands let go of her wrists now, climbed slowly up her back. Cold cold cold her spine screamed. The arms drew her into a bloody embrace. The lips parted and a tongue protruded from them and sought out hers . . . forced her mouth open, crammed them with a frozen perfume of putrescence . . . she felt herself gagging . . . she thrust her arms back . . . her fingers encountered the cheap plastic rosary . . . she yanked it loose from the telephone cord and whipped Aaron's face, again and again . . . saw the skin split open in gaping lacerations that spewed a dark dead blood . . . Aaron howled . . . retreated . . . rasped out, in a voice barely human, *"Catholic . . . why did you have to be Catholic? . . ."*

She flogged at the face again and again. Fury drove her. Blood spattered her face, her shredded blouse. The crucifix burned the flesh and cracked like thunder.

He backed away. His image receded into the mirror and she felt herself slump backward. Her head hit the edge of the nightstand. The rosary was half in, half out of the mirror. So was she.

From the waist down, she had vanished into the looking-glass world.

She could prop herself against the side of the bed with her elbows. I should be panicking, she told herself. It's the drugs. But they're going to wear off and then I'm going to scream and scream and I'll probably never stop screaming and oh God God . . . she tried to feel something in her toes but there was nothing at all, not even the phantom pain of amputation . . . the position she was in was excruciating, with nothing to rest her back on . . . what the fuck to do now, call a doctor, ask him *where's the rest of me* like a madcap Ronald Reagan? She tried to pull herself loose again. Nothing.

Nothing.

Nothing!

At last she took the phone and dialed the front desk. "You'd better send someone up," she said. "I'm not going to explain the problem because you're going to think I've gone insane."

She eased the suitcase under her to form a backrest. That was better. She felt among her clothes for the Fiorinals. Better not to think straight, she told herself. She only half believed this was happening to her. Thinking straight would only make her hysterical. Better to give herself up completely to unconsciousness. . . .

VISION SEEKER

"I think the circle is complete," PJ said. "I hear it in the thunder."

"Let's make love again," Chit said.

"I hate to think of you getting wet if it—"

"In the car then. So I can watch the rain pour down while you—"

"Yes. Yes."

SHAMANESS

"I think the circle will be complete soon," Simone said. "As soon as we anoint the last stones with blood. . . ."

But Marjorie Todd wasn't listening to her. She was watching Damien Peters preach his sermon . . . the first sermon of the new order . . . the sermon to herald the apocalypse. . . .

"Listen to me, Marjorie!"

"Yes. Yes. I saw him many times, you know. In Hangman's Holler. When I worked at the diner. Course, that was before I—we—became famous."

"The circle . . . the circle!" Simone whispered harshly, hoping that Damien's platitudes would soon come to an end.

ANGEL

"You think it'll rain?" said one of the production assistants.

"I'm calling it a day," said Jonathan Burr. "Nobody touch those marks."

Angel unfroze the beatific expression he'd been wearing for the long, lingering close-up of Timmy Valentine gazing at the setting sun.

. . . and the thunder came nearer.

13

TAMMUZ

PROPHET

And what a beautiful Sunday morning it is here in Hangman's Holler, all you people out there; God's morning; the air is humming with the riches of summer; I hope it's just as beautiful out there in television country, the country of my ministry, from sea to shining sea, I can feel the surge of power as a million hearts turn to hear the Lord's word, to do the Lord's work.

But I come to you with a heavy heart.

I've lied to you. I, Damien Peters, the one televangelist who's kept the faith, kept away from the demon booze and the demon adultery, I have told my flock a thing that isn't true.

Yes. I've lied. How can this be?

Because, my friends, it's not really a beautiful day out there. It's a dismal day. It's a-thundering and a-pouring as though we were on the brink of the very deluge itself, the time the Almighty punished man for his disobedience and iniquity and in his compassion saved only Noah and the creatures of the Ark.

But you don't have to look upon the thunder over Hangman's Holler, thanks to the miracle of special effects and high technology. I am standing before you at my lectern in a room in front of a blue screen, and my image is being combined electronically with another image that our studio's library has on file—an image of the finest, blessedest, most beautiful summer morning you're ever likely to see on God's green earth.

If you don't believe me, I'm going to ask the studio technicians to show you a glimpse through the window here at the studios . . . look . . . the lowering sky . . . the angry clouds . . . it is the face of God indeed, the face of God's wrath for has He not said, "I am a jealous God"? But let us not look upon the roiling thunder. Let us look on that summer morning one more time, my friends, let us gaze upon each precious leaf and flower as though it were the last time we were ever going to gaze upon such beauty. Because, I'm a-saying unto you, it may well *be* the last time. Because, as surely as I'm standing here in your living room in living, breathing, virtual reality, as surely as I'm speaking these words to you, my flock, my precious children, there's a storm a-gathering, and it's the biggest ol' storm that you're ever going to see, and the name of that storm is Armageddon.

The end of the world is nigh.

It's a time of reckoning. It's a time when we 'fess up to those little white lies that we've been telling each other all our lives. Even this harmless little illusion, showing you a beautiful day when in truth it's a-thundering and a-carrying on outside my window like the very day of judgment . . . it's still an illusion, my friends. And who is the master of illusion, the prince of disguises, the deceiving one? Why, you all know the answer to that as well as I do—it's Satan, the lord of darkness.

The devil lies, my faithful friends, but he also tells the

truth sometimes, and he mixes the truth with lies to confuse us, and to awaken in us a terrible despair.

Despair is the enemy, my friends! Do not despair!

Today's sermon is about illusion. It is about illusion as an art and as a science. It is about self-delusion and the delusion of other people. But most of all it is about the reality behind that illusion, which must and can only be the reality of our Savior Jesus Christ, who lives and reigns with Him in the unity of the Holy Spirit, world without end. Amen.

Today I'm going to level with you. You all know about these so-called scandals I've been involved in. You all know that Satan can take many forms, from the *National Enquirer* to the Internal Revenue Service. But I'm a-going to tell you all the truth, God's truth, His blessed truth.

The truth! The truth! The truth!

No matter what the cost.

No matter how great the pain.

Pray with me for a few moments . . . and if you are so moved by the power of His heavenly word, our number can be found flashing at the bottom of your screen . . . Visa and MasterCard accepted.

Our Father . . .

MEMORY: A.D. 130

Outside the pavilion of Caesar, the women wail for Tammuz. In the tent of the chorus master, the boys prepare for the performance of *Oedipus Rex* which will be both the mourning song for Antinous and the dedication piece for the new city that the emperor has decreed will be founded in this spot, a city to be called Antinoöpolis.

Days, the boy vampire who is now called Lysander sleeps buried in a sand dune just beyond the oasis, clutching in his hands a pouch of the ashes of Pompeii; he does not know why he needs this handful of native earth, but instinct tells him he dare not lose it.

Nights, Lysander waits until the darkest hour, when the Celtic boy, Cluelinus, has fallen asleep at Caesar's feet; then he steals in and plays the lyre in the purple-dipped tent of the emperor. Hadrian's grief has made an insomniac of him; he reads the classics by the flickering light of an oil lamp, seeking out comfort in the familiar words of the ancients: Homer, Alcaeus, Plato.

He sings the songs he learned long ago, before he changed; he sings in a Greek that already sounds antiquated, though it is but two or three generations old; the words themselves are older still, and no one remembers how they were originally sounded. But they are still beautiful:

> Like the wind from the mountain
> that plummets upon the oak-trees—
> Love shook my heart.

"Sappho is my favorite poet," the emperor says, and drinks deep of the undiluted wine in which he drowns his melancholy. "but what can *you* know of love, Antinous, who are so young? You are like an unfilled goblet; you must wait for the wine to be poured before you in turn can give wine; so it is with love; the young receive it by virtue of being beautiful; the aged give it for having lost their beauty. . . ."

"Yes, Caesar," says Lysander, not wanting to remind him that he is not Antinous, and that he is, indeed, older than the emperor. But he has still to give love to anyone. Alive, the goblet was never filled; undead, it remains empty.

"I am glad you've come to me now, though the requisite three days of mourning are not yet up," says Hadrian. "I was lonely. I know I cannot touch you, at least, not as before; you belong to Hades now. I am surprised that he even lets me look at you."

"I am not what I seem," says Lysander, knowing that he will not be believed. "Tell me about him. Antinous, I mean. Why did he die?"

"He threw himself into the river," says Hadrian.

"Was he unhappy with his lot, even though he was the favorite of an emperor? Was he ill, perhaps, despairing of a cure?"

"No, no, no, no . . . it was I who was ill . . . *am* ill . . . I and the entire corpus of my empire."

"Tell me of him."

"Do you know who the Christianoi are?"

"No, Caesar."

"They are an insidious religious sect. They worship Tammuz, like all the Levantine people. Nothing wrong with that, of course. Everyone knows that the king of spring dies each year and is reborn after three days, and renews the earth. It is only natural. But these people . . . they were so literal-minded, you see. They claimed that Tammuz was an actual person . . . not a metaphor, not even a priest who might take on the incarnation of the god for the purpose of the sacred rituals . . . but a person . . . a Judaean carpenter . . . a criminal they crucified a hundred years ago. If only you knew how terrible these people's madness is! They've taken poetry and turned it into shit. Taken the mystery out of religion, acted as though myths were no longer symbols of truth, but truth itself. Oh, we kill them, when we can find them; but they're a pestilence. They will last forever, and forever we will be trying to root them out; burn them alive, feed them to beasts, vivisect them in public spectacles. Unless, you see . . . unless . . ."

". . . you can create a better myth . . . something more beautiful."

"Antinous," says the one who will one day be made a

god by an act of the Senate. "He volunteered to do it one day when I was railing about the mystery cults of our eastern provinces . . . about how this cult of Jesus was perverting the truth, replacing the spiritual with the material . . . they believe in the resurrection of the body! We will have a world populated by vampires . . . by the living dead, whom the men of unconquered Africa call the *nzambi,* the ghosts who walk!"

Caesar trembles. Soundlessly, Lysander refills his wine *krater.*

"He killed himself that you might have a new Tammuz?" he says.

"He slipped away in the night," says Caesar, "the unblemished boy, the unwritten page, the unfilled goblet; he invoked Hapi, the Nile-god, and threw himself from the royal barge; then, only then, did I understand that he was capable of love after all."

Lysander, who does not have that capacity, can only listen.

"Oioioi, pheu, pheu," cries the emperor. It is the traditional Greek cry of mourning. "You loved me, Antinous. It was not that I am Caesar nor that I shall become a god after I die. You made yourself a god so that you would be waiting for me among the clouds of Olympus. You preceded me into godhood and it is thus that I know you are the elder god, born long before my birth, the god who dies and comes again; I knew that you are Tammuz and Adonis and Osiris; you shed your earthly form as a snake sloughs its skin; no man could have loved the world so much as you, who laid down your life to renew the earth."

He is raving, Lysander thinks. He has parlayed his unrequited love into some cosmic drama of gods and rebirth. I only serve to bolster his self-delusion. I have no independent existence. I am but a reflection of men's inner torments. I am the mirror of their souls.

Perceiving that Hadrian has sunk into silence yet
again, Lysander sings once more:

> The moon has set; so have the seven
> sisters;
> it is midnight; the night watch passes;
> I sleep alone.

And Caesar weeps.

PROPHET

And now I'm going to talk about false messiahs.

Once upon a time, before the true light came down and
was born among men, there were many false lights. And
they shone in the darkness, and because the people lived
in darkness, they clung to the light, any light, not knowing that the light was false. You all know how a drowning man will grasp at a straw. And a heathen will grasp
at superstition, being ignorant of the Lord.

Yes, my friends, ignorance is darkness.

I've been reading a lot of those secular humanist
books, and I've been watching the TV lectures of so-
called experts like Joseph Campbell, and as I was watching one last week it came to me in a vision that this was
the devil himself speaking to me, mixing lies with truth,
as I've said before. You see, they're talking about how
Neolithic man believed in a man who was made into a
god, and who was killed every year on Good Friday by
pagan high priestesses, whose body was ploughed into
the earth—and who came back to life on the third day.
They're a-telling us that this god, who was incarnated in
a living man, this heathen god who was called by a hundred different names, like Adonis, Dumuzi, Tammuz,
Osiris . . . that these heathen rites were what gave rise to

our Jesus' death and resurrection. They're saying that all mythologies are saying the same thing. They're saying that somehow, the coming of our Lord, the incarnation of God on earth, can be equated with heathen demons with a hundred arms and leering faces. They're a-telling us that the Easter bunny and the Easter egg are survivals of disgusting abominations they call primitive fertility rites. This, my faithful friends, is the kind of confusion those devil-inspired secular humanists are trying to foist off on us in the name of historical accuracy, in the name of multicultural fairness—well, I say unto you, such idle speculations are pure and simple *bullshit!*

Do not be shocked, my faithful friends. This foul language is the best that can be said of those who would seek to cloud the purity and clarity of our faith! I'm not going to bleep this word out. I want you all to repeat it after me—

Bullshit! Bullshit! Bullshit!

Get thee behind me, Satan!

My friends . . . you who are watching me now . . . I know you've been with me through thick and thin . . . I know you've been loyal to me despite the trials and tribulations of this ministry . . . the ill-fortune, the slurs, the scandals, the loathsome and unjustified charges that have been laid against me by those who despise and reject the work of the Lord . . . I'm going to level with you, my friends. It is a time for honesty. It is a time for truth.

I've had a vision.

Yesterday evening at sunset, I drove out into the hills beyond Hangman's Holler. I drove right up to the top of those blessed hills, far from the coal mines and far from the city; far from this temple I've built in Hangman's Holler with the help of each one of you faithful followers; far from anything made by man. I stood on the top of the hill and looked at the setting sun and I knelt down and prayed to the Lord, and I said, God, why, why have you sent so many sore afflictions to besiege your faithful servant? Why am I accused of fornication and of duping my flock and of failing to render unto Caesar what is Caesar's? I prayed and I prayed and I prayed with the tears streaming from my cheeks and I said, Don't turn your face from me, Lord, because I still love you, I can't stop loving you no matter what happens, because if I stopped loving you there would be nothing left in my life but pain.

And then I saw the gathering storm.

I saw the clouds roiling against the majesty of the setting sun. Beautiful and awesome is the handiwork of the Lord! Oh, I prayed and I wept, because I knew I was as nothing compared to the splendor of the heaven and the earth. And then the Lord blessed me with a vision.

He spoke to me, saying, "Damien, listen to me. I have something I want the whole world to know. I've brought you down low so that you can see the filth and the degradation of the human condition, so that when I raise you up high you will understand the true grandeur of My scheme. Now, Damien, listen, and listen good."

"Yes, Lord," I said, not daring to raise my eyes above the sod.

And the Lord said to me, "I am going to bring about a fundamental change in the nature of the world. And that change is going to happen at midnight, tomorrow night, Midsummer Day—a pagan festival to be sure, but I am the God of pagans as I am the God of the faithful; though they deny it, yet I am their one true God."

"And what will happen, O Lord?" I asked humbly. "Is this—the rapture that was promised? Is it the nuclear holocaust? Will you come down once more in glory to judge both the quick and the dead?"

And I felt the breath of the Lord upon me, and His touch trembled through every last fiber of my soul, and it was as though my eyes were opened wide and I beheld a great light upon them for the first time. It was as though I had been blind and deaf and now I could see and I could hear the music of the angels, and it's a pretty music, let me tell you; the rolling organ and the thousand-voice choir of my virtual cathedral are only the faintest echo of it. . . .

And though I dared not look upon His face, I knew that the Lord had smiled upon me. And He said, "You, my son, will lead my people out of the wilderness."

"I, Lord?" I said. "I am unworthy."

"Of course you are," He said. "Who among you is worthy? Who among you is without sin? But I have need of thee. From the hour I have named, until I come again in glory, there will be a new covenant. There will be a Third Testament. The mighty will fall and the last shall be first."

And then He told me about his grand plan for the future of mankind. But before I tell you about that, let us give thanks, and pray, and don't forget that number flashing at the bottom of your screen, because as you know, we have ministries all over the nation and all over the world, and your dollars are our life's blood.

MEMORY: A.D. 130

The funeral games for Antinous are Homeric in their austerity. Naked young athletes run a foot race and compete for a laurel wreath. Others wrestle or throw the javelin. Through it all, watching from the makeshift theater, put together with grim Roman efficiency, later to be refashioned in marble, the emperor betrays little emotion. Though the rites are Greek, the severity is very Roman.

He has asked the boy vampire to watch by his side, but Lysander has not yet learned to tolerate the sun. Instead he rests inside a sarcophagus. It is the sarcophagus of Antinous, the emperor's favorite. Perhaps Antinous, bloated by the river, is no longer beautiful enough to lie in state; Lysander has heard that the embalmers are already working on him, extracting his vital organs, stuffing him with saltpeter and spices and myrrh, readying him for his voyage to the west. The coffin stands in a place of honor beside the emperor's throne. But, with the attenuated hearing of his kind, the boy vampire cannot help but hear the sounds of the world outside his marmoreal confinement, even though he has passed into the sleep of death.

Now and then, the emperor pauses for matters of state. He signs documents held out to him by prostrate officials. He is, no doubt, impassive; his weeping has been done in the privacy of his tent; now he is every inch one-who-will-be-a-god.

Later, during the music contests, he seems more emotional. The songs themselves are trite; drinking songs, invocations to some facelessly beautiful girl or boy in the Aeolic style, pseudo-Homeric narratives. Although the music penetrates the cold sarcophagus, Lysander is unmoved. Only one song reaches into his dreamless sleep: a song in Celtish, sung by young Cluelinus, whose angular melody captures captivity's pain and alienation more poignantly than all the other songs with their smooth melismas and practiced coloraturas.

In the evening they perform the *Oedipus*. Caesar is steeped in shadow; it is easy for Lysander, transforming himself into a mist, to leak through the coffin seal and to seat himself, unnoticed, at the emperor's feet. Shifting, he becomes a shadow-creature, perhaps a raven. He worries at the bandages around Caesar's wrists. Soon there comes a trickle of blood. It is barely enough to assuage the hunger.

They perform the play by the light of a hundred torches. There are almost no people in the audience; how can there be? Antinoöpolis is only an idea in the mind of Caesar. Beyond the wooden scaffolding that suggests the skeleton of a real theater, there are a few palm trees, and beyond them, sand dunes; the desert wind is chill. The orchestra is shrouded in gloom.

The performances are lackluster. The carved masks are grotesque, exaggerated; this is not the way things were done in Pompeii. Times have changed, and Egypt is a country where the natural proportions of Hellenistic art are often transmuted into grotesqueries. The children of the chorus sing in a shrilling, ululating style calculated to rouse men's passion and terror; it is a hysterical rendition of Sophocles' tragedy, and the final lines fill Lysander's mind with bitter irony.

> Call no man happy
> Till he has crossed the bourn of life;
> Only the dead are free from pain.

If only the poet knew, if he had only tasted death before he wrote those lines, he would know that the bitterness of life is exceeded only by the bitterness of eternity.

Caesar calls for a fresh *krater* of wine. Fearing discovery, the boy shifts shape again, funneling into the dancing shadows cast by the torchbearers that stand at the four corners of the throne.

And now he is a black cat, clawing the gold thread from the imperial purple, climbing onto the shoulder of the god. The play is all but over; the self-blinded Oedipus is being led away by his young daughter Antigone, and behind them the chorus dances a slow dance, neither joyful nor funereal, a dance of intricate patterns that represents the workings of *moira,* that law of fate that neither god nor man may breach. The black cat laps at the emperor's ear; he nibbles; he draws blood; Caesar sighs.

"Antinous used to do that," he says, and for once there seems to be a human aspect to his remembrances.

No one is watching them. He becomes a boy again.

The emperor says, "You must rest. Tomorrow we are to perform a miracle, you know."

"I am to rise again from the tomb?"

"Yes."

"But do you really believe that I am somehow Antinous, come back to life a god?"

"Listen, Lysander. When I first saw you," Caesar murmurs, as the torchbearers stand, firm-jawed, just out of earshot, "I hoped it would be so. But I know now you are not Antinous at all. But there must be a miracle, you see. Oh, you should have seen his face when he told me that everything was going to be all right, that he was going to carry away all my pain and with it the suffering of my sundered empire. He was a child with a child's simple faith in miracles. But I know you are no child. Your eyes betray your true age. Antinous leaped into the Nile to show me that I'm only an emperor, but a boy could become a god, a redeemer, a supreme sacrifice. Oh, but he wasn't always so serious! He made me laugh; he made me foolish over him; he brightened my darkest moments. For his sake, I am going to make sure the miracle occurs. Tomorrow, the third day, Tammuz will rise from the grave. It doesn't matter that you are not he. Miracles are never miracles to those who perform them—they are only sleight of hand, but if they confirm men's faith, they are true miracles. You see, I've already drafted the Senate decree that's going to make him a god. I need you for the little charade. It's the art of illusion, you see."

And with those words, the music dies away and the actors come forward on bended knee across the wooden stage, hoping that Caesar will vouchsafe them something for their pains—a bag of *aurei,* an estate on Sicily, a brace of beautiful slaves.

The gifts are generous. The actors are barely able to cart them away. Bowing and scraping as they back away toward the exits, they vanish into shadow.

"You must go back into the coffin soon," says the emperor. "And then, after dawn, you shall have your freedom."

There is no one left in the audience now. Before dawn there will be a funeral procession to the place of entombment. The emperor will keep vigil beside the sarcophagus. Until the resurrection.

PROPHET

Welcome back to the virtual cathedral, my faithful flock, you have remained so loyal to me as the Lord tested my will and tempered me in the refiner's fire of temptation. I did not despair and neither did you, and now comes the time of our reward.

Sell your belongings! Give all your money to the poor, or better still, to our church! Say goodbye to those unsaved ones you call your friends and neighbors. Wait quietly at home. Mark the doors of your houses, as the Jews did of old, so that the wrath of the Almighty will pass you over.

It has come to be that the storm which will shake the world will start in a small town in Idaho named Highwater. There's a-going to be a gateway to hell opening up there in the mountains. They are making a movie there, but illusion will become reality quicker than they know it. There won't be any need for special effects once the demons of hell are unleashed!

After the night of terror, you and I and all the faithful will be clothed in glory. . . .

SHAMANESS

He's going too far, Simone Arleta thought, as she watched Damien's image on the portable television. But when she saw Marjorie Todd reach out and touch the screen as though it were a sacred relic, when she saw the hope surge up in the midst of her despair, she realized how Damien still had the gift of charisma despite all that had happened to him.

Still, he didn't have to finger Highwater. What if religious maniacs stormed the town looking for demons?

They would find plenty enough. . . .

MEMORY: A.D. 130

It is the hour before dawn. The sarcophagus has been sealed up inside a tomb hollowed out of rock. The women are wailing, shrieking, beating their breasts and tearing their hair. The boy vampire hears them clearly through the walls of stone. He hears the desert wind. He hears Caesar sighing to himself as he keeps watch. Soon the nights of terror will be over.

The stone is rolled away and he stands there.

This is what he sees:

The women—professional and amateur mourners, with their breasts laid bare and bloodied from the enthusiasm of their self-inflicted blows of grief—the members of the Praetorian guard, standing stiff and a little uncomfortable at these very un-Roman displays of emotion—the emperor on his throne, dressed in the attributes of Pharaoh, since it is as Pharaoh that he rules this province—the sky is gray, barely incarnadined by the impending dawn.

As they see him standing in the mouth of the tomb, the women become restless. The have never seen such a thing before. The rebirth of the god has only been a metaphor before.

He stands there, his shroud about his shoulders. He knows what they all see: a small boy, his skin suffused with a lucency not quite human, his eyes hypnotic. His dark hair is tousled by the chill wind. His pallor borders on the albino.

Confused, the women cease their chanting. Then one of them cries out: "Tammuz is dead; Tammuz has risen; Tammuz will come again. . . ."

One by one the women take up the cry. How much they believe this shallow deception! Oh, he is moved by their faith. He looks across the crowd into the face of Hadrian, and knows that the emperor knows it is all false; he has lied for the sake of making his beloved Antinous a god; truth has been sacrificed to make way for a greater truth.

Soon, before the sun's face shows, the boy must dissolve into the mists of morning, must fly across the sands to seek another resting place. He will find other cities, he will cross other oceans, he will suck the souls of other men and women yet unborn, and all to fulfill some part of their private mythologies. Perhaps it is true that he has become a god; like the gods, he has superhuman powers, and like the gods, his very existence has no meaning save in the context of the human condition.

The boy vampire knows he cannot escape the role he is to play in this and future dramas. Like Oedipus, he cannot outfox his own *moira*. He who died before he had time to know himself no longer has a self at all; he exists only as projection of men's beliefs, their horror of death, their fear of the unknown.

And the emperor too is trapped. But at least the emperor has a way to escape the perpetual illusion.

At least the emperor can die.

14

PYROTECHNICS

MIRROR

Pete Jamison, the bell captain, knocked on the door several times. He could hear whimpering. Maybe it was someone having wild sex. He didn't want to interrupt anything, but they had called down for help even though they wouldn't explain what they wanted. "Ms. Muñoz?" he called.

More whimpering. Shit, he thought, maybe she's being raped or something. He decided to use his master key. He burst into the room.

He saw Gabriela Muñoz—half of her—sticking out of the closet door mirror. The telephone had dropped to the floor. Rivulets of blood ran down the mirror. At first he could not believe his eyes. He just stood there staring like a fool. The woman was clawing at the ground . . . she was glassy-eyed, like she'd been on drugs or something, but drugs hadn't put her into the mirror. He didn't know what could've done it. There'd been rumors about this happening the week before to that writer guy, but now everyone was saying it had just been the effects people playing a practical joke.

This was no joke.

"Are you okay, Ms. Muñoz?" he said. Obviously she wasn't, but he was too dumbfounded to say anything intelligent.

"Get me out of here," she yelled. The bell captain grabbed hold of her arms and pulled. She was stuck. He pulled with all his might. She screamed at the top of her lungs and he was afraid he had dislocated her shoulder. He let go for a moment. Maybe there was some other way.

There was something clinging to the surface of the mirror . . . a rosary. He took it in his hand. It slid out of the glass. . . .

"Don't take out the rosary . . . it's the only thing that's holding him back. . . ."

Before she had finished her sentence she had begun to sink into the mirror . . . as though it were a pool of glycerine . . . she started to scream but before the scream was born she had already been sucked through. . . . He sat on the bed, staring at the rosary, wondering what he was going to tell them down at the front desk. . . .

They'll only say I've been hitting the bottle again, Jamison decided. Maybe it would be easier to blame his imagination. . . .

He pocketed the rosary and thought of the bottle of vodka he kept hidden behind the desk downstairs. . . .

PROPHET

Damien Peters was surprised to see another man being ushered into the first-class compartment of the plane, even more surprised to see that the man appeared to be a mirror image of himself.

Only when he looked more closely did he see that it was not himself. The ridges in the forehead were accentuated by some kind of makeup. The occasional nervous tic, the quick and flashy smile, these were studied mannerisms, so keenly observed and carefully reproduced that they were an almost too perfect re-creation of the original.

The mirror image seated himself directly across the aisle from Damien. The first-class compartment was in perfect lateral symmetry as they took off, since both men immediately began reading a copy of the *Wall Street Journal.*

As they reached cruising altitude, he could restrain his curiosity no longer. He peered over the top of his paper, only to discover that his double was simultaneously peering at him.

"I'll be hornswoggled," said the pseudo-Peters, "you are the real thing, by George, and here I am, method actor to the hilt, been stuck in this persona for a week now, ready for my big scene, and here's the genuine article. . . ."

"Why," said Damien Peters, "you're Jason Sirota, the famous character actor . . . the man of a thousand faces."

"That's right, and portrayer of a mad fundamentalist preacher in a movie called *Valentine,* presently on location in Idaho . . . and catching some flak, as I understand it, from the legal representatives of a certain Reverend Damien Peters, on whom the character is in no way, shape or form based. . . ."

"But you've got me down to a T!" said Damien, impressed in spite of himself. He didn't care about the lawsuit anyway; it was something his attorneys had devised to deflect the public from the sex scandal and to portray him as a victim of the media.

"I always model myself on the best," said Sirota. "And you are the very best, and it is an honor to know you."

"Why, thank you." They paused as the stewardess poured champagne.

"I much admired your sermon," Sirota said, "yesterday evening. I have, as you can imagine, been following your show religiously, if you'll excuse the expression. I can't believe that your operation is driven by anything other than the profoundest cynicism, and on those terms I admire it. That's all. Wholeheartedly. You're a great man, Peters, and a master of television, the ultimate snake-oil salesman . . . I wish I had your charisma. Then I wouldn't be stuck in these minor roles all the time . . . pivotal to be sure, but never any Oscar material in them—disgruntled sergeants, earnest high school principals, unprincipled police officers, sadistic pimps. . . . Mad priests have become a specialty, though I doubt I'd ever equal De Close in the remake of *The Blob*. My God, what a honey-roasted ham. You, on the other hand . . . the financial empire, the private network run as a personal PR service, the air-conditioned doghouse—"

"That wasn't me. Not the doghouse."

"Ah, but your fall from grace; positively Faustian. Your story is a paradigm of the human condition; my story is an endless round of 'doing lunch' and 'taking meetings.' "

Damien was unable to concentrate on his smoked salmon and capers. What this man was saying had a certain core of truth; that was what upset him the most. But all he could see was the manipulation of the media and the Machiavellian plotting; he couldn't see Damien's struggle with faith, the battle between God and Mammon which even now warred within him; he couldn't see Damien as anything but a bundle of motivations, neuroses and physical tics. He closed his eyes, tried to shut out the man's blathering, but in the self-inflicted darkness he saw . . . terrible things, hellish creatures writhing in pools of brimstone, garish visions out of Blake and Alighieri . . . so often in the past he had drifted away from an unpleasant conversation by concentrating on some biblical phrase and repeating it softly to himself like a mantra; but the word that came to his mind, again and again, echoing and reechoing, was *wormwood . . . wormwood . . . wormwood . . .* and he knew that to be a word from the book of the apocalypse, the universal deconstruction that he himself was helping to set in motion.

"I love leaving Hollywood behind," said Sirota, dropping out of character and betraying a more nasal voice, "and I understand that the Snake River country is very beautiful; do you know anything of it? I hope I can get down to the Craters of the Moon National Monument, you know; day after tomorrow, after my big scene, is a day off for me; perhaps you'd care to drive up with me? I do have a limousine at my disposal. . . ."

"I'll probably be occupied," Damien said.

"Oh, of course," said Sirota. "Armageddon will have occurred, will it not?"

"Exactly," Damien growled, and, not bothering to finish the smoked salmon, sought refuge behind his *Wall Street Journal* once again.

FIRE

97 EXT. JUNCTION—EVENING   97

As TAPPAN runs down Main Street, wild-eyed, brandishing his flaming torch, the FIRE follows him. WE HEAR EXPLOSIONS in the distance. FIRE races uphill toward the VALENTINE MANSION. The crazed preacher, barely ahead of the flames, batters at the wrought-iron gates of the mansion.

TAPPAN
(shrieking at the top of
his lungs)
Creature of Satan!

The gates fly open and WE FOLLOW
TAPPAN as he dashes for the front of the
house, with the flames rapidly gaining on
him. . . .

"Well, it's the dumbest pyro sequence *I've* ever seen,"
said Dan Osterday, head pyro guy for the production, as
he doled out the remains of the third keg of gunpowder
along the carefully marked pathway toward Valentine
Mansion Gate #3, the one perched astride a wheeled
platform that could be whisked aside at will, allowing the
camera dolly track to *rush* uphill toward the plywood
cutout of the mansion itself. . . . It was going to be quite
a shot, though its complexity smacked more of MTV
than a serious movie. It was one of those things where, if
they blew it, it would cost a cool million or two to set it
up again. Directors could be so stupid sometimes. They
never seemed to realize that effects rarely work correctly
the first time. They have to be fucked with until they
come out right.

This director, Burr, wasn't even planning to attend the
shooting of this effect; he was entrusting it to second unit.
Ruefully Osterday watched the stunt double, James
Torres, as he put on the gear and padding for the gag.
Torres was a scrawny man, with nerves of steel; he had
to be thin because, by the time he put on all the protective
clothing, he had to appear no bigger, from behind, than
the star, Jason Sirota, who would not even deign to grace
them with his appearance for this shot, since his line of
dialogue, the reverse shot, wasn't even going to be shot
until the next day.

Osterday finished laying the explosive charges. He

hoped it wouldn't rain, like that time two days ago, without even a warning from the weathermen; that would fuck up the whole thing and set them back a week.

"Or they can just write it out," he said to Torres, who merely nodded. "These green pages in the script are Maguire's; now that he's out of the picture, there's less and less green in each day's version. . . ." He held out the script, fanned the pages, making a rainbow out of them. Rainbow scripts rarely held together, but they were the rule rather than the exception in really big budget pictures.

Halfway down the slope, walkie-talkies were beeping and buzzing. "Looks like the second unit director's here," said Osterday. "I wonder which of the three turkeys they've assigned to this gag. . . ."

SHAMANESS

She sat in the armchair watching a peculiarly breathless CNN reporter discussing the Damien Peters sermon with Joshua Levy, some kind of cultural anthropology expert they always seemed to have on tap, who could always be counted on to say something stupid.

Right now, he was talking about millennial madness: "Well, Betsy, as we enter the final decade of the millennium, the amount of apocalyptic imagery in popular culture—and televangelism, distasteful though it may be to some, must be considered a manifestation of popular culture—must steadily increase, just as it did when we were moving toward the year A.D. 1000. That, too, was a fascinating epoch, with mass hysteria, suicides, end-of-the-world vigils, and hundreds of mad preachers roaming the streets of Europe prophesying doom and gloom. The interesting thing about today's version of millennial madness is the way it can reach into so many people's homes without the lifting of a madman's finger, you see.

A word which the Reverend Peters dropped during yesterday's ravings is *very* significant—he called his ministry a *virtual cathedral.* In other words, it is the illusion of reality transformed into hyperreality. Do you see what I mean? As we near the millennium, realities shift and blend and we could emerge with a wholly different reality—a magical transformation. I don't necessarily see the end result as a bad thing at all. That's where I differ from the Armageddon doomsayers. . . ."

Trapped in the crux of the pentacle of power, encircled by a line of chalk with four braziers of incense pointed at the four directions and each labeled with one of the four letters of   , the sacred name of God, was the former Prince Prathna. Its entrails coiled and thrashed about; its tongue whipped the air; a reeking mist circled about its head. She stared the monster in the eye; it would not do to betray any fear of one's minions.

When will you release me? it said.

"When your task is done," she said. "Now stop bothering me; I must concentrate."

You've promised me many things. You've promised me the living soul of Timmy Valentine for my delectation. You promised me food, but you only feed me scraps of shit.

"Shit is all you are able to devour in this form," said Simone, "and you know that as well as I do."

I don't want to stay this way forever. At some stage, my karma must work itself out and I must be released so that I can reenter the world as a human.

"Human!" Simone said. "There is some question as to whether you ever were human. . . ."

When I can have Timmy Valentine?

Simone turned her attention to the CNN interview, where the subject of Valentine had serendipitously come up. "Why," the squawking Betsy Snyderman was saying, "do you link all these millennial questions with Timmy Valentine? What can a pop-culture icon possibly have to do with questions of reality and illusion, and of—well, not to sound too alarmist about it—the end of the world?"

She treats Levy like a crank, and perhaps he is; but he's dangerously close to the truth, Simone thought.

"Well, Betsy . . . in the past I've spoken about the images of the young boy as angel of death that seem to have cropped up all through history—I've talked about the angel concealed in Caravaggio's *Martyrdom of Saint Matthew,* for example. I believe that this image is buried deep within the collective unconscious—I guess my philosophy is a kind of conflation of Carl Jung's and Joseph Campbell's—and that Timmy Valentine was the living embodiment of this image, you see. That's why his death (real or imagined) has propelled him into a far higher level of popular consciousness, and that's why his resurrection is going to herald something—I don't know—the renewal of the world, or maybe its utter destruction."

"Death and resurrection? Doesn't that seem kind of blasphemous, Dr. Levy? I mean, Christians believe that it was *Jesus* who—"

"I know, Betsy, but I'm a Jew."

"Yes, Joshua, but that aside—"

Angrily, Simone snapped him off with her remote.

Free me! shrieked the head of Prathna. *Free me, you sack of shit! Oh, shit shit shit . . .*

"Listen to me," she said, choosing her words with care—for as always with control of supernatural creatures one walked a tightrope—"we will feed you soon. You will feast yourself on the shit of a king—even though he is only king for a day."

For that was the next stage. For years now she had been working toward the fulfillment of some great plan, but the details would not come to her all at once; now it was crystal clear for the first time. Damien Peters had set himself up as a new messiah—if you will, an Antichrist. He had done so of his own free will, without any coercion from her. In ancient times, when priestesses ruled the world, that was how they had selected the one who would be king; a stranger, walking by chance into the village, would be chosen as incarnation of the living god. Now it was time for the ceremonial killing of the king—although, of course, a substitute would be found, for the forces of the universe were infinitely gullible, and always mistook the representation for the reality.

The false king was coming even now. She could hear footsteps. She wondered whom Damien Peters had managed to inveigle into coming up to the suite of his own free will. She hoped he had remembered to wear the charisma amulet with its belladonna dipped in raven's blood.

"Jacques!" she called out sharply, summoning the cadaverous servant from the inner room. "Bring the garbage bags."

He brought thirteen bags (one for each of the lunar months) and placed them concentrically around the circle of power.

There was a knock on the door.

She opened it, but did not remove the chain.

"It's me," said the Reverend Peters, "and I've brought you the prize, the pearl of great price itself." The glee in his eyes was sickening but strangely infectious. Quickly she drew the chloroform-soaked dishrag from her purse and held it up to the door; she opened it, smiling.

Damien Peters walked in.

Damien Peters stood outside.

The first Damien Peters said, "He's here of his own free will. And he's the perfect double."

The second Damien Peters said, in a voice uncannily like the first, "Why, Simone Arleta, queen of physics; I hadn't expected to find you here, but given the apocalyptic circumstances, I guess it was only reasonable—"

He said no more, for, as the first Damien held his arms behind his back, Simone shoved the rag over his nose and mouth. Then, as he slumped to the floor, she clubbed him over the head with a ceremonial mallet.

"How on earth—" she said. "It's perfect; absolutely perfect."

"It's Jason Sirota," said Damien. He took Sirota's attaché case and opened it. "Good," he said, "the script. I'll need this if I'm to go through with the plan."

She laughed. "I've never sacrificed anyone famous before," she said. "And he was doing *you!* Talk about method acting." She bent down over the prone body and teased at his hair. "Ah, the gray is fake; he's not quite as decrepit as you are; and"—she started to pull off his clothes—"he's a lot more firm; goes to the gym, I'd say."

The actor was now reduced to his B.V.D.s, which Simone removed with a pair of scissors. The *phii krasue* began to howl. "Help me lug this thing into the armchair," Simone said. They did so; the man stirred a little, and she gave him another whack on the head. Then she put on her ceremonial vestments—cloth of gold, blazoned with ancient sigils—and took from her trunk a paper crown, which she placed on Sirota's forehead. "You'll never know how great your last role was," she said, stroking his hair. Soft, soft; she wondered how many fans had fantasized about his hair. The crown was a little tacky; it was left over from a night out at Mediaeval Times, the live jousting dinner show down in Anaheim. But it was only the symbology that mattered.

"Hail, O King," she said, and knelt before the unconscious actor.

"Is all this really necessary?" Damien said. "I mean, a small amount of mumbo jumbo goes a long way, and—"

"No remorse!" she said. "This is it! Remember the god Osiris, whose death and rebirth we commemorate now! Remember Tammuz and Adonis! Remember Jesus, last in a line of god-kings that stretches back to the mists of time!"

Then, taking a dagger from her trunk, she carefully

disemboweled him, hara-kiri style, and tossed the steaming intestines into the circle. While the *phii krasue* was preoccupied with slurping up the offal, she got out her bronze *labrys,* the ceremonial double axe used by the moon-priestesses of ancient Crete, and hacked the actor into thirteen pieces. Blood spattered her vestments, her face. She remained impassive, although Damien looked as though he was going to vomit. She threw each piece at one of the garbage bags, and Jacques moved about soundlessly, stuffing the bags and sopping up the blood with sponges. When a sponge became full he thrust it into a trash can, carefully refraining from squeezing it. The room was eerily silent save for the frenzied feeding of the *phii krasue.* Last of all, Jacques held up the head. He whirled it around, letting the neck's ripped ligaments spatter them liberally with blood. Simone did not wince; the blood on her lips was warm and tasted of life, not death.

"Long may Osiris live and reign," Simone said.

Wordlessly, Simone removed all her garments and robed herself for the next part of the ritual, the grieving over the dead king. The robes were black and she had cut the rips in the fabric in advance to save time.

"The king is dead," she said. And she wept. There was no hypocrisy in her tears; as with everything else that flowed out of her magic, her tears fed on the dark truths within her, on distant traumas and childhood losses that she dared not bring to the surface of her consciousness. Perhaps it was her father she thought of. But she had no father, of course; biologically yes, perhaps, but women such as she were foaled by the western wind when the mares of darkness hunched their hindquarters toward the kingdom of the dead. She wept into a glass vial, and then she walked around the circle, making sure she spread one drop on every trash bag.

"All right," she said. "I believe we have all the ingredients; now, we're going to have load all this material into the car, so if you boys wouldn't mind grabbing a few of these sacks . . . and, for God's sake, try to act normal. . . ."

"That," said Damien, "is the most ridiculous thing I've ever heard."

"Save your sarcasm," she said. "We still have Angel's mother to deal with . . . she's waiting for you in her trailer."

VISION SEEKERS

Overnight: the Porsche parked in the shade of a tree, Lady Chit watched PJ build the structure out of stones and fallen branches. She fell asleep, lying back with her head against the front bumper; the sleep was dreamless; she was lulled by night musics she had never heard before, which nonetheless were as familiar to her as the lullaby her nanny used to sing, long ago, before she was sent to school in America.

Dawn: he woke her with a kiss and led her inside. It was a kind of sauna; steam hissed against hot stones; a smell of bitter herbs laced the air.

He said, "Some terrible things are going to happen soon. I want to take you to another country. When you come back you'll know many mysteries. I don't want you to face your grandfather before you do this."

She trusted him. She shed her clothes and sat down, in the *khatamaak* position familiar to her from Buddhist meditation. "Should I chant a mantra?" she said.

"If you want to. I guess this is kind of an ecumenical sweat lodge." He wore only a breechclout and his long dark hair.

She closed her eyes and let the heat seep into her. The heat came from the stones but also from the heart of the world. The heat oozed into her pores and kindled her inner fire. She did not know how long she sat there; it seemed as though aeons were passing. She knew only that the turbulence within her gradually subsided, and she found herself in a state of stillness; that though her eyes were still closed she could see; that in the silence she could hear even the thoughts of men, even the pinprick lives and deaths of the insects that swarmed among the trees of summer.

She felt him take her hand.

She opened her eyes and saw that she had left herself behind, and that the PJ who held her hand was not the one who kept vigil beside her in the swirling steam. The PJ who was leading her up the invisible staircase into the sky was a woman. She wore a deerskin dress and she had shallow breasts and she smelled like a woman, and into her hair were woven beads of many colors. The wind wuthered about her face, which was haloed by the sun.

"Come," said PJ. "I am still your friend, but now I'm also the *ma'aipots,* the sacred man-woman. I'm going to show you the world before the storm hits. You'd better look at the world now, because after the storm, the world may be quite different; you may not even recognize it."

She followed him into the sky. The clouds enveloped them. Hand in hand, a brace of she-eagles, they skimmed the high wind. They looked down at the mountain. There was the site of Junction, the old dead one and the new Junction of façades and soundstages. There was the sacred circle they had laid down together; in her vision she could see them glittering with an inner luster . . . what did they remind her of? The myriad lights on a landing strip in the middle of the night . . . She could see the film crew, doll-like, setting up for the scene of religious pyromania.

Then she saw the jaguar . . . was it a car or a beast? It bounded around the sacred circle. Here and there it stopped. A woman in black emerged. An acolyte assisted her, and she was accompanied by a man in the garments of a king. The acolyte handed the woman a bag. She could tell that it contained recently dead flesh . . . she knew the woman. It was Simone Arleta.

But how Simone had changed! When she had gone to see her in the Mojave Desert, there had not been this aura of evil about her. She had merely been a woman then—a wicked woman to be sure, and one who, like a vampire, enjoyed feeding off people's raw emotions. Now she was more than a woman. She had taken on the attributes of darkness—had become an actor in a timeless drama.

"It's the war in heaven," she said softly. "The battle for control of the universe . . . good and evil . . . light and darkness." She remembered such stories only dimly; her nanny used to tell her, as she lay in bed, a little girl of seven or eight, tales from the Ramayana, remote mythic beings with unpronounceable names. And then she understood why PJ had assumed the form of the *ma'aipots*. He was like the ancient prophet Tiresias, whom she'd studied in Mythology 101, who had been both a man and a woman. In the tension between yin and yang, he was the balance. So he too was part of the eternal drama, which the Greeks called *tragedy*.

PJ opened her arms wide, and with that her gaze widened, and she saw not only the Snake River valley, with its moonscape crags, its steep canyons, its twisted mountains, but beyond . . . she saw California, saw her trashed apartment in Los Angeles and her immaculate dorm room at Mills College . . . saw the great wide ocean and even, swathed in mist, Bangkok, with its medieval pagodas and its skyscrapers shaped like giant robots . . . she saw the world, and she saw, at the edges of the world, the black cloud that threatened to engulf it. . . .

"Is it about so much?" she said.

PJ said, "It is and it isn't. The war in our hearts and the war in the cosmos are the same war, you know. We've been brought to this moment by forces we can't control. You know you're going to have to kill your grandfather, don't you? Only you can send him home. It will take love to turn his path. But he's going to be difficult to love when you see him. You're going to have to remember the good feelings you had about him; you're going to have to dredge them up from your childhood."

"What about you, PJ?" she said. "Will all this free you too?"

"Yeah . . . when it's all over I won't be the world-magician after all; I'll just be another Native American artist hawking his paintings at the Saugus swap meet. And I won't be afraid anymore of waking up in the body of a girl."

"Show me more. . . ."

And PJ showed Chit the stars, the the gray spaces between the galaxies, and the country in the west where the buffalo have not yet died out, and the nine infernos of Dante Alighieri; but she told her that all these worlds would intersect inside the mirror world behind which stood the unborn shadow-self of Timmy Valentine.

And then they kissed, and she could feel the contours of PJ's body hardening; she could feel her breasts recede and the stiffness of his penis emerge out of the feminine mist; and when she opened her eyes they were inside the sweat lodge once more, and the magic they were making was the magic of earth and sky, rain and lightning.

ANGEL

The boy in the mirror reached out and gave Angel a knife. Angel hefted it in his left hand. It felt old. It was crusted with blood. Its hilt was studded with cabochon rubies, emeralds, amethysts. It was a knife that had killed before.

The boy in the mirror did not let go of Angel's hand; he was reluctant to relinquish its warmth.

Timmy said, "Angel. What is it you want most in the world?"

"To stop hurting, I guess."

"Do you know what it is I want?"

"I think," said Angel, "that you want to start hurting again."

"It can happen," Timmy said. "A war is being waged right now. A storm is shaking the world though the world knows nothing about it. And the epicenter of the storm is this movie set, where art and life imitate each other in such complicated ways as to unravel the fabric of the universe. That's it! When the cosmos is being ripped apart and put back together again, there are cracks big enough for you and me to escape through. But everything in the world has its blood-price. You know that, don't you? You know who you're going to have to kill."

"To stop the pain; yeah, I guess I do," Angel said.

Timmy let go at last, leaving a residue of cold against Angel's hand. The hilt of the dagger, too, was cold. But presently . . . almost as though it fed on all the anger inside him . . . the blade seemed to heat up. It was too hot to hold. He was going to burn himself. He was sure he smelled charring flesh. He dropped the knife and it clattered to the tiles. Only then did Angel remember that this was the bathroom, and that he'd come in to take a leak.

I don't need the fucking knife, he thought. I don't need any of this shit. I just wanna act my way through the scene and crawl back into bed and sleep without having any nightmares. . . .

He finished peeing and zipped up. I'll just leave the dagger behind.

Someone else can do the dirty work.

"You have a beautiful voice," Timmy Valentine said from inside the mirror. "Your voice deserves to echo into the far future."

He got to the door, turned; the thing was still there, glinting against the dark red glaze. He stood and looked at it for a long time. He thought about eternity. He thought about Errol in the cold earth. Jesus he hated Errol. If Errol were still alive there wouldn't be this sickness between him and his mother. Damn, he thought. I'm never going to get a life. The only way is to let myself die . . . and to kill the thing that's been eating away at me ever since we put Errol into the ground. . . .

And Angel Todd picked up the dagger, his heart pounding.

FIRE

"Hurry up, Torres," Osterday said. "The shot's all set up now." He banged on the door of the trailer where the stunt man was preparing himself for the gag. He'd been stuffing himself into the Sirota costume for some time.

The second unit crew were waiting at a safe distance. They wore heavy protective gear in case something went wrong. They seemed anxious. The heat was searing, oppressive; just beyond the set, the coolness of the forest beckoned.

Osterday knocked again; then he decided to go inside.

"Hurry the fuck up," he said. The stunt man turned around.

There was something different about Torres, he realized. This wasn't a scrawny man wearing layers of asbestos. This was someone else . . . it had to be Jason Sirota, the star. Actors were such a nuisance sometimes. They had an unhealthy obsession with themselves, and he'd probably been here, wasting the stunt man's time with dumb questions and slowing him down when he had a job to do.

Still, it never did to offend the star, so Osterday just said, "Hi, Mr. Sirota. Plane got in okay, I see. Have you come to see your stunt?"

Sirota—everyone knew he carried method acting to excess, but Osterday could have sworn he looked exactly like Damien Peters, the goofy televangelist—said, "There's been a change. I'm going to do the scene by myself."

Was it Peters or Sirota? It was uncanny. Osterday thought, he never watched those shows but sometimes Alice, his mother, would go on a religious binge and ruin a perfectly good Thanksgiving or Christmas by staring glassy-eyed at "The Hour of Heavenly Love." . . .

"You know you can't do that, Mr. Sirota. You're just joking, of course. What would your agent say?" But there was something in Sirota's eyes that seemed to mean business. Something not entirely human . . .

"Where's James?" Osterday asked.

"You won't be needing him anymore."

Osterday looked nervously toward the back of the trailer. There was a folding partition. James must be back there. He could hear something pattering. Gurgling. He couldn't figure out what the sound was.

"I ought to go back and see for myself," he said. The actor's eyes were cold—they never seemed to quiver—like the eyes of a statue. Why am I so afraid? Osterday thought. He could feel his arms prickling. It had suddenly become cold. There was a stench in the air like an unflushed toilet.

All of a sudden, the back partition slid open and James Torres fell out onto the floor of the trailer. He had been eviscerated. His intestines had been pulled out of his stomach and carefully wound around and around him. In his abdomen sat the bodiless head of an aged Oriental. The head was alive. Its tongue was buried deep inside Torres's guts, and it was feeding. Its entrails hung outside the cavity and quivered as they slithered over the carpeting. Blood oozed from a dozen shallow knife wounds. Torres's mouth and eyes were fixed in an expression of terror and disbelief.

Behind him stood a little old woman with a curved dagger in her hand. Calmly, she stepped over the body and that other creature in its feeding frenzy. She wore some kind of Egyptian costume.

"Who the fuck are you?" Osterday said. "What kind of a joke is this?" But he knew it wasn't a joke. He knew the difference between reality and special effects.

"Would you oblige us, Mr. Osterday, by beginning the effects sequence right away?"

"I'm . . . I'm waiting for the director's say-so."

"We have a new director now, and we are no longer making the same film," the old woman said. "The new movie is called *The Death and Resurrection of the Universe*. And it has a cast of billions."

"You're insane! You're some kind of psycho killer on the loose and—Mr. Sirota, help me get this woman to a—"

"I am not Mr. Sirota," said the actor, and, when he stared at him full in the face, it was clear that this wasn't any method acting; this was the real thing. They were both insane. Come to think of it, hadn't there been some kind of sex scandal or something? Maybe it had driven him over the edge. The woman looked familiar too. She was a TV psychic or something. Crackpots. Fucking crackpots.

"I'm gonna call security," he said, reaching for the cellular that stood just out of arm's reach, on the counter.

The woman, who barely reached up to his shoulder, stretched up and slapped his face. He could feel warm blood spurting from his nose. "You will be honored in the next world," she said, "for the role you are playing in bringing about the apocalpyse. . . ."

"What are you talking about?"

"Now go!"

The dagger was up against his throat. The mad preacher was behind him, and there was something in the small of his back that felt very much like the muzzle of a revolver.

"Back slowly out," said Simone Arleta, "and wave to the crew that it's okay to start."

There was another person with them; he had just emerged from the back. A skeletal figure dressed somewhat like a butler, he was silently cleaning up the blood and coaxing the monster into what looked like a hatbox. "Jacques," said the psychic imperiously, "make sure he doesn't try any funny business."

SHAMANESS

Simone was in her element now. The pieces were falling into place. These were the final stages in the grand ritual. Soon the line between illusion and reality would be so blurred that there would be a rift in the fabric of cause and effect which would allow a new reality to be forged. The truth could be remade.

The momentousness of what she was trying to achieve stunned even her; she wondered if she had finally fallen victim to hubris. But when she saw Damien Peters, who had been one of the world's most charismatic personalities, reduced to worrying about his sex life and his finances, when she saw how pathetic the other actors in this drama were—why, the great adversary was nothing more than a halfbreed swap-meet shaman, for God's sake—she lost her fear completely.

She stepped out of the trailer. The pyrotechnician followed her; now and then Jacques jabbed his back with gun to keep him compliant. Last of all came Damien, who was pretending to be a stunt man pretending to be an actor pretending to be himself.

Illusions within illusions! It was a delicious deployment of sympathetic magic. Never had there been such glorious confusion. This was the sort of confluence of fate that the Gods of Chaos had only played at creating. Poor Muriel Hykes-Bailey and her childish attempts at witchcraft, her "eye of newt" and "liver of blaspheming Jew"! She had never had any sense of history. She did not have what Catholics called the apostolic succession—the handing down of the sacerdotal mantle from the time of the earliest priestesses to the present. She was an amateur.

How the sun blazed!

"Tell them to start," she said impatiently to Osterday. "And explain to me exactly how everything works."

"Well, I've got to lay a few more charges." He was obviously temporizing. "As the stunt double—as the 'Reverend Tappan'—runs toward the gates up there, the camera crew follows him on that dolly track. I push these plungers—and the explosions go off in the distance. Tappan's waving a flaming torch and he's setting fire to things as he runs, but what actually happens is we turn on these gas jets . . . the pipes are concealed behind those hedges, you see . . ." He showed her some controls, dials that seemed to operate very much like the dials of a gas oven.

"All right. Start the explosions."

"You don't understand. First the ADs have to start barking orders . . . they roll camera . . . it's MOS so we won't have sound to worry about . . . then the second unit director will say 'Action'; *then* I get to start the explosions."

A production assistant came running up to them with the flaming torch. She handed it to Damien and left.

"Now," said Simone.

Damien took the torch and started moving toward the wrought-iron gates. She could hear the second unit director yelling, "What the fuck is going on?" but it did not matter. The explosions were beginning. The fire was starting to roar. Tongues of flame leaped up from the bushes.

"More fire!" she screamed.

"You want to burn down the set?" Osterday said.

"The world will be reborn in fire!" She pushed the pyrotechnician out of the way and twisted the dials higher. The flames spurted. She spread her arms wide and called upon the primordial fire, the fire from which the world was forged. She could feel that fire sweeping through her soul. She was focusing the fire as a magnifying glass focused the rays of the sun. The fire was rising out of the dark places themselves. The fire screamed in her. She was becoming the fire. The fire ran through her body like electricity. She watched as Damien strode toward the house. He was on fire himself, but the fire would not burn him, knowing he was its creature.

"He's burning up!" said Osterday. "We gotta call in the water truck."

She laughed.

And then she prayed: *O ancient Gods, unwakened since you were silenced by the abomination of Christianity, come forth . . . look with compassion on your servant . . . use me as a channel for your unspeakable powers . . . creatures beyond good and evil . . . surround this sacred place with the circle of flame . . . shatter the boundary between the real and the dream so that what is only dreamed of can become substance . . . give back to me the power of the creature I chained up in the land of shadow . . . give me that power a thousandfold, that I may serve you now and for all eternity. . . .*

She glanced at Osterday, feeding on the dark flames. Even her eyes could launch death, she realized. As the man felt her gaze upon him, he quaked, seeming to know it was the hour of his death. She felt the flames burst from the windows of her soul. Twin lances of flame spurted from her eyes and struck him. He recoiled. Even Jacques, who was used to supernatural manifestations, backed away.

Osterday backed away in the direction of the fire. Then he exploded. His head burst open and his brains spewed from his mouth and nostrils. His abdomen split and disgorged a tangled mass of intestines. His blood sizzled as it fountained. A severed arm flew in the direction of the film crew, knocking down the cameraman, who also burst into flames. The second unit director was trying to yell something into his walkie-talkie, which also caught fire. He hurled it away from him. A barrage of bone shards shrapneled his face and turned it into pizza. His scream could barely be heard above the hiss and roar of the flames.

Jacques let the *phii krasue* out of its box. It slithered toward the mass of flesh that had been Osterday and began to feed. She did not mind. Let it be satiated, she thought. It will need its strength for the final confrontation, for soon it would face the granddaughter it once loved, and there was always the possibility that it could be swayed from its true destiny. . . .

Oh, it was beautiful, Simone thought. Oh, there was poetry in it. How splendid Damien looked as he bore the torch of rebirth toward the image of Timmy Valentine's mansion.

The flames were spreading now. The flames were consuming the mansion's façade. And Damien stood there, holding aloft the torch, the fire dancing over his very flesh, exultant. The fire was racing toward the forest now. She turned the dials still higher. The façade, painted plywood, was crackling as the fire consumed it. The smoke had the acrid smell of burning paint, mingled with the sweet scent of barbecuing flesh. The forest was a mountain of kindling ready to go off. As the flames reached the edge of the wood, she could hear the crackle of dry twigs and branches. She was filled with a searing joy, and she could not refrain from weeping.

She ran to Damien, ran through the warm embrace of the fire. The magic protected them. Knowing its mistress, the fire had not harmed her; surrounded by the thirteen pieces of Jason Sirota, the fire thought Damien already dead. Magic, as always, was the art of misdirection.

The hot wind whirled about them. It felt good.

It was time to go on to the next stage—the rites of Xipe Totec, the flayed god, symbol of renewal. It was time to go to where Marjorie Todd waited, still glued to the television set and the afternoon rerun of Damien Peters' sermon.

VISION SEEKERS

"Smell the air," PJ said.

"I smell smoke," said Lady Chit. There air was suffocatingly hot. She could feel cedar needles pricking her face, carried on the burning wind.

"It's begun," PJ said. "Let's drive back before the road becomes impassable."

As they got back into the Porsche, embers were falling out of the sky like little stars.

FIRE

Brian and Petra were in the hotel coffee shop when it happened.

They were the only people there, and they had been waiting an inordinately long time to be served. They hadn't said much to each other. Brian knew they were both scared; they were afraid to articulate their fear because to do so might make it even more real. They had just been sitting there, looking at each other, smiling nervously.

Finally, Brian said, "I wanted to say that—"

"Yes?"

"I mean, if we live through . . . I mean . . ."

Their hands touched. Words had not been necessary after all.

At that moment, they looked up and saw Pete, one of

the bell captains. There was liquor on his breath. "Excuse me," he said. "but they're evacuating the town . . . there's a forest fire. No one knows how far it'll spread. . . ."

"Oh, my God," Petra said. "How far away is it?"

"It's up near Junction," said Pete. "They're gonna seal off the area and bring in helicopters. The movie people out there, well, no one's heard from them. . . ."

Brian suddenly knew that the battle was now joined. "We'd better go," he said. To Pete he said, "The roads, are they still open?"

"The roads? They've got buses lined up outside. They want everyone to stay at the town hall down in Riverview. No one can figure it out . . . sure, it's forest fire season, but with that big thuderstorm, no one thought that—"

"A lot of strange things have been happening," Brian said.

"Sure have," said the bell captain, and Brian got the feeling that he knew more than he was prepared to say.

"Let's get out of here," Petra said. "We have to reach them before it's too late."

"You're going to—"

FIRE

Holy shit! Look down there. Radio the other choppers.
The fire—it's a perfect circle—and bang in the middle there's a bald patch, untouched by the fire—like a huge flaming dartboard on the side of the mountain, and the bull's-eye is—
Junction.

FIRE

"Junction," said Brian.

PART THREE

❧ ❧ ❧ ❧ ❧ ❧ ❧

SMOKING MIRROR

Y el joven rígido, geométrico,
con un hacha rompió el espejo.

And rigid, geometric, the boy
With a hatchet shattered the
mirror.

LORCA

15

THROUGH THE LOOKING-GLASS

♣ ♣

MIRROR

Reality is set aside while a film is being made. Filmmaking is a fiefdom unto itself; the world beyond does not impinge upon it at all. Wars can be declared, plagues descend, tempests strike; on the soundstage the only reality is artifice.

Thus it was that, although a fire was consuming much of the forest around Junction, although towns were being evacuated and firefighter teams galvanized, no breath of these events reached the mirror room set of the soundstage, the set which stood at the exact center of the twin circles of power that had been drawn by Simone Arleta and PJ Gallagher in preparation for their apocalyptic struggle.

While Brian and Petra raced up the narrow road to Junction, the fire raged on either side. Trunks in flames crashed onto the road, but always behind them, never before them; their access to the inner circle was not to be cut off, only their escape. As they drove, smoke curled in through the vents. Petra was gagging. But Brian drove on. They could not turn back and the way ahead was miraculously clear.

They did not speak as they drove. The heat pounded at them. On the backseat was a black bag full of the tools of vampire hunting. Stakes and croquet mallets. Thermos flasks full of holy water. A bag of garlic bulbs. Medieval bullshit . . . the only truth left that they could count on.

And plenty of crucifixes.

At length they passed through the flames. At the center of the storm was an eerie quiet. They drove past the exterior set with its plywood façade of Timmy Valentine's house, now down to a cinder; a few small bonfires smoldered here and there beside the long uphill dolly track. Corpses lay facedown on the concrete.

Brian said, "I wonder who they are."

Petra said, "Don't stop. It's too late to help them."

Even when she closed her eyes she could see fire, dancing against walls of darkness.

SHAMANESS

Simone banged on the door of the boy's trailer. When no one came, she opened it and barged in. The woman was there, as she'd expected, waiting. The television was still on; on the screen was an aerial view of a mountain in flames. An announcer was droning on about the extraordinary news. In the side of the mountain was a circle of darkness, untouched by the fire; it was the circle Simone had drawn, the dark center of the firestorm.

Marjorie, of course, would not appreciate the ironic complexities of the situation. But her appreciation was not required, only her compliance.

It is feared that the cast and crew of Valentine, *including director Jonathan Burr, star Jason Sirota, and teen heart-*

throb Angel Todd, may all be stranded in the set of Junc-
tion. . . . Choppers have been unable to get through the
five-square-mile blaze. . . . Aerial photography shows the
former hometown of Timmy Valentine isolated in a bizarre
circle right in the middle of the forest fire. . . . Late in the
fire season, after the unpredicted rain . . . scientists say the
fire is a freak of nature. . . .

"We are here, Marjorie," Simone said softly. "Prepare
yourself."

The Reverend Damien Peters stood in the doorway. In
the far background, the burning forest glowed and made
him seem huge and black and demonic. Damien smiled
the unforgiving smile that only a god can smile, and
Simone knew that this was her master and her minion,
the great one who must always bow to the will of the
Goddess.

"Reverend Peters!" says the mother of Angel Todd.
"I've seen you on television." As if, thought Simone, that
only being on television could lend reality to the fleshy
shell that was Damien's earthly habitation. "I'm your
biggest fan." The woman spoke breathlessly, in a bizarre
parody of seductiveness, as though she had been ushered
into the presence of some movie-star sex symbol.
Damien, who was nothing like James Dean, spread out
his arms in the "crucified" pose and murmured a benediction.

"It's true," Marjorie Todd whispered. "You've come
for me. I just knew you would. I've been dreaming about
you. Oh, Lord, I want your mercy. I've done terrible
things, Reverend, terrible things, and I crave forgiveness."

"I've come for you," said the Reverend Damien Peters.

"Oh, I can feel the rapture seizing hold of me."

"That you can."

"Would you mind if . . . I mean, before it all starts to
happen . . . you think I could get your autograph?"

"Sure thing, ma'am." Once again the charisma. "You have a pen?"

The woman went around to the back of the trailer. Simone looked Damien in the eye. "Don't waver now," she said. Jacques was standing in the door now with the *phii krasue*'s hatbox in his arms.

"How can I?" said Damien.

The Todd woman came back. She had a ballpoint pen and a leatherbound King James Bible. She said, "Reverend, I know you didn't exactly *write* this, but near as I can see, you've done more to spread this word than anybody on this earth. I don't care about all them things they've been saying about you. I believe in you."

She was haggard and unkempt, and her eyes were red from weeping. But while she was in the back she had managed to put a little rouge on her cheeks, and she had drenched herself in a dime-store perfume. How unlike the mother of a million-dollar child star she seemed. Every gesture, every word betrayed her poor-white-trash origins. Yet out of this *thing* would come a glorious rebirth in blood and tears, Simone thought. I must treasure her. Truly, she thought, I must love her.

How fortunate that she has gone to seed this much, Simone thought; her skin sags and hangs in bunches on her flesh; it will be easy for her to participate in the ritual of Xipe Totec. Not like some others in the past.

Damien smiled and signed the Bible.

As he signed it, Simone motioned for Jacques to come forward. Jacques put the hatbox down on the table and held out a tray containing lancets, scalpels and paring knives of various sizes.

Simone concentrated. She drew on the power of the dark circle, and she stretched out her hands toward the Todd woman. She was innocent of all suspicion until that moment, but when she saw Simone's eyes transfix her, something must have stirred in her. She said: "Y-y-you're not a Satanist . . . are you?"

Simone howled with laughter. "Satan! The goat-king! Pan, the satyr, a minor deity in the majestic pantheon of eternity! Why not a Satanist then?"

"What church *is* this?" Marjorie asked. "You're really the Reverend Peters, ain't you? You ain't some kind of temptation sent to me by Satan?"

"We are all churches," Simone said, "we are the one true church; we are the god before all gods, the power that set the world in motion, the power that will dance at the world's destruction. . . ."

"You'll be all right, ma'am," Damien said, in a voice dripping with uneasy comfort, "you just stay still for a moment. I'll hold your hand if you want. It's for the good of the world. Trust me." And he touched the woman's hand, and she whimpered and went limp, allowing Jacques to slip around behind her and bind her wrists fast.

"Despair!" Simone cried, as she took the tray of knives from her manservant. And stared into the eyes of her victim with the full force of the ancient power. And saw despair, unconscionable, utter, transcendent despair within those eyes, and drank in that despair, drank her fill of the woman's hopelessness and disillusionment. Laughing, she drank her fill as she ripped open the front of the victim's blouse and began the careful work of flaying the whole skin from the living flesh.

MIRROR

99 INT. HALL OF MIRRORS—NIGHT 99

WE SEE TIMMY VALENTINE seated at a white piano that appears to be suspended in mid-air. There are mirrors on every side. Timmy is playing to himself—a haunting, quiet song quite unlike anything in his public

repertoire, an alien, alienating music. CAM-
ERA circles around him, moving closer and
closer, like a vulture wheeling over an undead
person. Gradually, WE MOVE INTO A
TIGHT SHOT of his face. He is wrapped up
in his music, his expression impossible to con-
strue.

ANOTHER ANGLE: TAPPAN

is seen standing at the far end of the room.
WE SEE TAPPAN'S REFLECTION over
and over, rearing up, surrounding the piano
like a predator preparing to pounce. He is still
carrying the BURNING TORCH.

> TIMMY
> (stops playing abruptly)
> Who are you? Why did you come?

> TAPPAN
> You creature of Satan. I've come to de-
> stroy you. I'm going to destroy the very
> idea of you, so you won't be able to cor-
> rupt future generations. . . .

> TIMMY
> (very softly)
> Why?

> TAPPAN
> Because you have no right to exist;
> you're an affront to the truth.

> TIMMY
> Why?

TAPPAN

Because you made me ask "why? why?"
just once too often. Because you made
me question God. Because when I questioned him I fell into despair. . . .

ON TIMMY'S EYES

which betray no trace of evil. He is a victim
because each sees in him the mirror of his
own inner torments.

TIMMY
(with an expression of wounded
innocence)

Why?

FATHER TAPPAN

hurls the firebrand at Timmy's piano.

"It's corny," said Jonathan Burr, "but it'll do the trick
. . . after we lard the scene with MTV-style editing and
gonzo effects. This Brian Zottoli's not a bad writer even
if sometimes you get the feeling that he's a little bit, you
know, in love with his word processor."

The new sides for the scene, delivered only an hour
before by a nervous P.A. who didn't look a day over
fifteen, were being distributed. Angel sat at the piano,
having some last-minute powder put on his face. He
wasn't much of a keyboard player—that was one thing
about him that was way different from the real Timmy
Valentine—and he was painstakingly struggling through
"Chopsticks" while the director stormed around the set
doing his thing.

"But where the fuck is Sirota?" Burr shouted at the
production assistants, who cowered nervously at the
edge of the set.

One of them said, "He was just at the second unit location . . . checking out the stunt, I guess."

"He shouldn't be checking out stunts! He should get his ass here before I—"

Angel pounded the keys. The waiting around was the worst aspect of filmmaking.

"Shut up for a moment, Angel," said Jonathan Burr.

He stopped playing. Stared at himself, reflected a thousandfold around him. This would be the hardest scene to film because of all the mirrors and the necessity of avoiding an accidental reflection of the camera in one of the side mirrors. Dolly tracks were being laid all over the Plexiglas ramp which covered the mirror-inlaid subfloor. Angles were being calculated; the director of photography wasn't leaving anything to chance, but measuring, testing, rehearsing every camera move.

"Where the fuck is Sirota?" Jonathan screamed. "Probably stalking around the mountains in some method-inspired funk."

"Five minutes," the first assistant director, Johnny de Rose, declared.

"Well, we can't just wait around for the fucker to show up," said Burr, popping a pill as he motioned for the P.A. to bring over his cellular phone. The phone was presented to him on a tray. He picked it up and tried to dial out. "The phones are out or something," he said. "Okay, let's go ahead a do some of the coverage on Angel while we're waiting. C'mon. Burning daylight here." He scratched his week-old beard and clapped his hands to get Angel's attention.

Angel had been staring into the mirror-polished ivory keys. He saw himself in every key. And he saw Timmy too, standing just over his shoulder; he could feel the chill of Timmy's unbreath brush his cheek; could almost feel Timmy's touch on his shoulder, could almost hear Timmy speak to him, saying over and over the words *deliverance, deliverance.*

"Okay guys," said the first A.D. "Ninety-nine-C—on Timmy. Get a move on, we're behind."

Then he heard, as from an immense distance, the familiar words . . . *rolling* . . . *speed* . . . *speed* . . . and began to settle into the persona of Timmy Valentine, could feel Timmy invading his fingers and his mind . . . softly he began to finger the keys with a skill he had never learned . . . *action* . . . and he played, and came closer to Timmy in his heart, and remembered the ancient knife that he wore on his person, concealed in the lining of his black velvet cape.

LABYRINTH

Brian and Petra reached the stage. There was no guard posted—why should there be, here in the middle of nowhere?—and they swung open the metal doors and entered. This was the place Petra had visited only days ago, when Trish Vandermeer had shown her the tinfoil caves, the model train layout, and the immense hall of mirrors.

"Trish?" she said. Her words echoed in a cavernous silence.

Where was Trish's office? The stage had changed since she was last here; the tinfoil passageways, freshly spraypainted before, had now been worked on so that they seemed to be coated with moss and to be oozing a viscous liquid from their crevices. Plywood-lined corridors, paint-flecked to resemble granite and marble, led nowhere or turned sharp corners to produce an optical illusion of going on forever. Overhead, in the dimness, catwalks and flies crisscrossed; a Styrofoam Anubis dangled on a rope. In the distance, she could hear voices. Somewhere in the labyrinth, filming was going on.

Brian said, "Where is everyone?"

"I'm going to look for Trish. The P.D. She'll know what's going on here and where everyone is . . . she's got an office somewhere in all this. I think there was a water cooler just outside it. . . ."

"Here's a water cooler," said Brian, pointing.

She turned. It seemed to have appeared from nowhere. There was a doorway, slightly ajar. It did look familiar. But it was encrusted with cobwebs, as though it hadn't been opened in a hundred years. As she stepped toward it, the cobwebs seemed to fade away. "My eyes are playing tricks on me," she said.

"Yeah," said Brian. "I thought I saw . . . someone who's been . . . dead awhile. Standing in the doorway."

"Who?"

"I don't want to say." She knew he was afraid that saying it would somehow make it real. Quietly she took his hand. They walked toward the office door, their footsteps ringing hollow on the concrete floor.

The door creaked open.

Trish's office was smoky and ill lit. A Macintosh computer, its screen simulating a fish tank full of belligerent Siamese fighting fish, sat on a starkly Scandinavian desk that was completely covered with papers, drawings, clay models, ashtrays and pencils. On a drafting table there was a sketch of the train layout set, the measurements of each prop notated in a precise, spidery hand. Leaning against the wall were shards of broken mirrors, doubtless left over from the mirror set Trish had been so proud of.

"Trish?" Petra said.

No answer.

"Let's go and look for them somewhere else," Brian said nervously.

Petra Shiloh . . .

Brian started. It wasn't her imagination then. It was Trish's voice.

"Where are you?" Petra said.

Petra . . .

The voice was barely audible . . . it seemed to be coming from the musty air itself . . . and then Petra saw something. A flash of light . . . a movement. In the pieces of broken mirror. All at once.

"She's trapped inside," Petra said. "They got her."

Brian said, "I can see other people in those mirrors . . . dead people. Lisa, my niece. I can see Terry Gish. I can see . . ."

More movement—a ripple of color—a dance of shadows.

Fire.

In the air, the faintest scent of brimstone.

And behind the fire . . . a boy hanging from a tree . . . his arms stretched out to her . . . calling out *Mother, Mother* . . . while maggots slithered in and out of his eye sockets . . . a fleeting glimpse of her dead son . . . the smell of citrus trees in the stifling summer . . .

"I see him—" she began, but she couldn't bring herself to say his name aloud.

"Someone dead?"

"Someone dead."

Petra Petra Petra Petra Petra . . .

"Let's go."

Brian took her by the hand and they left the office. As they stepped back out into the corridor, they heard another voice from behind the mirror, the voice of a young boy . . . and the voice said, *Deliverance.*

VISION SEEKERS

Holding hands, PJ and Chit ran from the Porsche to the soundstage. They did not stop to look at the corpses in the parking lot . . . they did not pause to feel the heat of the burning forest.

ANGEL

Another take. Angel was dressed all in white. A fan made his white cloak billow in an artificial breeze. Angel sat at the piano waiting for Timmy to possess him.

He was Timmy without even trying. He could see Timmy reflected in the keys he touched, funhouse-mirror-bent in the curved polished lid of the grand piano. He didn't have to think about the camera as it glided into a tight shot of his face; he just sat at the keyboard, looking inward, speaking to Timmy in his mind.

And Timmy said: *We're going to quench the rage inside you forever.* And he said, *We're going to fight our way through the flames and we're going to find a secret place, a place where you can be at peace. At last. At long last.*

Peace was in Angel's eyes. How the camera loved his eyes. Jonathan, crouching just out of the camera's range, was gesturing to him with his hands to tell him to keep up that dreamy face.

"Now," Burr mouthed.

And Angel said, "Why?"

Jonathan Burr motioned once more. There was supposed to be dialogue from the Father Tappan character here, but they'd cut that in later. Where was Sirota? Angel had met him only once, at a party at the producer's place in Malibu, the day before they set out for here; although Sirota was his nemesis in the story, they had few scenes together. Angel paused, reacting to the unspoken taunts of the mad preacher.

"Why?" said Angel in the voice of Timmy Valentine. He could feel the soundless catch of breath from the crew, knew that his mimicry of the vanished star was magical, uncanny.

A voice rang out from the back of the hall: "Because you have no right to exist; you're an affront to the truth!"

Startled, Angel looked up. A man in a minister's collar stood at the far end of the set.

"Cut, cut, cut!" Burr was shouting. "All right, go back to the first setup. It's about fucking time you turned up, Sirota."

The man was carrying a black leather bag in one hand and a flaming torch in the other. He was haggard and sweaty and his face was streaked with ashes; it looked like he had walked through fire to come to this place. There was a smell of burning sulphur. A woman stood behind him in the shadows; behind her was a man carrying a hatbox.

The man shambled toward the piano. He swayed like a drunkard, once almost keeling over into the camera as it was being pushed back to its first mark. Crew members scurried out of the way.

"What the fuck is wrong with you?" said Burr. He was losing control; Angel know that he couldn't let the crew see that he had no idea what was going on. The mad preacher gazed into Angel's eyes and Angel knew that this was no actor reciting lines from a script. Oh Jesus he's come from another world from beyond the grave from behind the mirror, he thought, and he wants to kill me for real, forever, dead, dead, dead.

"Why?" Angel said, although the camera wasn't rolling anymore.

And the mad preacher shrieked out the lines from the script: "Because you made me ask 'Why? why?' just once too often. Because you made me question God. Because when I questioned him I fell into despair!" And he began to wave his lighted torch so that the fire flickered from mirror to mirror and the room was filled with concentric images of dancing flame.

Burr interposed himself between them. "Jesus, this is brilliant!" he said. "But we're not rolling. Sirota, this is the deepest I've ever seen you get inside the skin of one of your characters, I mean, fucking Jesus this is I mean totally *uncanny!*" He turned to de Rose and shouted, "Get fucking rolling, for God's sake."

"Okay, guys, we're ready to go again now," the first A.D. yelled. Crew members hastened back into place.

"Jonathan," came the voice of the director of photography, "he's a mile off his mark and if we shoot him there we're gonna see the camera in those side mirrors—"

"Who gives a shit?" Burr raved. He was animated now, in a frenzy of inspiration or cocaine or both. "We can see the cameras; it'll be like more avant-garde, in fact we can tell the critics we're breaking down the interface between reality and illusion, I mean, look at *The French Lieutenant's Woman* and that threw realism out the window and see how they loved it and . . . keep going, keep going, we'll film where we can, this is top-drawer improv. . . ."

Angel listened to the director with only half an ear. Because the preacher with his flaming torch was advancing toward him. And his retinue, the woman in some kind of weird robes, the tall man who looked like a butler . . . they were right behind him . . . their faces as impassive as the preacher's was impassioned. And Angel knew he had seen that preacher before. It wasn't Sirota the big-name star. It was the man his mother loved to watch, the other celebrity from Hangman's Holler . . . Damien Peters. Of course he knew him. He was from his own hometown.

"Damien," he said. "What are you doing here?"

"I'm here to show you your dark self," said Reverend Peters. "I'm here to sacrifice you and rip out your still-bleeding heart. I'm a-telling you, the world has been turned upside down, and what was first shall be last and what was last shall be first!"

"Awesomeness!" said Burr. "I love this dialogue— don't know how much we'll have to cut, but—"

The witch woman lifted her arms up to the sky and began a wordless keening that sounded like the wind whistling through deserted canyons, through Arctic ice floes.

"Who the fuck is that woman?" Burr was saying, but no one seemed to notice him anymore. "Sirota—"

"I am not the person you think me," said the actor who wasn't an actor. His voice echoed, inhuman.

"Keep filming," Burr said to no one in particular. "Man's a genius. Is that woman a member of the guild? I don't want any trouble later."

"She's the witch woman," Angel said. "From the night I auditioned on television . . . the woman who exploded."

The witch woman glared at him.

Deliverance, said Timmy Valentine.

At that moment, Brian and Petra came rushing on to the set.

Brian shouted, "Stop the shooting! There are crazy people in here! They're trying to kill us!"

Petra ran to Angel's side. "Angel, stay calm," she said. "We're going to rescue you from all this. We're not going to let you get hurt."

Angel said softly, "Are you my mother now?" Years of anger seethed inside him. "Where's my real mother? Is she passed out somewhere, OD'd, dead?" Petra put her arms around him. But he would not give, although he knew she loved him, although he knew that he needed her. He made himself cold and dead inside. Like Errol. Like Timmy.

"Get these people the fuck out of here!" said Jonathan Burr.

"Be silent!" said the witch woman.

Before their eyes, the witch woman shrugged out of her ceremonial robe. She reached into her vagina and pulled out a squirming, newtlike creature. She held it in the palm of her hand and cried out, "Renew the world in blood." She wrung the amphibian out like a washcloth. There was more blood than Angel thought the creature could hold. The blood spattered the piano, sprinkled the Plexiglas floor, hissed as it spritzed Burr's face. And the witch woman declaimed, like a mantra, the words "Salamander, salamander, salamander."

Brian advanced toward the woman. He held a crucifix and and a flask of water. He started to asperge her as she stood there, chanting, screeching with laughter. The woman shrieked: "How dare you think that a little holy water can stand between you and the death and rebirth of the universe!"

And she hurled the salamander at him. It burst into flame. The flame was blood-red, brilliant. Brian recoiled. Angel felt Petra's hand clutch his. There was comfort in there but he did not choose to take it.

The witch woman laughed. The salamander blew up like a mouse in a microwave. The D.P. was going wild, trying to film everything; his grip was drenched in a shower of amphibian guts.

Above their heads, a thousand witch women shrieked and flailed their withered arms and shook their heads so their white hair stormed about their shoulders. A powerful womansmell streamed out of her. Angel knew the smell because it was the smell that emanated from his mother at particular times, the smell that told him that she wanted to devour him, ravish him, suck him back into her womb.

God, he thought, God, I remember how Becky Slade wanted to touch me and I turned away from her because I knew I was already taken, tainted, tarnished. And suddenly I want to hold Petra's hand again and I'm crying because of all the things that could have been, knowing what's gotta come and knowing the things I'll never have again. . . .

You come back and see Becky again one day you hear? When you be man enough.

He squeezed her hand. She said, "Help is coming." I don't know if I can believe her, he thought, I don't know if the help she's talking about can save me . . . maybe it can save the world but to save the world something's gotta die. Oh, shit shit shit I'm afraid.

The salamander had shattered into a thousand pieces and now every piece was alive, crawling up the camera, little red bursts of squirming, wriggling up the legs of the piano like living droplets of blood . . . there were tiny salamanders speckling the faces of the director and the director of photography . . . somewhere, one of the P.A.s was screaming.

Then two more people came onto the set. One was Premchitra; the other was PJ Gallagher, but somehow he had turned himself into a woman.

"Simone," he said. He danced over the Plexiglas, a whirlwind of feathers, beads and buckskin, his long hair whipping across his face. He danced and the salamanders began to shrivel into dust . . . they were absorbed into the polished white wood of the piano casing until they were like ancient bloodstains. . . . "Simone," said PJ. "I am the sacred man-woman from the dawn of time, the one who defeated you before and shall defeat you again. . . ." And he began to sing, a wailing melody in a quavering voice, as high-pitched as a child's.

Look at the way he moves, he thought, he's like that girl who was trying out for the Timmy Valentine role, he's completely buried his own sex and he walks, breathes, talks like a woman. . . .

"Sometimes the light wins," said Simone Arleta, "and sometimes the darkness. We have our own sacred man-woman."

Damien Peters handed the black bag and the flaming torch to the man dressed as a butler. Methodically, he unbuttoned his collar and peeled off his clerical garments, folded them neatly, placed them on the floor. He was naked.

Simone prostrated herself before him. "Hail, Xipe Totec," she said, "the flayed god, whom some call Jesus Christ."

There was chaos. Perhaps it was the certitude with which Simone blasphemed. Stunned, the crew watched. The camera went right on rolling. PJ went on dancing. Brian handed out crosses; the crew members took them numbly. Angel felt a cross pressed into his hand, stared at it curiously, half in a trance.

"Hail, staff of the world," Simone said. She took the preacher's rampant penis into her mouth.

The butler opened the black bag and took out a series of garments made of human skin, freshly flayed and drenched with coagulating blood. The preacher raised his arms and the servant slid on the skin of a woman's torso, the breasts sagging and hollow, the belly distended . . . I know that skin, Angel thought, I know every mole and pore of it . . . oh Jesus he thought, unable to look away, thinking he's turning into my mother he's turning into the mother out of my nightmares and. . . .

Carefully—with the old woman's lips still wrapped around his penis—the preacher lifted one leg at a time, and the butler slid on Marjorie Todd's legs like a pair of riding chaps. The empty breasts heaved up and down like half-filled water balloons. Damien Peters's eyes were closed in an expression of ecstasy and transcendent terror. Angel could see that, though the woman called him God, knelt before him, worshipped him, it was she who had the real power, she who held life and death. And Angel understood it because it had been that way with his mother; he was the precious jewel, he was the breadwinner, but she held all the power in the family, she held him to her with a leash of flesh and blood. The butler removed Marjorie's face, a mask with empty eyeholes, wrapped it around the preacher's head and fastened it in the back with a needle and thread. He crowned the preacher's head with Marjorie's frayed and bloody scalp. Then—as Peters pulled out his ejaculating penis and baptised the suppliant woman with his seed—he covered the male sex with Marjorie's genitalia, which had been spread out over a wooden frame, and fastened it about Peters's loins with a strip of skin.

"Behold!" cried Simone Arleta. "The *new* man-woman, symbol of the new order, dancer of the world's destruction!"

"Momma," Angel whispered.

The mother-thing reared up. It roared. It leered through flapping lips and glowered through shredded eyeholes. Angel shrank into Petra's embrace. The mother-thing seized the firetorch from the servant. Fire danced in its eyes.

"Come to me," it said, "come, my child, my child."

And Petra Shiloh said, "Don't look at it, Angel. You and I need each other . . . you've lost a mother, I've lost a child . . . this is all bullshit, Angel, these are illusions . . . we need each other."

The mother-thing stalked toward Angel, tossing the torch from hand to hand. "Stay away from him," said the other man-woman, "he's not for you. . . ." And she danced, and sparks flew from her eyes, and she spun a cool blue light from her churning hair, and her hands crisscrossed like the wings of an eagle, and her feet drummed the heartbeat of the world on the Plexiglas floor and made the thousand thousand mirror images vibrate. . . . "Listen to the words of *ma'aipots,*" said the one who possessed the body of PJ Gallagher, "for while you bring corruption and chaos, I bring balance and harmony. I became a man-woman when I sought a vision. You spurned visions and dredged your man-woman up from the carrion of your base desires."

I don't know what's happening, Angel thought, this isn't making sense anymore, it's like a bad dream that's leaking out into the real world . . . these two creatures are fighting over me somehow I've become some kind of pawn in this cosmic battle and I never meant to be anything more than some punk kid singing his heart out and now I'm someone else and I mean something different to every person who sees me and I can't ever be me again, I'm lost, I'm lost forever. . . .

The mother-thing's coming toward me and I have the dagger hidden in my cloak, the dagger from the other world, and—

She's coming toward me and I'm choking on the stench of her and I don't have anywhere to go—

To be free, I have to kill her, I alone, I, I, I, I have to—

The mother-thing hurled the torch at the piano! Fire leaped up! The soundboard cracked and clanged against quaking Plexiglas and the strings singed and became ropes of flame and the fire hurtled over the ivories with a tinkling, eerie music in a remote key . . . trying to duck the flames, the director of photography slipped, hugging the camera as it roller-coastered up the dolly tracks into the pyre, his clothes caught fire and his face turned black as the blood boiled to the surface . . . the mother-thing stepped through the flames . . . the *ma'aipots* danced . . . Angel wrested himself free from Petra's arms . . . ran toward the mother-thing with his dagger pointing at the creature's belly . . . the mother-thing parted the flames with its arms and Angel stabbed it again and again, and it roared out words of lust and shame to him, *Yes Angel fuck me again Angel fuck me go ahead fuck your mother fuck me fuck me,* and Angel thought, how can she say these things how can she let them know the shame the shame and he stabbed her and stabbed her as the tears streamed down and mingled with her blood, stabbed through the slick wet hide stripped from his mother's flesh, stabbed with all the hate that had hidden inside him for thirteen years, stabbed stabbed stabbed and—

"How can you kill me? I'm your mother. And I'm already dead anyway. And your dagger's only another kind of dick."

The mother-thing howled with laughter. And seized Angel in its arms. He breathed in smoke and vaporizing blood. He felt the preacher's cock throbbing beneath his mother's dead vulva. He could taste vomit at the back of his throat.

You a angel Angel.

Becky Slade's voice . . .

Come to bed, Momma needs you honey, come to bed, and don't forget the little blue pills and

And the mother-thing crushed him in its bleeding arms and—

"No!" Angel shrieked, and wriggled free. But there was nowhere to run. Nowhere except—

The mirrors.

He saw the mirrors. Saw himself. Saw the battle of the gods of chaos. Saw the flame-girt mountain capped with snow . . . saw Timmy Valentine.

And Timmy said, "Only you can break the spell. Only you can set us both free. . . ."

The dagger clattered to the ground.

And Angel ran toward the mirror. He battered against the glass with his fists. The mirrors shattered. All of them. All at once. Shards rained down, ripping at his face, skinning his knuckles, slicing at the backs of his hands. Fragments swirled like lethal snowflakes. A piece of mirror slashed the forehead of the key grip, didn't stop until it had sliced him in two. A volley of mirror shrapnel riddled a P.A. and turned her into a colander of blood. Mirrors impaled another man. A woman puked glass and raw intestines.

Behind the shattered mirrors should have stood the familiar labyrinth of artificial caves and prop rooms and narrow plywood corridors. It wasn't there. Instead, a hellish landscape opened out in all directions. Crags erupted from pools of brimstone. Demons with penile proboscises tormented herds of naked, screaming men and women. There was no sky. A wind of putrefaction wailed as it lashed at them. In a river of blood, bloated corpses swirled and eddied. In the distance, on a lofty mountain surrounded by circles of flame, stood the mansion of Timmy Valentine, its wrought-iron gates wide open.

The room of shattered mirrors was an island adrift on the currents of inferno. The charred hulk of the piano, the twisted dolly tracks, the melted-down pool of glass and metal that had been the Panavision camera, all these things seemed to float in the blood-tinted air.

For a moment all seemed frozen.

In the emptiness where the mirrors had been stood Timmy Valentine. And Timmy spoke to Angel, saying only the single word *deliverance*.

Behind Timmy were countless others who had passed beyond. . . .

There is no death, said Timmy Valentine.

Angel didn't hesitate. He ran into that emptiness, ran into the world behind the mirror.

And all the others followed him.

16

DELIVERANCE

MEMORY: 1519

The brightness of the air recedes: suddenly, as though a magician's handkerchief had been thrown over the sky and the sun whisked away.

The galleons are at the very edge of the horizon now; the boy vampire watches them only for a moment. They are his only link with the Old World. But that is past now. He is alone again, an ex–ship's boy, put ashore on an alien beach because he has been fingered as the source of a strange anemia that has infected the crew of the flagship. They have not even bothered to tell him the name of the country; he knows only that the island fortress that was their last port of call is named Cuba, and is part of the dominion of the king of Spain.

He has been left on the shore with a skin of fresh water and a sack of biscuits and a few shreds of salt pork. Only a chaplain has accompanied him to this barren place, and he has not stayed long; his boat has already been swallowed up in the twilight over the ocean.

The boy vampire remembers the captain speaking to him on the morning of his dismissal, the morning after the flogging of the seaman Diego. In his memory the wind howls ceaselessly and the ship rocks, creaks, and pitches. At the center of the fragile drifting island of wood the captain stands. His demeanor is impressive, though his armor is beginning to rust. Toward sunset, they will expose the boy on the shore—then they will continue toward the destination—an unknown country, described only in rumors of unthinkable riches.

The captain is saying, "I am sorry we parted this way, Juanito. Once, becalmed in the middle of nowhere, I came out onto the deck and heard you singing. It must have been a very old song; I didn't even know the language it was in. But it made me feel that somehow we would survive. And indeed, after three days, the calm lifted and we came to Cuba. I was not entirely convinced that this was due to witchcraft, and that your song was satanic in origin; but I must in all things bow to the opinion of the Dominicans."

"Why must you abandon me?" says the boy vampire who has named himself Juanito. "You know I have not really done anything."

"You drank the blood of young Vasquez. You were observed lapping at the lash wounds of Diego Almodóvar, flogged for sodomy and left tied to the mizzen as an example for all to fear, though some say it was not you but a . . . black cat. But you and I know better. You're a *vampiro,* a creature of Satan. It's bad luck to keep you with us, because we have come to the New World on a mission from God and his earthly representative, the Pope."

"Why do you say I am a *vampiro,* Captain Cortés?" the boy vampire asks. "We are standing here in broad daylight, and see, I do not seek the darkness. I'm not stuck away in a coffin somewhere, waiting for the sunset. I don't quail from the crucifix around your neck."

"How do I know?" says the captain. "The devil lies to us; but he also mixes the truth with lies, in order to make us despair."

It is true that the sun has never pained the boy as much, not since his encounter with Gilles de Rais in the last century and his discovery of the mutability of good and evil. Still, he is not enamored of the sun. He has always preferred the shadows. And his fear of crosses has begun to diminish as he has learned more and more about the hypocrisy of those who use them; still, he does not love the Church; he has been seen flinching from the consecrated host, although he proceeded to swallow it without grief, and later he attributed his flinching to the yaw of the vessel.

The captain says, "But perhaps, my child, perhaps one day we shall meet again. I will snatch you from the jaws of destiny as I did once, years ago, when I caught you fleeing the wrath of villagers in Spain."

"How can I ever forget that, Captain?" says Juanito. "They accused me of being a heretic." It is painful to remember that time when, speechless from the trauma of Bluebeard's castle, he wandered from forest to forest, surfacing now and then, within discontinuous fragments of time and place, drifting on the ocean of history. He has seen cities with buildings of a hundred stories, where men fly in birds of metal and drive chariots of steel; he has lived in a place of strange beasts and men with sloping foreheads, who have called him light-bringer, bringer of fire; he has journed through the Dream Time of an undiscovered continent, and lived among headhunters in a forest where the mosquitoes swarmed like rain, and where he himself, the blood-hunter, was called king of mosquitoes. Whether all these things happened before or after the meeting at Tiffauges he cannot tell. Time itself has become disjointed by his trauma. Though at times he has a memory of a future time also, when a woman, healer of minds, draws out these traumas by speaking softly to him as he lies on a couch, at war with the demon of compassion.

"I have a vision," says Cortés. "Perhaps I too, like you, am touched with divine madness. We cannot fit into the arbitrary paradigms dictated for us by church and state. When you sang the ancient song that day, I heard a music that others did not hear. I believe that I shall once more hear that music, even if I must journey into the jungle's heart to wrest it out."

Juanito does not know what Cortés is talking about. Humans are full of self-imagined falsehoods, he thinks, and the world they make for themselves is more than half unreal. "Goodbye, Captain Cortés," the boy vampire says, as the boat is lowered, with him, two oarsmen, and Brother Ortega, his face buried in an immense leather Vulgate, his cassock billowing.

In the sunset, the Dominican does not speak words of comfort to the boy. He only says, "May you never survive to curse the company of Christians. May you never live to blaspheme in the sight of men of God. I am sorry we have not had the pleasure of burning you at the stake."

Juanito has watched the oarsmen as they rowed the boat back toward the fleet, with Brother Ortega intoning into the wind, now and then making the sign of the cross.

Night has fallen.

The beach is desolate and the boy is hungry. He has not feasted since he drank the blood of the man beaten for sodomy, his back laid open by the lash, crisscrossed with rivulets of blood mixed with the salt and pepper ground in for added agony. Oh, that blood was bitter; it tasted like tears. Perhaps it was all the salt.

The air here bears no taint of the scent of blood. He sniffs the breeze from farther inland. There, he senses, is a forest, perhaps the same dark forest where, lost and nameless, he once encountered—or will encounter—the princess with the bound feet, the wild men of Borneo, the rishi meditating beneath a tree, the straggling survivors of a labor camp. The forest is always a place of renewal. He must go there if he is to find his name, his new identity.

Swiftly, silently, he runs toward the dark. The sand resists his toes. His feet begin to transform into paws, clawing up dirt, lengthening the spring and arc of him as his running slides into gliding. The earth is moist and pungent. He sniffs the soggy leaves, breathes in the compost of dead things that anchors the febrile upspurt of the living. In the forest the air is thick with insects and the canopy blocks out the moon and the stars. He runs. He is a jaguar now. His pelt is the night. The smell of human blood is distant, but clear as the lodestar on a cloudless night.

He runs.

At length he reaches a clearing the forest. There are stone steps, steep, in disrepair. Vines and shrubs thrust up through the cracks. He hears the slithering of snakes. In a shaft of moonlight he can see the stone face of a jaguar; his own face, hewn from the rock. There are other visages peering from the undergrowth—grotesque warriors, women with skull faces, feathered serpents. It is an abandoned city. It is so ancient that he barely hears the voices of the dead as they scream in their tormented slumber.

The jaguar moves off into the darkness, away from the moon that whitens the old stone and makes the vegetation glisten like wet silver. He runs. He exults in the ripple of muscle, flesh, sinew.

And then, without warning, comes the trap. He is caught and catapulted into the air. He tears at the netting, but it is tough. Darts fly through the darkness. Pain pelts him. He tastes his own blood. He roars, he growls, his jaws snap at the restraints.

Four men, two of them bearing torches, run into the clearing. They carry clubs and sharpened sticks, but in their ears and noses there are ornaments of gold, and their hair is coiffed with brilliant blue feathers. They speak in a language full of whistling consonants and twisty polysyllables. He cannot understand. But they have blood. The hunger swoops down on him and he transforms, weakened by the loss of blood.

And so it is that they see a jaguar caught in a net, but the next moment they see a naked child, with long black hair and skin so pale that it seems to draw its sheen from the very moonlight.

The savages—if that is what they are—murmur to each other. There is a curious lack of surprise in their voices. Perhaps there are many were-jaguars in this land. Perhaps it is so ingrained in their belief system that they find no surprise in it. At any rate, they lower the net, attach it to poles, and they start hurrying through the forest with the poles on their shoulders, moving at a brisk trot. The rhythm of their movement, the racing of their blood, the even pounding of their heartbeats, all feed the boy vampire's hunger. He waits for a moment to feed. Around them, the forest becomes ever more dense and the moonlight thins—only now and then does it glint on some lone leaf, some reptilian scale, some beak of a night bird as it swoops from perch to perch.

At last they reach the clearing with the temple, approaching it from a different direction so that the boy vampire realizes they have been running in a circle, that they must have begun stalking him even as he was in jaguar shape, prowling through the ruins.

Now they are carrying him up the steps. So the site has not been entirely abandoned; some practitioner of the old religion remains here, some guardian of an undead past. They begin to tire; the steps go on for a long time; the very air is thinner here, and it is laced with the scent of blood—new blood. He sniffs. The odor intensifies as they climb, and now it is mingled with copal incense, a maddening, intoxicating odor.

He has not had blood in several days.

They reach the top of the pyramid. They are above the forest now; the leafy canopy appears as a vast black glittering ocean, and they are drenched in starlight, for the sky is cloudless. There is an altar; behind the altar, a mirror, tall as a man, obscured by the incense that wafts from stone braziers next to the altar. There are more men with torches now, who emerge from a chamber behind the mirror. Quickly they assume various positions around the altar, some kneeling, some standing. At their head is a priest, wearing a robe of feathers—an old robe, tattered and gnawed at—and the priest holds in his hands an obsidian knife. His hair is long, knotted, completely matted with dried blood. As his captors release the vampire from the net, binding his hands with thongs, the bloodsmell comes at him from every side. There are pools of day-old blood at the base of the altar. The stones are soaked in it; blood has seeped into every pore and crevice of the ancient rock, and formed a coagulated sheath over every surface.

One of the vampire's captors is explaining, at some length, how the four of them stalked and netted the were-jaguar. There is much mimicry of the jaguar's walk, of the cries of nocturnal insects, of the growl and roar of the angry beast; then, it seems, he mimes the transformation into a boy. The gestures, the accompanying choral exclamations from the audience, are so stylized that the boy realizes he is witnessing an ancient ceremony.

They do not know how different I am, he thinks. Again, men see in me only what they wish to see. I hold to them the mirror of their own dark nature.

The high priest examines the boy vampire. Gingerly, he reaches out to touch him. He snatches back his hand; the vampire has stolen all its warmth, and he has felt only a preternatural cold. He measures the boy's head with a pair of gold-chased calipers. He nods approvingly. Physically, he has passed some kind of test.

It is now that the men try to bind the boy to the altar. They cannot hold him down; though he has the shape of a boy, he can summon the strength of the jaguar, the swiftness of the bat. The priest raises up the obsidian knife, and the boy senses that he wants his heart. Though the hunger pounds at him, he knows that there is a part of him that longs for death. For fifteen hundred years he has walked the forest of the night; could he not at last reach daylight? And so he does not resist at first. He lies back on the altar, bent over, chest thrust upward, waiting for the knife . . . until he feels the obsidian slice into him . . . until he smells his own blood, sluggish and old-smelling. It is then that the hunger seizes him. He cannot control it. He tears his bonds without effort. He is a jaguar once more. The priest steps back in consternation, and the vampire pounces on the young man who narrated the tale of his entrapment. His claws slide easily into the man's chest; he rips him open; his incisors chomp down to crunch through muscle and sternum to pluck out the heart, still fibrillating, spurting the quick, bright blood of the still-living. How good this blood feels! He drinks. The others do not flee. The high priest, far from retiring into his chamber, watches with fascination and adoration. He drinks. As he becomes satiated, the feline shape begins to waver and soon he is a boy again, a boy with bloodstained lips.

But now another of these captors has prostrated himself at his feet, offering himself as a sacrifice. And the others all seem ready, full of quiet joy, as though they had rediscovered some lost fragment of their past. The blood is running down the steps now; it will be absorbed by the porous rock long before it passes through the ocean of leaves and into the darkness of the forest. Against the rock's rough texture, in the glitter of a myriad stars, the blood itself seems spangled with points of light.

The boy turns to face the mirror. The copal smoke

roils and curls about the boy's face. Behind the smoke, of course, he casts no reflection.

He partakes of no particle of the sublunary; no mirror can show his likeness.

It is at this that the high priest finally gasps and falls to his knees in reverence. He is awed; it is though he has been waiting all his life for the boy to manifest himself. He has come to these lost people as a messiah.

Over and over the priest, pointing to the smoking mirror that is void of the boy's reflection, murmurs the name *Tezcatlipoca*.

And the others, taking their cue from him, repeat the name, so that the very forest seems to buzz with its harsh resonance:

Tezcatlipoca. Tezcatlipoca. Tezcatlipoca.
Tezcatlipoca. Tezcatlipoca. Tezcatlipoca.

The words, the first he is to learn in the Náhuatl tongue, mean "Smoking Mirror."

AVENGER

Brian burst through the shattered mirror with his bag in his hand.

He found himself running up a spiral stairwell . . . the back stairs of a hotel. Or maybe it was the stairwell of his apartment building in Hollywood. The stairwell went on and on. . . . Suddenly the words of the Red Queen in *Through the Looking-Glass* popped into his mind . . . "Sometimes it takes all the running you can do, just to stay in one place."

It seemed to that time itself had changed and that as he scaled the Escher-like steps, folding in and out of each other, time itself was twisting, mutating, Möbius-stripping until the upward climb becomes an analog of his life, an eternal present; he runs, and the infinite hallway echoes and reechoes with his feet on concrete and his hands slapping the cold metal banister.

In the eternal present, he sees, as though doorways were constantly opening and closing themselves along the landings of the stairwell, scenes that could be past or future. . . .

Uncle Brian . . . the little girl rising from the mist draped in seaweed with the brine pouring from her eyes and the holes in her side and . . .

. . . the stake tearing through the salty flesh in the glass coffin in the attic of the house that Timmy built and . . .

. . . piles of unbegun manuscripts lining unopened drawers and novels that were never started and rejection slips and strained conversations with editors and . . .

. . . Lisa . . .

I've gotta get off the treadmill, he thinks.

And forces himself to stop at the next landing, coming to a wrenching halt. Pulls open the first door, a hotel door like the ones at the Highwater Inn, and . . .

He sees a room, furnished in vinyl Colonial, and in the room is Aaron Maguire, tugging a woman through the closet mirror, and . . .

"Aaron," he says, and the writer turns and Brian sees that he has been laterally sliced in half, that the whole backside of his body is a mass of writhing musculature . . . arteries wriggling like snakes . . . blood drips from his outstretched arms like the fringes of a buckskin jacket. "Aaron, I—" Brian doesn't know what to say. "I feel terrible about getting your job this way—"

"Forget the fucking job," Aaron says. "I'm gone now, I'm just a loose end, an unfinished piece of business. Just kill me and move on . . . that's Hollywood."

As he speaks, he has pulled the woman through and Brian sees it is Gabriela Muñoz, the agent. "Gabriela!" Brian says. She stares fixedly at him. Her neck is bent at an inhuman angle. With a shock, he realizes that she is dead, and that Aaron is sucking the blood from the broken neck.

"Oh, God," he says, "can't we—send her back somehow—reverse everything—" He knows that in the mirror-world time has become fluid and nonlinear. Couldn't they change everything back to the way it was? "If you both step back through, can't you go back to the way you were?" he says.

But Aaron is greedily gulping down the blood that fountains up from the carotic artery. Brian opens his black bag. He is holding a cross now, and he is unstopping the thermos of holy water. He asperges Aaron and Aaron howls and the water fumes as it strikes him, lacerating his face, his chest, his arms.

"Free me," says Aaron Maguire. "Get me out of here—you can't believe the pain—"

Brian pulls out one of his sharpened stakes. He drives the stake through Aaron's chest. As Aaron falls to the ground, the stake pushes up through the body cavity and stands upright with the heart impaled on it, like a bloody shish kebab.

Brian steps backward through the open door.

Soon he is on the stairwell again, racing toward some unseen destiny.

VISION SEEKERS

Lady Chit finds herself in an elevator without buttons, without even the Up and Down arrows to tell her where she is going. She cannot tell if it is up or down; there is only the vaguest sensation of movement. Perhaps they have stopped altogether. Now and then the overhead lights blink. It is a plush elevator; the floor is deep pile carpeting, and a bust of some Roman general rests atop a *faux* Corinthian pedestal. It is a hotel, perhaps Claridge's, perhaps the Plaza . . . and she is a little girl again, being summoned into the presence of her grandfather. . . .

The elevator opens. She is in a hotel suite. Velvet draperies. Through the window, snatches of skyline. Traffic. It must be New York.

Prince Prathna is seated in a gingham armchair. "Hello, Premchitra," he says.

Chit presses her palms together in the traditional *wai* and kneels on the floor so that her head will not be on a higher level than that of her familiar elder.

"Come closer, my dear," he says to her. She inches a little closer. He smiles and she is thinking, I've heard so many stories about my grandfather and yet he seems a kindly old man, not at all decadent. I wonder why they tell those stories.

Lady Chit notices that there is a sacred cord, a *saisin*, stretched around the room. It loops through the armchair, around the legs of coffee tables, over the antenna of the television set. Her grandfather is within the magic circle and she is not.

"Grandfather," she asks him, "why is there a *saisin* around you?"

"It's for protection, my dear," he says, his eyes full of concern for her. "Terrible things have happened in the world. Evil powers have erupted out of the underworld, and they threaten to overwhelm the fragile balance of our cosmos. Come into the magic circle, Premchitra. You need to be protected too; you're young; America is a harsh place; I warned your parents not to send you to school there, but . . ."

The prince holds out his hand; instantly there appears on it a Barbie doll. "Here's something you've always wanted," he says, "which your parents never had time to buy for you. . . ."

Chit laughs . . . the little girl inside her laughs . . . unthinking, she runs across the *saisin*, runs toward her grandfather's arms, and—

The doll ages, withers, crumbles to dust, and—

She is standing in a cemetery in Bangkok . . . in the distance, monks are chanting mantras . . . a funeral pyre glows in the distance, beneath the shadow of a tall pagoda . . . her grandfather is no longer a kindly old man but a torsoless monster, dragging his entrails behind him as he lurches forward, his tongue propelling him closer toward her . . .

"Grandfather!" she cries out.

"This is all your doing," he says. His voice has become a grotesque rasp. "You were the one who wrote the letter to me from school in America, singing the praises of this Timmy Valentine . . . you caused the Gods of Chaos to set out in pursuit of him . . . *you* reduced me to this terrible condition. . . ."

"No!" she screams. She turns and runs. But the gap is closing. Again and again she passes the same marmoreal headstones, the same praying angels carved in granite, the same stone lions etched with Thai and Chinese characters. . . . I'm running in a circle, she realizes suddenly. I'm never going to escape. . . .

She feels the touch of the tongue against her ankle and . . .

Shit shit shit you fill me with hunger you fill me with rage shit shit shit why do you fill me with such rage shit shit shit I want you I want to devour you I want to suck the shit right out of your bleeding arse you human you sack of shit oh I'm hungry hungry hungry I want to devour your shit your shit your shit

Suddenly she remembers something. She thinks it is a memory. She is not sure. Perhaps a fantasy. She's lying in bed. She's seven or eight years old. The maid has rocked her to sleep with a story about a *phii krasue* and an admonition to beware of Si Ui, the serial killer who eats the livers of young children. She lying in bed in a cold sweat because she's woken from a dream and the air-conditioning has failed because of the monsoon storm that's taken out all the power on her street and then she knows there's a monster in the room, a monster that hunks over her, a monster shaped from the darkness, and she's telling herself *It's a bad dream, I don't want that maid ever to tell me those terrible stories again,* but it's no good because the monster won't go away and she tells herself *I know that there's no such thing as a* phii krasue, *not really,* but when she closes her eyes and squeezes them tight shut she suddenly feels the touch of something cold and wet against her cheeks, the touch of an alien tongue, and the terror makes her freeze and when she tries to scream a hand comes over her mouth and she's suffocating choking on her unborn scream and then she hears the voice . . . the rasp of the monster . . . and it's saying *oh you fill me with rage oh you fill me with hunger* and she retreats into a tiny part of her mind, far from the old man's touch and then she thinks *I'm dreaming I'm only dreaming. . . .*

In the cemetery with the monster grabbing at her and she cries out—

"No, Grandfather! It's time for you to die now . . . time for me to kill the memory . . . time for me to root you out of my nightmares and . . ."

The *phii krasue* shrieks! It keens! The very air shudders with his howling and—

"Go toward rebirth, Grandfather!" she cries. "Go with my forgiveness and with all my love!"

The howling rends the night air—

Suddenly she is outside the sacred circle of the *saisin.* And she is standing in an immense pavilion, watching the wooden barque that contains the body of Prince Prathna set alight within the compound of an ancient temple. Perhaps, she thinks, this is a vision of the future. She sees her parents, her mother dressed in a chic black Dior dress of mourning, her father in a white suit with a black armband; the monks are chanting words from the Buddhist scriptures:

Transient things are but an illusion;
Life is suffering.

The fragrance of incense and jasmine pervades the air.
The atmosphere is not one of gloom, for a Buddhist
funeral is a time of rejoicing, a time to celebrate the
passing of the soul to a more exalted plane of being.

"Go toward rebirth, Grandfather," she whispers, wiping a single tear from the corner of each eye.

PJ is beside her suddenly. He is there not in the flesh,
but in spirit, to tell her that the struggle is not yet over,
that there is a greater darkness to be vanquished before
they can escape from the world inside the mirrors. . . .

MEMORY: 1519

Time has passed; in that time the boy vampire has been
brought to Tenochtitlan, the center of the world. Those
who caught him in the jungle were half-savage villagers,
using the abandoned temples of ancient times for furtive
ceremonies, as a hermit crab uses the shell of a long-dead
mollusk. They are superstitious people, ignorant of the
philosophy, cosmology and theology that pervade the
great city to the north; but they know enough to realize
that they have found someone important . . . someone
who, if not a god himself, is too exalted for the likes of
them to deal with. And so they have delivered him to the
neighboring kingdom, which at least has a wall around
its chief village; they in turn have passed him on to the
state of which they are mere vassals; and they in turn
have sent him to the palace of Moctezuma, the first
speaker, ruler of the world.

Who, wakening from his nightmare of the return of
Quetzalcoatl from the east and the destruction by fire of
all the known universe, has seen in the boy vampire an

emissary of Tezcatlipoca, the god who speaks through a smoking mirror, who lives atop the great pyramid in the center of the city. Perhaps the boy—as yet unlearned in Náhuatl, the Aztec language—has come to counterbalance the destruction that has been foretold. And it is true that the boy is beautiful—unnaturally beautiful, with the pallor of the moon and clear, unflinching eyes, and with long dark hair sheened like a black jaguar's pelt. Moctezuma has heard that the boy transforms into such a jaguar at night and hunts for human blood. That is good. There is no need to manufacture miracles for the common populace when a real miracle is so readily available.

And so it is that the boy has come to live in the temple of Tezcatlipoca; that he is known by the god's name, and therefore does not need to invent one for himself; that he need not hunt for blood, for he is fed by his priestly attendants with fresh blood from the daily sacrifices; that he sits on a throne in the chamber of the Smoking Mirror that all may witness the marvel of his inability to cast a reflection. And so it is that Moctezuma, his litter borne on the shoulders of four noblemen, comes daily to ask him to intercede for him with the gods.

"I've had another nightmare, Smoking Mirror," he says to the boy. The two are alone together. The chamber, hewn from rock, is completely caked with generations of dried human blood. From just outside the door, every now and then, comes the wet thud of obsidian into human flesh. The boy drinks blood from a goblet. The room is dark with incense. Images of the god are everywhere, each image anointed with blood and flecked with copal ash.

"What kind of nightmare, First Speaker?" says the boy, who has in the intervening months become proficient in the language. "Is it the same dream as before?"

"Yes." Though he is not old, Moctezuma is weighed down with the cares of his kingdom. He knows he is a caretaker monarch, presiding over an age whose time is rapidly running out, for this is the year when, it has been prophesied for five hundred years, the god Quetzalcoatl will finally return and regain control of his stolen realm. "In my dream, ships with white wings are coming from the east. They bear the crest of the Plumed Serpent. They sweep into Tenochtitlan, sailing over land and sea. They eat the sweat of the sun. The people are struck down by terrible diseases even before Plumed Serpent arrives. He wears a skin of impenetrable metal and his soldiers are half man, half beast."

The boy who is now named for the god Tezcatlipoca says, "His name is Herman Cortés. He comes from a country called Spain. His men want gold; his church wants you to become Christians."

"I don't know what you're saying, little god; when you inhale the copal incense your words often become too dark for me to understand. I suppose these strange names and nonsense words of yours must be symbols of some kind."

The boy, used to being mistaken for someone else, merely smiles a wan smile and continues to drink his blood, which today comes from a beautiful virgin girl, daughter of a nobleman, a kinswoman to Moctezuma himself.

"You're so lucky," says the First Speaker. "In a few short months you will be sent to your namesake in the sky; you will join the company of the sun. While I—I must languish here on earth—and face the destruction that haunts my dreams."

"Why don't you simply fight them?" says the boy vampire. "They will only be a few hundred. But you could field a million men if you chose to. You could drive them back into the sea."

"You tempt me, Smoking Mirror," says Moctezuma. "I know you're just testing my resolve. Like all the gods, you think we are no more than ants, to be crushed, drowned, burned up in our thousands. I'm not going to give you the satisfaction. I'm just going to let the Plumed Serpent come into the city. The war is between you and him; I am only a man. And I'm a coward; I don't want to get involved in the cosmic battle."

"Cortés is also a man," says the boy vampire, knowing now that telling the truth only confirms Moctezuma in his illusion.

"The gods often come to us in human form," says the First Speaker, "as, for example, you, Smoking Mirror."

FIRE

The fire has broken through the protective circle. Helicopters are attempting a rescue. But the streets of the pseudo-Junction are empty, save for the burnt-up corpses of some crewmen.

VISION SEEKERS

And suddenly Petra sees her son swinging from a citrus tree, though the garden is not her garden, and the tree is not her tree.

The garden stretches far away, toward blue hills that ring the two of them. The lemon fragrance is as sweet and overpowering as an aerosol air freshener, but it cannot mask the stench of vomit and decay.

"Jason, Jason," Petra says. She fears the worst because she knows that all this has already happened, and yet she feels a kind of hope . . . perhaps in this replay there will be a change, perhaps she will reach him in time to cut him free, perhaps . . .

There is a ladder up to the branch where her son has hanged himself. A Timmy Valentine song plays with the quiet pervasiveness of Muzak. She grabs hold of the first rungs, heedless of the splinters that pierce her palms.

"This time I'm going to save you," she says.
She begins to climb.
"This time . . ."

FIRE

Fire on the mountaintops. Pines sizzle and crash.
Above the clouds, above the snowclad peaks, PJ and
Simone Arleta hurl thunderbolts and tear up mountains.
The battle rages. Two cosmic dances, two destinies at
war with one another. Thunder peals. Volcanoes erupt.
The Snake River Valley is all valleys, and the mountains
are all mountains where gods dwell: Olympus, Kailasa,
Popocatapetl, Kilauea.

The battle rages and the fire rages all around it—

ANGEL

And Angel finds himself on an Appalachian hilltop
just this side of the shattered mirror. Timmy is there. In
the flesh now, the two of them side by side, the human
boy just a hair shorter than his shadow self. I didn't mean
to cross over, he's thinking.

But Timmy says, "At last. You've come."

"Yeah, I guess I have. This was the only way left for
me to go."

"I know," says Timmy Valentine. "So often things
happen this way. You start off with an infinite number of
roads you can take. Then one by one they take away the
options and this is all you're left with."

"Did that happen to you?"

"Yes," says Timmy Valentine. "And now there's only
one way out for both of us. Do you know what it is?"

"Kind of."

"Come on." He takes Angel by the hand.

Jesus his hand is cold. I can't break free of his grip either, Angel thinks. And now he's leading me up the slope toward where the grass is thinner. We're running against the pull of gravity but somehow I feel so light I'm almost blowing away. And then the breeze lifts me up and I'm taken up, skimming the wind, oh it feels strange, like my blood is racing twice as fast and my heart pumping like crazy because I'm not human anymore, I'm surfing the airtides with huge black leathery wings . . . and when Timmy speaks to me again it's the high-pitched squeal of a bat. But I can understand him perfectly. "You'll be able to do this all the time," Timmy says. "You'll be all kinds of wild animals. Look! Feel!"

And Angel thinks, Now we're crashing to the earth, oh God, we're gonna die, it's like the worst roller coaster in the world I see the whole valley rushing up to meet me in a blur of green but now instead of crash landing our feet transform into paws and we thump against buoyant earth and we start uphill by leaps and bounds and we're roaring and we're mountain lions pounding the dirt and kicking up the soft clods, pissing our masculine pride into the damp tall grass.

Oh I feel free. More free than I've ever felt in my life. The closest I've ever come to feeling like this was when I was singing all by myself without anyone listening singing all alone alone with me without Momma without the memory of Errol to haunt me. Oh free free free. How can I stay this free? There's only one way. I began the process when I told on Momma to Petra. And then when I drove the dagger into the mother-thing I—

Stop.

They are standing at the summit of the hill now. Angel sees the old shack in Hangman's Holler, sees the ledge where you could look all the way down the valley to where Damien Peters used to drive by in his limousine on his way to the TV station and the virtual cathedral.

And they're in human form again. Angel marvels at

how different the two of them are, even though he's dressed as Timmy Valentine and he has on his Timmy Valentine makeup and he's dyed his hair the night-black of Timmy's hair . . . still they're not the same. I feel so young, he thinks, and although he and I look so alike when you look in his eyes you know how old he is.

"You don't know the half of it," Timmy says. "Come into my mind. . . ."

And he makes Angel see all of it . . . the child plucking the kithara and singing his heart out in the cave of the Sibylline Oracle . . . the child violated and robbed of his youth by the Sibyl and the Mage in the fire of a dying city . . . the child-god worshipped as Antinous and as Tezcatlipoca, as the Fisher King, as the Cornbringer, as the Flayed God, as the Angel of Death in the studio of Caravaggio, as the voice of the me generation in the person of Timmy Valentine; mistaken for the ultimate evil by Gilles de Rais, buried under the dead in Auschwitz, fleeing peasants with torches in Spain, singing the death-song of a Japanese Empress . . . he has lived through all this and so much more that the images kaleidoscope into confusion . . . two thousand years of having no identity save what the world chose to see in him . . . two thousand years of being the mirror of their private nightmares . . . two thousand years as the most real of possible illusions, as the most illusory of possible realities . . . Angel sees all these things, lives through all these things, and when the images begin to fade he feels an awful love inside him . . . the love of an apostle for his savior.

Angel says, "I'm sorry you've carried this burden so long. Do you want me to take it from you?"

"But," says Timmy Valentine, "you will have to become a vampire."

"You think I'm afraid of becoming a vampire, after all I've been through?" Angel says. "I know who the real vampires are. Not you . . . not me, even though I aim to spend the next two thousand years drinking human blood . . . no, I'll show you who the real vampires are!"

And he races down the hill toward the house and this time it's Timmy who follows him. I know this country, Angel thinks, this is my turf. This is one thing I'm gonna do for myself.

He reaches the place where they buried Errol. There's a shovel beside the old well. He starts digging. And digging. Sometimes Timmy pitches in, turning himself into a wolf so he can claw up the dirt.

First there's a pair of feet. Then the legs. Two palms pressed together in an attitude of prayer. And then the face . . . Angel's face. I thought he was a baby, Angel thinks, but he's kept on growing all this while even though he was under the earth. Look at him.

He's alive.

Breathing.

A stake and a mallet appear as in Angel's hands as if by magic.

You've been feeding on me all this time, Angel thinks. You've warped Momma's love into something shameful and cruel. Just one little blow of this mallet and you're gonna be history.

Becky Slade's voice: *You ain't man enough . . . you ain't a man, you a angel, Angel.*

But I am man enough, Angel thinks. And he steadies the stake over Errol's heart and brings the mallet crashing down and—

Suddenly there's a pair of gnarled hands grabbing the stake away from him. And when Angel looks up he sees the preacher from Hangman's Holler wearing his mother's skin—

"You let go," Angel says.

They struggle! Timmy stands by, unable to intervene because this battle is taking place inside Angel's mind. The mother-thing's hands are bloody. The skin is fastened with Frankenstein-style stitches, but his mother's real hands hang limp from the preacher's wrists.

The mother-thing says, "Love me, Angel. Love me forever."

He's trying to pull the stake away from her. But she has it pointed right at his heart.

"I'll make you love me even if it kills you," says the mother-thing. "You're all I got . . . it's you and me against the whole damned world. Oh, God, Angel, love me, love." The mother-thing weeps tears of blood as she tries to embrace him. But she never lets go of the stake, and he knows that if she embraces him the stake will pierce his chest and kill him.

They struggle—

FIRE

The Reverend Damien Peters is taking the stairway to heaven. It doesn't matter that the world is crashing into ruins around him. He is going into the arms of his God. Choirs of cherubim and seraphim chant antiphonally as he nears the throne of the Almighty. The pearly gates are swinging open . . . the wrought-iron gates that are strangely similar to the gates to the estate of Timmy Valentine. The hillside, the clouds, the house of the Lord himself are suffused with an eerie incandescence.

The Lord stands at the top of the endless steps. He speaks in a still, small voice. He is just a child. A child whose face is familiar to Damien from countless CD boxes, MTV videos, and teen magazine covers. A child whose eyes glow red, whose dark hair billows in the sunwind, whose lips are parted as though to kiss or to draw blood.

"Damien, Damien," says Timmy Valentine, "why persecutest thou me?"

"I didn't know!" Damien screams.

As the singing of the angels crescendoes, as the brightness increases, Damien can no longer bear to look. His eyes are burning even when he closes them, even when he buries his face in his hands.

At length comes darkness . . . and Damien realizes that, like Saint Paul, he has been struck blind.

FIRE

Simone battles the young *ma'aipots* shaman, but the greatest battle of all takes place within. So it is that, though she continues to act out the ageless drama, another part of her is journeying backward through the ages of man.

Simone has reached the morning of the world. Not the scientific dawn, with its Neanderthals and saber-toothed tigers, but the mythic dawn, when the stars were diamonds mounted in the sphere of the sky, when a mighty serpent guarded the tree of knowledge. The knowledge is all there, waiting to be plucked. It dangles, red and juicy, glistening in the humid summer air.

The snake, coiled around the tree, sheds its skin. Within that skin is the man-woman with whom she has been at war.

"You?" she says, more in wonderment than fear.

"Yes," says the young shaman who is both man and woman. The shaman comes toward her with an apple in his hand.

"I don't need more knowledge," she says.

"Ah, but you do," says the shaman. There is still something of the serpent in the way he moves, in his sinuous gestures. "There is one more thing that you do not know, that you fear to know—isn't there?"

He toys with the apple. It catches the light like a burnished copper mirror. He throws it from hand to hand.

He juggles. Suddenly he has a hundred hands and the apple he juggles is the world.

And Simone is tempted.

MEMORY: 1520

Spring has come to Tenochtitlan. All over the kingdom they are performing the rites of Xipe Totec. Priests are donning the flayed skins of their sacrificial victims to celebrate the death and rebirth of the world, the planting of the corn, the successful return of the gods from the Narrow Passage between the world and the land of the dead.

The people have been rejoicing. They dance in the streets through the night . . . they feast on the fresh meat of slain captives . . . there are many weddings, for it is an auspicious time to celebrate fertility. Lord Snake Woman, the First Speaker's chief minister, is full of gladness.

Only Moctezuma is troubled.

He knows that Quetzalcoatl is returning to reclaim his kingdom. He knows that the time will soon be upon them. It is a time to mourn. These rites of Xipe Totec may well be the last.

Moctezuma has sent the god an invitation, but it would have made no difference. The gods always come and go of their own free will. The god is coming to the heart of the world of the Fifth Sun. He comes to dance the world's destruction, and the First Speaker knows that there is nothing he can do.

And so it is that he spends his days in the chamber of Smoking Mirror, atop the great pyramid that overlooks the city on the lake; he speaks only to the boy who speaks in riddles. And the vampire who is known as the Unblemished Boy, the one who cannot be seen in mirrors, the one who speaks for Tezcatlipoca, answers his questions, in these last days, in the only way that he can. It is getting on toward night. The sounds of sacrificing still go on, as they have been going on all day long, for these are dark times, and the gods cry out for appeasement.

"What will happen when Plumed Serpent returns?" Moctezuma says.

"All is illusion."

"I know, I know. But I can't shed this illusion the way you can. They call me a god, but I'm not godlike enough to *know*, empirically, that the cosmos doesn't exist."

Suddenly they hear a tumult down below. "What is the matter?" says Moctezuma, calling out to his priests. Slowly he raises himself from his throne—he cannot move quickly or he will damage the cloak of a hundred thousand quetzal feathers that he wears—to face the eldest priest, who anxiously prostrates himself. He is in tears.

"We were afraid to summon you from your conversation with the god," says the priest.

"What is it?"

"They have come. They are sweeping through the city, leveling, destroying, burning up. The drawbridges have been destroyed and still they come. In a few minutes they will reach this plaza and this temple."

"Dry your tears, priest. Let there be no regret." Motioning that the boy vampire should follow him, Moctezuma leaves the smoky inner chamber. The boy steps out into evening. The sunset pains him a little. He stays under the shade of an immense statue of a skull-faced deity.

There is commotion at the top of the steps. A priest, half in, half out of the freshly flayed skin of a noblewoman, jumps up and down in order to force the skin's thin buttocks over his own. A man lies on the altar, awaiting the knife, but because of the confusion he has not yet been sacrificed. He pleads not to be deprived of his rightful honor, which he won in a contest of skill during last year's javelin-throwing festival. They are standing ankle-deep in gore that flows over a sediment of coagulated blood. From somewhere far below they hear the clank of metal on stone and they know that the pale gods from across the sea are on their way.

"Quick!" says the First Speaker. "We've no time to lose!"

He seizes the obsidian knife from a frightened priest and himself dispatches the victim, slicing through the chest cavity and with a single deft movement plucking the heart out by the roots. Jets of blood stream from the palpitating heart, spattering his face and splashing the garments he has so scrupulously sought not to damage.

He throws the heart to the boy vampire, who fastidiously laps at it like a kitten licking its paws. The energy surges through the boy. He peers over the edge of the pyramid and sees the Spaniards in the square. The horses are pawing the stones and the surrounding city is aflame. Men and women are fleeing from the buildings like bees from burning hives. They hear the roar of cannon above the death cries, but it is all far below, in miniature. It is the burning city that illuminates the spectacle. Even the lake seems to be on fire, for every canoe, every islet, every bridge has been set alight.

"It is glorious," says Moctezuma. "It is beautiful. It is the consummation of our entire civilization, this mad oblivion."

Another prisoner is placed upon the altar. Passionlessly, as though he were merely sliding a lobe ornament into his ear, the First Speaker kills, rips out a heart, tosses it to the boy vampire. Others are cutting up the carcasses and heaving the jumbled body parts down the thousand steps, as though the offerings had the power to stop the coming of Quetzalcoatl. But there will be no stopping; that is already clear. The horses have reached the base of the pyramid. The boy vampire can see the Spaniards swarming uphill now, their armor glittering with reflected fire, swords drawn, flying the insignia of the king of Spain. Cortés is at their head.

Moctezuma recognizes the god. He turns to the child-god beside him and says, "If things had been different, you would have reigned until the end of the sacred year. But now we have no choice but to sacrifice that which is most precious to us. Do not be sad."

"You do not know," says the boy vampire, "how much I welcome death."

The tramp of boots of stone continues. Nearer, nearer, nearer. With frightening rhythmic precision.

"Lie down on the altar, then."

The boy stands like a doll while the priests remove his robes of godhood. Naked, he lies back against the cold stone. Death is not something that he fears. He has passed through death before. The incense rises from four braziers at the corners of the altar and blurs the moon.

He thinks: My death will not stop the destruction of this world. He knows it and I know it. But he has to go through the motions. As must I, as always a player in someone else's drama. At least, this time, I may actually die. Why not? I came to being in a city's death throes; why should I not die the same way?

Flash! The knife descending, a quick glint of moonlight through veils of incense, then—

The footsteps very close now.

A hand seizes the First Speaker's wrist. Sacrilege! The priests gasp.

"Get up from there!" A rough voice. Suddenly the boy recognizes it as from a half-remembered dream. "Get up, Juanito." It is the Dominican, Brother Ortega. "So this is how we find you—participating in heathen rites—indulging in the devil's own abominations—"

"No." He hears the quiet voice of Cortés.

The boy sits up. The First Speaker's wrists have been bound, and he is being held by two men. The priests are weeping. The one wearing the noblewoman's skin is being poked and prodded by a curious squire. The Speaker and the God from the Sea look at each other and they can see that this is more than a clash of men; it is indeed a battle between worlds, between gods.

"Isn't this creature of hell proof enough that these people are incorrigible heathens?" cries Brother Ortega. "And we thought we were rid of him forever."

"I think our rediscovery of him a good omen, Brother." Cortés turns and smiles at Juanito. "Condemned to death by me, snatched from death's jaws by me; what an irony."

"I tried to tell him who you really were, Captain; he only listened to his own illusions."

"We will see about those illusions."

The soldiers shove Moctezuma, who attempts to retain his imperious demeanor, into the inner chamber.

"Show me these devils of yours!" cries Brother Ortega. Soldiers are carrying a great wooden cross up the the steps of the pyramid. "We'll see how they can stand up to Christ and the Madonna."

The boy vampire follows them inside. Their feet are slick with human blood. They step over limbless torsos. Decapitated heads stare at them from wooden poles. The priests have thrown so much incense into the burners that the men are choking. The gods can be seen only dimly—here a leering rictus carved out of gold, here a stubby arm from which depends a human skull, tied to the fingers by a single forelock, there a woman-goddess with pendulous breasts. And in the back of the chamber, the mirror through which Tezcatlipoca has always spoken to his people, draped in smoke.

And the boy thinks: I will never escape. Eternity is in my veins. I will go back to Spain. I will wander the world forever, always ancient, always a boy. And always I will hunger for a shadow of life's remembrance. The thirst for blood is an addiction, and each taste brings less satisfaction and greater thirst. . . .

Moctezuma says to the boy vampire, "Go back through the mirror! You are fated to lose this war . . . your age is over."

The boy stands in front of the mirror . . . staring . . . he has seen . . . fragments of other past, other futures . . . he gazes transfixed, while around him the soldiers are casting the gods from their thrones, calling on Saint James and the Virgin Mary to witness the abominations they are rooting out.

The boy vampire sees someone much like himself. He is standing on a kind of stage, but it is not a theater he has ever seen before. He holds a metal tube in his hand, and he is singing. The voice is much like his own, but it is tempered with a mortality, and an incipient manhood, that he knows he can never possess. Who is this youth? A circle of light follows him as he dances to a jangling, alien music.

And suddenly the other boy has seen him across the chasm of time.

And holds out something to him, whispering, "You *can* be free! This is the secret. . . ."

And Juanito sees that it is an apple.

Shiny. Red as blood.

He reaches into the mirror—

"And is this mirror your god?" Cortés shrieks at the priests. "I will show you how your god answers you!"

And he takes a stone Madonna from one of his men. Wielding it like a club, he shatters the mirror. Brother Ortega jumps up and down on the shards of the mirror as though stamping out a fire. The soldiers cheer and the priests cringe and prick their own flesh with thorns and daggers, hoping to expiate the sacrilege.

"Timmy," says the boy in the mirror as his image splinters into a thousand images.

"Timmy?" says Juanito. "What is that?" Suddenly he knows that where the other boy stands, another citadel is burning. But perhaps that citadel is a mere illusion. . . .

The apple rolls to his feet across the gulf of space-time, and—

SERPENT

—and Petra has climbed up to her son, and feverishly she unties the knot around his neck, and calls his name again and again as though he could hear it in the world beyond and come rushing back to life—

—and she hugs the corpse, trying to warm it back to life with her mother's warmth . . . she kisses the cold lips and tastes only gall and caked vomit but she doesn't care because it is her son—

—life is stirring inside him! The lips are moving, gasping for air! And then at last his arms move on their own, clutching her tighter to him, and she whispers, "Jason, oh, I'm sorry, I'm sorry, Jason," and words come wheezing to his parched lips—"I'm gone, Mom. I'm gone. You have another son now."

And the skin begins to peel back from those lips, to shrivel and slough off like the skin of a snake, and there is another boy inside the flayed skin of the dead boy, a boy who's still alive, who desperately needs her, whose own mother has betrayed him the way she never could betray a son. . . .

Mother, behold thy son. . . .

And all at once she understands that Jason is dead. Truly dead. He is beyond forgiving her. She must forgive herself.

I must lay my son to rest, she says. And look to the living. . . .

"Angel," she says softly, as the tree dissolves in smoke and she finds herself—

VAMPIRE JUNCTION

—Darkness. "Where are we going?" says Damien Peters. They are moving. He hears the clatter of a train. "Are we traveling somewhere?"

He feels a hand in his. "I've come to guide you." It's the voice of the boy who was God. "Until you can see again."

"I don't want to see again. I want to wander in the outer darkness, a-weeping and a-gnashing my teeth until the end of time."

"But that is not to be."

"Why?" says Damien Peters.

"Because you have only assumed the mask of the deities in the eternal battle for control of the universe. You are not the deity itself."

Damien weeps from his sightless eyes.

VAMPIRE JUNCTION: TUNNEL

—on a slow train winding up the mountain.

"Where are you taking me?" Petra says. They are in a tunnel. Utter darkness. Now and then, a mural is illuminated—fragments of her own shattered life.

"To Brian," says Angel Todd. "That's what you really want, isn't it? Come on. I promise you I'm not going to be jealous anymore."

VAMPIRE JUNCTION: SHAMANESS: TUNNEL

The Waldorf salad in the dining car tastes sour. But Simone devours it greedily. The train clatters on. She picks out the walnuts and concentrates on the slices of apple.

The truth in the apple is bitter.

As she swallows the flesh of the fruit she knows that the godhead is leaving her. She knows that she is just an empty skin. Once she was filled with power, but the power was borrowed, not hers to keep. The drama will soon be over and she will only be an old woman, useless, spent.

She cannot bear to be powerless. Power has been her life.

She watches as the chunks of apple harden. They turn sharp-edged, like shards of the broken mirror. Still she eats. The glass slices her tongue. She is numb to the pain as the pieces lacerate the lining of her cheeks. Blood gushes from her mouth, her nostrils, from the ripped flesh of her face.

She eats, knowing she is consuming herself.

The last piece of the apple lodges in her throat. It severs her trachea and she stops breathing.

The train to Vampire Junction reaches the end of the tunnel.

VAMPIRE JUNCTION

And the train, hurtling toward the light of the burning world, and—

MEMORY: 1520

As Juanito bites into the apple he sees a vision of his release. How he must walk the earth for a few more centuries yet, until he can find someone who truly desires to take the burden . . . how he must reach out to him through the mirrors within mirrors, through the worlds between worlds, and—

VAMPIRE JUNCTION: ANGEL: MIRROR

"You came!" says Angel, pulling the boy through the mirror. "Out of the past or something."

"There is no time in the Looking-Glass Country."

"Listen. Listen."

It's the clatter of the train, the metallic heave and stutter of it, as they pass from the tunnel into a landscape of faery radiance.

"Do you know what we're going to have to do?" Angel says.

"Yes. We have to transfuse our blood into each other."

"Okay."

"I love you," says Timmy Valentine. Perhaps, Angel thinks, he has never said this before to anyone.

The two move closer to one another.

"How're we gonna do this?" Angel says softly.

"Bite me." Timmy smiles with his eyes. "On the neck, stupid." And he laughs a little. The laughter is tinged with such sadness as Angel can never know while he is still human.

The two touch, only the tips of their fingers at first; Angel feels a vague sexual stirring at this, but it isn't what he felt when he was with Becky Slade, scared of being discovered, or with Marjorie, ashamed of being used. The sexual feeling soon dissipates because what they are about to do is more than making love; it is transubstantiation. Angel takes off the vampire cloak of his costume; Timmy takes off the feathered cloak he brought with him from beyond the mirrored mirror. He doesn't take his eyes off the boy vampire's face as he slowly undresses and casts his clothes behind him, on the many-patched vinyl seats of the old train. Light streams in. They embrace. The sudden cold of Timmy's flesh burns only a little. The vampire inclines his neck and Angel's mouth seeks out the jugular vein, missing it at first until Timmy, wrapping his arm around Angel's head, pulls him toward the proper place. The skin breaks easily and the blood comes, sluggish at first, purpled by death; the touch of the chill rheum on his tongue is like an opiate, drawing him down into a bottomless well, a dark place he has always known but never dared look upon. He drinks. And as he drinks the cold becomes warm. And then, cupping the vampire's head in his hands, he too offers him his neck. He feels the prick of Timmy's hunger, feels the soul sapped from himself, feels no regret, feels only a savage joy; feels truly that he has killed the past, killed Errol, killed his mother and the mother-beast that wore his mother's shape, killed the old Angel in him; he mourns the dead, he mourns himself, but knows he must go on. He sucks in the death's blood and the death force from his dead friend. Oh, he devours the cold. He is steeped in cold. The cold drives fuselike through his veins. Oh cold cold cold. Oh cold. But beneath the cold a distant warmth, the fever of transient life perceived through the cold lens of eternity.

VISION SEEKERS

Brian has reached the last landing at the top of the stairwell. He opens the door and finds himself on a train. The train moves through darkness. He cannot find his compartment. He inches down the corridor, moving in contrary motion to the hurtling train.

As he opens a door between cars, he almost collides with Petra and a boy. Is it Angel or is it Timmy Valentine? Petra's cheek brushes his. He finds her in his arms. They kiss. The boy smiles; Brian feels a little embarrassed and pulls away.

Lisa! Brian thinks. The past is like a vampire. It steals your will to live. It's time to kill the past. He looks at the boy and the woman and realizes how much they need him. How the boy needs his manhood, his reassurance; how the woman needs his empathy, his gentleness. We could be a family, Brian thinks. He says, "What are we gonna do now?"

The boy who has come to him with Petra says, "The rest of them are getting off at Vampire Junction. But we're gonna keep going. For a while longer . . ."

VISION SEEKERS

PJ sees the witch woman dead, sprawled over a table in the dining car, the final piece of the fruit of knowledge stuck in her throat.

He feels no rancor, only a profound sorrow at the passing of his enemy.

"Goodbye," he whispers to the last of the Gods of Chaos—the only one who ever possessed a true shred of the gods' power.

As he gazes down at the witch woman, PJ feels a lightness of being. He is having a vision within a vision. His soul is soaring to the place where he went on his first vision quest, when the woman-spirit who visited him gave him the bitter gift of seeing, coupling it with sexual ambiguity. . . . Now the spirit has come again. He sees the spirit, clothed in clouds, shining like the sun. He is overwhelmed with joy, for he knows that the time of his deliverance has finally come.

"Do you know why I have come?" she says.

"Yes. You're going to take back your gifts."

"That's right. You don't need them anymore. They've been a burden to you. That's all right, I understand. No human should have to do the things you've done."

The spirit woman touches him three times. At the first touch his womanliness leaves him; at the second, he begins to fall back to earth; at the third, there is no more magic.

The spirit woman has departed. But in her place there is another woman, young and vibrant and full of love for him. He takes her in his arms.

"Chit," he says, "Chit, Chit . . ."

"I've killed my grandfather," says Chit. "I've sent him on to his next life. . . ."

"I'm not a shaman anymore," PJ says. "The gift has left me."

"But we're still trapped in this vision . . . we're still inside the mirror world. . . ."

"But not for much longer. Listen. I can feel the train shuddering to a stop."

"Oh . . . PJ . . . make love to me now! Quickly! Before the vision ends."

DISSOLVE: PROPHET: VISION SEEKER

Slowly, Damien Peters opens his eyes.

The witch is dead. *Ding dong,* he thinks, smiling a little to himself, knowing that they will soon leave Oz behind forever. . . .

MEMORY: 1520

And the boy says to Moctezuma: "Rejoice, First Speaker. You were right. This is no time to mourn. I have learned that all things end . . . even the empire you sought to preserve, even the eternity I am doomed to suffer through."

Above the screams of the dying, the hiss and roar of the flames, Moctezuma says, "Are you truly the god, then? Have you fought Plumed Serpent and lost?"

"We have all been gods once in a while. But godhood never lasts." To Cortés, he says, "Farewell, Captain."

"Where are you going, Juanito?" says the captain.

"You must come back with me; the irony of your sentencing and your rescue will be a fine tale to tell at the banquet tables in the courts of Europe. We are all rich now."

"I am returning to the dark forest of the soul," says the boy vampire, "and when I shall come again, no one shall know."

At these words, Moctezuma lets out a bloodcurdling cry, knowing for certain now that the god has abandoned him forever.

"No, no," the boy says gently, "rejoice, First Speaker."

And, as is the wont of his kind, he dissipates himself into the copal smoke and, in a thousand misty tendrils, funnels into the shattered pieces of Smoking Mirror.

VAMPIRE JUNCTION

The train pulls into a country station. It is night. The first to leave is PJ; he holds out an arm to steady Lady Chit. She is beautiful in the full moon's radiance. PJ will always treasure the memory of their last lovemaking . . . the love between them the only truth they could cling to in the kaleidoscope of the fading vision.

Next is the preacher, Damien Peters. He looks as though he has harrowed hell, and to tell the truth he has, though it was a hell within himself. "The world's a hell of a different place than what I thought," he mutters to himself.

"Are you going back to Hangman's Holler?" PJ asks him as he steps onto the platform.

"Don't rightly know," says the Reverend Peters.

Then comes Timmy Valentine.

Timmy doesn't say anything to anyone for a while; he just stands there. He is pale in the moonlight, but he no longer seems bloodless; and there's a half-laugh in his eyes that PJ doesn't remember ever seeing before. At first

PJ thinks it must be Angel. But when Timmy finally speaks, the voice is unmistakable.

"I feel like Pinocchio," Timmy says. "Real at last."

"No regrets," says a voice from the window. Angel. He is standing there, between Brian and Petra. They are an unholy Holy Family; Brian is an unshaven, starving-writer-looking Father, Petra a politically correct Holy Ghost in her batik pants suit; Angel's face has acquired the phosphorescent pallor of the undead.

"Aren't you gonna get off here?" PJ says.

"Nah," Angel says. "Maybe at the next station. Maybe not for a while."

"But Brian—" PJ says. Brian's look speaks of all that they went through together; but he slowly shakes his head. And then the three of them embrace as the train pulls away from Vampire Junction, toward the distant sunrise.

"Let's go home!" cries Timmy Valentine. And laughing, he leads the way toward the labyrinth of the broken mirror. . . .

DISSOLVE

Out of a clear blue sky there came a storm to end all storms. Water poured down over the burning mountain. The rain turned the fiery forest into smoldering mush in a matter of hours. The freak weather was a nightmare for meteorologists, forcing them to question the very fundamentals of their science.

When the choppers landed in Junction, the rescue teams found dead people everywhere, charred beyond recognition. But at the bull's-eye of the circle of fire they found a miracle. The main soundstage was undamaged; indeed, a skeleton crew had apparently been filming through the entire crisis, oblivious to the world outside.

"But didn't you *hear* anything?" an incredulous rescue worker asked Jonathan Burr, the director.

"Hey," he replied, "we were *jamming* on that set. I mean, we shot footage that most directors would willingly die for. Actually a few people *did* die I guess. But you know, sometimes art is worth dying for. Well, when we see the dailies we'll know."

Among the dead were the mother of the teenage star, Marjorie Todd. She could be identified only from dental records; somehow her entire skin had been burned away. The dead also included stunt coordinator James Torres, pyro coordinator Dan Osterday . . .

"The insurance companies are going to go insane," said Burr.

. . . and veteran actor Jason Sirota, who was slated to play the role of Father Tappan, a mad priest who—ironically—burns down the entire town of Junction in a religious frenzy. To the astonishment of the rescuers—and later of talk show hosts, "Entertainment Tonight," and CNN—the Reverend Damien Peters, televangelist embroiled in an IRS and sex scandal, happened to be at the set, and filled in Sirota's part at short notice—especially amazing since he had come to Junction to gather evidence for a lawsuit which he and "attorney-to-the-stars" Morgan Weintraub had already instigated, alleging libel and defamation in the script's portrayal of the Tappan character. . . .

"It's not that surprising," said Burr later on "Geraldo." "When you're being hounded by the feds *and* by the scandalmongers, acting often seems the only way out. Some people, they bitch and moan, but you put a camera in front of them and they're just born hams. . . ."

Since Sirota was demonstrably dead at the time, the Taft-Hartley law allowed the Reverend Peters to perform without being a member of the Actors Guild.

Still missing from the location as of the close of shooting were Petra Shiloh, a journalist, and screenwriter

Brian Zottoli, who wrote the final draft of the script and was, in Burr's words, "indispensable . . . he totally *shaped* the artistic vision of the final product."

In the most bizarre twist of all, Angel Todd, the young star of the film, shortly became heir to Timmy Valentine's estate. Rudy Lydick, the executor, revealed that a clause in the will granted full control of all Valentine's assets to, "at the sole discretion of the executor, such person as may possess the exceptional ability of duplicating Timmy Valentine's achievements and abilities." Angel Todd changed his legal name to Timmy Valentine shortly afterward. . . .

"Life imitating art," said Jonathan Burr when interviewed for HBO's "Valentine—the Making of a Cult Classic." "To quote one of the Senseless Vultures' old hits:

'Death is an Illusion.
The mirror is blood.'

"I don't know what it means, but you know, they used to be the warmup band for Timmy's act. Where the hell are they now? I'm sure there're plenty of people who'd like to know."

17

VALENTINE–THE MOTION PICTURE

PROPHET

I can't believe I'm a-standing before you today: me, Damien Peters, ex-preacher, ex-snake-oil-merchant. Me, Damien Peters, Ladies and Gentlemen of the Academy, holding in my hands the Academy Award for best supporting actor in Jonathan Burr's movie *Valentine.* I hardly know where to begin.

A year ago I preached my last sermon. I said that the end of the world was coming. I named an exact manner, time, and place for the world to end. But, you see, I was wrong.

The world didn't end. Or did it?

Maybe there was some terrible conflict between good and evil that took place that day. Sure, there were signs and portents. Sure, there were conflagrations and there were freakish thunderstorms and other miracles of nature. Maybe the world did end that day. Maybe we're already in the middle of a new age. Or maybe the war ended in the only way it could end, with good triumphing over evil, with the world being preserved, healed, made whole, for us to enjoy for generations to come. I'm still a Christian—though not, God knows, a very good one sometimes—and I *have* to believe that good is stronger than evil. I *have* to believe there's only one outcome in the great battle.

Did the world end?

For me, in a way, it did end. I went to Junction to stop a movie from being made. And then, while the fire raged outside up and down the mountain, while the rescue workers desperately tried to get to us, I found myself inside the set of the movie. I saw that my whole life had been a movie up to that point. I had bought my own hype. I saw that I'd been a fool, that God wasn't going to come down and bail me out of the corner I'd backed myself into. As it says in the Good Book: "He saved others; himself he cannot save."

The movie changed a lot of things in my life. I haven't abandoned the Lord, but I think I'm doing a much better job serving Him than in the past. I've sold all the assets of the ministry and satisfied the IRS as well as compensating the victims of my sexual indiscretions. I've donated the rest of the church's money to several charities and to AIDS research. I'm clean now, thanks to the revelations I had about reality and illusion.

I would like to thank Jonathan Burr, my director; Brian Zottoli, the screenwriter, who can't, unfortunately, be with us tonight; and I want to give special thanks to a woman killed in the fire, renowned psychic Simone Arleta, whose insights into the dark side of human nature helped me come to terms with the mess I'd made of my life.

Thanks, also, to Timmy Valentine. I used to preach against him as a creature of darkness, a Satan, but now I know that the devil you have to fight is the one in your own heart.

DISSOLVE

Lady Chit had spent her whole life moving in privileged circles, but she'd never dreamed that she would one day be coming to the Oscars. It was particularly ironic that this year the Oscars had been moved to the Lennon Auditorium, the place where it had all begun. She and PJ had come in Timmy's limousine, and they were dressed in a way that would surely have affronted her mother's idea of good taste—she in a neon pink Thai silk gown that punkishly exaggerated the sweeping, angular shoulder pads of traditional Siamese court dress, he in nouveau Native American, a fringed, buckskin tuxedo, eagle feathers, and a wampum cummerbund. Timmy was the most plainly dressed of them all; he wore black. It was the priciest black money could buy.

Stupendous Pictures had rented a box for its nominees—seven of them!—and their friends. Damien had been the first actually to win something. PJ squeezed her hand as Damien walked down the aisle, gold statuette cradled in his arms. "I'm scared," she said. "I keep seeing him flouncing about in the flayed hide of that woman. . . ."

"Do you still have nightmares?" PJ said.

"Yeah." But she didn't want to talk about the nightmares. They were part of her now, and no therapy, no exorcism, could ever make them go away. She was happy with her life, even with the darkness it contained.

Her return to Mills College, after the many traumas of Junction, was anticlimactic. The activists were out in force there, protesting the new coed policy. She realized that she didn't have much in common with these people, and—politely but firmly—told her mother that she was going to try for somewhere a little more populist. Like Berkeley.

Taking PJ back to Thailand to meet the parents had not been nearly as bad as she had thought it would be.

For one thing, *Dances with Wolves* had been playing in Thailand for several months, and PJ soon became a smashing success with society chic, partyhopping with the best of them, being universally praised by her relatives for possessing the elusive and untranslatable quality of *kreng jai,* which few white people were ever known to evince—a kind of intuitive empathy that preserves other people's face as well as one's own. The relationship was, after all, not entirely out of the question. Her family were, in the final analysis, more forward-looking than she'd anticipated. And why worry about marrying a man with no money, when there was plenty to go around, what with her father's acquiring the chairmanship of seven Japano-Thai corporations?

And when the strangely charred remains of Prince Prathna had finally been exhumed from a ruined house in Junction, and given the proper funeral rites, and sent to the next world in a burning ship on the grounds of the family temple, all her relatives had agreed that PJ's comportment was exemplary. He had also asked the right questions of the Buddhist monks, and seemed ready to enter a monastery, for a while, himself, the better to come to an understanding of the illusory transience of the world.

"Can I sneak a glass of that red wine?" Timmy said.

"But you never drink . . . wine," said Jonathan Burr, who had been sitting a couple of seats away, nervously drumming at the armrest. When one's picture is up for seven Oscars, Chit thought, one certainly becomes a nervous wreck.

"I do now," said Timmy Valentine. "What are they gonna do, card me?"

"Okay," said Burr. "But wait until those TV cameras are turned the other way. We want you to be a good role model to those millions of teenage kids who are watching tonight."

"Bullshit!" said Timmy. How like a kid he sounds!

Chit thought. After two thousand years without a child-hood, he's certainly ready to become all boy. Timmy's childish defiance made her laugh. He turned to her, guzzling the whole glass in one gulp. "Hey, I gotta have *some* fun," he said. Then, sliding across the seats so he was right next to PJ and Chit—who were, after all, the only people who knew the whole truth about him—he added, "Becoming mortal didn't give me *everything* back, you know. I'm still a eunuch. But hey, career-wise, it's not a bad thing. I'll be able to sing soprano for a long, long time . . . long after I turn old and wizened and unsexy."

PJ said, "You'll never turn unsexy, Timmy."

"You old flirt," Timmy said. The three of them embraced, laughing.

Damien was sidling back into the box now. As he sat down, he said, "No more mushy stuff, kids; they're about to announce the best screenplay award. . . ."

The winner was Brian Zottoli.

DISSOLVE

Brian has asked me to accept the award for him . . . he's out in the middle of nowhere, traveling the earth, trying to find himself or something . . . I received a letter from him postmarked "Timbuktu" the other day. I'd love to share it with you.

Let me just shake out the sand. . . .

[LAUGHTER]

Here goes.

Dear Jonathan:

Things are pretty bizarre here in the middle of nowhere. But at least they're a little quieter than in Los Angeles. I don't expect to be back for a long, long time. I hear I'm up for an Oscar—they have CNN at the hotel, believe it or not!—but I know I'm not going to win. So I'm not going to write out a speech for you to read on my behalf at the awards ceremony, even though I'm going to to ask you to accept the award for me if I do win, ha, ha, ha. I mean, come on. If you had to choose between those candidates, would you pick *me?* I didn't think so.

Having a great time, wish you were here; there's no toilet paper so I'm having to conserve my notepaper which is why this missive is so short.

All my best,
Brian Zottoli.

[LAUGHTER]
Well, I know that Brian would want to thank his remarkably understanding, cooperative and undemanding director (he says modestly)—
[LAUGHTER]
I do have something to say about the effects in the film, though. A lot of people have asked how we did that hall of mirrors sequence. Well, there were no *Terminator 2*–type exotic computer programs. There were no teams of puppeteers operating vast robots.
It all really happened.
Really.
Really!

DISSOLVE

"Great speech," Timmy was telling Jonathan as he slid back into his seat, mopping up the sweat with a silk handkerchief.

"I tell you," said Burr. "That was a tough one. I had to make up the letter, of course. We still haven't located Brian."

"But you never found his body," Chit pointed out. She

did not know where Brian had gone, but she knew, as
surely as she knew her own name, that neither Brian nor
Petra had disappeared completely.

One day they were going to come back out of the
mirror world. And Angel, too. Angel Todd, the eternal
vampire.

"Oh, my God! Look at all the glitterati," Damien was
saying. "Is that Ronald Reagan down there?"

"No, it's Sylvester Stallone," said someone else.

"Oh, come on; they don't look anything alike."

Lady Chit looked out over the multitudes of celebrities.
The journalists were swarming about them in a veritable
feeding frenzy. So many gaudy clothes! So many sequins,
spangles, boas, furs, tiaras, diamonds, diamonds, diamonds! Angel's mother would have loved it. Angel, probably not. Angel's idea of heaven would have been to wander
alone through the forest singing some Appalachian folk
song to himself. Once, she remembered, she'd stumbled on
him doing just that. She still remembered the song's elastic
melody and wayward turn of phrase:

> 'Tis the gift to be simple,
> 'Tis the gift to be free. . . .

And she remembered, too, the way that Angel sang
those words. It was as though the mere utterance of them
was enough to set him free from all the cares of the world.
She loved the way he sang to himself; it was only when he
was alone, without an audience to please, an audience that
possessed him and chained him, an audience that was
somehow an extension of his mother's obsessive and oppressive love, it was only then that his singing approached
the crystalline purity that was the peculiar gift of Timmy
Valentine. She missed Angel, she decided. She hoped he
would come back soon . . . although she knew that, even if
Angel were not to come back until she was an old woman,
waited on hand and foot on some estate in the hills of

Chiangmai, he would still be the same as when they had parted. Only she would have aged.

"Are you thinking about Angel?" Timmy asked her, when they had all sat down again, and they were all watching an elaborate song-and-dance number choreographed from the score to one of those Roman Numeral movies—*Rocky XVII* or *Home Alone V* or some such thing.

"Yes, I guess I am," Chit said.

"I can tell," said Timmy. "You know, whatever he's going through—I've been there."

"They'll be back," Chit said with calm conviction.

PJ said, "I understand that Jonathan's unlikely to win for best director—a lot of people seem to think his sensibility's too off-beat for the mainstream. . . ."

"Well, I'm not gonna win best actor either," said Timmy. "I mean, kids don't win that award—and they don't know any different. Do they?"

"Yeah, but you still might get to go up there . . . there's also best song . . . you know that," said Chit. "And you're the one who wrote the title song in *Valentine*. And you know it was number one for ten weeks. And you know that . . . in fact . . . oh, my God, they're just about to announce that category! Hold still, everyone!"

She saw that Timmy's hands were shaking. He must hardly remember what it's like to feel the rush of adrenaline or the sand-in-your-mouth stage fright or the dizzying palpitations in your stomach . . . these little terrors that every human knows. He's enjoying his nervousness, she thought, reveling in it. I can't blame him.

"Jesus, I can't fucking stand the tension!" Timmy whispered to himself.

"I love you, PJ," said Lady Chit softly to the shaman who had lost his powers.

"Me too," said PJ.

"The tension! The fucking tension!"

"And the winner is . . ."

18

LAST IMPRESSIONS

❦ ❦

MOSAIC STONES

Sissy Robinson, age 13:

And when I saw him, like, at the Oscars, on television, he was all different. He was still cute and all but there was something more. He wasn't just pretending to be Timmy Valentine. He *was* Timmy Valentine.

I loved him.

That's why I finally took down my Freddy Krueger poster and put up a larger-than-life full-body picture of Timmy that fills up the whole wall. I mean, I had to buy ten issues of *Raving Teen* magazine, they only had a part of the picture with each issue, it was like "See a different part of Timmy every month. . . ." You know what I mean. It was worth it.

PJ Gallagher, artist; Native American activist:

The last time I saw Angel Todd, it wasn't even in the real world; it was the world of visions. It's a world my people share with the Australian aborigines, who call it the Dreamtime.

Angel wasn't getting off the train. Angel had become a vampire.

I don't know if he realizes what this means. He was a kid who had a dreadful life. Traumatized by his twin brother's death, smothered by his mother's unhealthy attentions, sexually terrorized, the only thing he had going for him was his death wish. At least, that's probably what the shrinks would say about him. To me, it was more like he'd never been given the chance to dream. Others did all his dreaming for him. It got so he wanted to die. And so he did die. Kind of.

I think about all the other people who crossed over: Shannon; her mother; the crazy shamaness; Aaron, the writer; Gabriela, the money-grubbing agent; and all those others. They won't be coming back.

I think of all my childhood friends in Junction too: David and Terry, and Naomi, and even Mr. Kavaldjian the undertaker. Mr. and Mrs. Gish. And the woman who ran the general store. And my Mom and Dad, Kyle and Shannah. And all the kids who used to hang out in the arcade where we played Bloodsucker until we turned the machine over, and over, and over. Crossed over. All of them.

And I think: if the powers of the universe are locked in an endless, timeless battle, and all these people I've known, loved, hated, are just casualties, stray-bullet stoppers, roadkills, slain by friendly or at least indifferent fire . . . what does it mean?

I used to know the answers to these questions. I had a gift. Now I don't have the gift anymore. But I do have my art. . . .

Jonathan Burr, director:

Okay, so I didn't get the Oscar. It's kind of tough when you're up against Polanski, Spielberg, and Kurosawa.

But I got a multimillion-dollar three-picture deal out of it, so you can hardly say I failed. Nah.

I've never talked about what happened in the hall of mirrors. About those so-called "effects" which the camera so faithfully captured, because they went on running, reliably powered by our generators, long after the whole shoot had descended into pandemonium. No one else has talked about it either. I know I saw things—amazing things—things you'd maybe call psychedelic if you'd grown up, like me, in those good old days.

These things sure as hell weren't in Brian Zottoli's script.

It was like watching—no, physically *experiencing*— say, the ending of *2001—A Space Odyssey.* And the other thing was, I was only an observer. The movie I was watching wasn't about me. It was about these other people, this Damien Peters dude, this Indian shaman, this Queen of Hollywood Psychics, and about Angel and Petra and Brian and the spirit of Timmy Valentine. I know I learned the answer to the riddle of Timmy Valentine, but I also know that I've forgotten it. It's been wiped from my memory. Probably for all time.

And then, the next time I saw Angel Todd, he wasn't Angel anymore.

That I do know.

Petra Shiloh, journalist:

The last time I saw Angel Todd? I'm seeing him now. We're at the beginning of a new life. I know it.

Brian Zottoli, novelist:

She's right. We're at the beginning.

We're the last people left on the train, and we've left behind the last known station on the railroad. Now the tracks are roller coastering down the mountain, and the trees of the forest are rushing by so thick and fast we don't even have time to count them.

We sit. We laugh over old times. Sometimes Angel starts to talk about the things he used to do when he was still alive. It's good he's coming out of his shell.

Sometimes I talk about Lisa too, about how I couldn't save her. And Petra talks about her son. We have a new son now, and he's never going to die on us. Because we're going to protect him. This time we're going to make it work.

Angel is scared of crosses and of sunlight. I tell him he'll gradually get over those phobias. Timmy did, even though it took him fifteen hundred years to lose his fear of the sun. Angel is hungry all the time and there is no blood here, except, of course, mine, and Petra's. I wonder how long he can hold it in. But sometime we're going to emerge from this forest. We're going to surface somewhere in the world, walk out through a mirror, go on living, or unliving, as the case may be . . . one of these days.

Until then, we travel in a perpetual dreaming.

Timmy Valentine:
The last time I saw Angel Todd . . .

I felt tired last night. That was new. That was exciting.

This morning I tripped and I hurt my shin. That was exhilarating.

This afternoon I looked at a girl and I felt a different kind of hunger.

That was breathtaking.

Yes, in a way, I do envy him.

Still.

I envied him before, gazing at him across the gulf between the mirror-worlds, knowing all the things he was capable of feeling, of which I knew only the faintest echo of remembrance; I envied that. I envied the darkly sexual thing that lay behind his mask of innocence. That is still denied me. I can regain what I once had, but I can never recover what I never really possessed.

Oh, Angel, Angel, how I still envy you.

But even the envy I feel is an exciting thing—an envy that comes with prickling skin and accelerating pulse. I couldn't feel that kind of envy before.

I envy the adventures you will have. I envy the ages that stretch out before you, time enough to heal, to learn compassion, wisdom. To be human is always to live half-blinded, yearning to see what cannot be seen, to control what cannot be controlled, to conquer death; to live with the sizzling intensity of the mayfly, which is born, lives, procreates, perishes in a single day. You will not have this. Your enemy will not be time.

But men will be your enemy. They will hunt you down. They will worship you. They will desire you. Always you will be the object not attained, and it will drive men mad. I know. I was that object once. And you attained me, and in doing so relinquished your humanity.

Humanity itself, however, you cannot relinquish. We need each other. We nurture each other as the night nurtures the day.

The last time I will see Angel Todd has not come yet.

But time has no meaning in the Looking-Glass Country. By the time I see you again, I'll probably be old. I'll be a wizened miser sitting in my Malibu estate, or maybe Monte Carlo, counting my ill-gotten gains as I watch the life force drain from me.

Oh, Angel, you will come to me as the Angel of Death. To take me to the other side. You will hold the mirror open for me, and I'll see the one great truth that only the dying can see.

And I'll be ready for you.

—Los Angeles, Bangkok, 1990–1991